LADY
MOSES

A NOVEL

LUCINDA ROY

A *Virago* book

Published by Virago Press 1998

First published in the United States by
HarperCollins 1998

Copyright © Lucinda Roy 1998

'Solstice' from *The Black Unicorn* by Audre Lorde. Copyright
© 1978 by Audre Lorde. Reprinted by permission of the
Charlotte Sheedy Literary Agency.

A CIP catalogue record for this book is
available from the British Library

ISBN 1 86049 287 8

Typeset in Melior by M Rules
Printed and bound in Great Britain by
Clays Ltd, St Ives plc

Virago
A Division of
Little, Brown and Company (UK)
Brettenham House
Lancaster Place
London WC2E 7EN

For my beloved Larry and Joseph;
for Jane and Bob, whose faith and encouragement
made a difference; and for my mother and father,
whose spirits guide me and make me strong

may I never lose
that terror
that keeps me brave.

— FROM 'SOLSTICE' IN AUDRE LORDE'S *The Black Unicorn*

. . . the worst is not
so long as we can say 'This is the worst.'

— FROM SHAKESPEARE'S *King Lear*

Thanks to my wonderful agent, Jean Naggar, for believing in this book, and to her staff for their invaluable assistance. Thanks should also go to Jim Whitehead, Heather Ross Miller, Miller Williams, Carolyn Forché, and Bill Harrison, who taught me, years ago at the University of Arkansas, to strive for excellence. A special thanks to my editors at HarperCollins, Joelle Delbourgo and Leigh Ann Sackrider, for their careful suggestions.

Thanks also to Tim Duggan at HarperCollins for his assistance with all the editing details; and thanks to Ellen Brown and Siobhan Dowd, who read the manuscript with keen critical eye and who never wavered in their friendship. My thanks to Sally Abbey at Virago for her enthusiasm and guidance. Thanks to Dean Robert Bates and my friends in the College of Arts & Sciences at Virginia Tech for their support while I tried to write *Lady Moses* and serve as associate dean at the same time. And thanks to Virginia Tech for the research leave that enabled me to continue with this project.

Heartfelt thanks to Sally Harris, whose encouragement and feedback were crucial. Last, but not least, thanks to my family and friends, especially Larry, Joseph, Bob, and Jane for their love and support, and for never doubting I would find a way to tell Jacinta's story.

PART I

L O N D O N

1

Louise Buttercup Moses is dead. She was the beginning of my story and she shaped its middle. She has left me to write the end of it on my own. Her thin English hair, coiled by the chemotherapy, hugs her skull like the fuzz of newborns; her eyelids don't flutter anymore; her chapped lips are slightly parted, as if she's come in from winter to warn me about the chill of the outside world. But dead parents don't speak in the literal sense. So I force myself to dream the words from her mouth and give them the appropriate intonation: *I love you, Jacinta,* she says. *The world is only cold if you forget how to light a fire. You will be lucky.*

It isn't the way I thought it would be. In my rocking chair by the hospital bed we set up for her in the living room, I sit and stare at each contour of her face. I want to carry it with me on the rest of my journey because, in death at least, it is full of tenderness. I look at her expression and see it recede from me into memory even as I stare at it. I hope that, when the pain lessens, she will have left something in her wake for me to steer by. On this day in April, I hold Lady, who is crying with the strength of all her nine years and telling me it isn't fair. I, a daughter no longer, hug my daughter and try to tell her in words she'll understand that justice is as transient as innocence; and that Mama Lou loved her; and that love, in the end, always has to be enough.

Later, when I am alone again, I sit with my mother's corpse in the dark. I reach out to touch her, but jerk my hand back. She is cold. Her skin reminds me of plastic. I shiver and rock back and forth to nowhere, and pull the blanket Alfred gave me tight around my neck.

Louise Buttercup Moses is dead. I, Jacinta Louise, am still breathing. Once again that small detail means that I am the one left behind. It was Easter when I sat in the dark with the dead before. I try not to remember. This is another place. This is another Easter. Circles are not always nooses. Coming back to the past can be a way out of the present. We must believe that; we have no choice.

The grayness of London seeps in through the drawn curtains in the sitting room where Louise went mad, casting a light that will forever remind me of weeping. In this room in London, on this day, after thirty-six years of playing Mother and Daughter, she has finally escaped from me. I call out her name: *Louise! Louise!* But no one resurrects the dead unless it's in a story.

First we are together on the pages of a narrative, and then, a few pages later, when I was comfortable in the role of my mother's mother, she dies. I feel cheated. In spite of what I said to Lady, I am angry, angry, angry. I want her back. It was too soon. The system was rigged with a virus. Someone should have told me.

When she told me she was dying, the ocean crackled between us and, in an aside, casually, as though I should have expected it, she mentioned that, if the chemotherapy didn't work, she'd have about six months. 'What a nuisance,' she said. We made jokes, the way we had learned to do when life sucked so much you wanted to kill something. She told me she could get the wig on the National Health. 'I don't want the Maggie Thatcher look,' she said. 'Her hair looks sort of concrete, doesn't it? I like the queen's hairdo; I could live with that.' She told me I was very brave. I tried hard to keep breathing. She told me she was proud of me. 'America's so much better than here,' she said. 'Everything's rotting in Britain.' Then she thanked me again for not making a fuss and said she was going to Salisbury Cathedral the next morning on the coach. She wanted to visit Salisbury because it made her happy to know how spires felt. When I put the phone down, I was a 'little coloured girl' again instead of a woman of color, and everything turned to dust. It hurt so much I cried out like an animal and terrified Lady.

Nothing is more potent than exhaustion, not even fear. I am tired. I long to be back in Virginia where spring is green and where the ghosts from two continents cannot find me. I look at my mother's sweet face as she sleeps. In the dark recesses of the room, regret scratches around in the corners. I lean back in the chair. Sixty-six. Not a lucky number. Our ages play with each other. Three is half of six. At thirty-six, I am half the woman she was. What she did I probably could not have done. She left and then came back, denying the sweet pull of insanity for nearly thirty years.

Alfred comes in. *Come and have some tea, Cinta,* he says. *Come and have a nice cup of tea.*

But tea won't help this time. Alfred knows this. He comes into the room and pulls up a chair, which scrapes across the carpet in a sound reminiscent of the word 'hush.'

Hush. The Mother-Baby is sleeping – coaxed into death by the final lullaby. This room on Lavender Sweep in South London is her sepulchre. A few cars rush around the bow of the street; we barely hear them. Lavender Sweep has been Louise's home for forty years. There is nothing glamorous or grand about it. It is an ordinary street in an ordinary part of South London that had, for a few decades (I force myself to believe), some extraordinary residents.

Alfred takes my hand and that is the only cue I need in order to let go. Pain spills out of me like blood. When I speak, my voice has to climb stairs.

She was better than this. If only . . . if only . . .

Alfred kisses the hand I burned as a child because it had sinned, and places it over the golden key that hangs from a chain around my neck.

We'll write it down, he says, barely audible. *Amazing things happened in this house. You know it will heal us if we write it all down.*

He thinks I don't hear him. But way down where I am on the

bottom rung of the ladder, my strong left hand reaches for a pen.

If life is only a brief journey toward great loss in a small room, what will I tell my child when she asks me again, just as she did when she was five years old, 'What is the meaning of life, Mama?'

There has to be more than this paltry death. My answer to my daughter must imply that there is glory to be found if you look for it hard enough. If mortality is to be borne, it needs a frame of reference. Perhaps courage comes in the construction of one.

You know it will heal us if we write it all down.

I start with the capital letter 'I.' It begins in the sky with Louise and ends on the earth with me and Alfred years ago when Simon was with us – before Lady, before Manny, before Esther, before John. Before something terrible transformed Easter.

Back to a time when Louise and Simon were alive, when there was joy and grandeur in the world, and I was a small coloured girl riding my father's elephant among the traffic on Lavender Sweep.

2

I began on Christmas Eve. I slipped out of the womb with astonishing ease. My mother turned to the midwife and said she wouldn't mind doing it again tomorrow.

They christened me Jacinta Louise Buttercup Moses after my mother (Louise Buttercup) and an aunt in Africa named Jacinta.

God only knows where my African aunt got that name – my father never could remember. According to the stories, my aunt was wild: she ran off into the bush with a Temne man and returned with three girls and an attitude. She became a devout Catholic long enough to receive typing lessons from the nuns. Then she announced one day that she was walking to the capital with her daughters and never coming back. The village life bored her, she said, almost as much as the nuns. She was the first of my father's family to venture out beyond the village and try to discover what was on the other side.

Years later, Simon Moses, now grown and intellectually gifted, and a man (which gave him a distinct advantage over his sister), got a scholarship to go to a university in London where he met Louise Buttercup. Few English people had seen an inter-racial couple before: I can still remember people staring at them as they pushed me along in the pram. (Alfred claims I have an astonishing memory even for things that didn't happen. No one remembers things from when they were a year and a half, he says. But I do. I remember everything. It's all in sharp relief – as if my vision has been honed by scalpels. It's the clarity that delights and terrifies, the clarity that can tear you away from reason.)

My father had a sense of humor. He had to. It was only a few years since Hitler had been defeated, and he was a black man married to a white woman – the first black man some English people had ever seen up close. He used to lick his lips when passersby stared for too long, and then they'd take off with all their fears confirmed. Luckily, my mother despised humanity, so she didn't give a damn what anyone thought. She raised me to believe that most people were cows in a field. 'Look at them,' she'd whisper to me as we sat in a pew at church, 'cows in a field.' It never struck me as paradoxical that she hated humanity most when she was at prayer. Catholicism has always had an elitist foundation. There's the Pope and the cardinals, the monsignors, the bishops, the priests, the nuns, and then the plebs. My mother said we weren't plebeian or working-class even though we were as poor as church mice; we were classless because we were Bohemian, on account of the fact that my father was a genius and she was a failed actress. All during primary school, I told my friends I was from Bohemia. She often confused me, my mother, because she refused to talk down to me.

Because I admired my mother with a passion, I never wanted to be a cow in a field. At night I'd end my prayers with a fervent plea: 'Don't let me be a cow in a field, Lord! Please!' To my great misfortune, He must have listened. Maybe my mother's loathing of bovines stemmed from the fact of her name. She too must have been teased at school for having the name of a cow.

My father was a little over five feet, two inches tall – though most people who knew him swore he was much taller. He'd been a fighter in his youth, and he was almost as broad as he was tall. He had a beautiful, dark face, and a gentle spirit typical of Mende people. He sang the songs he'd heard from his mother growing up, but he never wrote them down, so they were lost with him. But years after he left us, I'd rush down the stairs of our terraced house to try to catch the thread of song I'd hear weaving its way home to Africa. Louise would shout after me: 'Where are you going?' and I'd say, 'I'm going to catch him, Mummy. He's singing again.' And she didn't try to stop me. And that's the best thing about her – that all through the years, she never tried to stop me.

On Saturday mornings, Simon, Louise, and I had our Red Sea Radio Hour. We called it by this name because my father said that the Moses clan danced so magnificently that we could tame the elements if we wanted to. 'We've parted the Red Sea once!' he'd cry. 'Let's do it again!' This was the time when we turned the large dial on the old radio to the BBC and listened to a selection of music played by a man with a reedy voice who sounded like the Queen's butler, or so my mother claimed, though this was probably mere speculation, none of us having been introduced to either of them. Nevertheless, Sidney Purcell took on that persona – here was a man who never demeaned the Queen's English as I did by leaving off my 'g's and 'h's.

'Now, ladies and gentlemen-n-n of the airwaves,' he'd say, 'we are going-g-g to listen-n-n to *Carmina-a-a Burana-a-a* by Carl Orf-f-f.'

When the music played, my father and I danced. Sometimes my mother danced too. But not often, because as she said, she was happy just watching us. My father said it wasn't the same as dancing in Africa but that it was close enough. Often, we didn't dance in time to the music at all. Looking back, it seems to me we danced instead to the rhythms inside Simon's head. We'd close our eyes and let our hips shake and turn our legs loose to his memories. Our feet would pound the floor of the tiny living room-kitchenette at the top of our flight of stairs on Lavender Sweep. Once in a while the next-door neighbors would pound on the adjoining wall. 'Keep it down in there, bloody nignogs!' Mrs. Midwinter would shout. Then Simon would dutifully go to the radio and fiddle with the dial. Sometimes the dial 'got the better of him,' and simply refused to turn the right way. Then my mother would cover her mouth and laugh because the music was turned up even louder and my father was dancing in the character of Irma Midwinter, pinching up his face as though we were a stench she wanted to avoid smelling.

When the Red Sea dance was over, I'd sit on my father's lap again, and Louise would bring us lemonade, if we had some. If not, it was water. If there was one to spare, I had a sugar cube in my glass, and I'd watch it dissolve slowly until it became invisible. Then my father would stroke my hair and my mother would draw up a small, three-legged stool and lean into him too, and we'd all three sit in the afterglow of the dance, not saying anything, simply happy.

My father's hands had boomerang thumbs, or at least that's what I called them, because they bent right over as if they had decided against staying with the other fingers and were off to find adventures of their own. His palms were very pale (my mother said it was because he worked so hard at the Brillo factory, but Simon only laughed), and in his dark fingernails there were half-moons or white suns just about to set. In those moments after the whirl of the dance, there was nothing more I wanted than to be there on my father's lap with my mother next to us in our tiny living room. Even at five, I was acutely conscious and self-aware. I knew I was blessed with a fair-skinned mother and a dark-skinned father; and I knew that our conjuring up of West Africa in the small room at the top of a house in Battersea was significant.

My mother and father were in love for eight years. It was a Cathy and Heathcliff kind of loving that was premised upon desire, but it lacked the violence often associated with extreme passion. They were tender with each other. I know that, not just because I remember it myself, but because of the letters she showed me later. Very few couples know what it means to be tender with one another. But to Simon and Louise, tenderness seemed to be at the center of their passion for one another. When my father called to her, the call was a question rather than a command. It was almost as though he was afraid that, one day, she wouldn't be there to answer him. I believed that nothing could touch us. I believed that we were rich because we had the power to conjure up a continent in our kitchenette and dance to music only we could hear. I stuck out my little chin in pride and felt sorry for plebeians, cows, and everyone who didn't come from Bohemia.

Passion ruled in our house on Lavender Sweep. Although my mother confessed in later life that she'd never seen my father naked – that he always wore a vest to bed – she didn't hide the fact that this in no way inhibited his performance. When, as a grown woman, I gazed at his photo and admired his perfect teeth, she said she suspected they were dentures. She never did know for certain, however, because he didn't take them out at night. He was a man of mystery.

During the day, as I mentioned, my father worked in a Brillo factory. He had a bad heart, so the strenuous factory work was ill advised, but we needed the money. Sometimes I'd creep out of bed at five A.M. and run to the front-room window to watch his back disappear around the curve of Lavender Sweep. There was no heat in three of the four rooms we occupied, so I'd stand at the window and shiver, my breath making mist circles on the glass. In the distance was the rattle and rumble of trains from Clapham Junction, where he was heading. I hated Brillo pads for years afterward and refused to use them to clean pots. Those paltry little cleaning pads had taken my father away from us. For years they epitomized to me the injustice of capitalism.

In order to make ends meet, my mother did some secretarial work at home, typing books about mythology and folklore for a warlock named Ruskin Garland. Later it struck me as odd that she typed books for a warlock; still odder that Ruskin liked to spend his vacations at a nudist colony near Liverpool, where it was often exceedingly chilly. But my mother didn't think it was worthy of note, so Ruskin was just Ruskin, and that was that. He happened to be my godfather, though he vehemently denied the existence of an orthodox deity. He once drew a beautiful flower using the blood that dripped from his nostrils during a particularly severe nosebleed – one of the earliest examples I can remember of a creative approach to recycling. He caught the blood on the paper on which he was writing letters, and improvised the way only he could. My mother said that this action was the hallmark of an artist. I lay in bed at night and wished for nosebleeds.

Ruskin Garland was my father's intellectual companion and Alfred Russell-Smythe was my mother's emotional one. For years I thought he was in love with her; but Louise only laughed at me. Ruskin and Alfred hated each other's guts. It gave me real pleasure even as a tiny child to watch them carry on. Once, Ruskin broke a teacup on Alfred's head – which, believe me, is very hard to do. Alfred rented a tiny flat from us that consisted of two rooms on the lowest floor of the house. He proceeded to become almost as good a friend to me as my parents were. Later, when I needed his friendship more than anything else, he never let me down.

Apart from Ruskin and Alfred, there was what seemed to my childish eyes to be a constant stream of visitors to our one-hundred-year-old terraced house in Battersea. They came to hear my father speak, or to hear him read his stories. Men from Nigeria and Ghana, Sierra Leone and the Congo entered the small rooms bringing the land with them in their flowing robes and embroidered hats. Some of them would cry when he read; some of them just smiled. I sat on his lap and felt the beat of his heart as he read the words. It quickened at the dramatic climax of the story, then returned to normal. Sometimes men and women from the West Indies would show up. If the Africans brought their land in their clothes, then the Jamaicans and Bajans brought it in their voices – island voices that sang rather than spoke.

After the stories, it was time for bed. Louise tucked me in, but I could still hear the excitement in the other room as people argued about politics and religion. My father's voice was the one the others seemed to return to. It would be end-stopped by Ruskin, who always seemed to want to have the last word. I knew that some of the Africans hated Ruskin, but he made my father laugh, and that was enough for me. My mother said my father was a Communist, but that didn't mean he was a bad person. 'There are lots of good Communists,' she said. 'I proba-bly would have been one myself if I'd grown up where he did.' She told me not to mention it to the nuns, who probably wouldn't understand. So, at the age of four and a half, I began to carry secrets around with me. They felt good and warm, like small animals tucked up inside my blouse. They weren't lonely secrets; they were shared with Louise or with Alfred or with

Simon. My parents and their friends trusted me. I carried the secrets with a care that could easily have been mistaken for pomposity.

So my mother and I were Catholics and my father was a Communist writer. Alfred explained to me that writers couldn't be Catholics because their minds were too broad for religion. It made sense to me; my father's forehead was indeed broad, to match the gorgeous width of his nose. My mother wouldn't talk about religious differences. For her it would have been like talking about the details of lovemaking. But she didn't seem happy when Simon stayed at home on Sunday morning listening to jazz on the radio or playing his Paul Robeson records. They didn't argue in front of me, and Simon could always displace her anger by twirling her around or telling her a story. Alfred said I had the most charming parents in London, and it didn't matter whether or not we went to church together, like most of the white people I saw in the pews, because Simon prayed when he took up a pen. When I told my father this, he roared with laughter and said that Alfred Russell-Smythe was a very wise man and that I should always remember to listen to him. Then he brought me up close, checked to see that Louise wasn't nearby, and spoke in a low voice:

'I am not a Roman Catholic, little one. I am a socialist. Some would say I'm a Communist, but that is only because it is difficult for people to understand what socialism means. I am a socialist, but I know God. He is here.' He put his hand on his heart. 'And when I have you and your mother in my arms, He is there too. And if I write a story, I find Him in the pages. And when I die, He will call out my name like a song over my land, and my beloved will hear the word "Africa," and hear the word "glory," and remember that it is the same thing. Do you understand?' I nodded. And later on I found the same words in one of his stories, and I circled the words spoken this time by an old man who was trying to explain to his wife why she should not weep when he died. 'You and I are the first Moses to be from many lands and many peoples. It is our job to tell the story of what this is like because it is important. You do not know the language here' (he pointed to my head), 'but you do know it here.' (He pointed to my heart.) 'That is what matters. When we go back to Africa, the land will come to you as a friend and welcome you home.'

'Why are we important, Daddy?'

'Because without our story there is a big hole in the world, and people will not know how to talk to each other. And people will not remember to cherish what is different. And then there is nothing but fascism and Holocausts.'

'O,' I said, trying to look as though I understood. He told me I'd find all this in the Jacinta story he'd written if I looked hard enough. I was already reading on my own. I took the book to bed with me that night and fell asleep over the story, looking for clues.

Simon Moses and Simon Moses' stories were the same thing when I was young. When I looked back on our time together, I couldn't separate the man from the narratives he'd weave. From within the web of Simon's stories, I learned about good and evil, glory and despair. I learned how to live with courage, and how to love the land we came from although I had never seen it with my own eyes. Simon's eyes saw it for me. The voice in his stories comforted me. I could lie down in the hammock of his words and listen to Africa calling my name. When little Jacinta ran away to ride on the elephant, and when the elephant, huge and ponderous, and as slow as prehistory, let her step up onto his back, and when she dug her fingers into the leathery folds of his skin, it was me riding up there through the bush. And, as a little girl, I never doubted that, one day, it would be the Real-Jacinta instead of the Story-Jacinta riding up there on his back, surveying the bush from the top of the world.

At night, when my father crawled home through the dank, South London streets after a twelve-hour day, he'd sit down and write at the old Remington. The keys would click far into the night, like my mother's stiletto heels, and I'd go to sleep to the tune of words.

On Sundays, if I was lucky, he'd read me what he'd written during the week, or read to me from his 'undiscovered collection,' which had been passed from editor to editor for four years. Some of them told him he was not cut out for writing. Others told him no one wanted to read about Africa in that way, and recommended the Tarzan series. Others praised his use of language but said he needed to make the stories more commercially appealing. And one or two said they'd publish it if they could, but they didn't know where the market for black books was in Britain. One small collection of his work was published by a West Indian press; and, when we got the fifty-pound advance, he made an African stew with beef in it, and palm oil, and we all danced around in our kitchen in the sky, told each other we were famous, and planned our trips to visit the queen and her butler at Buckingham Palace, and to go back home to West Africa.

Because my favorite story was the one about the elephant named Asunu and the girl named Jacinta who tried to find him before the hunters did, Simon told that one over and over again. Full of repetition and twists and turns, the story reversed back on itself and caught me off guard each time. At the end I'd say, 'Daddy, I want to be Jacinta. I want to ride up high on the elephant and see the high palms and feel the breeze of the flapping ears,' and he'd say, 'You *are* Jacinta.' And, for many years, I thought he was making a joke.

Then one day something terrible happened.

I was five and a half years old and, according to Ruskin, so bright that the nuns were already trying to think of ways to quell my spirit. I was eating breakfast with Louise; I assumed that Simon had left hours beforehand the way he did on weekdays to make the long journey across London to the Brillo factory. But my mother didn't answer me when I spoke to her. And she spilled the cornflakes and the milk and then swore loudly enough for me to hear it. Then she sat down at the table and I saw that her hands were trembling. I was five and a half, and I wanted to say, 'I am five and a half. Remember?' But she was spilling things and saying words that didn't sound like her, and the room was getting smaller on me, and I wanted Simon to come home. She took me on her lap. I felt her heart beating the way my father's did when he got to the best part of the story. But I knew it wasn't the same.

My mother said my father had had a heart attack. She asked if I knew what that was, and I told her I did. It was a half-truth, as I thought she meant that someone had attacked his heart, and I couldn't imagine who would want to do it, or how I would get revenge. She said he was very sick. I told her he would get better and she squeezed me in reply, so I said it again. She told me I didn't have to go to school – that I was going to the hospital to see him. I jumped off her lap and spun around with my arms flung out. 'No school! No school! Yippee!' She said I'd have to be very good and quiet because children weren't allowed in the wards. She said she planned to get me in anyway and no bloody twerp of a nurse was going to stop her.

I wanted to make a good impression, so I reached into my mother's wardrobe for my First Holy Communion dress. It had belonged to a girl named Lottie Driscoll whose mother gave it to my mother when Lottie outgrew it. Soon I'd be old enough to wear it, to take the vows and suck on the host. The dress was white, of course, though there was a small yellow stain on the bodice where Lottie had dropped the yolk of the soft-boiled egg she had had for her First Holy Communion breakfast. I wanted to ask my mother if I could wear it to the hospital even though it was several sizes too big. I wanted to take it from her wardrobe, which smelled of 'Je Reviens' perfume, open the box, unwrap the tissue paper, and put the dress on in honor of this special trip. But Louise didn't hear me when I asked in my best voice, with all the consonants sounded out at the ends of words, so I had to make do with my Duckie dress, which had a red zigzag border and blond girls herding ducks across the hem. It had a stain too, on the skirt, where I'd sat on one of my father's fountain pens, but I still wore it because I had only three dresses, and besides, Alfred assured me that anyone would mistake the stain for a snippet of summer sky. So I put on the dress with the red zigzags, the ducks, the blond girls, and the sky fragment. Then I yanked on my yellowed ankle socks to see if I could get them closer to my knees, and slipped my arms into the hand-me-down coat we'd bought at a church bazaar – one Alfred claimed had, in all likelihood, once belonged to Elizabeth Taylor, the nylon fur collar being so elegant – and stood in front of my mother as she put on her lipstick and combed her straight, fair hair.

We walked to the hospital. It was about three miles away and the journey down to the Northcote Road and up the steep hill toward Wandsworth Common was a tiring one, but I was too excited to complain. I chattered all the way there. The sunshine made me want to sing. I sang the hymns I'd learned at school and then went on to sing some tunes from *Snow White*, which I liked better. We passed women with shopping bags and baskets-on-wheels. Many pushed small children in prams or pushchairs. My mother cautioned me about the dog turds, which were everywhere, as usual, but I didn't step in any of them. She said people in London shouldn't have dogs; it was a health hazard. I suggested they clean up after their animals. My mother laughed in a hollow way and said, 'That'll be the day!'

The streets were lined with cars, and I wished for an automobile so that we wouldn't have to wait at bus stops in the cold or walk so far. I closed my eyes so that I could picture the three of us inside a Rolls-Royce. My mother pulled on my arm. I barely missed planting my foot in an especially runny dog doo-doo.

'Watch where you're going, Jacinta!' she snapped.

I focused again on the pavement. Then I turned to her and asked once more why Daddy was at St. Jude's. She told me he'd had a heart attack on his way home from the Brillo factory. I chalked up another black mark to Brillo. She said he'd turned the corner from Lavender Hill and was at the house at the end of Lavender Sweep, which had the brick wall with the broken glass bottles cemented into the top. Alfred said they did that so that children's knees would be scooped out and cats' limbs torn off. He said it should be banned. He called it the Wall of Cruelty. It was just next door to the Hilarious House with the pink door, turquoise doorstep, and yellow shutters. My mother said that my father had just fallen down there, next to that awful wall. She said it as if it were the wall's fault, and I didn't doubt that somehow it was.

'The Wall of Cruelty,' I said in my most grown-up and serious manner. It felt good that she was talking to me like this. It felt as though I were Betty Lemon, who lived downstairs and who sat with my mother and talked in a low voice about things that were not for young ears.

'But something told me to go outside. Something pulled me out into the night. And then I went to fetch Alfred, and we both searched for him because it was getting so late. And then we found him behind that hedge next to that awful wall . . .'

'The Wall of Cruelty.'

'And he hadn't cried out or anything. I just knew he was there. And then we called an ambulance and Alfred stayed with you, and I went to the hospital with Daddy.'

It seemed funny to me that I hadn't woken up when so much had happened. I loved to look at ambulances, and now I'd missed the flashing light and the siren and everything. I was angry with Alfred. He should have woken me up. But I was glad that my mother had found my father and couldn't imagine what he had been thinking of, falling over like that and not getting up again when my mother was waiting for him with a shepherd's pie she'd made that day. And it had minced meat in it too, and carrots. If he had known, he would never have been late like that.

I told my mother she was very clever to find him, and that I would have found him too if I'd been awake.

'Yes,' she said, smiling. 'You're probably right. We Moses find each other no matter what. You see what love can do, Cinta, don't you? Love can let you move mountains if you believe in it enough. We're going to believe, you and I. And we're going to move mountains.'

'Yes!' I said, clapping my hands. 'We *can* move mountains, can't we?'

By the time we got to the hospital, my mother seemed much happier. But as soon as we stepped inside the Victorian brick building, she began to tremble again.

In the lobby, nurses looked at me with disdain. They looked at my mother the same way. One nurse with a face like a pinched nerve told her she couldn't bring *that* in here, meaning me. She said it was too early for visiting hours, and we'd have to wait for another forty-five minutes. My mother trembled more than ever, and I held on tight to her hand so that she wouldn't fly away.

A doctor came out and told us we were making too much

noise. But he wasn't mean like the nurse had been, and he smiled at me. He said I could stand in the doorway at the end of the ward and wave to my father. He said that was all he could allow. My mother wasn't standing up straight the way she always told me to do. I wanted to tell her to pull her shoulders back because if you slouched like that you couldn't get into the army or anything, but I knew this would be a bad time. She positioned me in the huge doorway that was the entrance to the men's ward where my father was. The doctor said she could go in even though it was early. She walked slowly down the wide aisle. She was wearing her best high heels, which must have hurt her feet on the journey. Her legs looked like a movie star's legs, and one man sat up in bed and whistled. His whistle sounded eerie as it floated up to the high ceilings. It was like whistling in church, and I felt ashamed for him. The windows were high on either side so my mother was caught in a wide shaft of light that traveled the length of the ward. I wanted to stare at her forever. I didn't want what was going to happen next. I knew it would be something bad. I didn't know what it would be, but it would be bad. I tried to run after her, but my legs wouldn't move. And then I saw my father.

For some reason, Simon Moses didn't look much like Simon Moses. He looked small. Like a small old man in a big white bed. My mother had turned to the right, and was standing at the foot of his bed, pointing to me so that he could wave. He tried to sit up, and she rushed to help him. He was smiling. He had striped pajamas on and his face looked very dark against the white walls and the white sheets. No one else was black there except for me. I wished his African friends could have visited this morning too. He lifted up his hand and waved. Later it seemed to me that he waved in slow motion, but I don't know whether that was true or not. But I could see his hand – the palm pale and strong – and I could see how handsome he was. I think I waved back, but I could never say for sure, which made me feel guilty later because I wanted him to know how happy I was to see him. Then the nurse came and took me away to a damp waiting room of bare brick walls where a man coughed up snot into a brown handkerchief and a woman smoked a whole pack of cigarettes before my mother came back.

The woman in the waiting room had a child with her. His name was Simon too, but she usually called him Si which sounded to me like 'sigh.' Each time she called to him in a raspy voice he sighed as if he too knew how appropriate his nickname was. I told him my father's heart had been attacked by Brillo. He said his granddad had pneumonia. He wanted to play with me, he whispered, but his ma wouldn't let him play with wogs. I said that was okay. I didn't want to play, anyway. He pointed to the ink stain and asked me what I'd got on my dress. 'It's the sky,' I said. 'Don't look nuffink like the sky,' he told me. He had a point. Then he went back to sit with his mother, who was sucking another cigarette down her throat, and we stared at each other across the dingy waiting room, and I wished Louise had let me wear Lottie's First Holy Communion dress so that I looked less like a wog and more like the Jacinta-in-the-Story.

By the time my mother came to collect me, I was angry with her on account of the dress. I was angry too that she'd left me there with the mean woman and the Sigh. Before I could stop myself, I waved goodbye to the Sigh. He began to wave back, but his mother slapped his wrist and he looked away from me.

Louise said we could catch the 49 bus back because her feet hurt and it was too far to walk. I forgot about the little boy in the waiting room and danced around clapping my hands. I asked if we could ride on the top deck. She didn't hear me. I didn't care, because we were riding the bus! We walked to the bus stop and waited. Soon we could be riding on top of the world! Alfred said I was a genius. He said normal five-year-olds couldn't read the things I could read. He said they wouldn't know the difference between Earl Grey and English Breakfast if it spat at them. I knew it was true. Other children just didn't seem to think the way I did. Some of them didn't even talk correctly. Some of them were just plain stupid like the Sigh had been today. No imagination. I, on the other hand, never stopped thinking about very difficult conceptions, Alfred said, or some such thing, which made me a genius and not a wog after all. No wonder God was rewarding me with a ride on the 49 bus.

I caught sight of the swings in the distance, at the far end of Wandsworth Common. I asked my mother if we could go there because it was a holiday.

'No!' she snapped. I didn't ask again.

The bus roared up to the stop and we got on. Louise forgot that I had a problem with the big step on to the platform and I nearly fell over as she dragged me on to the bus. By the time I realized we were sitting on the lower deck, it was too late to say anything. Louise fumbled in her pockets for change.

The bus conductor was Indian. He came up to us and asked where we were going. My mother said, 'Lavender Hill, please.' But the fare had gone up since we had ridden the bus and we were threepence short. My mother turned to me and asked if I had threepence. My mouth fell open. I had never had threepence in my life, except for one time when we went to the museum and Ruskin gave me two threepenny coins for my birthday.

'How far can I get with this?' Louise asked the conductor, opening the palm of her hand to show him the coins.

'I tell you what,' he said, in a low voice, 'I will let you and the little girl travel to the Northcote Road. But do not tell on me, Missus. I could lose my job, and there are many children to feed at home.' He punched some numbers into the machine around his neck, rolled out a ticket, and gave it to us. My mother gave him all the money she had, and then she bit her lip and pulled on her wedding ring finger and kept saying that Simon should have told her about the fares going up. Then suddenly she stopped saying anything at all and just sat like a stone. I had to nudge her hard when we got to the Northcote Road because it seemed to me she was just sitting there like a dead person, which made me annoyed because she was supposed to be the grown-up.

We got out at the stop by the fishmonger's, but she nearly left me on the bus, and I had to call after her because she had gone already and I was left behind.

When I caught up with her, her face from the side looked strange, so I tried to check that she was still Louise Buttercup Moses by getting in front of her and walking backward. When she nearly tripped over me, she dragged me back to her side. Her fingernails dug into my arm and I cried out.

'You little fool!' she said. 'What do you think you're doing? It's late. I have to get you home and then come all the way back. Just try for once to behave yourself, will you?'

We walked along together in silence. Then I hit upon a great idea. I would sing the well song again from *Snow White* because it always cheered her up. I'd include the echo too. Alfred said that I was as good as Shirley Temple, Ella Fitzgerald, and Judy Garland all rolled into one. He'd been urging my parents to have me audition, but Simon only laughed at him. I began to sing. I sang with gusto, knowing how much she liked my voice.

All of a sudden we had stopped walking and my mother had turned into someone else who was shouting at me and shaking me and calling me a silly little fool. She said I didn't deserve a day off from school. She said she didn't want to hear any more of that ridiculous nonsense – meaning my singing. And she said that the nurses were right not to let 'coloured' children in the wards if they didn't know how to behave. She'd never called me a 'coloured' child that way before. It made me shrivel up and remember how white she was. It made me want straight hair and a nose as thin as a knife. She was holding my hand so tightly that I thought my fingers would break, but I was afraid to tell her because she was walking faster than I could run, and I'd never seen her like that before.

When I looked around, the shoppers along the Northcote Road were looking at us. Women's white faces staring at the little coloured girl who was a fool, not a genius, after all. I didn't know what to do. I wasn't a coloured child. I was Jacinta Louise Buttercup Moses. I was the Jacinta-in-the-Story. I bit my lip and tried hard not to cry, but it spilled out of me anyway, and I hated the sound of me crying like a baby. I kept running along beside her, and all I could see were my yellow socks and the thin line of blood on my mother's instep where her high heels had cut into her foot. I stepped on all the lines between the pavement slabs because she was pulling me along so fast.

When we got home she made a cup of tea and let me have some in a saucer. But the house looked strange, like my mother had looked when she was shouting at me. It seemed darker than before, and the hallways were narrower. It was like going into a tunnel. And it was very cold because there was only one heater upstairs, and, before I could stop myself, I was asking her when Daddy would come home. Instead of shouting at me, she said she didn't know. I told her it would be soon. At last it was the right thing to say. She didn't seem to remember that she'd been angry with me. I was confused. She didn't talk much all the rest of the day, and I kept out of her way and played with my Tressy doll because I could turn a key in her back and make her hair grow the way white children's hair grew all down their backs. I almost wished I'd gone to school after all.

Then it was time for visiting hours again, and she left two hours too early, Alfred said, so that she could see him again.

Alfred put me to bed and tried to read one of Simon's stories, but it sounded strange in his voice, so I pretended I'd fallen asleep.

That night, or perhaps the next one, I dreamed Simon died.

When I woke up, my mother was standing by the bed. She kneeled down and took my hand in hers and said, 'Daddy is dead, baby.' She hadn't called me 'baby' in a long time, and I liked it. I said, 'I dreamed it.' She didn't seem to hear me.

I wasn't allowed to go to the funeral. I stayed home with Alfred because he said he was too tenderhearted for grief. We played Monopoly. The 'chance' and 'community chest' cards got all soggy because Alfred wept over everything. I tried to ignore it. He kept telling me that Simon was his best friend, which I knew was a lie because my father's best friend was Ruskin Garland. I didn't tell him that because I was trying to work out how to make money. I decided to ask Alfred about it, as he was very knowledgeable about things like that even though he never had any himself.

'Are we on the dole, Alfred?'

'What?' he said.

'Are we on the dole? You get money that way, don't you?'

'Not exactly. It means you are unemployed and you have to go and get some money from the government.'

'And they just give it to you?'

'Do you have Park Lane? O dear,' he sniffed.

When Alfred cleared his nose, it was a cold, cavernous sound, and I imagined his snot forming huge stalactites in his nose – the kind I'd read about with Simon in my science book.

'You should blow it,' I said. 'Mummy says you can get a nose-bleed doing a sniff like that.'

He blew his nose. Then he told me all about the time he'd met my father and my mother. But I knew the story already and I wanted to get back to making money. I had to listen, though, because I was five.

'And there I was on Clapham Common, speaking to the only black man I'd ever seen up close in my life,' said Alfred, 'because he was the only person who took the time to ask if I was cold, or if I was hungry, or what was the matter with me. And I told him, as you know, that I was down and out and brokenhearted to boot, and hungry on top of all that. And he said, "I can't do much about the broken heart, but there's food on the table and you're welcome to share it with us. Come home with me and meet my wife." And I went, even though I thought he said, "Come home and *eat* my wife." I went anyway because I was so depressed it didn't much matter to me whether he was a cannibal or not. And of course he wasn't. Nothing like. Simon Moses was a gentleman and a scholar. And then there was your mother. And she was white and so lovely, and he was black and lovely too, and I was an out-of-work thespian and it was *Othello* all over again. They fed me breast of lamb and roast potatoes. Then the Chief told me a story. Just from his head. And Jacinta, it was the most beautiful thing I'd ever heard. And I remember thinking about beauty and grief when I heard it, and about the way each one lives inside the other. I remember thinking that –'

'How do you make money?' I said.

'What? Why do you want to know? Look at the hundreds of pounds you have right there in your hand. You're too young to be thinking about –'

'This isn't *real* money,' I said, throwing down the Monopoly money. 'Everyone knows that. I want to find out how to make real money, Alfred. Okay?'

'Why do you want the money, child?'

'So that I can buy things, of course.'

'What do you want to buy?'

I thought for a moment. 'A car.'

Alfred nodded. 'Anything else?'

'A dress for me and a dress for my mum.'

'Anything else?'

'A new house.'

Alfred smiled. 'All right,' he said, 'I'll try to explain how people make money. But I don't think you'll like it.'

He went on about education and training and all kinds of things you had to do before you could make money. It seemed as though no one allowed you to make anything at all until you were about thirty, or even older. I didn't want to wait for years to make my money and I told him that. I said I needed it now, but he just shook his head and looked sad. I think it may have been the first wall I ever came to that I couldn't knock down.

'Are we poor?' I asked him through my teeth. There was a kind of fury in my voice, and it was hard for me to open my mouth wide – hard to speak at all.

'It depends on what you mean by poor.'

'I mean poor, like Oliver Twist or someone.'

'O no, Cinta, nothing like that. I work occasionally. Bit parts mostly, but I can pay the rent. And your mother, she is very talented. Very talented. Types up all those manuscripts and can recite Keats in a way I've never even heard done before. Extraordinary talent.'

'I want more money.'

He looked away and said, 'That would be nice, Jacinta, but, for a while at least, you'll have to learn to settle for what you have. Which is more than many and less than some. It's the way of the world, I'm afraid. We all just have to grin and bear it.'

I don't know if it was the tone of his voice that made me so sad, or whether it was the fact that the Wall of Cruelty had appeared in front of me and there was no way to scale it to find my father on the other side. It may have been the fact that Simon Moses would never take me on his lap again and make me the

Jacinta-in-the-Story; or it may have been the fact that I wouldn't be able to ride an elephant any longer or remember the rice fields or find Africa without him. Whatever it was, I didn't yet have words to tell it. All I had were two things: fear and sorrow.

'O,' I cried out, as though I weren't a child at all but an old woman. 'O, O, O.'

I didn't know then about the round and perfect holes of suffering, but I said them anyway, letting them well up from my throat like large round stones.

Alfred held me. We said we were sorry, though I didn't know what we were apologizing to each other for. Now I believe a part of us was sorry for something other than my father's death. I think we were sorry for the injustice of death itself, which grabs us by the hand and won't let go. We were sorry on account of the pain and on account of our own mortality and that of all those we loved and ever would love. We were sorry that being sorry didn't make a damn bit of difference. We'd witnessed the passing of something amazing. My father and Alfred's best friend was dead. He would never come back.

By the time the mourners came back from the funeral, the Monopoly game had been put away, we had dried our eyes, and Alfred and I were standing sentry over the ham and cucumber sandwiches and the small angel food cake my mother had bought in his honor. It was too expensive, she'd said, but people expected something at a funeral. Alfred had bought some digestive biscuits. We saved two for ourselves on a saucer and stashed it away in the kitchen behind the bread bin. Alfred said it was what Simon would have wanted.

About two hundred people tried to fit into our house after the funeral. People kept kissing me on the cheek and ruffling my hair, which I hated. Ruskin seemed to be holding my mother up. I asked her if she was going to fall down if he let go of her elbow and she laughed. I'd learned in the past two days to make an effort around her – to try to remember that I had to say the right thing. I'd said the wrong thing on the way home from the hospital and it had been terrible. She'd looked at me the way Sister Maria sometimes looked at me. She'd said my singing was nonsense. She'd called me a 'coloured child' and made me ashamed. I never wanted that to happen again. Louise Buttercup Moses had to love me. Always.

That night I lay awake for hours after my mother put me to bed and thought about Simon and Louise and Alfred and Ruskin. For the first time I saw them as people who could leave me and I was afraid. I couldn't articulate the fear, but I knew it was there – a small, vicious dog waiting to devour my heart. Anyone could die. Anyone. It didn't matter how good you were, or how wonderful the stories sounded, or how much someone prayed for you. You still died. Neither Louise nor I could move mountains with our prayers after all.

Suddenly I sat up in bed. The room was faintly lit by the hall light, and I could make out the shadows of people in the door crack as they wended their way down to the front door. I heard my mother say good night to Alfred. I heard him blow his nose in his flat downstairs. Then it was quiet. Just my mother's footsteps coming back up the three flights of stairs. Only my mother's footsteps coming up the stairs to our part of the house – past the rooms we rented to the Lemons, who were going to move next week because they'd found a council house, and then what would we do? (I heard my mother say on the phone to Ruskin) and on up to where we lived – Louise and Jacinta Louise. No Simon Moses anymore.

She stopped at my door and I heard her sigh. I was afraid to tell her I was still awake. What if that was the wrong thing to say? I had to be careful from now on. She continued on up to the small kitchen at the top of the house. We were the only people I knew whose kitchen was up near the birds. I heard her turning the tap on at the sink – maybe washing her face. She said we'd get a bathroom one day. I wished for money so that I could buy it for her tomorrow. I'd find ways to make a fortune. The house was quiet. No typewriter.

I found myself whispering: 'My mother is Louise Buttercup. I am Jacinta Louise Buttercup Moses. My father is Simon Moses. My father is dead.'

Way down below us, Alfred blew his nose. Stalactites. I lay down and closed my eyes. The dark brushed my face like fur. I didn't want to open my eyes again. I didn't want to be Jacinta

Louise. What do you do when you don't want to be you any-more? How do you bear it when you are five years old?

I heard my mother's footsteps outside the door. Then she crept in and I squinched open my eyes from the safety of the covers. One false move and all hell would break loose. I could make out her figure in the dark. She had a pillow and a blanket. She put them on the floor by my bed. Then she lay down. I wanted so much to say good night I thought I'd burst, but I didn't say it. I prayed silently to Jesus: 'Don't let me be a cow in a field, Lord. *Please.* Especially not now.' I suddenly wondered whether I could pray to Simon, now that he was buried and everything. The words were out before I had a chance to think. But my mother was sleeping, and her steady breath was the only sound I heard echoing around our house. Very softly I sang the wishing well song from *Snow White* before I remembered how angry my mother had been when I sang before. I mouthed it into the pillow instead, and then tried to imagine myself counting the paisley swirls on our stair carpet – the swirls that looked like fishes' hands – because it usually worked better than sheep.

We needed to find new renters. If we didn't find them soon, we'd have to go to the poorhouse like Oliver Twist did in the film. They'd take my mother away from me and feed me gruel. We had to find renters. Alfred only paid two pounds a week as a controlled tenant. It wasn't enough. I'd heard my mother say that to my father. It wasn't enough. I thought of all the people I knew. None of them were homeless. It was depressing.

And then, out of the dark, I heard my father's voice saying, '*You are Jacinta. You are Jacinta.*' And, for some reason, it made me feel better. I repeated it to myself like a lullaby: '*You are Jacinta.* You *are.* You *are.*'

Suddenly I remembered my fifth birthday, when my father had taken me down to the Northcote Road to get my ears pierced at a jeweler's shop. It was a pawnshop too, and it was crammed full of interesting things like old fur coats and paint-ings in huge gold frames. An old man had pierced holes in my ears with a special gun, and I hadn't cried once. My father had said he was proud of me for not crying. He said African girls in his village always had their ears pierced, so now I was an

African girl. He bought me a tiny pair of gold 'sleepers' and I was told to remind Louise to turn them every day so that the holes didn't close up on me like they did on some little girls. I had to keep everything clean and not touch my ears, said the old gentleman in the shop, or my ears could get infected, swell up, and drop off. Simon said that wouldn't happen to my ears because I was a very clever and careful little girl. My heart swelled with pride when he said that.

On the way home, he bought me a teddy bear iced lolly, and I sucked off the arms first, then bit off the vanilla cream head the way I always did so that only the squat little body was left. My father took my hand as we looked at all the shops along the Northcote Road, and stopped at some of the stalls where they sold vegetables and fruit. We bought a mango and some plantains for a birthday feast. We spent a fortune just on the mango, but my father said it was a good investment because I had come of age. 'You are African now, Jacinta,' he said. And we stood in the middle of the Northcote Road and remembered the rice fields and the sunsets and the people and the land in his stories. And gold hung from my ears, and my hand was hidden in his dark hand, and we took the mango and the plantains back home to Louise.

I twisted my sleepers round in my ears. No infection. I was a clean, careful, clever little girl. Tomorrow I'd find renters for my mother. I'd ask around at school. There had to be someone looking for a place to live. In our advertisement in the paper we said we'd take a black family. But we'd take a white one if that was all there was – I was certain of it. And I'd be six on Christmas Eve. I could make anything happen if I tried hard enough. Maybe I could dream myself into my father's stories and then they'd be real, just like the dream I had that he died and then he did, which was real and not a story. I squinched up my eyes and tried to be his Jacinta. But the elephant was too high, and so I couldn't get on and ride the way she did. The next thing I knew, my mother was rocking me in her arms. When I told her I couldn't ride the elephant, she smiled again. I'd said the right thing. Tomorrow I'd find a family to live below us and begin making fortunes.

I felt good and bad at the same time. There were things to be done. I had to hurry. People died on you if you didn't keep an eye on them.

I held tightly to my mother's hand.

If she flew away, she'd have to take me with her.

3

The Lemons moved out two weeks later, and a white family, the Beadycaps, moved in. Alfred found them. He bumped into Lily and Harry Beadycap at the fishmonger's on the Northcote Road. They happened to be looking for accommodation. My mother said the Beadycaps were a gift from God, but she soon changed her mind.

I was greatly relieved that I didn't have to find renters after all. I was sorry we hadn't found a coloured family, because it would have been fun to have some people in the house who looked like me, especially now that Simon was gone. But it would be fun too, my mother reassured me, getting to know all the Beadycap children. At least one or two of them were close in age to me. We could be friends. Reassured by her words, I forgot about my schemes for making money; but, every so often, they'd surface again as the years went by.

At first we were grateful when the Beadycaps liked the three rooms on the ground floor of the house – but then their daughter Mary filled my little school hat with spit. She claimed it was meant to have been vomit, but she couldn't get her finger far enough down her throat for that. My mother was horrified, and it was only our 'dire straits,' she said, which kept us from booting them out.

The Beadycaps lived on the main floor of our old brick house.

They were on the same level as the front door, which meant their rooms were always drafty and inhospitable. Their few sticks of furniture were covered in dirty clothes, piles of them. Lily said there weren't enough wardrobes in Battersea to house her six children's laundry. Most things weren't washed; they were worn again the next week or the week after that, once they'd been 'aerated,' Lily said, on the furniture.

Louise and I lived fairly quietly in our four rooms. We'd hear the Beadycaps below us and Alfred below them, but in London you become accustomed to domestic noise. Only when violence broke out between the twins or two of the other siblings would we rush to the landing and yell down to Lily or Harry to put a stop to it. Often, no one replied. After a few months we didn't tell them when Maurice was putting Mary's head in the toilet, or Kevin was trying to throw the toddler downstairs. My mother intervened only when necessary and washed her hands after she touched them. From her, I learned to be a social and intellectual snob. The Beadycaps were dirty. They paid rent. We had to put up with them but we would never, never approve. I held my little head up when I walked down the stairs to the front door and rarely deigned to look down at them. They were not like us. My daddy had been a genius; my mother was a former actress. They were below us in more than the literal sense. I think they were a little afraid of my mother. She swiped at them once in a while and could swear like a trooper. The children singled Alfred out for especially cruel torture. They made fun of his huge nose and wispy hair; they laughed at his affectations; they hooted at his clothes. I learned the word 'queer' from Maurice and the word 'queen' from Mary. Once in a while it thrilled me to observe them taunting him. I wanted Alfred to fight back, but he wouldn't. I thought he was a coward. When I visited him in his tiny flat, I'd ask him why he didn't tell them off. 'I'm a paci-fist,' he'd say, standing over his copper kettle, waiting for the water to boil so that he could have his English Breakfast or his Earl Grey, disappointing me once again.

There was no shower or bathtub in our house. None of the houses on Lavender Sweep had been built in the days when these were common, and we'd never had the money to add one.

I washed at the sink. I was too big to sit in it anymore. And there was a big metal bowl I'd stand in sometimes so that Louise could sponge me off. I wished for hot running water and bubble baths.

Worst of all, we had to share our toilet with the Beadycaps. Maurice always missed the bowl. Alfred said it was because he couldn't stand still. Alfred said he (Alfred) had to hold on to something sturdy whenever Maurice entered the room because the Troubled Boy (I called him T.B. for short) gave him the illusion of being on board ship.

'The boy *sways* so much,' he said.

It was true. Maurice could never stand still. A great, hulking boy of nine when he moved in, Maurice ate five sausages and six rashers of bacon each morning for breakfast, even though his mother and father were almost penniless. 'The boy's eating us out of house and home,' Lily Beadycap would say, nodding in his direction with great pride as her son thrust another Harris pork banger in his mouth. Maurice also ate his boogers in public. (Being a lady, I only chewed on mine in the privacy of the bedroom.)

After Simon's death, I spent much of my early childhood living inside the pages of books, or inside the black-and-white Rediffusion television set Simon had bought for us just before he died. It was encased in dirty-cream plastic housing, and it opened up the world to me, and made me ache with desire for material wealth.

There were two channels on TV, and each time we watched in those early days, we did so reverentially, not comprehending how they could have done something as amazing as squash actors into a little screen and bring them to our living room. I watched *Bonanza* every week, combing my hair carefully before the show came on because I thought Little Joe could see me. When Alfred told me he couldn't, I only half-believed him. I'd seen Little Joe's eyes. I knew he recognized me each week. Like most people in America, the Cartwrights were rich and lived on a great big farm and rode horses that carried them across the prairie faster than the wind. Unfortunately, the farm was often on fire at the beginning of the show, but they simply rode into the flames as fearlessly as ever and put them out with their cunning and bravery. They couldn't afford new clothes because they had a cook who obviously cost them a great deal because Chinese cooking was the best in the world. So they wore exactly the same outfits every week. When I pointed this out to Alfred, he said it was a convention and was not supposed to be a realistic depiction. I didn't let on that I couldn't speak French and so couldn't understand a word of what he was talking about. He treated me like an equal and I didn't want to jeopardize anything.

Once in a while, Alfred suggested to my mother that we invite the Beadycaps up to watch television with us. They couldn't afford a telly, he said, and the children longed to see a few programs. But my mother was horrified. She said she'd have to disinfect the chairs if they sat on them. She said they had fleas. Alfred looked very distressed when she said this. If I hadn't known him better, I would have sworn he was angry with her. But I sided with Louise. *Bonanza* and some of the other programs on television meant more to me than anything else in the world (apart from my mother and Alfred, and Simon's stories). I had no intention of sharing such a keen pleasure. So the echoes of other worlds tumbled down the stairs of the old house and entered the Beadycaps' dingy, furnished rooms to plague them. We had a television and a phone (though we couldn't really afford to use it). We had a gas heater in one room rather than a coal fireplace. We had worn carpet on our floors instead of the bare, warped floorboards and rag rugs they had. We were better than they were. Everything in my mother's expression convinced me of that. Everything in Alfred's suggested otherwise. I ignored him. The Beadycaps were dirty, and cleanliness was next to Godliness. Their fingernails were caked in what looked like soot. They spoke like commoners. They never enunciated like we did. Their consonants were a mess and their vowels were as distorted as their ugly mouths. They were not like us. Worst of all, they were prejudiced. They used words like 'wog' and 'half-caste' all the time, and the language they used to describe Alfred's frilly lavender shirts and high voice couldn't be repeated. Louise made me wash my hands whenever we went down to the front door because they might have touched it. Their mother, Lily, seemed like a pleasant woman, but she didn't understand the depth of her children's evil, my mother said. I barely glanced at the Beadycaps because they were not worthy of my attention. Alfred said I was turning into a snob. Louise reinforced my behavior: 'Don't go near them. They carry germs.'

During these years, my diary was another of my friends. In it I explored my hopes, fears, and dreams. I wrote my first poems in the diaries (nonsense rhymes, then couplets, then fourteen-ers, then a sonnet or two), and logged my major achievements. Sometimes I'd read parts of it to Alfred or my mother, or even to my Jamaican friend, Alison Bean. Mostly, however, I kept it to myself. It was the Secret-Me in there, and I knew instinctively that sharing secrets could be dangerous. Sometimes, especially after a moving sermon in church, I'd address my entries to God or Simon. (Sometimes I got the two confused.) Often I'd return to the theme of escape and liberation. When Alfred told me about slavery, I began to write from the point of view of Sojourner Truth. When I was nine, I wrote out the entire hymn 'O Come, O Come, Emmanuel' because the words drew me in so powerfully. As 'captive Israel mourned in lonely exile' I thought about all the coloured children across the world who were mourning too. Jews and black people had a lot in common, I believed. I planned revolutions where we would help each other escape persecution. I pictured Emmanuel as a beautiful man with wavy blond hair, just like the portrait of Jesus in the hymnals. He would come to us because He had been promised. I prayed so fervently that I got headaches. When Alfred learned of their cause, he said the nuns were fanatical about prayer, and I should remember my father's Communism and take a leaf from his book. So I prayed more discreetly because I didn't want to be thought of as a fanatic, or, worse still, a potential nun like the sisters at the convent school. Although they lived in a posh area of Clapham Park, the nuns weren't allowed to wear high heels or lipstick like Louise did, so their faces were as bland as baked potatoes. Mind you, Louise didn't wear heels anymore, or lipstick, for the most part. Her hair was getting limp because she didn't curl it with water the way she used to, her stomach was beginning to protrude like Lily Beadycap's, and she looked nothing like Merle Oberon, the movie star Alfred said she favored.

So I turned to the church to hold me up. When Louise and I entered St. Vincent de Paul's, which sat in the center of the mundane Altenberg Gardens like a Gothic anomaly, the drab domesticity of our lives – the dirt, the Beadycaps, the shared toilet, the threadbare carpet, the frigid and tiny rooms – all of it was washed away by the shadowy, incense-filled place of worship. It was possible to believe that life was grand in church. It was possible to believe that even the most lowly of us could become a god. Although my father's death made me a little skeptical about some of the claims made by Father Moth, on the whole I reveled in things like transubstantiation and penance. The only place that could rival Simon's stories was church with its tales of Samson and Delilah, David and Goliath, the Virgin Mary, Mary Magdalene, Pontius Pilate, and, of course, Moses. Sometimes it worried me that Moses didn't dwell in the Promised Land after all. Why had the Lord said to him 'I have let you see it with your eyes, but you shall not go over there'? Could it be a curse being named after someone who never reached the land of his dreams? My father had borne that name for more than forty years. He hadn't been able to get back home either. Every so often, the fact of my name was troubling. I didn't want it to claim me. As Alfred said, people were more than the sum of their parts. 'Moses' was a small part of me – that was all. It wouldn't proscribe my life. When Simon was alive, he and I had parted the Red Sea with regularity, I reasoned. I could do so again.

By the time I was twelve and a half, life had settled into what seemed to me to be a boring routine of Latin, history, physics with chemistry, mathematics, English literature, geography, biology, and French. *Bonanza* and *The Big Valley* made it all bearable, and Alfred helped me see things in perspective. I knew we lived on the rim of poverty. I knew there was no money for new shoes or new clothes, for ice cream or chocolate. For someone who wanted a baby grand in the parlor (a room we didn't have), life wasn't easy. Lavender Sweep, as I told Alfred at least once a day, was a *complete* dump. No one who was anyone lived in Battersea. My only friend in the whole road (apart from Alfred) was Alison Bean, and she was two years younger than me, and she was going to go to comprehensive school because she wasn't academically gifted. Alfred said there was more to life than a little intellectual trickery, which I thought was extremely mean considering the fact that he had taught me to value erudition.

In spite of our poverty, I could have borne the Sweep better had it not been for the Beadycaps. By the time I was twelve and a half, Maurice and Mary, the Beadycap twins, were sixteen. Their enormous size was enough to make you swear they were five years older; and they swaggered in and out of the house at all times of the day and night.

It was early summer when I got up one morning – the beginning of the school holidays. Alfred and Louise were both working – Alfred was auditioning for a part in a denture advertisement (he would be the 'before' model); Louise had to drop off a manuscript at Ruskin's because he didn't trust the post office. Alison and I had the whole day together. Louise got me up before she left and gave me Kellogg's cornflakes. I chattered away as usual, and she stared off into space as usual. There were bags under her eyes because she'd stayed up all night working on Ruskin's novel and had worked all day yesterday cleaning the house of a woman who lived in Clapham Park. Her breath smelled of stale coffee, and she sighed a lot and repeated questions I'd answered before. Every so often she'd twirl her hair around her fore- and middle fingers. Sometimes I'd catch her staring at me. There was something eerie about it – as if she were looking at me through a two-way mirror. When I asked her why she was staring at me, she jumped up and told me to stop being silly. A few minutes later, she was back twirling and gazing off into space. I was secretly glad when I heard the front door slam shut. Louise needed to pull herself together. New curtains would help matters, I thought, and so would a new carpet. I'd show her the pictures Alfred and I had cut out from the women's magazines, and the article we'd found about how to make the most of thinning hair. I made a mental note to do that tomorrow.

I rushed to our bedroom. My mother's bed was a mattress on the floor and mine was the bottom bunk from someone's old set of bunk beds. My mother's mattress hadn't been used last night because she'd been typing for Ruskin. I'd begun to hate having her sleep in the same room as me. She had given up the room she slept in with Simon because of rising damp. The plaster was peeling, and a man who came to look at it had told us it would cost hundreds, maybe even thousands of pounds to repair. But I didn't think Louise wanted to repair it. For some reason she seemed to like sleeping in my room in the middle of the floor on a mattress. But I liked privacy. She needed to find her own place. I'd suggested the front room on a number of occasions, but she never seemed to hear me. I tore open one of the drawers in the old chest that Alfred and I, in a flurry of bad taste, had painted pillar-box red last year in one of our 'overhaul' periods. If it had been ugly before, it was grotesque now. The cheap paint was peeling and chipping everywhere. Looking for comfort, I reached down into the chest for my diary, but, no matter how much I searched through my underwear drawer, I couldn't find it. I must have put it somewhere else. It could take days to find it in Louise's mess. I slammed the drawer shut. The house was a dump. Lavender Sweep was a dump. I wanted to go to America and ride across the prairie on my ebony stallion. I wanted to be Cathy on the moors with Heathcliff. I wanted to have a real steak in a real restaurant in Soho. I kicked the dresser and cursed Louise.

I'd wanted to look through my diary entry again. It had been especially good last night, I thought. I'd written it with biographers in mind, elevating the tone and employing a string of new words:

1. I am a coloured girl living in a white country. If I have a child by a white man, he'll be a quadroon.
2. London stinks.
3. Alfred is my best friend. He is also a graphic homosexual. And a very pleasant person.

4. Josephine Marsh is my other best friend. She is a white girl with long fair hair. She wears it in a ponytail. It reminds me of the Tressy doll I used to have whose hair grew. I still remember the ads with the American woman's voice telling me about the doll's secret, telling me that my doll's hair was magic. If I found the secret I could wind out her hair from the hole in the top of her head. I could make it grow the way white people's hair grew. I'd have power.

5. I am the brightest girl in my class – though no one seems to know it. Especially not the nuns, who think I'm disrespectful just because I argue with them about metaphysiology.

6. I am a bit ~~fat plump~~ voluptuous.

7. My father was a genius. If it's hereditary, I have inherited it.

8. Shakespeare was the greatest writer who ever lived, apart from Simon Moses and (in the future) Jacinta Louise Buttercup Moses (i.e., *moi*).

9. Louise Buttercup wishes she could climb down into the grave with my father. I found her diary. I'm not enough.

10. We are very poor. No one in my class at the convent is as poor as we are. I liked primary school better. People were like me there. We have carpet on the stairs that is so worn through that the pretty print with the fishes' hands is all gone. Just commas now. Faint yellow ones. I miss the fishes' hands. I want to KILL someone when I look at our house. Barbara Allnutt is rich. Her father drives a car. I'm a Communist. During the revolution I plan to take Barbara's car and drive it down her throat during our victory parade.

Motto for this year – <u>Blessed are the poor. They shall inherit the earth.</u>

It was a good entry, but I wanted to add some things about God and religion because I had been tempted again last night, and I needed to know what to do when an urge came upon me.

Father Mulroon told us that 'it' could make you blind, or at least result in perversion of some kind. We all knew what 'it' was, and I was doing it regularly. I knew it was wrong, but I couldn't seem to help myself. Thinking it through would be good, I thought. Mind over matter. I could reason myself out of desire if only I tried hard enough. But where was the bloody diary?

The doorbell rang. By the time I'd run down three narrow flights of stairs, Alison Bean's little brown finger was wiggling frantically in the letter box slit in the door.

'Let me in, Jassie!' she cried. 'It's your friend, Alison Bean from Jamaica!'

In spite of myself I laughed. Alison seemed to believe I was in danger of mistaking her for someone else. When I opened the door, she snatched her finger out just in time and nearly fell into the hallway.

'Summer 'olidays! Summer 'olidays!' she cried. 'And it's sunny, Jacinta! The sun is shinin'! No school! No school!' She twirled about like some kind of nutcase, and I shushed her quiet because there was no telling when a Beadycap would crawl out from under the woodwork. Alison was one of the quietest people I knew, except when she was excited about something and then the girl lost control. I looked at her huge brown eyes and tiny braids that stuck out from her skull like antennae. As she stood in the dismal hallway of the house, I remembered why I'd chosen her to be my friend. In spite of her dirty feet and her poverty, little Alison Bean was beautiful enough to make you swallow hard. When it snowed once, I made her lie down in it in the middle of Lavender Sweep so that I could remember how beautiful she looked.

'Let's go to the Common!' she cried.

But I didn't want to go anywhere. And it was me who decided what was what. 'No,' I said firmly. 'We'll sit on the stoop and watch the world go by.'

'All right,' she said, acquiescent as always. 'I don't care what we do long as we does it together.'

'*Do* it together.'

'Yeah. Sorry.'

She took my hand.

'Best friends, ain't we, Jassie?'

'Let's go and get a book to read,' I told her. '*Great Expectations*. I have to read it for English lit. I'll read it to you.'

'Out loud?'

'Of course.'

'Will you do the accents and stuff?'

'Yes. Of course.'

She smiled. 'I love the accents and stuff,' she said. 'You ain't got no bread, 'ave you, Jassie? Or a glass o' lemonade?'

Alison lived in the Hilarious House, the one whose colors clashed so badly it made you wince – the one right next to the house that had the Wall of Cruelty around the handkerchief of green that masqueraded as a front garden. Alison had so many brothers and sisters I'd stopped counting. But she let me put coconut oil in her hair, and she liked to sing with me. She agreed with everything I ever said and told me I was the best thing ever to happen to her. I liked her adoration. It made me tall.

We sat on the front doorstep as I read from *Great Expectations*, explaining it along the way. Once in a while I'd stop reading, and we'd watch the cars or the people.

The Sweep looked as dull as ever. No lavender. No chimney sweeps. Nothing romantic at all. When I sat on the front step and leaned forward, I could just see the tip of the Wall of Cruelty with the broken glass bottles glinting in the sunlight. But I never looked down there because of what the Wall had done to Simon. I'd kick it once in a while as I shuffled past, and there was a dent in the old brick that I liked to think I'd made. At the other end of the Sweep, curving round away from us, way down at the end of the road, was Dr. Murphy's office – a terraced house converted into a tiny doctor's office. In between us and him were about a hundred houses, all linked together like Siamese twins, all with skinny rooms and emaciated hallways. There was only one group of houses that didn't look like the rest: these were the Bridge Work Trio, Alfred said. The three houses looked like three false teeth because they were newer than the others, built when a bomb took out the old ones during the blitz. They had flat windows instead of bowed ones, and they had a 'modern' feel to them. Lottie Driscoll lived in one of them with her mother. Her father had left them for a younger woman and was now living it up in Margate. Lottie had a room all to herself with white wallpaper covered in little bunches of lilacs. She had a bathroom too, with fancy faucets and a large mirror on the wall. She had central heating and a mother who remembered to listen to her.

Apart from the cars and the distant rumble of trains, the scratching sound of Hubert Butcher as he tore along on his single roller skate was all we heard. Alison called out to him.

'Hello, Hubert. Ain't it a lovely mornin'?'

'Hello, Hubert,' he replied in his usual monotone. 'Lovely morning. Lovely morning.'

I wished Alison wouldn't speak to him. Hubert Butcher was more than twenty years old, but a hunk of his brain was missing. Sometimes he fiddled with himself right in front of you. Sometimes he just stared. His mother was a child minder; but, as Louise pointed out, Mrs. Butcher needed to look out for her own child before she took in anyone else's. They lived a few doors down, but sometimes you could hear Hubert all the way up and down the street when he had one of his 'conniptions.'

I looked at Alison. She was beaming. She didn't see what I saw. To her, Lavender Sweep was a place of wonder. She'd told me as much. She'd talk about her half-mile trips down to the Northcote Road as if they were expeditions to Africa. I planned to mold Alison in much the same way as Eliza Doolittle had been molded. We practiced 'The Rain in Spain' frequently, and I'd noticed some improvement. For a moment, I envied her. It was a fleeting thing, but it would haunt me later. Alison had what I did not possess: contentment. She found joy in small things. Sometimes I could too, but often my tremendous craving for beauty got in the way. 'You're lucky, Alison,' I said before I could stop myself.

'Lucky? Me?'

'Never mind,' I said. 'It's nothing.'

I opened up the book again.

Just then, the door swung open and Maurice Beadycap, huge

and hulking, appeared in the doorway. He stood there with his legs apart like Colossus. Alison cringed as though he'd already hit her.

'Hiya,' he said, trying to sound American rather than Cockney.

'Hello,' I said disdainfully. 'Why don't you come and improve your mind, Maurice? We're reading *Great Expectations*. It's all about a boy whose expectations are greater than his circumstances. You'd enjoy it.'

I giggled. Alison joined in, though I was confident she didn't get the joke. She loved watching me slay Maurice with my wit. It was nice to have an audience. All Alfred did was disapprove.

Maurice stepped over us so that he could block the view of the road. We could smell him. It was a musk smell. I didn't like it. For some reason, it embarrassed me. His silhouette eclipsed the sun, and Alison and I had to squint to make out his face as he spoke down to us.

'Birds of a feather,' he sneered, looking from one of us to the other.

Part of me wanted to deny the association. My mother was white, after all. But Alison was my friend. Why did I feel ashamed? I hated him for making me feel that way.

'Go away, Maurice. We're having a *private* conversation.'

'Right you are, Cinta. Be gone in a mo. Got loads to do. In fact, I've decided to read a bit. Found a lovely little book to flip through. The girl who wrote it is a genius. It's hereditary.'

I think my heart must have stopped. I don't know what happened to my face, but Alison gasped when she looked at me, and reached out as if she were saving me from a great fall. It must have been several seconds before I found my voice.

'Where did you get it?' I was whispering, and there was a sob at the end of the sentence. I stood up. My knees were wobbly. Alison stood up too and took my arm.

'Found it lying around.'

'Liar! Bastard liar! You went into my drawers!'

Maurice began to laugh. 'I wish that was true, Cinta. I tell you, I've wanted to do that for years.' He looked me up and down and laughed some more. I tried to grab the book. He put it behind his back and twisted my arm.

'You're hurting me!'

'You need to behave yourself, little girlie. I'm twice your size. I could crush you in the blink of an eye. Get it?'

I was crying. Alison tried to punch him with her little fist. But she was only ten and very puny. He pushed her away. She fell off the stoop and grazed her knee.

'Alison! Are you hurt?' I turned to Maurice and screamed in his face. 'You pig! You horrible pig!'

I kicked him hard in the shin. He grabbed hold of me and lifted me so that I was pressed up against his body. Fear held me. I had never in my life been so close to a man who was not my father or Alfred. And Maurice had suddenly become a man. He jammed me up against the brick and looked into my face. He spoke softly – his hips slammed into mine, his breath hot on my face.

'Tell you what, Jacinta Louise. Tell you what. 'Cos I'm such a bloody gentleman, I'll let you have this book back.' He shoved into me again. My feet were off the ground. I felt something hard below my waist. He must have the diary in his pocket, I thought. I tried to reach down and grab it. To my amazement he didn't try to stop me.

'You wan' it, don'tcha?' he whispered, guiding my hand down, down.

I jerked it away, but not before I'd found out it wasn't the diary. I screamed.

'Shut up, you little bitch!'

He was carrying me inside. Alison was following us, calling out for help. He planted me down in the hall and swore at both of us to shut up. We clamped our mouths shut. My mother was at work; Alfred was out too; and Maurice's parents were God knows where. The hallway was dark. Out of the corner of my eye, I saw a door crack open. Mary's eye appeared in the crack. The eye was smiling.

'I toldja I'd be a gentleman, didn't I?'

Maurice was breathing fast. He was shaking too, and his eyes looked wild. I saw the stairs behind him going up into the gloom of our rooms. The fishes' hands looked pathetic – worn away to nothing. Maurice stood in front of me. Nearly six feet tall. Barbara Allnutt had seen him once. A 'dish,' she'd called him. 'Like one of those movie stars. A dish.' I felt the skin on his face when he'd brushed it against me. Stubble. Rough. Nothing like Louise's face or Alfred's. Rough.

'What do you want, Maurice?' My voice was far away. Someone else must be speaking.

'Tell her to get lost.' He flicked his head over at Alison Bean.

'Go away, Alison,' I said.

She just stood there.

'Go away, Alison! He won't give it back unless you go away!'

Her eyes were so wide I thought they'd fall out. She turned slowly, looked back once, then went out through the front door. Maurice closed it behind her. The slab of light that had flooded the hallway before was gone. We were all left in the dark. My pulse was an anvil in my head and something was happening to me between my legs. Something terrifying I didn't want to stop.

'You want the diary back, Cinta? Do you?'

I nodded.

'You can have it.' He thrust the diary under my face. 'For a kiss.'

'A kiss?' My voice was weak. I thought I was going to faint.

'Yeah. You know what those are, don'tcha? I mean, the nuns do teach you about the French, don't they? Just a kiss, Cinta. You'd like it. You know you would.'

He was up against me again. Lifting me with his hips so that I was up off the floor. And then his lips were on mine, and the shock of his tongue. Fat. So fat and brutal, finding places in my mouth to lick. My hands did nothing. They were paralyzed. Something terrible was happening to me and Maurice Beadycap was the one making it happen. But I was a good girl. I'd always been a good girl. And now I was sinning with Maurice in our hallway and Mary was there looking at us. His saliva tasted of grease – sausage and bacon grease. His tongue was in the back of my mouth. He was licking my tongue, and I was letting him do it even though I was a good girl.

He pushed me farther into the wall. In a moment I would disappear into the floral wallpaper. Nothing left of me but a burned outline in the faded sunflowers. He pushed again and lost his balance. We fell over and somehow jammed up against the door where Mary hid.

'Jesus bloody Christ! My nose!' she wailed.

Maurice looked up to see his twin sister standing in the doorway with her hand cupped over her nosebleed. Her underwear was down around her knees and she was panting.

'I wasn't doin' nothin', honest!' she pleaded, crazy with fear, sensing the danger she was in.

She tried to jump over us in the cramped hallway and head out through the front door, but Maurice caught hold of his sister's leg and she came crashing to the ground. I felt the walls shake when she fell and saw her white buttocks exposed. They were bruised and scarred as if she'd spent her life bouncing from A to B on her bottom. Then her brother was upon her, and they were biting and kicking, and Mary's blood and saliva was all over the carpet.

'Bitch! Bitch! Pervert! Get yer own, why don'tcha?' Maurice screeched.

I fled. Not upstairs to Louise's rooms, but down, down to Alfred's. Down where I belonged. His door wasn't locked. I fell inside and locked it behind me. My teeth were chattering. Above me I could hear the twins tearing each other's hearts out. Something in me had been sleeping. Something in me had been thrust awake. I would never be Jacinta Louise of the diary again. The nuns were right. Hell was fire. Hell was hot. Hell was saliva and hips and hands. Hell was as dirty as Maurice Beadycap's lips.

I found Alfred's old dictionary, sat down unsteadily on his bedsettee, and flipped the pages to a word Josephine Marsh and I had found two months ago and giggled over in class – 'nymphomaniac.' Dear God, help me. I found my hand between my thighs and jerked it away again. What was that saying in the Bible? If your hand offends, cut it off. Yes. Cut it off.

I closed the book and stood up. It was quiet upstairs. Just the sound of a girl crying.

I squeezed into Alfred's kitchen and lit one of his two gas rings. The flames were blue and gold. They danced and teased and pulled me in the way fire can.

Carefully I lowered my right hand down over the flame until I could hardly bear the heat. I thought about Maurice. His tongue inside my mouth. My mouth open for him. My legs wide. Dirty. Dirty. My mother's voice telling me who we were, who they were. My father's sad face, looming regretful from the grave.

The last thing I remember before passing out was a sweet smell of burned flesh and a flimsy hiss flying up toward the ceiling – a signal to someone who would never be there to hear it.

4

London succumbs to the dark and to the fog. It's a real pea-souper outside, Alfred tells me. I draw back the lace curtains at the bow windows. The headlights from a few passing cars are barely visible outside; their cones of light dissipate into the fog. There is an eerie quality to the Sweep, which wears my mother's death like a mantle. Again, I return to the rocking chair by her bed. Alfred whispers because of Louise.

'They will come for her tomorrow. Lady is fast asleep. You sleep too, Cinta,' he pleads. 'You're exhausted.'

I shake my head. I don't need to tell him that these are the last hours we'll have with her, or that I want to burn every line of her worn face into my brain so that I can carry it back with me across the ocean.

It is at this time in the vigil, when we have both settled into the folds of our grief, that the 'formal feeling' spoken of by Emily Dickinson takes a firm hold at last. It is a relief to feel suffering take shape inside you, scoop out a place in your heart, and take up residence for the rest of your life. Better than fury; far preferable to madness.

I was alone with her when she died. Alfred asks me what she said. I lie.

'She said she wanted you to continue living in the house, Alfred. She said it was yours to live in until you die.'

'I can't –'

'Yes you can.' My voice is calm, authoritative. A professor's voice. 'I get the life insurance. It's all arranged. Besides, what would I do with a house in South London? I live in Virginia now. No point holding on to the past.'

'You could sell it.'

'One day I may if you ever come back to America with us. But for now it's yours. It's your home. Lady and I will visit.'

We both know that neither of us will leave our homes. I left England twelve years ago with a pretty man from the New World. Why would I come back? Why would Alfred leave? You stay where your dreams are buried or where you believe you can best resurrect them.

I don't tell Alfred what really happened. There is no point. I don't tell him how she sat bolt upright in the bed a few hours before she died; how she pointed to the blocked-up chimney and called out Simon's name in a voice that already belonged to the dead; how she turned to me with rage in her eyes and poured what was left of her energy into loathing; how she accused me of deceiving her, of driving her to the asylum.

'You little bitch!' she cried, looking past my body into my conscience. 'You drove me to it! You read it! It was mine! You little cow! The only secret . . . you read it! Sin! What would Father Moth say to you, my girl? You drove me to it! Knock down the walls! God is dead! Knock down all the walls . . .'

Then she lay back on the pillow like someone who has been pulled from the water, and the trembling began.

I don't tell Alfred this. What good would it do? The house closes in on me with its secrets and its betrayals. It's a warren, not a home, as small and tight as young Queen Victoria's bodices. Big dreams in little rooms. Dangerous. A very dangerous combination. Where is grandeur now? After sixty-six years of living, she dies in the house that drove her mad. Or was it me? Was I the one who sent her spinning off into oblivion? Was I the one who made her yearn for the comfort of the double-depth grave she longed to share with Simon? Was I the evil one, or was it Maurice after all? Why weren't you there, Louise, when he stuck his fat and greasy tongue in my mouth and clamped his hips over my innocence in the squalid hallways of this house?

'We had such happy times here,' Alfred says. 'Didn't we, Cinta?'

I nod. He goes on, 'In spite of everything, I think the Sweep's been good to us. And now for your mum there is peace. Not a bad ending after sixty-six years.' His voice is shaky. It's clear he's trying to convince himself of something he's unsure of.

In an abrupt movement, I stand up. Alfred is startled.

'It's okay. I just need to check on Lady.'

'But she's fine –'

'I know. I just want to check for myself, Alfred, okay? I'll be back in a moment. Would you like a drink? Tea? Something stronger? Mum has . . . had . . . some gin, am I right?'

'Gordon's. In the cupboard next to the sink. But I think a nice cup of tea would be . . . if it's not too much trouble . . .'

My mother and Alfred have shared all three floors of the old house for several years. They tried a series of lodgers, but eventually gave up. For the pittance renters brought with them in terms of rent, my mother claimed it wasn't worth it. So Alfred and Louise shared the house with two cats and a budgerigar named Ollie Owl. The bird is annoying. It sounds like Hubert Butcher and speaks in a high monotone. I go into the kitchen where Ollie Owl swings on his little perch. 'Ollie Owl! Ollie Owl!' he screeches. 'Isn't Ollie a good little bird? Is he a paragon? Is he a Prince Charming?'

We have a real kitchen now, in a bi-level makeover of the room where the Beadycaps used to sleep and Alfred's old flat. There's even a bar with bar stools, central heating, olive green Venetian blinds at the newly installed French doors, and a double stainless-steel sink and fitted cabinetry from IKEA. It's the kitchen in the magazines Alfred and I used to pore over until our eyes hurt. Beyond the French doors, out there in the fog, is a tiny patio with a birdbath, watched over by a statue of St. Francis of Assisi. I peer out into the dark and think I can just make out the shape of him as he bends stiffly over to comfort the weakest of God's creatures. I put the kettle on and catch myself singing an old song my mother used to sing to me:

Polly put the kettle on
Polly put the kettle on
Polly put the kettle on
We'll all have tea.

Every so often I'm struck by how easy it is to slip into nor-
malcy again and forget the horror that awaits me. Here I am
singing about some twit named Polly when my mother died
without blessing me. I clamp my mouth shut and focus on the
tea.

In spite of the radical home improvements, it's not difficult,
when you concentrate, to remember the way this used to be
when Louise was young and the Beadycap children roamed the
hallways like manifestations of ignorance and want. I am afraid.
What if I carry her corpse around with me, hidden in the folds
of my flesh like a tumor? What if I can't get over it?

I watch the flames as the kettle boils. I feel the ridges in my
right hand where the skin is pulled up like a tiny swastika. It
was in this room, on an old gas stove, where I held my hand
over the flame and smelled my flesh as it liquefied. It was here
that obliteration was, for a while, preferable to survival. The
imprint of my body is in the walls of this house and underneath
the new layers of paint and wallpaper. Louise's screams and
mine are etched into the plaster along with our laughter,
Simon's stories, and all the ghosts who made us.

The kettle whistles shrilly and Ollie Owl joins in. Maurice is
standing over me, telling me nothing is an accident. No one's a
victim, he says. Remember that. I reach out toward the dial on
the stove to twist it to the Off position. The flames dance, blue
and gold, in the semi-darkness, licking the wounds of this
house.

5

The first thing I saw was a large woman dressed in white. She was joined by other large women dressed in the same way. They floated around me like white balloons. Once or twice the balloons smiled at me. There was another large woman who wasn't like the balloons because she wore a belt and a little white halo on her head. She appeared several times. She was in a hurry, and I had done something wrong. There was a smell of disinfectant. Someone was cleaning up after Maurice Beadycap, but they'd never get rid of all the germs. No siree. Too many germs wherever he'd put his hands. I tried to explain this to them, but they were all very stupid. Everyone was as pale as ghosts. All I wanted was a bit of color. My eyes found a calendar pinned up on the wall beside a bed. There were pictures on it of Stonehenge. There was grass in the picture and a blue sky. The gray stone slabs reminded me of something large I had forgotten, but I didn't know exactly what it was. Then one day it wasn't Stonehenge anymore. It was Salisbury Cathedral, and the spire rose up against the sky. But the sky was white this time and there was no grass. I wanted Stonehenge again because of the blue sky and the green grass, but nobody listened when I asked them to flip it back to the Celtic ruins. No one wanted to go back in time.

Suddenly Louise was there beside me. Then she was gone

again. Then she came back. Behind her was the gray stone spire. It sat on top of her head and made her look like a wizard. Louise was white too, of course – her face made even paler by the disinfected light of the hospital. The sheets were white. Everything was white except me. It was like living inside the glass snow dome Alfred had given me for my seventh birthday, although it never snowed, and there was nothing grand about it and absolutely no snow.

Louise looked down at me and smiled. I was numb. She said I was a good girl and that everything would be all right. 'It'll be all right, Jassie,' she said. Then she was gone before I could ask her anything, or let her know that my hand hurt so much I wanted to beg her to cut it off. When I tried to call after her, it was suddenly nighttime, and a stranger came and gave me something to help me sleep. 'You mustn't wake the others,' she said. She was referring to the white balloons. 'They need their sleep.'

Slowly things came into focus. Often I tried to push them back into the White. I didn't want to remember. Once the woman who became the nurse asked me why I was crying. I told her I wasn't. She shook her head, and I knew I'd given the wrong answer again.

Little by little I came back. Only a few days, after all. A few days of summer drifting back from Whiteness into the scalding fire of the present tense.

I was quiet when I realized where I was. Simon had died in this hospital. I'd been kept away from him because I was a coloured child. I glared at everyone. They thought I was mad. I didn't care. Madness was rather nice, in many ways. It added drama to my life.

Alfred's twin sister came to visit one day. It must have been more than a week after my arrival, but I never was able to pin time down during my stay at St. Jude's. It kept changing its clothes and masquerading as something else. Alfred's sister's visit took me by surprise. I hadn't known he had a sister. Her name was Alfrieda; and, even among the balloon women, she'd win the prize for the largest boobs in the ward. They were so massive, in fact, that she had to keep shoving them out of the way to make room for her arms, which she used in a Mediterranean fashion to emphasize her main points.

Alfrieda wore a straw hat with plastic fruit on top: two neon-yellow bananas, a bunch of blood-red cherries, and a pair of enormous apples – rosy enough to tempt Snow White. Her dress was covered in either brown flowers or small mammals, it was hard to tell which; and she carried a black bag with a gold parrot clasp on top. Each time she opened her bag she had to tweak the parrot's beak. I thought perhaps it made her happy because the parrot looked a bit like Alfred and there could have been some rivalry there – I'd read about that kind of thing in Homer or someone.

Alfrieda (she spelled her name out carefully for me, but my head hurt so she had to repeat it four or five times) sat by my bed for what seemed like hours and told exactly the same stories Alfred told. Alfrieda seemed to know I'd been sad. She said I should be happy from now on and laugh a lot because laughter made the world go round and tears rusted it. Besides, she said, I was killing my poor, sainted mother by being depressed. Alfrieda said she was Alfred's elder sister by four minutes, and that she loved me just like he did. She said he couldn't come to visit at the present time because men weren't allowed in the maternity ward for reasons she couldn't fathom, for weren't we all God's creatures and weren't men equally responsible for the miracles taking place in these women's wombs? I said I didn't know, because I hadn't realized miracles were taking place in their wombs. Alfrieda told me to talk to my mother soon.

At last I understood that the balloons were pregnant. There were sixteen balloons and me. They all looked revolting. I never wanted to be that fat. They rolled around in their white nighties like big old cows in a field. They talked about breast feeding and bottles all the time and spoke as if their bodies were only vaguely connected to them. Only two of the balloons wanted to breast feed. Everyone else, including the matron, said it was bad for the baby. There were more vitamins in bottled milk, she said, so the baby would grow taller.

In order to provide me with reading material, Alfrieda

brought along Alfred's dictionary. I found the word 'mammary' and wrote in my makeshift diary that the mammarian talk was making me depressed. I hadn't thought of myself as depressed until Alfrieda used the word. I liked the idea. It made me resemble Jaques in *As You Like It*. It made me special. I hadn't thought to keep a diary again, after what had happened with Maurice. But I was writing on scraps of paper before I could help myself – observations, ditties, short poems – and then it was too late because I'd started writing and I couldn't stop. Writing for me was like peeing after you've held it in for hours. You just have to go. And the sweet release makes it all worth it. That's what writing was like. When I put pen to paper I was the Jacinta-in-the-Story. I was the child my mother had hoped for. I was Simon's little angel. I was close to God.

The women in the maternity ward often had cigarettes dangling from their mouths – though they were only supposed to smoke in the hallways. Some had pink curlers in their hair, even during visiting hours, and a few of them called me 'luv' and 'duckie' and felt sorry for me, as I hoped they would. The rest ignored me, for the most part. I wondered if they would have been kinder had my skin been like theirs.

As things came into focus even more, the pain in my hand set in with a steady vengeance, and I asked for painkillers every hour or two. Often they wouldn't give them to me, and then I'd wish I were dead because the recurring pain in my hand was excruciating, and the headaches joined with it to take up a kind of refrain of suffering.

I began to suspect they'd put me in a maternity ward on purpose. Supposing Maurice Beadycap had made me pregnant! He had done that funny kissing with his tongue while it was as fat as a sausage. Josephine Marsh had told me to be careful of deep kisses. They led to disrepute, she said. The nuns told us to watch out for things like that too. Men were everywhere, according to Sister Eileen, and many of us were willing victims, especially if we wore miniskirts. I wore miniskirts. My heart turned over. When Alfrieda came to visit again, I'd ask her about it.

My hand was heavily bandaged. I was glad. I didn't want to

see it. When they changed the bandages, I looked away. I imagined there'd be a scar there riding across my palm like a swastika. I knew about the Nazis. Louise talked about them. Everyone in England over a certain age talked about them. It was boring but educational. Alfrieda said I'd hit my head on Alfred's stove. She said I was lucky to be alive. When she said the word 'lucky,' it seemed to spiral up above her hat and hover there like the Holy Ghost before flying right out of the window. Above my left ear under still more bandages was what felt like a dent.

I wasn't sure whether or not I felt happy to be alive. If I'd died, I'd be with Simon. There would be the stories again that would take me to Africa. I'd ride on an elephant like Jacinta-in-the-Story, and I'd be as happy as a lark, the way I used to be before he died. Or maybe I wouldn't know him even then. Because no one really knew what happened when you became the dear departed. Even the Church told you one thing and then told you the other. And maybe I'd have to burn in hell for a while because of what I'd done with Maurice, and the bit with my hand too. In spite of what the Bible said, I had a feeling that self-mutilation was at least a venial, if not a mortal sin.

Louise came to visit soon after I'd decided that death stank as much as life did.

I'd found out what the days were at last. It was a Monday when she visited this time, and I was able to piece together the fact that she and Alfrieda had visited yesterday and the day before. That was about as far back as I could remember with any clarity. It was unusual for me to struggle with my memory. It was always clear. But I liked the fuzziness produced by the painkillers. It was like living in one of the fogs you see in London, when shapes become ghosts and nobody recognizes anyone else.

Louise came in with the other visitors, so I saw her walk down the long aisles between the twenty or thirty beds in the ward. I had a chance to study her, and I began writing a diary entry in my head. She'd changed in the seven years since she'd walked into the ward to see my father for the last time, leaving me alone behind her.

Louise Buttercup Moses still has good legs. Pretty ones. She's wearing shoes with a slight heel. But she looks poor. Anyone seeing her, especially the girls at school, would notice it immediately. Her cheap nylon dress is too tight and the stomach she no longer bothers to hide sticks out as if she, like the rest of them, has a bun in the oven.

For a moment I panic. Ruskin Garland, the writer-warlock, has been sniffing around her lately. I'm still not quite sure what you have to do to get pregnant. Maybe she's done it. The word 'hussy' comes into my head.

Louise's hair began to grow thin as soon as my father died. It turned gray too, so she dyed it. She went from blond to brunette and back again. Once she bought really cheap dye and it turned her hair bright purple and she began to cry. She washed the color down the kitchen sink and it ran down the drain as a shade of plum. She always rinses her hair religiously with vinegar and water because it's meant to strengthen the shafts. She smells a bit like a fish 'n chip shop. Today her face is beautiful, as always. But she looks tired. And her eyes don't shine anymore. And I wonder why, when husbands die, the light goes out of their wives' eyes even though they have children to make them happy.

Louise was wearing a scarf. It had a paisley pattern on it – just like our stair carpet used to before it had been worn away to nothing. And she was wearing lipstick in my honor. But she'd put it on in a hurry and it had smudged beyond her lip line. Everything about her said 'I am poor.' I wanted to smack her.

'Hello, darling,' she said, pushing the wild, African hair back from my face. I tried to shy away, but it hurt my head when I jerked it back so I surrendered to her fussing.

Some of the other visitors stared at us when she greeted me. They always did. They expected my mother to look more like me. But she was white, with a straight little nose and small lips with a lipstick smudge, and I was a coloured girl, and that was that, and if they didn't like it, they could all go and lump it was what I said because that's what Simon used to say when people said things to him. I tried to pretend they were dead. I tried so hard it gave me a worse headache than before.

I wanted to know whether she had a gift for me. She pulled out two magazines and a Cadbury's chocolate Flake bar. I knew it cost her money she didn't have. She probably skipped her lunch to pay for it. Instead of making me grateful, it made me angry. I flipped through the magazines and threw them aside. I wanted revenge because she hadn't been there to save me. I wanted revenge because the light had gone out of our lives when Simon died, and she hadn't been able to bring it back. We lived in the cold, round breath-circles of our house. Alfred was the only one who still believed in glory. Louise had given up on it. Louise had given up on me. I could tell by looking at her watery expression, and her pale skin with the spider veins, and her knuckles that bled in the winter because of the cleaning she did for other women. Out of the blue I asked her why we lived in such a dump. She drew back as though I'd hit her. It felt wonderful.

'What?' she said, her voice far away, as if she were trying to catch up with it.

'I *said* why do we have to live in such a dump? I hate it. I hate the Beadycap pee on the toilet and the tiny rooms and the cold and the carpet without the fishes' hands –'

'The what?'

'Nothing. I hate it anyway. Josephine Marsh, my best friend at school, she has a lovely house. It has a garage attached to it like a room. And she has –'

'What is the matter with you? You're hysterical. Keep your voice down. You want the whole world to hear us air our dirty laundry?'

'Our dirty laundry! What about the *Beadycaps'* dirty laundry? It's everywhere. It makes me sick. Sick, sick, sick! They make me sick too. Why can't we just have the house to ourselves? Alfred can stay, but we don't need them. Why do we have to live cramped up in three rooms at the top of the house? They have the best rooms. Why don't we pay the damn builder to fix the damn house so that it doesn't rot around us? I *hate* small rooms. I'm claustrophobic. I *hate* it!'

I looked her straight in the eye. A sad wisp of hair fell across her forehead, and she pushed it back absentmindedly. Her lower lip was trembling. Again, I had an almost uncontrollable urge to slap her.

'I don't give a good goddamn about anything anymore,' I said, using one of Ruskin's phrases in order to get on her nerves. 'I don't! I don't want to go back to Lavender Sweep with you. Battersea is a hell-hole and you know it. The only pretty thing there is Clapham Common. Everything else is Ugly. I hate Ugly, do you understand? Ugly is making me go mad. I want beautiful things like the girls at school have. Even the nuns have beautiful things. They have the chapel and they have those wide corridors in the convent. You never give me anything beautiful. I want to go away and live with' – I pulled a name out of the air – 'Ruskin Garland.'

'Ruskin Garland!' She was genuinely shocked. I was filled with triumph.

'Yes. Ruskin Garland,' I said with emphasis, as if I were talking about some movie star.

'Why Ruskin of all people?'

'He's rich.'

'No he's not.'

'He's richer than we are. He has a car.'

'Jacinta, I don't know what's got into you. It must be the medicine. I'll ask them to lower your dose. But I want you to pay close attention while I tell you a few home truths because you have no right talking to your mother like this. No right at all. You are *never, ever* living with Ruskin Garland. You have no idea what he's like. I do. And it's my responsibility as a mother to protect you for as long as I can. . . . Sending a twelve-year-old child to live with a man like . . . Well. It would be over my dead body and there's an end to it.'

'*Protect* me! Ha, ha, ha! And bloody ha, ha!'

People looked around. I'd raised my voice. I wanted to make Louise feel ashamed. She stood up quickly and drew the curtains round the bed.

'They can still hear us,' I taunted.

She was as white as the sheets I was lying in. Ghost white. As white as death.

'White is a damn ugly color,' I said, then wished I hadn't. She knew what I was referring to because she let her hand brush her cheek, and then she looked down.

I wanted to stop. I'd gone too far. But I couldn't stop. Sinning had felt bad the first time around; now it felt good. Sin was hot and warm; it carried with it the scent of vengeance. I lowered my voice a little because I didn't want the balloons or the matron interfering before I had a chance to thoroughly humiliate her.

'I'm black, not like you. I don't ever want to be like you. When Daddy died you gave up. You flattened out like a . . . like a . . . pancake or something.' I knew the simile was poor. It made me as mad as hell. I pulled out my trump card. 'I've read it, you know.'

'Read what?'

'Your diary, Louise. That's what.'

She didn't flinch. I said it louder.

'I've read your diary, Louise.'

She hated it when I called her that. But still no reaction.

The ward around us seemed to be listening. A huge pair of British ears in a voluminous hospital gown.

At last she looked up. 'Why?'

Her question was so soft I could barely hear it. I wanted to cry. I think I was crying; I don't remember. I told her I knew all about her. About the way she wanted to climb down into the grave with Simon and leave me behind by myself. And about the way she put his old cardigan on at night so that the smell would make her dream about him, and the next day would be bearable for her with me. I said I knew that her love for him was like fire, and that everything else was burned up now that he was dead. I told her I'd read the poems – her poems. I knew everything.

'Why don't you go and put more flowers on him, Louise? Why don't you do that instead of wasting your time here? Do you want to know how *this* happened? Do you?' I held up my hand. It was thick with gauze. I began to pull it off. She tried to stop me, but I wouldn't let her. We both gasped when the bandages came off.

My palm was pulled up into a mass of scar tissue. The scars and swelling looked like a mountain ridge in the shape of a spider. I fingered the skin. It was still red and raw. They'd put some kind of ointment on it and the smell was terrible. I cried out and my mother took me in her arms. 'I was trying to get away . . . from Ugly!' I sobbed. 'And now look what's happened! Why didn't you come and save me, Mum? Why didn't you c-c-come?'

'I'm sorry, Jassie,' she said.

She rocked me until I was quiet. She asked me what I was thinking of, playing with fire like that, and neither of us pursued it again because how could you pursue despair? It would eat you alive. Best to leave it behind. We'd already been swallowed up by too many ghosts on Lavender Sweep.

My mother called the nurse, who put new bandages on my hand and told me I was a naughty girl for taking them off. They wanted to give me something to make me sleep, but, for once, I asked them not to. I said in my calmest voice that I was fine. I had to have a clear head to think. I wanted to be left alone, but Louise wasn't finished with me. When the nurse had left us, just as visiting hours were over, my mother took my good hand in hers and leaned over me.

'I know you're hurting. And I'm sorry for that. Something wonderful happened to us when your father was alive, and it's hard to believe that it will ever happen again. But it will for you, Jassie. You must believe that. Some man will come along and sweep you off your feet the way Simon did me, and it will be just like all those fairy stories you've read and –'

'You mean I have to wait for some *man* to make my life bearable?' I almost spat the words into her face.'Not bloody likely.'

'Jacinta, that's enough.'

I didn't know what to tell her. I didn't know how to say what I felt in my heart about being a girl who would be a woman who would spend her life praying for a man to make life wonderful. I stuttered out a wish:

'*I* want to make life wonderful for me, Mum. I don't want to wait for someone else to do it. *I* want to make life wonderful.'

She smiled down at me. I didn't know what the smile meant, but I accepted it anyway and smiled back. She still wasn't finished, though.

'You shouldn't have read my diary. I'm not angry. I just want you to know that you shouldn't have done it. How would you feel if I read yours?'

I swallowed hard and thought of Maurice Beadycap with my diary in his hand.

'There are only a few things in this world you are allowed to keep to yourself. A diary is one of those things. It's not meant for other people to see. It's where you can write things down without thinking you'll be judged by someone for what you've written. No one grades it, or critiques it, or gets angry at you for what you say in it. It's yours to keep.

'I can't pretend I don't still love your father. Maybe you will be able to make life wonderful all by yourself. Some people can – especially men, I think. But I'm not very good at it. I think about him every day. Every hour. He's in my soul. He was my great love. Heaven protect you, Jacinta, from a love like that. Because there's no going back from it and there's no comfort when it's gone. And, at some point, loving that much is a kind of violence – like doing violence unto yourself. I know you won't understand that yet, but someday, if you're anything like me or your daddy, you will. We can't love a little, we Moses. We love to the ends of the earth and don't stop there.

'But you should also know that I love you more than my own life. I wouldn't set foot in this stinking hospital if I didn't love you. I swore I'd never come here again after what they did to him. . . . But you're our baby. Our bodies made you. I see him in you. In the way you write and speak and sing. Each day you grow more like him and it makes me glad. And you grow more like yourself too and that makes me even happier.'

She rose to leave and it was difficult to hear the rest of what she said, so I leaned forward in the bed to catch her.

'I've been sad for too long. Much too long. You mustn't hate me. If you hate your mother, you wind up hating yourself. We need to be patient with each other. There's many a day I want to fling myself into the fire and –'

She stopped short and looked at me as if to say 'What are you doing here?' Then she gathered her composure around her like an actress, and I could see the training she'd had on the stage, and I think a great part of me admired Louise Butterercup as she said, 'I'd be ashamed of you, Jacinta, if you were to give up without a fight. I'd have to say you were never the daughter of Simon Moses if you admitted defeat on account of a bit of wallpaper or a few small rooms. You're more than that because he was.'

She turned to go. As she drew back the curtain, she looked around one last time: 'And never touch my things again without permission or I'll skin you alive.'

The curtain swayed where she dropped it behind her – the only evidence that she'd been there at all.

I looked down at my hand and slowly turned it over. They'd covered up the scar, but I knew it was there. The burn had destroyed my life line. My palm would either heal or fester. I had disfigured myself in Alfred's squalid kitchen, but perhaps I could heal myself also.

Gently, very gently, I tried to flex my thumb and forefinger. The pain was like dying. But I could move my fingers. I hadn't destroyed my hand even if I'd have to rely on the other one for a while. Besides, I was ambidextrous like Simon. I still had at least one hand to write with.

I remembered what I'd said to Louise about the house. She'd never forgive me. Why had I said it? It was Maurice Beadycap. He was the root cause of all my misery. I sought him out in my mind with the diligence of a spider and pictured myself running my nails down his cheek. He'd be disfigured too. I'd attacked the wrong person. Someday I'd make him pay.

By the time Alfrieda arrived the next evening, I'd planned the rest of my life. I would make money somehow, buy Louise a modest mansion, lynch Maurice, and endow a nunnery with superfluous funds. But when Alfrieda reached the foot of my bed, I forgot about my plans. I was livid. This time I wasn't going to let the other patients enjoy free 'coloured' entertainment. 'Close the damn curtain, *Alfred*,' I said.

He pulled them around us without commenting on my language and sat down on the Spartan hospital chair by my bed.

'You look ridiculous.'

'How did you know?'

'How did I *know*!'

'All right, all right. It's a little overdone, but how else could I get into a maternity ward in this day and age? Only the dads are allowed, and then only at special visiting hours. It's absurd. I needed to see you, Jacinta. You're my best friend. I promised your father I'd look after you . . .'

I looked at Alfred. He was right; he was my best friend. Better than Josephine Marsh at school, who only deigned to speak to me if I helped her with her English lit or Latin homework – better than Alison Bean, who was too young to understand what yearning was.

I tried to keep scowling, but I'd caught sight of the fruit on Alfred's hat. It looked so silly that I began to laugh. Alfred began laughing with me. Before long we were giggling so much that matron had to pull the curtain back and tell us to be quiet. When we were certain she'd gone to her post at the end of the ward, I asked Alfrieda to tell me where she found her bosoms.

'Balloons,' she said smugly. 'Pear-shaped balloons. I don't blow them up all the way, of course. The tips have to endow me with a certain shapeliness, if you get my drift.'

'Are they uncomfortable, Alfred . . . Alfrieda, I mean.'

'Only on the 49 bus. It was terrible. I was scrunched up against this man with pointy elbows. I was afraid I'd burst.'

We chuckled again. It was hard work because we didn't want matron poking her nose round the curtain a second time. I snorted with laughter so much that snot came out of my nose and my ears popped.

'Do you think matron suspects us, Alfred?'

'Not in a million years. I modeled my physique on hers, you know.'

'I love the hat.'

'*Moi aussi.*'

'I love the bananas.'

'O yes. Aren't they lovely? Arding and Hobbs. On sale.'

We stopped laughing as suddenly as we'd begun. I don't think either of us knew why. Sometimes it's just time to stop laughing, that's all.

'What did you say to your mother?'

Alfred had on his serious voice now. He wore it about once a week. Usually I could ignore it, or make him go off on a tangent. I knew that wouldn't work today.

'Nothing. Honest. I didn't say a thing.'

He sat back and shook his head. The enormous apples rolled back and forth across the brim of his hat.

'Your apples are loose.'

'Don't try to change the subject, Jacinta. Why did you do it?'

'Do what?'

'You hurt her very much.'

'She shouldn't have told you. She's a baby. She goes running to you whenever she's got a problem –'

'Louise didn't tell me a thing. Just that you'd had words, that's all. And that you wanted to leave home' – he swallowed hard – 'with Ruskin Garland, of all people! Jacinta, I couldn't believe my ears! Why Ruskin Garland? The man's . . . well, he is certainly strange, and that's putting it kindly.'

'*He's* strange!'

'I don't mind telling you, I've never trusted the man. Never. Always sucking up to your father as if the two of them had secrets ordinary people couldn't understand. The man's an intellectual snob and a misogynist, if you ask me.'

'What's that?'

'A woman hater.'

'He likes Louise.'

Alfred pooh-poohed the idea. 'Ruskin doesn't like anyone except himself.'

'He likes me too.'

'Jacinta, has he ever –'

'No. Of course not!' I was highly embarrassed. I was certain Alfred knew all about Maurice's tongue. He probably thought of me as some kind of harlot. I wanted to die all over again.

'Your poor mother thinks she's failed you, Jacinta.'

'She has.'

Alfred unlocked the parrot clasp on his handbag and reached in for a handkerchief. He was still trying to do Alfrieda's voice. Only sometimes he'd forget so he sounded like a boy whose voice keeps changing. It got on my nerves.

'Here, take this,' he said, trying to hand me his huge hankie.

'Don't need it.'

'Yes you do. Blow your nose.'

I blew it. I felt like a child. 'She *has* failed me, Al . . . Alfrieda.'

'In what way?'

'By being mean.'

'When has Louise Buttercup ever been mean to you?'

'You don't know anything, Alfred.'

'*Alfrieda!* Please! I'll get thrown out on my arse if you're not careful.'

'You shouldn't say that word. Louise doesn't like it.'

'Why are you being such a bitch, Jacinta?'

'You shouldn't say that word either. I'm a child, remember?'

'Look, I don't have time for this. I came here for a nice little visit. And to see if there's anything I can do to help you. I think you're in serious trouble, Miss, and I think you'd better sit up and take note because, if you're not careful, you'll wake up at forty and realize you've wasted your future by looking back at what you never had.'

With biting sarcasm I asked, 'Is that what happened to you?'

'Yes. It did. In a way. At forty I realized I would never have my dreams. And so at forty I stopped dreaming – for myself anyway. Now my dreams are for you, and for your sweet mother too.'

Alfred answered me with grace. It made me ashamed. I didn't know what to say, so I said what I always said when things were hard: 'It's not fair.'

'Nothing's fair, little one. Nothing. Never has been. It's not fair that people are starving in Biafra, or that Jews are dying in the USSR, or that one man has the power to press a button and send us all to kingdom come, or that I never did get the part of Lysander in *A Midsummer Night's Dream*. It's not fair that Simon Moses died before he had a chance to know his beautiful daughter, and that he left no money for his family, and that his wife has to grow old cleaning other women's houses when she has more brains and talent in her little finger than the lot of them put together. It's not fair, is it, Jacinta, that her hands are raw from the harsh cleaners she uses, and it's not fair that she still loves your father the way she does after all these years of him being under the earth. It's not fair that the Jamaican Beans run around with nothing but little sandals on their feet in winter. It's not fair that Mrs. Butcher gave birth to Hubert twenty-nine years ago, and that she is still waiting for him to grow the part of his brain that's missing. All along Lavender Sweep life's not fair. The Beadycaps know it, you can be certain, when they sit down to yet another meal of fatty bacon and toast and dripping. And do you think the rich bastards across the Thames don't know it when they sit down to their Scottish salmon and caviar, their champagne, and their lovely little chocolate bonbon affairs with the chewy centers and the raspberry-cream filling? Of course they know. There's never been justice in this world. Never. Look at Jesus.'

'I thought you were an atheist.'

'He had all kinds of problems. No one understood socialism back then, you see. Still don't.'

'Why bother, then?'

'People never understand the implications of – what?'

'I said, why bother, then? If people are so stupid and life stinks so much, why bother to hang around?'

I must have asked the question with unexpected seriousness because Alfred came down from his podium and spoke to me like a friend.

'You bother because you must, Cinta. Do you see that? That's what it means to be brave and to be good. It means you bother – about yourself and about other people. You take time to love them, if you can. You tolerate them if you can't. All you need is patience.'

'We've got enough of those,' I said, indicating the ward with my bad hand.

I sighed an adult sigh and looked up into Alfred's rouged and powdered face.

'Life sucks, Alfrieda.'

'Indeed it doth sucketh the big one at times. Not to change the subject, but the Beatles have a new one out. Thought you'd like to know. Can you get any of the pirate stations on that little transistor radio of yours?'

'Sort of. S'a bit fuzzy, though. What's it like?'

'Not as good as their last one. I confess I bought the record, though. Couldn't help myself. They're a phenomenon, those boys. Their records will be collector's items one day. I like that John Lennon, especially. He was on the BBC the other night. Very articulate. Said some interesting things. That McCartney fellow is as light as air, but Lennon – now he's going to be a force to deal with. You mark my words. Tired?'

'Mmm.'

'I'll tuck you in. Lie down. There. Why did you do it, Cinta? Were you so unhappy?'

'Do what?'

'Your hand.'

'Was an accident.'

'Maurice had to break the door down with his head. You locked it. You never lock the door. What happened, Cinta? You can tell me.'

'Nothing happened. I promise. I swear it didn't. I was just careless, that's all.'

'Your mother suspects you did it on purpose.'

'Louise is an actress. She always dramatizes everything. You know how vain I am. Do you really think I'd do something like that to myself on purpose? Pills maybe. . . . Only joking . . . really. I'm just teasing, that's all. Did he really break it down with his head?'

'What?'

'The door. Did Maurice really break it down with his head?'

'Yes. . . . No! I can't remember. What does it matter? Don't get me on the wrong track. I want to help you if I can. You would tell me, wouldn't you? I mean, we've never had secrets between us, have we? We're best friends.'

'Abso-fucking-lutely.'

'Jacinta!'

'Sorry. It slipped out. The girls at school say it.'

'Some of the girls at school are cretins of the first order. Go to sleep.'

'Alfred?'

'What? And don't call me –'

'I know. I know. I'm not going to have a baby, am I?'

'What!'

'They put me in a maternity ward. Everyone here is going to have . . . I mean . . . just wondered.'

'O, you sweet child! No. No, no, no! Of course you're not. Not for a good many years I hope. They're overcrowded, that's all. This is the only female ward where there are beds to spare, what with this flu outbreak going around. Jacinta, you do know about the birds and the bees, don't you?'

'Sort of. Josephine Marsh says –'

'Jesus, Mary, and Joseph! If you got your information from that girl, you probably think women deliver at will. Look, there's a show on the telly I'll let you watch. It's all about that sort of thing. Very tasteful. I'll tell your mother about it. You need to be educated, my girl. It's 1967. No time to dillydally.'

'Alfred?'

'Lie down and go to sleep! Look at those covers. I just spent forever tucking you in and now you –'

'I didn't do it on purpose. Do you believe me?'

'Yes.'

'But I *was* sad. Will you always make me laugh? I'll be okay if you do that.'

Alfred held me close to his ample bosoms.

'I'll make you laugh for the rest of my life, Cinta. I promise I'll make you laugh until the tears come.'

He squeezed me hard and I squeezed back one last time. The twin explosions echoed round the ward like gunshot. Why matron didn't come running I'll never know. Maybe she suspected all along and was just humoring us. Maybe she was deaf. I laughed so much my throat ached. I could hear the women and their visitors tittering beyond the curtain, but I didn't care. Alfred had made things better. He would always make things better. He was different, like me. We'd scaled the Wall of Cruelty and escaped from Ugly for a while. I was grateful to have such an extraordinary friend.

A little later, when things had died down, Alfrieda took her leave. No one except me seemed to notice that she was missing two apples from her hat as she swept out of the ward like a queen.

6

At thirteen I had a loud voice and the highest grades in Form III alpha. My attitude vacillated between irony and superciliousness. Alfred's influence was evident in me too. It caused me to weep buckets over *Romeo and Juliet* and grind my teeth in fury at the injustice portrayed in *To Kill a Mockingbird*, one of Alfred's all-time favorite books. Louise, despite what she'd said in the hospital, didn't reassert herself as the primary mentor in my life. She existed only in my peripheral vision. She'd been an absent mother for years, evident only in the flesh, floating around the house like a fragment from something grand. But now the moments of animation, the times when she saw me, listened to what I said, became even more infrequent than before. My mother was semitransparent – an outline filled in with whatever color I chose to throw her up against. I ruled the roost now, and made many decisions usually made by adults. I should have known better, but I assumed Louise would continue to become a smaller and smaller fixture in the landscape, and that I would become a bigger one. I was going to be a great politician, or an actress, or a writer. I became strong – far stronger than I'd been when the flames of Alfred's gas rings drew me in. My hand was scarred, but it functioned well. And there was a certain fascination in the scars. Now my body told a story. Tragedy was written in my palm.

The three of us – me, Alfred, and Louise – watched television shows together, and it was one of the few times when Louise seemed to be able to concentrate. Alfred's passion for the BBC adaptations of Austen, Dickens, and the Brontë sisters had not waned. The three of us saw the Olivier version of *Wuthering Heights* whenever the BBC reran it, and my mother would tell us how she'd been in a play with Olivier's wife, Joan Plowright, just after the war. She said it wistfully, as if she'd missed some incredible chance that would never come back to her. I told her I'd got 95 percent for English literature – an unheard-of score at my convent school. She said Merle Oberon was a real beauty; you didn't see women like that nowadays. I told her the nuns thought I could be a writer; she said Heathcliff and Cathy were lucky to find each other even in death. I'd tell her we could spruce up the fireplace with a new brass fire screen; Louise would finger her thin hair and talk about the time it took to curl the hair of movie stars with paper curlers and water. Alfred didn't pay attention during these interchanges. He had *become* Cathy and Heathcliff by that time. There was no pulling him back from bliss, and no pulling Louise closer to attentiveness.

Conversations with Louise over the next year or two were much like that. We shared things, but she seemed far away. I decided to take over, hoping I could make her see how good life could be if we made a few improvements. I began by making curtains. We didn't have a sewing machine, so I had to do it all by hand. The first few attempts were pathetic. Later on, I got pretty good. Even Louise said our rooms looked better now that there were nice curtains at the windows. But the bold floral prints on cheap cotton fabric didn't help much in the winter when the wind whistled through the old house, and I spent my waking hours wishing for central heating.

But I was indomitable. We could lift ourselves out of shabbiness if only we tried hard enough. I got books on home improvement and read them with Alfred. He always liked impractical things like footstools and grand pianos. Whenever there was a photo in some book that included a grand piano, he oohed and aahed over it for at least three minutes. I told him we needed a washing machine and a refrigerator, as well as a vacuum cleaner and an electric food mixer long before we invested in something as bourgeois as a piano. He told me pianos had never been bourgeois – only the dolts who played them. We went back to wallpaper samples.

Some of the things we tried didn't work. The dark red paper Alfred and I hung in the toilet was downright strange. It had these black and white swirls on it that were meant to represent ballroom dancers. But several people, including the man who came to read the meter, said it made his head spin being in there. Alfred said he assumed that's why the man had missed the toilet bowl altogether.

That same year, we had a real bathroom put in.

We got a grant from the council. They paid for more than 70 percent of the cost of installation. We were able to pay the rest off in installments. I thought I was in heaven until Louise explained that we'd have to share it with the Beadycaps. I took baths at five in the morning and midnight so that I wouldn't run into Maurice. I hadn't said two words to him since he'd flung me into the flames of hell, and I didn't want to begin now.

Bathing delighted me. I bought cheap bubble bath with my pocket money and sat for an hour at a time in the water dreaming about where I'd go when I grew up. I decided on America, in part because of Little Joe in *Bonanza*, in part because of Heath in *The Big Valley*, and in part because everyone in America seemed to live in houses with rooms of a half acre and more. In *My Three Sons*, for example, the rooms were huge, they had old white men as servants, and the father wasn't even supposed to be a millionaire. I decided that, if I were ever rich, I wouldn't buy a car or keep lots of money in the bank. I'd give it all away instead – apart from the money I'd need to purchase a modest mansion. I pictured myself as a female version of Martin Luther King. But I wouldn't be a reverend because religious women were always too humble for my liking. I knew for a fact that I wasn't a humble person. I was proud and willful – that's what the nuns said, and they were right. I was like Satan in *Paradise Lost*. Alfred said Blake said Satan was a hero. Made sense to me. Alfred told me I probably shouldn't mention it to the nuns.

In the bathtub late at night, or early enough in the morning that the sun hadn't yet risen, I dreamed my favorite daydream: 'Going Home.' In that dream I returned to Africa and found the land swathed in the luminescence my father had written about. I found myself as I knew I could be, if only luck had been a more significant player in my story. Simon was there too. He took me on his lap and sang to me while his mother brought me bitter leaf soup and foo-foo, and wrapped me in an African gara cloth large enough to hold all yearnings. I rode the elephant as Jacinta-in-the-Story, and felt the folds of his skin between my thighs and the flaps of his ears slapping the wind like applause. In the bathtub, Africa could find me in Battersea and take me home. It was in the bath that I made the pact with myself to go to Africa as soon as I was twenty-one. A pact I sealed later with Alison Bean. She would go back to Jamaica; I would go to West Africa. Then we'd visit each other. Being from the same place originally, we were bound to feel at home in either destination. Alison said she'd follow me anywhere. I said I knew that. And it was true because she was my friend, the only black friend I had in childhood.

My period began the same year as the bath was put in. I was fascinated by the way the water changed to a pale pink if I had a bath when I was having my period. I was only allowed two baths a week because it cost a lot to heat the water, so I never missed one because of my female condition.

I'd carefully lay the sanitary pad on the edge of the bathtub, knowing I had to make it last even if it was fairly soiled, because pads were expensive. I didn't want to have to use rags like Mary Beadycap because she was always leaking on everything. Then I'd step into the hot, bubbly water and feel its warmth on my naked body. In the winter, the bathtub was the only warm place in the house. I'd sit in it and watch my breath rise into the cold air. Circle after circle of breathing.

In the bathtub, I'd practice kissing. Sometimes I used a sponge, but the best thing to use was the plunger because it was all rubbery. I always scrubbed it well first and then I brought the rim together like a mouth and put my tongue inside. I wasn't sure whether girls were meant to do that, or if they just had to endure it while boys did it to them. When I mentioned it to Alfred, it set him off on a sermon about the male and the female and what stereotypes were. He wasn't helpful at all. Kissing the plunger reminded me of Maurice. I'd felt his swollen tongue in my mouth. I never looked at his mouth anymore because all it seemed to be saying was the word 'lust.' Maurice Beadycap was one of the seven deadly sins; in fact, he was probably several. I read about him in *Pilgrim's Progress* and prayed during mass that he would find hell especially warm.

Our only regular visitor during these years was Ruskin Garland. He came to see us about once a month. He always brought chocolates for my mother and balloons for me. I tried to get him to bring me bubble bath, but it was like talking to a wall. He and Alfred were the same: once they'd hit upon an idea, there was no shifting them. When I was five, a balloon had thrilled me. Ever after, Ruskin Garland brought me red balloons. It drove me crazy.

Louise never encouraged me to hang around with her and Ruskin anymore. She used to let me sit with them and sip tea while they had a glass of the Harvey's Bristol Cream sherry Ruskin gave her for Christmas each year. But after I got back from the hospital, she didn't let me spend time with them. Alfred said it was because I'd made that ridiculous comment about living with Ruskin, and now my good taste was in question. I told him he was jealous of Simon's *best* friend, and that I knew *for a fact* that Mr. Ruskin Garland, writer *and* warlock, would be *delighted* if I were to turn up on his doorstep at *any hour of the day or night.* Alfred said I'd probably find ten or twelve other convent schoolgirls there with him, and I said, 'That just goes to prove how kind he is.' Alfred rolled his eyes to heaven and gave up on me.

There was one occasion, however, when I was allowed to spend time with Ruskin. And that was my mother's birthday, the last time for a long while that we celebrated anything together.

My mother was born in June in 1926. It was a general strike, or what I used to call the Great Depressing, when she was born, so she claimed that even then she'd been in the wrong place at the wrong time. We decided to do something special for her forty-second birthday. It was my idea. I kept thinking about what Alfred had told me about people who got to be forty and had all their dreams shrivel up on them. My present to her was a Dream Book. I made it myself. It was a large scrapbook filled with pictures of pretty rooms and elegant houses. There were photographs from magazines of gardens and roses and my mother's favorite trees – oaks and weeping willows. I wrote poems on sheets of bond paper – some of them my own, some I stole from famous poets – and glued them next to appropriate pictures. On the cover was a photo of me. I had only eight photographs of me altogether, as we didn't have a camera. Six were school photos and two were taken at Brighton when we went on a day trip there with Alfred one summer. I liked the last school photo best, so I glued it to the cover and surrounded it with plastic flowers from Woolworth's.

When she saw the book, my mother cried. She said it was the most beautiful gift she'd ever received. She said she hadn't realized I wrote poems, which made my heart fall to my knees because I'd shown her several of my best ones over the past few years, and she'd told me, albeit with the usual far-off look in her eyes, that they were wonderful. But still it was good to see her reacting to something at last. And when she spent most of the evening leafing through the book and reading things over and over again, I was almost completely happy.

Because it was my mother's birthday, we had angel food cake and digestive biscuits, which we dunked in our tea, and I tried to forget that we'd had angel food cake when Simon became an angel, even though Alfred kept bringing it up.

Ruskin talked about my father. He (Ruskin) had been to Africa too, years ago. He talked about Nigeria and the Ivory Coast. He said the women there usually went around au naturel. My mother changed the subject. I managed to get him talking about Africa again, though, later on. He told us about some of the secret societies and why tribal cultures were more in touch with their spirituality than western ones. I swelled my chest and tried to look tribal. Alfred tried to participate too. He said he'd been to France just after the War, and that he'd certainly encountered primitive society there too. He was trying to be funny, but no one thought his joke was very good.

Ruskin said he'd been at a ceremony once in West Africa where a man in one of the secret societies had cut off his penis. My mother was shocked into exclamation. 'His penis!' she cried. It was the first time I'd heard her utter that word. It was more shocking than Ruskin's story. Ruskin, reveling in Louise's reaction, said the man had disappeared into the bush and returned with his penis reattached. No scars. Nothing. I asked him how the man did it. Ruskin said it was a question of mind over matter. Alfred said it was a load of balls. Then everyone laughed, and I joined in because life seemed so good just then.

I even drank a small glass of sherry. Louise said I could because of the Dream Book and because I was growing up. Ruskin smiled at me for a long time, then said I was turning into a beautiful young lady and that all the men would be after me. It was the wrong thing to say because it made my mother fidget and Alfred scowl. Soon afterward, Louise said it was time for bed. I don't think Ruskin meant any harm. But then I was thirteen, and I knew there was a lot I was missing.

In bed I lay awake for a long time listening to the melodious contralto of Alfred's speaking voice and the bass intonations of Ruskin as they filtered down through the ceiling. Ruskin always employed the declarative and imperative modes, at least according to Alfred. He rarely employed the interrogative, and, when he did, it was for rhetorical purposes. Ruskin could not countenance disagreement. 'Close your eyes and think of Hitler,' Alfred once said about Ruskin's voice after a particularly trying visit from the warlock. 'And there you have it – Ruskin Garland's voice all dressed up with a Nazi salute.' Tonight I could hear the two of them arguing about something as usual. I guessed it had to do with spirituality. Being a warlock, Ruskin claimed a close relationship with the spirits. Being an actor, Alfred claimed an even closer relationship with the soul. Once or twice I heard my mother's voice, but then it was gone before I had a chance to savor it. I think I heard her laugh a few times too, but it was laughter as thin as smoke, and it swirled up and away from me, however much I strained to hear it, and floated out above the chimney stacks of South London, and up into the night.

I must have fallen asleep because, when I woke, two voices were outside the door. One was Ruskin's, but changed. His voice was not imperious anymore. No imperatives. No irrefutable statements of fact – just the pleading tone of a man who is very tired of asking the same question. Ruskin was begging my mother to let him kiss her. He said something about eight years, something about getting old. There was a long silence and the sound of a man making a kind of grunting sound. Then I think she must have pushed him away because he said a bad word. Then I heard Alfred coming up the stairs and saying, 'Is everything all right, Louise?'

Ruskin said, 'Bloody hell,' and then he apologized. I felt sorry for a grown man who behaved like Maurice Beadycap. More and more, men were looking like fools to me. The only man I knew who had any sense at all was Alfred.

Louise made Alfred go back downstairs. Ruskin was just leaving, she said. Alfred muttered something I couldn't hear, and then headed back downstairs to his flat. I thought that would be the end of it, but Ruskin started pleading again a few moments later.

'I've waited so long, Louise,' he said, his voice shaking like a tree in a storm. I sat up in bed and tried not to breathe because I didn't want to miss a word. 'I need you. Please. *Please*!'

My mother's voice was flat when she said, 'Go home, Ruskin. It's late. And you're drunk.'

'He's not going to rise up from the grave, you know, Louise,' Ruskin said, his voice louder than before. 'Isn't it time you pulled yourself together?'

Louise must have jerked her shoulders back and stood up straight before she replied because her voice was tall when she said, 'He rises up every night, Ruskin. And every night he's with me in ways no man living can ever replicate.'

And then there was a pause. I heard Ruskin turn and shuffle down the stairs. He closed the door gently behind him.

Ruskin didn't come back for quite a while; and it was then, just after that birthday celebration, that Louise's descent began.

Alfred noticed it first. He kept asking me how Louise was today. When I'd say 'same as usual,' he'd look at me as if I were a fool, and tell me to look after her.

I've asked myself a thousand times why I didn't see what was coming. It was true that any little thing would set her off, but I'd always thought of my mother as volatile, in spite of the fact that she was often in her own little world. In sentimental moments, I called her flighty because, ever since that time when we walked home from the hospital after seeing my father, I knew she couldn't be trusted to stay on the ground. In my harsher moments, I said she had a screw loose. To myself, late at night, I didn't have a name for her state of mind at all because the depth of my need and the permanence of her apathy dumbfounded me. I reassured myself that we'd seen the worst. When I told Alfred, in a wave of optimism, that I thought she was 'on the mend' he said, 'The worst is not so long as you can say/"This is the worst,"' which was about as helpful as nothing.

In those last few days before the tumult, I'd find her next to the radio, weeping. Sometimes the weather set her off and she'd fly off the handle because it was drizzling again – as if that were a rarity in London; at other times a comment by one of the neighbors would make her storm inside as though the final deluge had already begun. I postulated in my diary that Louise was undergoing the 'change.' I wrote a particularly bad poem about it called 'Menopausal Musings.' In it, Louise was thinly disguised in the second person singular. She wandered around smashing things hormonally, and spoke in iambic pentameter with occasional spondaic substitution and end rhyme. By the time I'd finished reworking the poem, I'd convinced myself that the 'change' was the cause of Louise's frequent changes of mood. When I mentioned it in passing to Alison Bean, she told her mother, who told her to tell me to make sure my mother ate plenty of red beans and rice because they calmed the flesh. Seeing as how Louise's flesh had been calmed to the point of being semi-comatose for the past decade, I didn't try the red beans and rice. I continued to turn her pain into poetry until my diary was fat with it.

At the same time I continued honing my obsession with do-it-yourself projects. I was determined to make the house more attractive. I wanted snobby Josephine Marsh and the other girls at school to come to Lavender Sweep and coo with delight at our tasteful stair carpet and expensive-looking draperies. I designed plan after plan that always included knocking down two or three supporting walls to make the rooms less claustro-phobic. Alfred said none of the designs would work, but he was forever helping me sand and strip and paint. We papered the room I slept in with a bright pink and yellow wallpaper. The woodwork we painted pale green. The curtains we got from Arding and Hobbs as remnants; they were orange and blue. Louise said, in her faraway voice, that it was very colorful. Mary Beadycap laughed outright when she came up to my room in the middle of our decorating weekend to demand the use of the phone.

'It's bloomin' awful,' she said on her way out. 'Looks like a bloody birthday cake. You wogs is all color blind, me dad says. Look at that Alison Bean's house. Pink and blue and yellow all over! Yuk!'

I threw green paint all over the front of her skirt. I think she would have killed me if Alfred hadn't intervened.

Alfred said Mary already drank too much. 'You should make allowances for those who imbibe,' he said. 'It's not really their fault.'

'She doesn't have to drink that stuff if she doesn't want to,' I said. 'Where's her willpower?'

Alfred said I was too young to understand where it was, and that, if I were Mary, and I had to work from nine to five six days a week at the underwear counter in Woolworth's, I might be a drunkard too. I told him everyone had a chance to improve themselves. I suggested that Mary go back to school and learn the queen's English, as education was the key to success. Alfred said I was becoming as obnoxious and class-bound as Josephine Marsh. He said I'd be voting Conservative next. I told him it was a possibility. He didn't speak to me for two whole hours, until I took it back.

One evening in October, after several weeks of moodiness on

the part of Louise, I decided to help my mother spring-clean our kitchen. We'd scrub the stove till it shone, then we'd scour the sink and mop the lino. The kitchen was about ten feet by twelve feet. It was also our dining and living room, and the only room with a real gas heater. Our original living room was in the front of the house, where Simon used to write his stories; but it was so cold in there that glasses of water froze in the winter. Louise and I rarely used it, preferring the warmth provided by the sturdy old gas heater in the kitchen. The television was up in the kitchen too. I told Louise we wouldn't call it the kitchen anymore because it didn't really look like the kitchens in the magazines. Only the sink and the stove were kitchenlike, I said. We'd call it the studio-living room because that sounded much better. No one had kitchens at the top of the house, anyway. Maybe we could change the rooms around some time when she saved up enough money; then we could put the kitchen downstairs in the big room with the bay windows.

I rattled on as I scrubbed the sink. I didn't look around as I spoke because I was concentrating on getting rid of the brown tea stain that had been a permanent mark on our sink ever since I could remember. I wanted Louise to see how beautiful a clean sink could be. She was letting the house go to rack and ruin. There was dirt everywhere. I could never bring Josephine Marsh to a place like this.

I scrubbed and scrubbed. Nothing happened.

In fact, the more I scrubbed, the worse the stain seemed to become. Gradually, as the scouring pad from the Brillo factory that had killed my father left its copper threads in the small cuts on my hands, I felt a hatred swell in me until I found myself trembling with shame. After more than thirty minutes of scrubbing, I flung down the wire wool in fury.

'*Damn* this sink!' I cried. 'It will never, *ever* be clean! I *hate* this house! It's like trying to make a silk purse out of a dog's ear, working on this! It's driving me crazy! When are we going to make some real improvements to this dump? I need more space. Look, why don't you think about that idea I had? We could knock down that wall between my bedroom and the front room. It's got so much junk in it. All that stuff daddy collected. What did he want with a Buddha anyway? And why hang on to those bags full of papers? I've made some plans. There'd be room if we knocked down that wall – space to move about. All the new houses are open these days. It says so in the magazines. Then we wouldn't have to live all cramped up like we do and get on each other's nerves, and the Beadycaps could move out and stop peeing all over our toilet seat, and stop leaving soiled sanitary pads in our bathroom. This sink is never going to be clean, you know. Not ever! What we need is a new one. One of those stainless-steel sinks they have in –'

I turned around to see if she was listening.

My mother was standing over me like a demon. Her whole head was shaking, as if she were on some crazy ride at the fair. Her mouth was going too – open, shut, open, shut – and she looked like a fish. It shocked me so much to see her that way that I nearly said, 'You look just like a fish, Mum,' but I couldn't speak. Someone had slipped his hand down my throat and stolen my voice. Louise's mouth was going and going – open, shut, open, shut. Her head was shaking her mind loose. Her hands rubbed against her thighs as though they were on fire and she was trying to put them out.

We must have stood like this for several seconds.

Then, as if someone had fired a starting pistol, she pounced.

She pushed me up against the wall Alfred and I had begun to strip in preparation for the fruit-basket wallpaper we were buying in stages from the do-it-yourself shop. She had her hands glued to my shoulders and she was pushing me against the wall with all her might.

'You want to knock down the walls, do you?' she shrieked. She banged me hard against the wall. A bit of plaster was jerked loose. It fell down the neck of my shirt and crushed against my skin. It felt like someone's ashes.

'You want to knock down the walls? Fine! Fine! Let's do it, then.'

She kicked a piece out of the wall by the sink. She kicked it again and a big chunk of plaster fell at her feet. She laughed the way Rochester's wife did in *Jane Eyre* when the fire was engulfing their house.

'Each day you want this and you want that! Who's meant to pay for all this, girl? You? I clean and scrub bitches' houses for a pittance, you know that? I type Ruskin's books for him and he gives me fifty pounds after months of work! Months! Look at my hands, you bugger! *Look!*'

She held her hands a few inches from my face, then jammed my head back against the wall. I felt something warm trickle down my neck. Her hands felt like sandpaper. I wondered why I hadn't remembered that. I'd forgotten something important and now this was happening. If I'd remembered to buy her hand lotion, none of this would have happened.

She was looking at her hands again. The sight of them seemed to make her even more angry. She could hardly speak. Her words rushed out all at once between sobs, and I thought of small animals caught in traps when I heard her.

My mind was surprisingly clear. I was terrified, but I was observing everything as it happened. An imprint of the scene was being burned on to my memory. I'd forgotten something important; now I had to pay. Just like I'd paid as a 'coloured child' when Simon died. I'd miscalculated her despair. If I survived this, I'd never miscalculate anything again. I'd be attentive to her pain. I'd be good. I swore it. I'd be good.

My mother grabbed hold of my throat and began shaking me. Her fingers tightened around my neck.

'I'm going to shake the living daylights out of you, Jacinta Moses! Bitch! Bitch! Don't you think I try? Don't you think I'd rather die than live like this?'

Her fingers squeezed even harder. I was coughing and spluttering, but I didn't care. I wanted only to be quiet while she did this because then all this would go away into darkness, and I'd be in the light with Simon, away from the horror of my mother.

When her hands suddenly jerked loose from around my throat I blurted out, 'It's okay, Mum! It's okay. I don't care. You can do it. It was all my fault. I didn't know. Don't cry. Please d-d-don't cry like that. I don't want new walls. I promise I don't. I love this house. We're in it together. We'll be okay as long as we're together. Don't be sad. I'll make it b-b-b-better. I promise.'

And suddenly Alfred and Lily were there. They never asked

me exactly what had happened. My mother was sobbing. I thought she would never stop. I thought the walls of the kitchen would have that sound etched into them. I'd hear it whenever I got my cereal or washed my hands, screeching down upon me like ruin. Lily swooped Louise up and took her downstairs to the front room to lie down.

Alfred stayed with me until I could stop saying I was sorry. It took a long time because I was like a record stuck in a groove, and I couldn't seem to climb out of it.

I could hear the hum of Alfred's voice, but none of his words came back to me later. And I could hear Lily Beadycap's voice too. I want to say that she was singing – that it floated up through the floor to the attic kitchen where Alfred and I held each other. It was an old war song she sang called 'Pack up Your Troubles' – only she made it sound like a lullaby.

Lucky Mary, lucky Maurice, I thought. Their mother still sings to them. What woman will sing to me?

That night Lily stayed with Louise, and Alfred slept upstairs on a chair in the kitchen. I wanted to see Louise again, but Lily said I could see her in the morning. I'd only set her off again if I pestered her now. Alfred told Lily to hush up – that Louise would love to see me in the morning.

In bed I could still hear Lily humming a tune once in a while to calm my mother.

Dear God, I thought, *my mother tried to murder me.*

It was a large thought. Too big for a thirteen-year-old to hold on to. At one time, when I'd let myself care about her, getting Louise Buttercup's attention was all I'd wanted. Tonight I'd finally gotten her to listen to me, and what had happened? Tonight my own mother had tried to strangle me.

The hardest part was that I didn't know whether or not she'd heard Alfred and Lily coming to my rescue – whether that had made her stop, or if she would have stopped of her own accord.

I did know something for certain, though: Louise Buttercup Moses was mad.

My father was dead and my mother was insane.

I lay awake most of the night listening to my mother's moans and the frequent scurrying of Alfred and Lily. Once in a while they'd whisper together in the hallway outside my room, and I heard Lily say something about a mental hospital and a woman who would care for 'coloured girls' like me. Alfred got angry and said I was his child too because Simon had bequeathed us to him and he wasn't going to let any bloody fool of a social worker take me away. Then Louise moaned again and they rushed in to calm her down.

Sometime before dawn, Ruskin Garland arrived. I heard him at the front door. He didn't ring the bell, just knocked quietly. Alfred hurried downstairs to open the door.

Having Ruskin in the house made everything seem possible again. He began ordering Lily and Alfred around, and they didn't seem to mind. When I stumbled out of my room, he patted me on the cheek, said, 'Poor thing,' and handed me a red balloon.

I was so happy that he didn't hate me for what I'd done to Louise that I put my arms around him and begged him to save us all. He seemed embarrassed but he didn't push me away.

They let me see my mother later in the day. I didn't have to go to school; they said I could stay at home as long as I didn't make a lot of noise.

Louise looked very pale on the bedsettee she occasionally slept on in the front room. I wished she were back on the mattress on the floor in my room. I wished we could go back in time and be with Simon again, dancing to the memory of Africa, which still lived in his movements and in the sound of his voice. The electric portable heater was on, and the thin orange bar gave off a faint heat that got lost in the high ceilings. I glanced up at the fluted plasterwork, mostly because I didn't want to look at Louise. The incongruity of the cherub-and-grape frieze work left a bitter taste in my mouth. It was odd to see this delicate work in a house as run-down as ours, in a road filled with those who never had enough. I forced myself to look again at the woman who had tried to murder me the night before.

Louise was wearing one of Lily's nighties. It was much too big, and she had to keep pulling up the sleeves so that she could see her hands. Whenever the sleeves rolled down again, she got distressed, and Ruskin would have to lean over her and pull them up. I couldn't understand why she would want to see her hands when they were so ugly. I decided to go out and buy her hand lotion that very day. If her hands were beautiful, maybe she'd get well again – or at least settle back into sleepwalking.

She didn't seem to see me; she looked right through me into the blocked-up fireplace at one end of the room.

'He's going up the chimney,' she said, in a matter-of-fact voice. 'He looks like a comma or a question mark. See. There he goes. Do you see him, Ruskin? Did you see him that time?'

Ruskin said she needed to rest. I was there to see her, he said.

She looked at me for the first time with some recognition. I reached out to take her hand, but she moved it away.

'I'm sorry for what I said, Mum. I didn't mean it.'

'Go and clean your room,' she told me. 'It's a mess.'

Outside, Ruskin explained that she was sick. I mustn't pay any attention to her, he said. He told me it would be a good idea if I didn't mention what had happened to anyone. He knew of a nice little hospital in Somerset where Louise could stay until she got better. Ruskin said I'd be living with Alfred while Louise was away. I could stay in my own room and Lily would look in on me too.

'I can look after myself,' I said.

Ruskin smiled at me the way adults do when they think you're talking rubbish. He didn't offer to have me live with him and I didn't ask. I'd been rejected enough for a lifetime. I didn't plan on asking anyone else to love me. Not ever again.

So Ruskin bundled my mother up late that night and drove her away to a place near Bath in Somerset. It was called St. Augustine's Sanitarium for Nervous Disorders – he'd written it down with the phone number on a piece of paper for Alfred. I made a copy of the name and phone number of the place and kept it under my pillow. It was now official: my mother was a Nervous Disorder. I wore the shame on me like the badge of Hester Prynne. Only Lily, Alfred, Ruskin, and I knew where she was (though I assumed that other members of the Beadycap clan knew something was up). For more than six months it was our secret. I lived on Lavender Sweep without her. During that time I never called her on the phone or visited her at St. Augustine's. In fact, I hardly let myself think about her at all. In my fantasies, I was an orphan. In my fantasies, Louise was tucked away with Simon in his custom-made, double-depth grave, her flesh worm-eaten like the love between her and me. If my mother didn't want me, I didn't want her either. I had Alfred Russell-Smythe; I had Alison Bean. Those two would have to be enough, I said, making the last grave mistake of my childhood – assuming once again that I had seen the worst.

7

At first, the period when my mother was a Nervous Disorder was unexpectedly peaceful; I hadn't realized how much energy it took to counteract the weight of her sorrow. When the weight was lifted, in spite of the guilt I carried, I felt liberated. The first few months of her leaving were almost joyous. In my diary that April fourth I marked the one-year anniversary of the assassination of Martin Luther King with a poem called 'Free at Last!' It was supposed to be about slavery and the civil rights movement, but it was really my freedom I was celebrating. There was no pall over our house anymore. I think that Alfred was also a bit relieved. We kept the rooms reasonably clean, tried to avoid too much home improvement because that seemed to have triggered her breakdown, and lived in a state of reasonable contentment now that Louise didn't breathe grief down our necks. Of course Alfred never said this. But I could tell. In a secret place in my heart, I began wishing that Louise Buttercup Moses would never, ever come back to Lavender Sweep.

Springtime in Battersea brought with it a brief prettiness. Alison claimed it was 'the most beautifulest' time of the year. She looked up and down the street and saw loveliness everywhere. I realized that the axiom was true: beauty was indeed in the eye of the beholder. And my eyes were as open as Alison's this particular spring.

Dreams seemed achievable and everything was young. Three more months until the warm weather (if it made an appearance at all) would turn dog turds into stinking mounds of shit. We had three months before the summer when, Ruskin threatened, Louise could come home. But he'd been saying that for ages, pushing her return farther back, into a distant future. He couldn't scare me anymore.

April with Alison would be particularly good, now that I could stay out as late as I wanted and mingle with children who had germs. Alison herself was growing into loveliness, and my craving for all things beautiful made me ache to be near her. I liked it when she sat next to me on the front step and her darker-than-dark skin and quiet profile eclipsed my view of the Sweep. I liked it too when she lay her head on my lap and let me plait her tight, African hair, and sing songs to her from *South Pacific* or the Catholic hymnal. Often I'd take her to the Africa I'd pieced together from Simon's stories, and she'd take me to the Jamaica she remembered as a young child. In those months I learned to take up the remnants of my life, the stories left to me by my father, the morals taught me by Alfred, my own unquenchable optimism, and sew them all together into a crazy quilt that made sense only to me. Alison and Alfred helped me sew it together. From October to April, they became the thread.

Almost every afternoon after school, and most of the day on Saturdays, if it was warm enough and the rain held off, I'd sit with Alison on our front step. Lily polished it with bright red boot polish. It was the one area of the house she took some pride in. I overheard Maurice taunting his mother once, saying the step looked like the mouth of a whore, an observation that elicited the worst string of swear words I'd ever heard from a woman's mouth.

Maurice and Mary were still at home. To everyone's amazement, Maurice was becoming something of a mathematics genius. He was going to the London School of Economics. It was hard for Alison and me to imagine him as anything other than Maurice of the Sausage Tongue, however. Behind his back, I still called him the Troubled Boy, and mocked him for his ignorance; and he still swayed constantly as if he were aboard a ship. Alfred said he'd probably enter the navy at some point, as he had a genetic disposition toward imbalance.

When Alison and I sat together on Lily's red stoop, we could see Mrs. Gem's corner shop on the inside part of the curve the Sweep made just before the bus stop. Mrs. Gem had Gobstoppers and Candysnakes; she had a Penny Tray we could mull over for hours, trying to get the best sweets possible for a penny. Alison didn't get pocket money. Since Louise had been taken away, my only source of pocket money was Alfred. He was out of work more often than not now that the film business was, as he put it, 'in the doldrums.' But he still got the occasional bit part in a television production, so I'd get a sixpence now and then. He had the classic Dickensian face, apparently. He'd been told that Americans in particular would be thrilled by the antiquity of his features. Whenever he heard someone with an American accent, he asked them if they were in films. It was embarrassing.

If we followed the Sweep to its Clapham Common end, then walked alongside the common for about two or three miles, we'd enter one of the Christopher Wren sections of South London. It was a huge leap from Lavender Sweep to the majestic flats on that side of the common. It was like stepping out of one rhythm and into another. The flats had bars on their windows to stop people like us from getting in. Alfred said it was where the bourgeoisie repelled the proletariat. He said bars on windows were a sickness, and that people like that were simply too rich. Wealth needs to be shared, not hoarded, he said. Yet he loved the houses themselves, saying they were fashioned by God, who'd come down as a bird. It was a pun on Christopher Wren's name, but I didn't get it for several years. 'The man was a genius!' he'd say. 'Imagine the dome of St. Paul's! Imagine designing that! It takes a special kind of mind to be able to envision perfection. You stand in St. Paul's and you think you're at the point of all horizons. You know that feeling you get when you're out at sea and the world falls off around you like a huge eye? I know you haven't sailed anywhere yet; but, mark my words, when you do, Jacinta, it's just like the dome of St. Paul's.

You begin to understand what infinity means. And that's the point where existence is blessed by pure beauty – a beauty so profound that it eclipses time, and all that remains are alleluias. That's St. Paul's, Jacinta. That's why I take you there every Christmas to see what beauty means.'

But, even in the spring, Battersea wasn't beauty or infinity for long. It was 'finite rooms hemmed to finite rooms.' When I read that line from my diary poems to Alfred, he said I was very advanced for my age. He was certain I'd grow up to be Shakespeare's sister or a malcontent. He said it was in the stars.

Sometimes I'd point out places of architectural interest to Alison. She always seemed to enjoy it, though when I'd quiz her later she never remembered any of the names.

'John Francis Bentley lived here,' I'd say, pointing to a large eighteenth-century house in Clapham Common Old Town. 'He designed the Catholic cathedral at Westminster, you know.

'Tennyson actually walked in Marianne Thornton's school on Acre Square!

'Some of the houses are Georgian, of course. I love that period – windows with little rectangular panes of glass – everything formal – as though it will be that way forever.

'Did I tell you about the plague pit on the Common? It's right there under the pond. Really it is, Alison. Imagine all those *bones*.'

Alison's eyes would grow wide and she'd say things like 'Cor, blimey,' and I'd be as happy as I could be, given my circumstances.

Clapham Common itself was my favorite place to be. I'd go with Alison and sit on the bench near the old air raid shelters – huge concrete mounds where Alfred said he'd seen men and women firing the big guns up into a network of lights during the War. At other times, we'd sit by the dancing trees, as Louise used to call them when Simon was alive, near the narrow footpath where Louise and I used to walk before she became distracted.

I didn't tell Alison Bean about my mother. Alfred said you couldn't trust anyone. If I told, then I could be taken away to a 'home.' I made up elaborate stories about how Louise and I were doing one thing or another. One weekend we were going to Salisbury Cathedral on the coach, I told the girls at school, because my mother loved spires. The next week I told them we were spending a quiet weekend at home playing poker.

Because Alison was younger than I was, she seemed to believe everything I said. She didn't ask too many questions, and she rarely wanted to come in to the house to play because of Maurice and what had happened before. I was happy around Alison Bean. Apart from Alfred, Alison was the person I felt most relaxed with.

Sometimes we held hands when we talked. Alison had a small hand. It looked very black in my brown one. On the Common, we must have looked like two small specks on the expanse of green ringed by the South Circular Road, traffic whizzing round the edges of what I called 'tranquillity.' The breeze made my cheeks red, and Alison's eyes water. We strolled down toward the bandstand as boys on roller skates, mothers with prams, and old people passed us by – all out enjoying the mild afternoon. I told Alison we needed to cele-brate the life of a King. She thought I meant Jesus.

'I love Jesus,' she said.

'No. Not Jesus. Another King. Jesus was the King of the Jews, but Martin Luther King was the King of the Blacks. He was assassinated a year ago, you know. Which leaves a big hole in the movement, Alfred says, and means that someone has to rise up and take his place.'

'Who?'

'Me maybe. I want to go to America, you know. After Africa, of course. There's so much to do. People are rioting over there, you know. Alfred says it's the most violent nation in history. He says the United States is predicated upon – that means "based upon" – suffering. He says it was the Indians who were slaugh-tered first and now it's the blacks. He says that Simon said the Little Rock Nine – you remember, Alison, I told you that story last time – anyhow, the Little Rock Nine symbolized some-thing . . . I forget what it was exactly, but it was very important. Something bad about the West. Someone needs to go there and clean up the mess. It really is messy over there, Alison. I plan to go after Africa. There's so much to be done. Sometimes it's a bit overwhelming.'

The wind picked up and blew in our faces. My hair stood up on my head because I'd forgotten my hat. Alison's short hair didn't move. I admired the Africanness of it. It reminded me of Simon.

'You can come to Kingston with me one day, Jacinta. If you like.'

'I think I'd like that,' I replied.

'Yeah. You would. It's super-calla-fraga-listic-expi-ali-docious!'

We laughed. It had taken Alison two weeks to get her tongue around the word I'd taught her from *Mary Poppins*. It had since become her favorite adjective.

'What would I like about Jamaica?' I asked.

'Plantains.'

'What else?'

'My granny.'

'Are there beaches with yellow sand? That's what I'd like more than anything. And coloured people everywhere. Here, there, and everywhere. Lots of poor ones too so that I could do good works.'

'O yes, Jassie. There's lotsa those – poor people *and* beaches. Sometimes the poor people are *right there* on the beaches, so's you don't never have to even go lookin' for 'em. Lotsa them don't 'ave no shoes neither. You'd love it, Jacinta.'

I looked up at the trees. A few had blossoms on. Most were losing them to the wind.

'"April is the cruelest month,"' I said.

Alison looked at me.

'We learned that at school,' I told her, 'but I don't believe it. I think April is the happiest month because of the spring and all the buds and everything. You know what I mean. New beginnings. Time to start over. Anything can happen in the spring!'

Alison nodded. Then she uttered one of the longest and most complicated series of sentences I'd heard from her in a long time.

'I'm going home one day. To Jamaica. Just like we said. You can come too. Mum says I'm a Cockney girlie now, so they won't reckanize me. But I think they will. Plantains are great. And there's no Maurice Beadycap over there. I hate him. He's a bad, bad one. One day something terrible's gonna happen to him. Mum says so. I like the trees too. I like pretty things. You're really pretty. I could look at you all day. My granny's pretty too, in a old way. She has the best smile and the best rice in town. She smells like . . . like . . . smiling.'

'You know, that was a simile, Alison. Well done!'

'It was!'

'Yep. You said "she smells like smiling." You compared one unlike thing to another. You did something else unusual too, in a rhetorical sense, but I don't quite know what it is. I'll have to ask Alfred. Poets use figures of speech like that, you know. I'm going to be a poet someday.'

'I used a sim-le!' Alison said. She was beaming. She asked me if I'd be her best friend. I told her I could be *her* best friend, if she liked, but she'd have to be my *second*-best friend because of Josephine Marsh. I didn't tell her about Alfred or my other friend Julie Russell because I thought it might hurt her feelings. She said she'd be really happy to be my second-best friend. I took out a safety pin I always carried just in case, and we did the Indian blood-brother ceremony. I pricked my forefinger and squished some blood out. She pricked her forefinger too, though it took her five tries because she was so afraid of the sight of blood. Then we held our fingers together and recited a rhyme I'd made up.

If all the mummies loved you,
and all the dads were good,
then life would be like dreaming,
and they'd do what they should.

If all the friends were like you,
and all the kings were queens,
how happy we would be on earth
because we all could dream.

We held hands some more and sang 'Yesterday' in parts. We got very emotional when we got to the bit about people leaving. I thought about Louise, and I almost told Alison about it. I knew she'd understand and that she could keep a secret. But still, I had to be careful. I could ruin everything all over again by speaking out of turn. I didn't know what Alison had lost, but I thought perhaps it was her granny in Jamaica because when she spoke about her she always seemed to be writing her name in capital letters, the way I did in my head with Simon – and now Louise.

Just then, a woman went by with a baby in a pram. We rushed up to look at it but the woman shooed us away.

'Get out of 'ere! I don't want no coloured's germs on my baby!'

We were stunned for a moment. Then we looked at each other and looked at her. The woman was filthy. Her hair was so greasy it looked wet; her face had smudges of black on it; and there was snot running from her nose, which she wiped away on her sleeve. We began to laugh. We laughed and laughed and laughed. Alison mimicked her voice as we danced in circles around the pram:

'Coloured germs! Coloured germs!' we sang.

The best part of all was that the woman seemed to be afraid of us. Her eyes got big and she took several steps backward. I felt myself growing taller.

'We eat little babies,' I said, remembering the way Simon used to lick his lips to chase rude people away. 'We're cannibals!'

'Yum, yum,' Alison added.

The woman swore at us, then took off at about ninety miles an hour.

'Ha, ha, ha! Ha, ha!' The wind took our laughter and whipped it up around us like blossoms.

'We shoulda *breathed* on it,' Alison said.

'Or sneezed!'

'Yeah! Even better!'

'Hee, hee!'

'Ha, ha, ha!'

'You know, Alison, I don't like white people much. Except for my mother and Alfred, of course.'

'I don't like 'em either. They look at you funny. Me dad says don't none of 'em like us much. They're out to get us, he says.'

We looked at each other. 'Yum, yum, baby meat,' I said, and we fell about all over again.

'Do you like being black, Alison?' I asked, suddenly serious.

'I s'pose.'

'Do you ever wish you were white like the others?'

She stood for a while frowning in concentration. Behind her, about a mile away, matchbox-sized cars tore along the distant road – cars driven by people who didn't have to wait for buses, driven by white people who had found a way to get away.

I waited to hear what she would say. I wanted her to give the right answer, though I didn't know what it was. At last she looked up at me and her face broke into a smile.

'If I was white, then I wouldn't be like the others, Jassie. Me brothers 'n sisters would all look at me funny. When I went back to my granny, she'd say, "Who are you, Missy?" I'd be the odd man out.'

'Yes,' I said, understanding for the first time that our homes were places where our skins belonged. 'Yes. You're right. You're abso-effing-lutely right!' Alison gasped in horror at my language, then covered her mouth with her hand and giggled.

I continued: 'Who wants to be freckly and pointy-nosed anyway? Who wants to have greasy wads of hair and fat babies that look like loaves of white bread?'

'Not us!' Alison cried.

'Who wants to be slave owners and racists and wealthy bastards living in Chelsea with our caviar and champagne, our color tellies and our Rolls-Royces?'

Alison gave me a puzzled look. Color televisions and Rolls-Royces were too appealing to pretend we didn't want them. I needed to make whiteness less attractive. I thought for a moment, then hit upon exactly the thing that would convince her.

'And who wants to be doomed to hell because of all the centuries of crimes you've committed as a white supremacist?'

'Not us!' Alison said emphatically. Hell was terrifying to her. It was where Mrs. Bean said all her children would go if they didn't attend church every Sunday.

'We're lucky, Alison. We're lucky because . . . we're lucky because . . .'

'Because we're not white?' Alison suggested timidly.

'Yes! Exactly!'

I grabbed hold of her hands and we spun around so that the sky twirled above us and the ground spun under our feet.

'Yum, yum, baby meat!' we chanted to the canopy of dancing trees.

We were so happy we never heard Maurice and Mary behind us until it was too late.

We spun around and saw them standing in the middle of the narrow path, which led from the main road to the bandstand. The cars that circled the common were whizzing behind the twins too, and I had to concentrate on standing still so that I wasn't swaying in time with Maurice, now that our spinning was over.

Normally, seeing the Beadycap twins barring my path on Clapham Common would have been enough to set my knees shaking. I hadn't spoken three sentences to Maurice since he kissed me. They were both even bigger than before. Even Mary was about twice my weight. This time, though, we'd made a white woman run away. We had power. We stood our ground.

'Go away, Maurice Beadycap,' I shouted into the wind. 'We were having a private conversation.'

Maurice just looked at us. It was impossible to tell what he was thinking.

Mary began cursing us, calling us wogs and coons.

'This is our country,' she said, 'not yours. Go home and swing on trees, why don'tcha?'

I leaped before I knew it. Alison followed suit.

We both went for Mary's eyes. She kicked and spat and we didn't let go. Something told us Maurice would never help her.

She didn't even bother to cry out for help. It would have been useless to do so.

The funny thing is, we were both laughing. Hooting with laughter, in fact. We laughed even more when we yanked up her skirt and found her navy blue knickers under the ugly yellow petticoat she was wearing. We each grabbed hold of the elastic and pulled them down to her knees, her ankles. A few bloody rags fell out. Alison slipped the knickers off while I tickled her. Mary was a sucker for tickling.

We took off for home. When we looked round, we saw to our horror that Maurice was chasing us. Behind Maurice we could see Mary on the ground, her legs wide open, her shock of pubic hair reddish-brown against the green of the grass. The wind caught the hem of her skirt. It ballooned around her head. She didn't look like a living person; she looked like a corpse. A few passersby stopped to stare.

We did that, I thought. I couldn't feel anything. I wanted to feel sorry for her, but I couldn't. Maurice had stopped in his tracks when we turned round. We were all caught in a moment of indecision. He didn't seem to know what to do, but there was a terrible look in his eyes, and I knew we'd taken as much away from him as we had from Mary.

'Run!' I said.

We ran and ran and ran.

The busy intersection ahead of us seemed to get farther away rather than closer. Behind us was Maurice Beadycap. He was screaming, 'I'll murder you!' I thought of Louise. I ran faster.

I reached the road first and dashed across. Alison was on the other side with Mary's knickers in her hand. Maurice was a few feet behind her.

'Run!' I cried. 'Run, Alison! He's right behind you!'

She ran.

I didn't think the bus had hit her at first. She was there in front of me, then the bus was there, then she wasn't there. I looked around. She was lying in the middle of the road and there was a deafening screech of brakes. I'd heard the sound of flesh against metal, but it had been a small sound, almost gentle.

A kind of 'poof' really, like the sound you hear when a bean bag is dropped on to the floor.

The world hushed up, and I could hear my blood pumping through my body, throbbing as if it wanted to get out. I walked out into the road and stood over her. Her dress was up around her waist and I could see that she had pink knickers on. Mary's blue ones were still in her left hand. There was a tiny trickle of blood coming from a place above her right eye, and more coming from somewhere else because soon there was a bright puddle around her, as if she were lying on a scarlet mirror. Her eyes were wide open and it occurred to me that she'd just learned a most amazing secret.

Maurice came up beside me and adults began giving orders. Maurice's eyes were almost as big as Alison's. He was breathing fast and hard. He put his arm round my waist and pulled me toward him. I thought for a moment he planned to comfort me. I let myself sink into him. He was big and warm and smelled of men.

He whispered into my ear: 'You did it.'

I jerked myself away and began to shake. I shook so much my teeth chattered. I wanted to say it was his fault – that Maurice was evil and he'd taken something away from me again. I reached down and took Mary's knickers from Alison's hand just before her father got there to rock her little head in his hands and cry like a baby over her body. 'From Kingston! For this! For this!' He turned to people in the crowd and made a sweeping gesture as though he were pushing a curtain aside.

I was led away by someone. I think it was Lily Beadycap, but it could have been Mrs. Butcher.

Alfred met me at the corner of Lavender Sweep, not far from Mrs. Gem's sweetshop. He was running toward me. He looked like a stick man. I was afraid he would shatter in the wind. He wrapped his skinny arms around me and whisked me up into the house. He sat me down in the kitchen with the fruit-basket wallpaper and the dents in the wall where my mother had kicked out a hunk of it. He made me a cup of English Breakfast tea and spoke about death and dying. He never asked me whose fault it was. 'Dear God in heaven,' he repeated over and over.

'When will it end? One thing after another. You think you've seen the worst and then – poor little Alison. Poor Mr. and Mrs. Bean. When will it end?'

I trembled for two days.

Four days later I was back at school and Alison was in a small plot in Wandsworth Cemetery. I didn't go to the funeral. No one said I had to.

Maurice disappeared on the same day that Alison was killed. Lily was frantic. She said he was a genius and their ticket to better days. He had no right to go off on his own like that, she said. There were rumors that he'd joined the merchant navy. I hoped he was in hell. His words burned in my head. Maurice was evil, not me. Him. I hadn't done it. He had. He was the one with the tongue and the hands. He was the one we were running away from. Yet I'd made Alison cross the road. It was me. But only because of Maurice. He'd made me do it, just like he'd made me burn my hand that time. Maurice was the devil. If you got in his way, he devoured you. I needed to find someone to protect me. Louise was worse than useless. Alfred wasn't capable of hating anyone, and you needed to hate someone like Maurice, otherwise he'd win. I prayed for a champion to come and save me. I prayed to Simon to send someone who would never be afraid of Maurice Beadycap.

Then, one evening a few days after I'd returned to school, there was a knock at the door. Alfred was trying to make me eat some cod and potatoes. He said if I didn't eat soon I'd waste away. He went down to answer the door. 'Eat that up, young lady,' he said. 'I'll be back in a minute.'

When Alfred returned he had a white woman with him in a brown suit with gold buttons. She looked organized. Even her hair was organized into a taut brown bun, stuck through with large black hairpins. She had a small briefcase in her hand, and she looked weary, like the women in the offices where we went to get vouchers for shoes, or help with the heating bill. Alfred was crying.

'Now don't worry, child,' he said. 'I'll get you back. Your mother will too. It's a free country and they can't go against your daddy's wishes like that. You'll be back on Lavender Sweep in no time. You'll see.'

I got up slowly and began to pack my bags. I didn't feel a thing. I knew that one of the twins had called social services. I knew it for a fact. I felt as though I'd known the secret was out as soon as I saw Mary's pubic hair on Clapham Common. You always got punished for things like that.

Alison Bean was dead. So was Simon. My mother was as mad as a hatter.

A glorious numbness set in. Everyone flew away. It was only a matter of time. The more you loved them, the more likely it was you'd lose them. The joke was on me. I should have known I'd seen this episode before. It was a repeat, but I'd forgotten to change the channel.

I smiled to myself. They could send Jacinta Louise Buttercup Moses wherever they wanted. The only person they could never touch was me.

Alfred has fallen asleep in the chair next to my mother's deathbed. I leave his English Breakfast on the side table next to him. I cover it with a saucer and creep back out again into the narrow hallway. At the foot of the stairs is where Maurice pinned my small body to the wall. The flowered wallpaper is gone, of course; now there is wine-colored paper and white woodwork. Yet, when I inhale deeply, I can still smell Maurice and his siblings, the urine-soaked mattresses, the grease from Lily's sausages and bacon.

Upstairs, Lady sleeps in the room that used to be mine. I think I hear her cry out. I creep upstairs; the old stairs that had once been covered with paisley/fish-hand carpet creak under my weight. I push open the door to her room.

All is quiet. She sleeps without nightmares. I kiss her gently and am awestruck by the beauty of my daughter's face. Who would have thought that nightmare could translate itself into blessing? I am my daughter's mother. Will I be a good one? When she is thirty-six, will she turn to me and demand the same kind of answers I demanded from my poor mother only days ago?

I creep out again, go downstairs and take my coat from the closet in the hallway. Outside the fog is beginning to lift, but the dampness puts a deeper chill in the air as the sky readies itself for dawn.

The fact of my mother's breast cancer has cast everything in a new light – as if her life and mine are foreshortened somehow by this circumstance, so that what is close up is large and intrusive, and what is far away a trick of the light. In the fog I see her clearly. The past few days shove me into a recognition of who we were.

In her final days, my mother was still an actress. When she told Lady one of the stories my father wrote, her voice took off into drama. Lady curled up on Louise's hospital bed – her whole body listening for clues. She looked just like I did when Simon told me the same story years before.

My mother told the story of the elephant – my father's story, but with different intonations because my mother was the storyteller this time, and she was a white Englishwoman, and he was a black African man, and that makes all the difference. I tried to listen, well knowing that soon it would be me doing the telling.

My father's in print again. A new edition of his stories was published by Faber and Faber a few years ago. Everyone is praising his prose. He is fashionable at last. I become Simon Moses' daughter all over again. My mother has carried a copy of the stories in her bag ever since it came out. She carries it everywhere, together with a copy of my first book of poems. She tells me our styles are the same, but it's hard for me to see it. She likes my poem about my father's death best. 'It sounds like holes,' she says.

In spite of the pain, my mother laughs so much during her last few days on this earth that she often lets out a series of enormous farts that she blames on the chemotherapy. We have a few days together before the pain turns my mother inside out. Up until that time, Alfred, myself, and the hospice worker control it with painkillers.

I sleep in the rocking chair beside her bed and chart the course of her breathing.

One night I wake with a start. Louise is looking at me. Before I can stop myself, I begin telling her about my dream, knowing she won't understand how closely it resembles my first and last Easter in Africa.

'I was lying in the earth – sort of – only there was this huge tree on top of me. I could see its branches and it – are you tired, by the way? 'Cos I can stop if you are.'

'No, no. I'm wide awake. So you were looking at this tree. Then what happened?'

'Well, it just seemed to me that it was very dark. Almost pitch dark. But I could see the tree, as I said. And it was lovely – the loveliest of trees. And I thought, "I don't mind being under the earth if I can see trees like that." And then it occurred to me that it wasn't the branches at all, it was the roots! Only things were upside down because it was the sky behind them, I knew that for certain. Weird, isn't it?'

'What happened then?'

'I began to think about dying. And about the roots of things. I can't explain it very well. And then I got scared. And then I woke up. What do you think about dying, by the way?' I realize I'm being anything but subtle.

Louise doesn't say anything for a while. But I know she's thinking about it. What she says next surprises me.

'You shouldn't be afraid of death, Jacinta. It can be a wonderful thing if the timing's right. If life didn't make us hate it, then how would we let go? But then there's Alfred. And he's getting so old. And London's a hard place for someone like him to be alone in. Even harder than it used to be. And he's still an extrovert, in a way. Still wears those lavender shirts with the lace. And the occasional dab of lipstick, you know. He got stoned the other day by some awful skinhead types. Did I tell you? Nothing too serious, but still . . .'

I want to shake her. I remember her diary. How much she wanted to share my father's grave.

'You're *not* going to die!' My voice is so loud it makes her laugh.

'You can't command someone to live, dear! It doesn't work that way.'

There's joy in her voice. She is happy. My mother is *happy* to be dying!

'You *want* to die, don't you?'

She stops laughing. 'No,' she says. 'Not really.'

'You wanted to die when I was a child, though, didn't you?'

'I suppose I did,' she says. 'I was lonely.' Her face is softened by the dim light in the room. The edges of her pain have been smoothed down by drugs. She seems to be at peace. I am compelled to try to ruin it.

'I'm never lonely with Lady,' I say. It's an accusation.

'You are you and I am me. Maybe you didn't love your husband the way I loved your father.'

I am stunned. She said it as a matter of fact; she didn't intend to be offensive. But she's hurt me more than she realizes. I wish I'd had the guts to tell her years ago about that Easter in Africa.

'You don't know,' I say, my voice trembling, 'what my husband was to me. You barely even met him. You don't know what happened over there. You've never even asked. You don't know what I've been through to get here. You don't have a clue. I wanted to be a good person, and it got all messed up. Just like that. And I forgot about all those things I was going to do for other people, and all that was left was . . . making do.'

'You know what it's like, then, Jacinta.' She lies back in the bed and sighs. 'And you mustn't resent your mother for wanting to let some of it go. Sometimes life's a bitch. You're right. I don't know anything about your husband or your time in Africa. Just those things you told me about Simon's family and that strange story about those friends of yours – and of course the accident. But you kept the details to yourself. And I didn't mind. Everyone needs some privacy. If you don't have any privacy at all, how can you learn to respect yourself? Your father used to say that's how they managed to control the slaves. Their main weapon was denying them privacy. Herding them together in their little cabins. Naming them publicly with a branding iron. The poor don't have privacy and neither do the insane – not in the old days, anyway. Privacy is for the middle class.

'Sometimes,' she says, more to herself than to me, 'you look at your child and it seems like a lot to bear – that responsibility, you know. You know what it's like. When Lady was born, remember? You wanted to die. And you wouldn't let any of us near you. You're like me that way. When times are really bad, you just stop. Like a watch or a clock that hasn't been wound. You just stop. Sometimes you look at your child and you think it's just not worth it.'

I *am* worth it, I think. Don't give me your despair. I have to have something to give to Lady.

'Is that why you left?' I say out loud.

'When?'

'When I was a child.'

'O.'

'Is it? I wasn't worth it, right?'

She sighs. I want to have mercy on her, but I can't. Something in me pushes hard. 'I wasn't worth it, was I? Was I?'

'I love you, Jacinta. But I had to go away for a while and . . . think.'

'They sent me to live with –'

'Don't you think I know that!'

She sits up in bed. At last she's angry. I'm glad. If she's angry, she's not dead already. Rage, rage, against the dying of the light, Louise.

I say I'm sorry. I can't see whether she's crying. I move to hug her, but she pushes me away with what little strength she has left. I can tell she wants to say something. I wait for her to speak.

'You need to remember, Jacinta . . . you need to remember . . . whatever it cost me . . . I came back for you.'

The fog is lifting. I can see the rooftops in a zigzag outline against the brightening sky.

It occurs to me that I have taught students about my notions of 'beauty' and 'truth' for more than twelve years yet I know nothing. I don't know what propels evil; and, if you don't know that, how can you ready anyone else for an encounter with the world? I want to make a pattern out of my life. I need to do that if I am going to make sense of any of this. A part of me thinks life is a trick. Stephen Crane was right about the indifference of God. Events are random; fortune is blind. You're blindfolded, pinned to a wheel, and spun round like a top. 'Nothing comes from nothing.' You eat, you sleep, you suffer, you die. You love, if you can, in the margins.

I need to make a pattern in my head. I need to make a pattern.

I take out the small journal I still carry around with me. On the doorstep of Lavender Sweep, nearly a quarter century after I sat there for the last time with Alison, I open it up and try to write down what I know. I write this.

If I were to make a Life Quilt, the center would be a circle of fire. People looking at it would wonder whether it was the flames of hell or the flames of passion. Sewn into Greeting Squares would be the people I've loved. Lady is in the middle. Nothing is symmetrical in my quilt. The whole pattern slips off to one side like a bad actor's hurried exit. Lady's difference is obvious but not shocking. We are laughing: Alfred Russell-Smythe, Alison Bean, Emmanuel Fox, John Turay, Louise Buttercup, Simon Moses, Esther Cole. I join them to each other but it's me they've made. Interspersed with the colorful squares are oblongs of stark white with nothing in them but a word. The white squares say 'Maurice' over and over again. There are some other squares too. In one is a red mirror; in another, a lost arm. Around the edge of the quilt are the Wing Squares, cut out from gold the color of Lady's skin. They take the Life Quilt up into the air. It rises in front of me and takes off.

I'm not afraid. I've been to hell and back at least three times. I know the cost of resurrection. I cannot change my story so that it fits my dreams better. I look for the links between Maurice and evil, the rich and the poor, Africa and Europe, America and a colored girl born on Christmas Eve. Maurice shoves himself to center stage. He's hanging from a beam in some old motel room. Something tight around his neck, his hand where it shouldn't be. His eyes are popping out of his head as he swings back and forth, his feet drawing an invisible smile in the air. The clarity of it frightens me. Can you wish death upon someone if you try hard enough? Lady's voice pushes him aside. I rush inside and up the stairs.

'*Uno!*' she cries in her sleep, playing the game she and Louise played right up until the last day or two of her journey.

The child's voice seems to echo round the house: 'No! No! No!'

I go in and take my little girl in my arms in much the same way as Louise did once, just after Simon died.

'Is Mama Lou really dead?' Lady asks. 'I dreamed she died. Is it true?'

'Yes,' I say, remembering how often our dreams are the same – Lady dreaming she caught five moons, all of them striped except one; me dreaming five lunatics out of captivity, one of them myself – 'Yes, it's true. But she left us something.'

'What did she leave us?' Lady asks, scooting back in the bed so that she can look up into my eyes.

'Her strength,' I say.

'I miss her,' Lady tells me.

'Me too.'

'She was one of my best friends,' Lady says.

'Best friends are hard to come by, Lady. It's good you recognize that she was one of them. You have to find a way to get best friends back when it looks as though they're gone for good.'

'But how do you find them when they're dead, Mom?'

'You find them by looking back to where they used to be. Little by little they begin to join you where you are, as long as you look back without regret. And then, one day, the past and present meet, and the line we call death dissolves. At least, that's sort of what your uncle Alfred taught me, in a way.'

Lady is comforted. Soon I am listening to her rhythmic breathing. On the way downstairs, I crack open the bathroom door where I used to kiss the plunger and conjure up what remained of Africa after Simon's death. There was glory here too, Alison, I say to myself. Why was I too stupid to see what you saw? Alison's voice joins mine. I sweeten the words between us. Not my second-best friend, Alison. Never only my second-best friend. You who let me dream aloud. You who sent me spinning into joy when only absence was real.

Downstairs I hear Alfred stir. I'll show him what I've written. He's right. It will heal us on this new day, and give us time to make room for the necessary waking of our dead.

8

I spent the night in a children's home in Clapham Park. I barely said a word. No one took much notice because the place was crowded: four new arrivals in one day, they said, three of us 'coloured' children. They made me wash my hair with a lethal-smelling shampoo and comb it with a metal comb, as a precaution against lice.

That night in the narrow bed assigned to me by a Miss Murphy, I hovered above everything, and observed the night-mares of lonely children. 'I am not Jacinta Moses,' I whispered. 'I am Simone Madagascar.' It was a ludicrous name, but it felt good to sever my connections to Lavender Sweep, to Maurice Beadycap, to Louise Buttercup, and even to Alison Bean (who would never lie down again in the snow so that I could marvel at the exquisite blackness of her against the white earth). I chose Simone Madagascar because, although she wasn't me, she had enough of Simon in her name and enough of Africa to be dif-ferent. People could call me 'Mad' for short. With a mother in a nuthouse, I reasoned in my self-induced calm, I would be pre-disposed to insanity. On the other hand, if I kept the name to myself, it could always be mine alone.

Ruskin appeared the next morning. I didn't react when I saw him because I didn't care what happened to me anymore. I hadn't felt much of anything since I stooped down to remove a pair of blue knickers from the stiffening fingers of Alison Bean.

Everyone made a fuss when Ruskin appeared. He could do that to people – make them believe he was someone important. Alfred was prone to say, grudgingly, that Ruskin was fairly good-looking for an adult past his prime, and one of the women at the home remembered seeing Ruskin on some show about the 'primitive' broadcast by the BBC so they hurried us through the paperwork.

Although I was too numb to feel much, it would be a relief to go home. I needed the space of the three rooms without Louise. With Maurice gone, nothing would disturb me.

When we got outside to Ruskin's Volkswagen, he paused, then placed his hand on my shoulder and tilted my chin so that I had to look up his nose. There was a huge booger in his left nostril, but I didn't comment because I didn't give a damn. He was talking about something. I caught him in mid-sentence once I stopped focusing on the booger.

'. . . Alfred's qualities are certainly endearing,' he said as I watched the way his tongue moved in his mouth, 'but he's not suitable as a guardian of a lovely young thing like you. As I said, your mother is still under the weather and –'

'Insane, you mean,' I said mockingly. (Simone was looking down at us both. She could see the bald spot on Ruskin's head. It didn't interest her in the least.)

Ruskin continued: 'Therefore we've managed to convince the authorities to let you run around with your friends in Battersea just a few doors down from where you lived before. It took a lot of persuading to convince them to agree to this. In fact, I'm behind on my next book, what with your mother's illness and all this to deal with. But a few words in the right ears and, Bob's your uncle, there you are. Installed just a few doors down from your own home in Mrs. Butcher's –'

My heart must have stopped because I nearly fell over. Ruskin reached out to grab me.

'You didn't, did you, Ruskin? You didn't . . . I mean, you couldn't!' I cried. He'd stolen the only thing I had left: my numbness. He'd found a way to open me up like a wound. I wanted to kill him. I was spluttering like a fool.

'Now get a grip on yourself, young lady. No need to throw a tantrum. It's only for a little while until your mother comes home, Jacinta.'

'Not Jacinta! Simone Madagascar!' The name was out before I could stop it. I tried to take it back. 'I mean . . . it's just a nickname. That's all. Something the kids gave me.'

Ruskin was chortling. 'Why Madagascar, for God's sake? It's the most ridiculous name I've ever –'

'Shut up! Shut the fuck up and mind your own damn business! I was just playing, that's all. Just do what you came to do and then go to hell.' My voice steadied itself. I couldn't remember being as rude as this to an adult before. It made my skin tingle, and it obviously threw Ruskin off balance. He drew back from me, his eyes on fire. His hand seemed to be itching on the ivory head of the cane he always carried with him.

Hit me, please, I prayed. *If you hit me I'll have to go to the hospital again. I'd be safe there in the white sheets. Hit me, Ruskin. Please.*

I opened my eyes. I must have closed them when I began praying. Ruskin was looking at me strangely. I think I noticed horror in his face, then I thought it was rage. It was as if an artist had begun by painting one expression on him, then toyed with the idea of another. He looked all higgledy-piggledy caught in between like that. It almost made me laugh.

'Jesus Christ! You want it, don't you? You *want* me to hit you!'

He caught me by the arm and began to propel me toward the car: 'Come on, my girl. One mental case in the family is more than enough. We're going back to Lavender Sweep.'

'I won't live with her,' I said, my voice remarkably steady. 'She's dirty and smelly, and Hubert makes me sick,' I yelled.

'Mrs. B. is a nice woman,' said Ruskin, but I could tell he was hardly listening so I shut up. How would Ruskin Garland the writer-warlock ever understand what it meant to be me or Simone Madagascar? I'd realized early that no one knew anyone else from the inside. You could guess at things sometimes – have a rough idea about what people were thinking, but you never really knew. Ruskin was white. Ruskin was a man. Unlike

Alfred, Ruskin stayed Ruskin. I didn't know quite what I meant by that. But I did know that Ruskin Garland would always be a man talking about the Primitive with a capital 'P.' He'd always be someone I could recognize. For a brief moment, I felt sorry for him. Then the merciful numbness came back, and I rose above us and was dissipated into the air just above the Volkswagen.

Playing the role of Jacinta again, I climbed into Ruskin's car, and we drove back through Clapham Park round by Olde Towne and on by Clapham Common toward Lavender Sweep. He talked about his warlock activities, but I didn't pay attention. He took to embellishing things in order to impress me.

'We're naked, of course,' he declared at the traffic lights opposite St. Mary's. I thought of the candles my mother lit inside the church and the votive offerings she used to make to the Virgin Mary. In my mind I saw the pink face of the Virgin staring down at me from her pedestal – her blue robes covered in stars, as if she were the night itself made human. It would be interesting to open the door and leap out. I could curl up under the feet of the statue and be taken to heaven in my sleep. Another Ascension Day. I thought of my mother's urgent whispers coming from the wooden confessional box. I heard the priest's voice telling her to be sorry. I thought of my own sins. Playing with myself in the bathtub; planning how to kill Maurice Beadycap; calling to Alison Bean to cross the road; wishing my mother was dead; sending her to the insane asylum . . . I was so full of sin now it hardly mattered what I did next; I would go to hell anyway. I leaned back in the seat and closed my eyes.

'Yes, it's part of the ritual, Jacinta – I mean, Simone.' I opened my eyes and he winked at me. 'Clothes are an impediment to the spirit. There's a tremendous misunderstanding between those in and outside the Order.' He sounded just like Sister Maria. I didn't tell him that, of course. I pictured him naked. It was unpleasant. I dressed him again.

'Do you like nudity, Simone?' he asked, looking down to where my bosoms were just beginning to 'blossom.'

I shrugged. I was thoroughly bored.

'Little girls your age usually do. They are still pure – untouched by the perversions of a society racked by guilt. They accept the body in a way that is totally uninhibited. They know their femaleness and it thrills them. What we need right now is a female prime minister. I know it's radical, but I'm right. A woman would put us all in our place. We could obtain succor at her breast.' He was looking down at mine again. I shifted in my seat. 'Put a woman at the helm and let the female spirit enlighten us and what have you got then?' He put his hand on my thigh. 'You've got joy, Jacinta,' he said softly. 'Pure joy.'

'*Simone*,' I whispered. 'Not Jacinta.' But my voice was too low to be audible.

Ruskin went on to speak about flower power and its limitations. He had the answers to everything. When he wasn't changing gears, he'd rest his hand on my thigh. Once in a while he'd squeeze it. I tried to pretend it wasn't happening, but gradually I began to feel it. It was as if my whole body had become the area where his hand was. I didn't know whether it made me smaller or larger. I did know it made me feel guilty, something I'd escaped for a while. I hated him for pulling me back.

Ruskin quoted Sartre, Orwell, Aristotle, Darwin, Jung, Freud, and, most of all, himself. In his books, he claimed, he'd found the engine that drove the universe. It was what the Nazis had been searching for, he declared. He didn't say the word 'Nazi' the way Alfred said it. I wondered whether he liked Jews.

All at once it came to me again that we were heading toward Mrs. Butcher's house and that his fat, hairy hand, now that it had been on my thigh, would always have been there. He was making me the girl with the swastika on her palm; he was turning me back into the girl who drove her mother insane, the girl who killed her best friend before she could tell her she was her best friend, and not her second-best friend at all. At the next set of traffic lights, I swiveled round to face Ruskin. He scooted his hand up my thigh so that he could pull at the lace on my knickers. Sometimes he'd inch his forefinger up around the lace and I was reminded of Maurice, and of the great sin that befell Catholic girls if they didn't keep their guards up. I was trembling. I thought of Alison's knickers and Mary Beadycap's knickers, and my knickers. People were always finding ways to pull them down. I tried to numb myself again, but it didn't work, and I came back to Ruskin's hand down there, more urgent than before; and all I could think of was how I had pried Mary's knickers out of Alison's hand, and how soiled and pathetic they were; and how all of this had led to where we were now, driving in a car heading in the direction of hell.

We pulled up at a traffic light, so Ruskin jerked his hand away because people were walking by – white people with the grayness of London in their expressions.

I sank back into the seat again. I didn't want to admit it, but part of me missed the warmth of his hand. It was the first touch I'd allowed myself to feel since Alison's death, and it made me want to cry.

We both remained quiet until we pulled up in front of the house. I sat there glued to the seat. Ruskin got out and came over to my side of the car. In my distress I'd forgotten to savor what it was like riding in the front seat, but it hardly seemed to matter. Out of the blue I turned to him and pointed out the fact that he had bad breath and a booger hanging from his nose. I said it softly so he had to bend down to hear it. I could see the sharp hairs in his ears. When he realized what I'd said, he jerked his head up so fast that he cracked his skull on the door frame. I looked him in the eye.

'You shouldn't have touched me like that, Ruskin. You know it was a sin.' My voice carried along the Sweep, and Ruskin looked around nervously.

'Look, I tell you what, Jacinta. You keep this as our little secret, and I won't say a thing about your name. How's that?'

'What name?' I said.

When he spoke he directed his words to the windscreen, perhaps remembering what I'd said about his breath.

'Be careful, Jacinta. This isn't a game anymore, and you're not a child. I can easily take you back there to the home if I feel it's in your best interests. I had to work hard to get you a place with Mrs. Butcher. You're indebted to me, you know. By all accounts Mrs. Butcher is a good foster mother. Dozens of children have passed through her home. She knows how to take care of young people. She'll look after you until your mother comes home. None of us gets what we want when we want it.

You wait for the thing you've longed for all your life and then, one day, when you think you've almost got it, she turns round and disappears on you. And all that's left is a shadow of . . . anyhow. . . . You've got to grow up, that's all there is to it, young lady. We all have burdens to carry. Yours is not exceptional. Mrs. Butcher has taken in many coloured girls and done a fine job with them.'

'I don't want to live with a white woman,' I said.

He looked stunned. 'Your mother's white.'

'So what? I'm not.'

'You're a half-caste, Jacinta. And that makes you part white, my girl.'

'I don't like that word.'

'What word?' His hand twitched on his cane.

'Half-caste. It's rude.'

'Mulatto, then. Whatever. Look, I have to get going and –'

'Mulatto's awful too. I'm a mule, that's what they're telling me. Do you know about mules? I do. I'm not going to be one and that's that.'

'O, for God's sake! All right, all right. What then? What do you want me to call you?'

'Nothing.'

'What?'

'Nothing. Don't call me anything. I never want to see you again,' I said. 'You're old and dirty. You're a dirty old man.' The words leaped out of my mouth and skipped down the street like a girl playing hopscotch. I thought of the way Alison Bean used to play hopscotch long after dark, while I went in to do my homework; how I'd hear her outside on the pavement, skipping over the concrete slabs, the click of the pebble landing on the next square she'd drawn, and then the next one after that. Hop, skip, skip, hop, hop . . . and back to the beginning.

Ruskin Garland spoke again, more wearily than before.

'To tell you the truth, I don't want to see you for a while either. Perhaps we both need a holiday from one another. Give you a chance to grow up. Now, get out of the fucking car before I use this.' He smacked his cane on the pavement.

His language made my eyes sting. I blinked, then climbed out slowly. We walked up to Mrs. Butcher's front door and Ruskin rang the bell. Nothing happened. He rapped loudly on the door. Still nothing.

'Damn the woman,' he said. 'She knew what time we were supposed to be here. Where is she?'

Just then the door opened. A small black child with a dirty face and torn trousers opened the door. He was about five – maybe six. He looked up at us without saying a word.

'Is your . . . is Mrs. Butcher home?' Ruskin asked.

The child nodded.

'Go and get her for me. Tell her Ruskin Garland is here.'

The child didn't move. He just looked from Ruskin to me as if he couldn't imagine what planet we'd come from. Ruskin swore again, then planted the boy to one side, took hold of my arm, and marched on through the house. The first open door we came to was to the right. It opened up into the front room. Ruskin walked in without knocking. I followed.

'Phew!' he said before he could stop himself. 'It stinks in here.'

We looked around. Half a dozen cribs. In each one a child. But not a sound. None of them crying. None of them laughing or talking to themselves. They just sat there and stared.

'What's the matter with them?' Ruskin asked, backing toward the door.

'How should I know?' I replied, speaking more to calm myself than as a response to his question. 'Maybe they've just woken up.'

But we both knew that was a lie. Something about the way they sat up in their cribs, their small faces pressed against the bars, or lay down staring up at the bare lightbulb swinging from a cord in the middle of the room convinced us that this was how they lived at Mrs. Butcher's.

There were posters around the room, tacked up with tape. The edges of the posters were curling up with age. One showed a thatched cottage in the country. It said VISIT THE WEST COUNTRY in large red letters. Another was a photo of a bottle of Guinness. GUINNESS IS GOOD FOR YOU! was written underneath. There was an

OXFAM poster with emaciated children with large brown eyes holding up bowls to the camera; and there was a picture of an ice-cream sundae with a huge red cherry on the top. A small plaque over one of the cots read HOME IS WHERE THE HEART IS. The carpet was frayed and soiled. There were greasy handprints on the woodwork. A small portable heater whirred in the background and above us on the next floor we heard the sound of children arguing with each other.

Just then, a voice behind us made us jump.

'What a state! What a state! Mr. Garland, I am so sorry! Whatever was Michael thinking of letting you come in like this unescorted? How do you do? We met when I visited poor Louise when she was taken poorly that time. Vera Butcher never forgets a face. And how are you, my pet? Pleased to be back on the Sweep, are you?'

'No,' I said as coldly as I could.

'She's a little out of sorts, Mrs. Butcher,' Ruskin said. But his voice seemed weak. He'd gasped when we'd entered the room, and now it was clear he was having second thoughts about the appropriateness of Mrs. Butcher as a temporary foster parent. She must have guessed what we were thinking because Mrs. Butcher launched into a description of her child-rearing skills, and stressed how 'handy' it would be, my living there, what with my old home being just down the road, so to speak. Why I could trot along down there and visit that nice Mr. Smythe at any time, she said. She'd raised forty-seven children for at least part of their young lives, and although she knew the facilities weren't luxurious, they were homey. There was a girl, Sheila, who came in to help. Yes, the babies were always well-behaved. Nice and quiet like this. They liked the quiet. Too much stimulation could injure their little nerves. No. They weren't all foster children. Most belonged to someone. The mothers had to work, so they left them here for a small fee. 'Hardly worth my while, really. You can't make money on child minding. I do it out of love,' she said.

We looked around at the doleful faces of the infants, then looked at each other. Ruskin cleared his throat.

Behind Mrs. Butcher we heard a voice. She introduced it to

us before we saw what it was attached to. But I knew. I'd recognize Hubert Butcher anywhere. He'd been scooting up and down Lavender Sweep on his single roller skate ever since I could remember. It was he who terrified me the most. What if he tried to do what Maurice had done? People like Hubert were dangerous. Everyone knew it.

He came into the room. We tried to take a step back, but we jammed up against the cribs, causing one of the babies to start whimpering.

'Hubert, this is Mr. Garland and Jacinta Moses. You know Jacinta, don't you?'

'You know Jacinta, don't you,' Hubert replied in the disturbing monotone of a man who only partly comprehends what he is saying.

'Mr. Garland, this is my son, Hubert. I think you may have met him once. He's not quite right in the head. But it's nothing contagious. He's a good boy. His mum's pride and joy ever since his poor father took sick and left us for a better world.'

Hubert began to speak. He didn't stop speaking for the rest of Ruskin's visit. Mrs. Butcher ignored him, for the most part. Every now and then, when Hubert forgot he was in public and began to explore his trousers, she'd say, 'Stop that, you horrible boy!' Then she'd turn back around to us and smile broadly. Ruskin kept clearing his throat. It was clear he hated being near Hubert. Ruskin looked at him with disgust. Hubert yanked on his crotch again. His fly was partly open. I shuddered and looked away. Mrs. Butcher slapped his hand.

'Jacinta will only be here for a little while. Just until her mother comes home.'

'Till her mum comes home,' echoed Hubert in a monotone.

'O, she'll be all right, Mr. Ruskin . . . er, Garland, I mean. You can trust me, don't you worry. I've seen Hubert through thirty years of nappy changes, and I'm sure I can do well by a young lady like Jacinta. Don't you worry. And there's no colour bar here, Mr. Garland. None at all. We're all the same under the skin after all, aren't we?'

'Well, I must be going. I have a long journey back to –'

'O, Mr. Garland! You must at least come into the kitchen and have a nice cup of tea? No one leaves Vera Butcher's residence without refreshment.'

We were hurried outside into the hallway. Ruskin insisted he couldn't stay, but she made him wait by the front door while she went off to fetch lemon cupcakes for his trip. He stood impatiently in the hallway, rubbing his hand against the leg of his pants as if he were really nervous. It was now or never. I had to ask him. In spite of Louise's and Alfred's warning, in spite of what he'd done to me in the car, he was the only one left. I grabbed hold of his hand.

'Ruskin, let me live with you.'

Behind us, through the open door to the front room, the silent black, brown, and white babies stared up at the plasterwork. From the kitchen came Hubert's frantic voice. 'No cupcakies for the Ruskin! No cupcakies! Hubert's lemon cakies!'

Ruskin edged toward the front door. 'I'm sorry, Jacinta. It wouldn't . . . it wouldn't be right. You're close to home here. You're strong. You'll be fine. Don't worry.'

'You promised my mother you'd take care of me!' I cried, my composure deserting me completely.

'Jacinta, I'm telling you once and for all that it wouldn't work.'

'Why not? I'll cook, I'll clean. I'll be so good. I'll never be rude again, I promise. Ruskin, please! Please don't leave me here!'

I was leaning up against the wall. I could feel the grease on the wallpaper as it entered me through my blouse.

'I wish I could take you,' he said. I'd never heard him use that tone of voice before. He sounded like Alfred. I wanted him to hold me. 'But I can't, Jacinta. You're too pretty and I'm . . . as you can see . . . I need to be alone. It's for the best. I promised your mother I'd never . . . I'm sorry. Tell Mrs. Butcher I had to leave.'

He made a single gulping sound in the back of his throat, and then he shoved me out of the way and dashed through the front door. I couldn't stop him. He was gone. I felt sick. I held on to the banisters leading to the upper floors. My teeth were chattering.

Mrs. Butcher arrived with the lemon cupcakes. She began talking when she was still in the kitchen. It was only when she reached the front hall that she realized Ruskin had left.

'Well, bless my soul! And I picked out some of the nicest ones for him too. Would you like one, love?'

'No!' I cried. I was going to run away. One night, two at the most, and then I'd be gone. I could go back to Alfred and hide in his flat. No one would catch us. I could go up to Piccadilly Circus on the bus and live with the street people. I could run away like Maurice had. I could kill myself.

'Well, I know I don't have to ask my Hubert twice if he'd like to have a cupcake, do I?'

Hubert leaped for the cupcakes. He stuffed a whole one into his mouth and spoke at the same time.

'And he does, and he does, and he does love his lemon cup-cakies.'

Mrs. Butcher sighed. 'Don't you worry, love,' she said. 'You'll fit in here in no time.'

I began to bawl. I bawled and bawled. 'I don't want to-to-to be Jacinta Mo-Moses anymore!' I cried.

'There, there, there,' Mrs. Butcher said. 'Who else would you be, love, if not yourself? That's the way the world works. We're who we are and we make the best of it. The sooner you learn that, the better you'll be. Now come back into the kitchen with me and have a cupcake.'

'And he will, and he will, and he will have another cup-cakie!'

'Yes, Hubert, you too. Sheila!'

A girl came running down from upstairs.

'See to those babies. It stinks to high heaven in there. No wonder Mr. Ruskin hurried off like that. It's a disgrace. I thought I told you to change those babies hours ago! Sheila, what are you thinking about, my girl? Get your head out of them clouds and join us here on earth for a while. C'mon, luv,' she said to me, 'you come with me. It's not a palace but it's not a prison neither. Come and have a nice cupcake.'

'And me?' Michael said, appearing out of nowhere.

'Yes, yes. You too, Michael.'

I let her lead me to the kitchen. My heart was broken. Nothing could ever happen that would make me smile again.

Hubert Butcher believed that there were trains in his head.

He'd believed it for decades, Mrs. Butcher said. She remembered the day it began 'as if it was yesterday.' They'd been sitting together in the front room. She wasn't a child minder then, and the furniture was new-looking and sweet-smelling, she told me. She and her husband knew there was something different about Hubert. He was six and talking the way he did now. He never used the 'I' word, Mrs. Butcher said. But she and her husband thought it was just some eccentricity. Her cousin was eccentric, she said. Bought twenty-seven canaries and kept them in her upstairs loo. Mrs. Butcher thought Hubert might be taking after the cousin. But that day he was in her lap in the rocking chair when, all of a sudden, he looked up at the ceiling and seemed to notice the cracks.

'It was then that things took a turn for the worse, Jacinta. Because it was then that I knew for certain something deep was amiss. A train was going past and we could hear it in the distance as it rumbled into Clapham Junction. It'd never bothered me before. Hardly noticed it, really. But this one was loud, an express, maybe. Anyhow, my boy looked up at that ceiling and a terror spread across his face like a blanket. "Mum! Mum!" he cried, stuffing his fists into his ears. "The trains are comin' in me head!"

'At first I was really chuffed. You see, he'd referred to himself as "me," don't you know? And that was a kind of miracle. But then it dawned on me that he wasn't going to believe me when I said they weren't. I took him outside, you see, and tried to point to where the trains were over the rooftops, but it was no good. He was screaming and carrying on so bad we had to get the doctor. And that was the day that Dr. Swan told us he'd never be right. I tried to tell him he was wrong. I tried to tell him about Hubert saying "me" like that, but he said it didn't make any difference. So we went to one doctor after another and they said the same thing. They gave him a name. He's a "mosaic" – isn't that a strange name? I wanted to tell the one who called him that that he was a boy, not some bloomin' pattern. But you can't fight too much against what must be, Jacinta. You do that and you're lost.'

I took a sip of tea. We were sitting by the gas fire in Vera Butcher's kitchen. I'd been living there for several weeks. Every day Alfred came to visit me. I had smiled five times so far. Mrs. Butcher said I was on the mend. She said that children had the capacity to heal themselves more quickly than adults, which I took as being a veiled reference to my mother; and indeed, I was surprised at the way my spirits began to improve.

'Was it the cracks in the ceiling that made Hubert think the trains were in his head?' I asked.

'I don't know, dear. Could be. I'm not sure Hubert knows where he begins and where he leaves off.'

'That's awful.'

'Yes. It is in a way, dear. But you know, in another way, it's not so bad. You take Hubert out for a walk on a nice summer day and there's never been such a happy boy. He *is* the day, you see. He's not the way we are. The day doesn't have to happen to him, if you see what I mean.'

I told Alfred what Mrs. Butcher had said about Hubert. He said she was a rare woman. Much wiser than most. He told me to listen carefully to what she said, then asked me if I liked it better there now.

'I suppose.'

Alfred was visibly relieved. 'I'll tell Ruskin,' he said.

'No! Please don't, Alfred. Tell him . . . tell him I'm sick and thin. *Please!*'

Alfred tapped his nose with his finger in a gesture that meant he'd keep my secret. 'The nose knows,' he said. 'In point of fact, you *are* looking somewhat pale. I'll make sure to let Mr. Ruskin Garland know that as soon as possible.'

The Butchers and I got into a kind of routine. I helped out with the children. Mrs. Butcher was distressed at first because I played with the children and it made them livelier than before. After a while, though, she told Alfred she liked having me there. The mothers had commented favorably on their babies' moods;

if they (her customers) were happy, she was. Alfred said Mrs. Butcher wasn't a bad woman. But her lack of training made her dangerous as a child minder. He said we'd been too hard on her in the past. (He really meant that I had been too hard on her, but he didn't say it because he knew I was still fragile.) I said I'd never put my baby with someone like Mrs. Butcher to sit all day long and stare up at a lightbulb. Alfred said he hoped I'd have the money to retain my high ideals. I told him I would because I was getting an exceptional education, which would stand me in good stead later on. He said only time would tell. Adults regularly resorted to cliché when all else failed.

Nothing dramatic happened at Vera Butcher's. We simply became easier with each other. Once in a while a great bitterness would envelop me, and then Mrs. Butcher knew it was best to leave me alone. But I didn't surrender wholly to it because there were always things to be done, and the sense of pride I felt when I saw I could make things better encouraged me to want to do more. About once a week at first, and then more frequently, I felt almost human. More than anything else at that time I wanted to live within some kind of routine. In spite of her faults, Vera Butcher gave that back to me.

Alfred usually stopped by Mrs. Butcher's house at seven-thirty. By then we'd had tea – a meal that always included some kind of cupcake for dessert – and those children who were fostered had been bathed and put to bed. Sometimes I'd be late coming down for Alfred's visit because the children made me tell them stories. Once they found out I knew so many, they would beg me each night to tell them a longer one. I used Simon's stories of Africa. Most of the children were West Indian, but they didn't know anything about Africa – nothing at all – and it made me sad. Little Michael asked if Africa was hard to carry, as he wanted Santa to bring it here for Christmas. When I asked him why, he said the weather would be hot then and his nose wouldn't run all the time. Then he wiped the snot away with the back of his hand and asked me to tell another story.

The stories I told them surprised me. I hadn't realized how many I still had in my head. When I spoke the words, something strange happened. It was as if it wasn't me talking at all, but my father. My mouth moved, but it was his voice that came out. It was deep and reminded me of the chords an organist can play on those huge organs in cathedrals. I made parts of the stories up. They became mine too. I inserted songs into some of the paragraphs and had village girls singing such things as 'I'm Gonna Wash That Man Right Outta My Hair,' and village boys singing 'Maria.' Simon's stories had lacked romance. I shoved it into his plots relentlessly. I made the children characters in the stories too: Michael slew a lion once, but I had to change it because he began to cry when the lion died from the knife wound he'd inflicted. So Hubert was transformed into the African Wizard-Chief 'He-Who-Speaks-in-Tongues' so that he could restore the lion – minus teeth and claws – to his former glory.

Before I moved to Mrs. Butcher's, I hadn't realized I liked children. The summer holidays gave me a chance to spend the whole day with them. Many had less than I did. Some had lost their parents; others were put on hold while their parents served time in prison, or were in rehabilitation. Most of them were from the West Indies, but two were mixed race, and the rest were white. When they got to know me, they sat on my lap, asked me to comb their hair and tell them stories. I pretended they were my real brothers and sisters. I made the disheveled ones more presentable because Mrs. Butcher didn't seem to notice when their shirts were hanging out or their noses needed wiping. I cleaned up the ones who soiled themselves by accident. Mrs. Butcher said I ran rings around Sheila. I was a born nurse, she said. I told her I planned to become a flying doctor.

The children opened up to me. I heard Michael's stories about the children behind the plaster. He said he saw them at night. They came out like people coated in self-rising flour – he insisted it was self-rising. The kind you use in cakes, he said. They rubbed on you at night, those white ghosties, and gave you the Itchy-Fidgets. It had happened to him before in another house – white ghosties rubbing on him all night. That's why he'd been taken away, he said. Mrs. Butcher said his father had a 'penchant' for poodles. She said Michael didn't say a word for a year, then he opened up to Hubert one day and he'd been asking for cupcakes ever since.

From the children I learned that there were worse situations than the ones I'd known. Before Mrs. Butcher's, I hadn't realized that there were tragedies more compelling than my own. The stories I told the children brought Simon back. For some reason, I could tell them better when I wasn't living in the house where he wrote them. I could make them mine in a more profound way. Gradually I began to realize that my mother's house on Lavender Sweep held me in like a corset. It was there that Simon's ghost lived. It was there that the flames on Alfred's gas ring had drawn me in. It was there that Louise had gone mad. Alfred's presence was not enough to redeem the house. 'It was a palace of doom,' I wrote in my diary one day, in spite of my vows never to write again. I was glad to be out of it – happy to be living with sane people at last, even if one of them had part of his brain missing, and the other didn't have a clue how to rear infants.

The spirit I'd managed to quell for a while rose up in me again and reasserted itself as a do-it-yourself fiend. To my delight, Mrs. B. liked my ideas for home improvements. Soon we were stripping and sanding, painting and wallpapering until her front room became a brightly colored nursery. I asked for some posters from the Battersea library. I went in and told the librarian that we were all orphans and that the only posters we had were alcoholic. She gave us glossy new ones depicting Peter Rabbit and Peter Pan, Winnie the Pooh and Pinocchio. I pinned them up above the cots and framed them in squares of cardboard that had been decorated by the children.

At Mrs. Butcher's I didn't have to be anyone but Jacinta Louise Buttercup Moses. That was who I was and it was enough.

In the morning I'd get up earlier than the other children because there was only one bathroom for all nine of us, and I was too old to line up the way the others did to have my mouth and underarms wiped by Mrs. B. I'd wash quickly and then write in the new journal Alfred had brought me.

I hadn't planned on keeping up with my journal. It forced

you to see how dismal your life was, how absurd your wishes for the future. My old diaries depressed me. I thought of Maurice's hand on the pages and it made me want to throw up. Yet I was drawn to cataloguing my achievements and recording my own growth. Occasionally, I could still weave magic into the pages. So, every morning, I confided my life to the pages of my journal.

After that, I helped Mrs. B. with breakfast. We had a fixed routine. Everyone had either porridge or cornflakes. Michael always tried to sit next to me, but I never sat down for long. Mandy would drop her spoon, or Irma would need help getting down from her high chair. Then the babies would arrive during or after breakfast, dropped off by mums who had to work at Woolworth's or at Marks and Spencer, at the hairdresser's or the dry cleaner's.

When my summer holidays began, I convinced Mrs. Butcher to get two extra prams so that we could load up all the children and take them for walks on Clapham Common after breakfast. At first she hated the idea. They would catch cold, she said. With the child minders and the fosters there would be too many children to take out all at once. What about Hubert? But we found a way, the older children helping the younger ones. And we played rounders and piggy in the middle; and we flew homemade kites that never would stay up in the air.

In the afternoons, the youngsters napped and I cleaned or redecorated. Then the mums would come and we'd be left with only nine of us, which seemed like a much more manageable number.

Then we'd have supper and I'd tell stories to the children and they'd fall asleep. I had never had much of a routine before. It blessed me and gave me time to think. I began to believe in hope again, though I wouldn't admit it to anyone. Every so often hope would catch me unawares and another layer of sorrow would slough off me like old skin, and I'd find myself humming some tune from *South Pacific* or *Showboat*.

At Mrs. Butcher's I dreamed of princes and palaces, of white beaches and designer clothes while I scrubbed the floors or sewed a frill for the bathroom sink. I watched the black-and-white TV with the same steady concentration I employed when I watched it with Louise and Alfred, only this time I watched for a reason: to learn. I learned from the BBC how to behave if the queen invited me to dinner; how to dress appropriately for the ski slopes; how to rebuff the attentions of the Prince of Wales; how to smile demurely when heads of state asked me to sleep with them; how to use the proper fork at banquets; how to redecorate a room with just the right chandelier; how to use my body to obtain my desires; how to kiss; how to reject; how to gain power. I took to writing the word 'power' on the backs of envelopes and the undersides of chairs I liked to sit in. It elevated me, that word. It made me feel that Ruskin Garland could never again put his hand on my thigh without permission. It made me certain of the fact that Maurice Beadycap's tongue would be bitten off the next time he tried to force it into my mouth. But power wouldn't bring back Alison Bean. And power couldn't make my mother whole or my father breathe. Power was limited. I always came back to the walls.

Louise didn't write to me. She sent messages via Alfred. Every so often over that summer he'd ask me if I wanted to go and see her. I said no. He didn't ask me why at the time, and I was grateful. We almost got right through the holidays that way. In late August, however, during one of his after-dinner visits, he brought the subject up again.

'I'm going to visit your mother, Jacinta. Would you like to come?'

Vera Butcher looked up from her sewing. I cursed Alfred silently. This was neither the time nor the place to mention my mother.

Mrs. Butcher put in her penny's worth: 'O, Alfred. Wouldn't that be nice? I know the poor thing misses her mother. Is she better now? How's the TB?'

Mrs. Butcher spoke frequently about my mother's 'indisposition.' I never found out whether or not she really knew what had happened. I was grudgingly grateful to her for handling the situation with a modicum of grace – which was a lot more than I could say for Alfred at that moment.

'I told you, Alfred. I'm busy with things right now.'

Mrs. Butcher wouldn't hear of it. 'But, Jacinta! You *must* go and visit her. What would she think if you didn't go? It's the summer holidays. And besides, you could take your books with you and study on the journey. She really is such a brainbox, Alfred, did you know that? Going to sail through those O levels, I'm sure. Not like the rest of us, struggling with the two times table. O, no. She's going to be an air hostess or a doctor of some kind, you mark my words.'

Alfred smiled. He looked at me again. His huge head and straggly hair made him gnomelike. I was still trying to hate him, but each day it was getting more difficult. If he kept on like this, though, I'd be able to hate him again in earnest.

'I won't be going, Alfred. I'm busy, okay?'

Mrs. Butcher gave Alfred a look. They nodded to each other. I was about to change the subject when something else did it for me. A train rushed by in the distance. Mrs. Butcher put her hand on Hubert's knee to steady him. 'If he has another conniption about those bloody trains, I'll go off my flippin' rocker.'

But Hubert was good this time. His eyes grew wide and he breathed harder than usual, that was all. Then the train noise disappeared into the dark, and we were left the way we'd been found.

'Trains,' said Alfred, knotting his forehead as if he were look-ing at a mathematics problem, 'trains are odd phenomena. There's something about them, Vera, that excites even the most placid of us in England. Something that reminds us that there are other places out there – other sights to see. They emphasize distance, in a way. Make it more significant, more prominent, if you will.'

I looked at Alfred's nose. It was a prominent nose. A promon-tory. I wondered what the distance was from his hairline to his nostrils – several feet probably. Then I wondered about the dis-tance between his eyebrows. A centimeter, if that. His brows were a couple, he used to say; they held hands over the bridge of his nose.

'I know what you mean, Alfred. I do indeed. Do you think that's what Hubert hears? The distance?'

'Could be. I don't know.' Alfred smiled over at Hubert. Hubert asked for a cupcake. 'Maybe it awakens in him the same kind of yearning we all feel when we're trapped in a place we can't escape from. You hear life rushing past you and you think, "I need to be a part of that rush." But you can't be. Circumstances won't let you. So you stay here and dream. And on the edges of the dream is the sound of the trains rushing through you like heartache.'

I didn't know how it had transpired that Alfred and Mrs. Butcher had become friends. He'd hated the idea of my moving here as much as I had. But something changed once I arrived. Vera Butcher began to look forward to Alfred's visits. Once she asked if he was 'on the lookout for a good woman.' I told her he was – that he never left the lookout unmanned for fear of being pounced upon. She thought I was joking and began to dress up before his visits. In the end I had to tell her. It was too sorrowful watching her string her false pearls around her neck and clip on her gold-tone earrings.

'Homo . . . homosex . . . homosexual,' she said, plopping down on her bed like a sack of potatoes. 'Are you sure?'

''Fraid so. I thought everyone knew.'

'Yes. I suppose . . . I mean . . . I heard rumors . . . but then you don't like to believe . . . Are you sure?'

'Yep. We talk about it once in a while. He had a great love called Lipton, but it didn't come to anything in the end. Lipton was in the army. He went overseas in the end and Alfred never saw him again. Sorry.'

Mrs. Butcher slowly unwound the pearls and took off the earrings.

'Well,' she said, 'as my dear husband always told me, "You lose a few and then you lose a few."'

Suddenly she turned round to face me. Her voice was urgent and her bottom lip was trembling.

'It doesn't mean he's not a gentleman, though, does it? I mean, he could still be a . . . gentleman. Couldn't he?'

'Yes,' I said. 'In fact, he's the most gentlemanly gentleman I've ever met.'

'Yes. He is, isn't he? And there are all sorts of ways to love someone, aren't there? And you don't need to . . . I mean, after a year or two it doesn't amount to much anyway, does it? A little cavorting under the sheets – it's not much really. Men never know what to do anyhow. All thumbs they are. There are other things, aren't there? With a man like that.'

We never spoke about it again. And I never saw Mrs. Butcher in her jewelry after that day.

I was staring into Vera Butcher's gas fire, thinking about Louise and Hubert and Vera and Alfred and Ruskin and Alison and Maurice and Mary and Me. I thought of e.e. cummings's poem about Maggie and Milly and Molly and Mae who go down to the beach to play one day. Why were they lucky enough to find such treasures? Would I be lucky too? Vera Butcher hadn't been lucky – or had she? Was I a lucky person? Did you know that kind of thing when you were a teenager or was it something you could only know much later on? Who else was out there for me? Who else would I meet who would change my expectations and make me into someone I hadn't been before?

'If you'd known what was going to happen, would you have done it?'

The question slipped out before I could stop it. I was speaking to myself or to Louise. Perhaps to Simon. Alfred took a deep breath, but Vera was the one who answered me.

'You mean about Hubert,' she said.

'O no! No! I just meant in general, that's all.'

Mrs. Butcher raised a hand to quiet me. 'It's a good question really, love. The thing is, you don't know. You don't. And there's an end to it. If you knew, you probably wouldn't do it. That's why people don't jump off those diving boards. At least not people with any sense. You know what could happen, and it makes you think twice. But in life you don't know that. So you just keep going. I don't regret giving birth, myself. But I do wonder what will happen to my Hubert when I'm dead and gone. Often I pray he'll go first. I'd follow soon after, I know it. He's my life now, you see. Him and the children. We're not much, the two of us, but we're sufficient for each other.'

I could see Alfred was crying. Mrs. Butcher didn't notice; she was in her own world. And all Hubert did was rock in his invisible rocking chair – back and forth, back and forth, as if he would get somewhere someday if only he rocked hard enough.

One Sunday in early September, Mrs. Butcher came into my room at seven in the morning. I slept with three of the other girls, but they were much younger and struggling with their potty training, so they were all together in a double bed. I had my own single bed shoved up into a corner of the room.

'Get up, Jacinta!' she whispered. 'There's a surprise waiting! Get up! Get up!'

I rolled over and tried to go back to sleep, but she threw back the covers and the room was frigid. I groaned. She urged me to get up again and see the surprise. She literally dragged me out of bed. I told her it was Sunday. I'd go to mass at nine-thirty, if I had to. Just not now. She threw her housecoat over my shoulders and propelled me downstairs.

Alfred was waiting in the kitchen. He was standing up as we walked in – standing on tiptoe as if he were looking over the top of a high wall.

'There she is!' he cried. Then disappointment spread across his face.

'Vera! She's not dressed!'

'She's got the housecoat on. She'll be all right.'

A look from Alfred told her I wouldn't be all right after all. She hurried me back upstairs to get some clothes on.

As she helped me pick out my best dress, I guessed their secret. Two weeks before, I'd entered a contest at school. The winner would be notified by post within fourteen days. The letter must have arrived yesterday at 161 Lavender Sweep, the address I still used. It was a poetry competition. I'd written a poem about suffering. It was set in Africa and the rhyming words included 'wicker,' 'thicker,' 'snicker,' and 'bicker.' I felt sorry for the other contestants as I affixed the stamps at Her Majesty's Post Office. They didn't stand a chance.

Alfred was still waiting for me on tiptoe downstairs.

'The nose knows,' he said gleefully, rubbing his nostril.

'The nose knows,' I said, smiling in spite of myself.

The prize was fifty pounds. Fifty pounds! I had never seen that much money in my life! Ruskin sometimes carried a wad of notes around, but he'd never let me count them. He was as tight as Eartha Kitt's underwear – or so Alfred said.

Vera Butcher waved good-bye to us at the front door. Hubert was calling to her from his bedroom. The words 'tea' and 'cup-cakie' floated down on us from above. She took her handkerchief from her pocket and waved it up and down as if I were going away forever. It made me laugh. I laughed out loud. Alfred laughed too. 'How did you know?' he said.

'The nose knows,' I said, laughing even more, and ran on ahead.

I rushed through the door and up the stairs to our rooms. I passed Mary Beadycap on the way. She smelled like a brewery. 'Knickers,' she said to me as I took the stairs two at a time. 'There's no future in 'em. Dead end, that's what they are. Knickers.'

'Get an education,' I called down sweetly to her. 'That's the key.'

She launched a projectile in my direction. Her saliva hit the worndown stair carpet with the paisley pattern or the fishes' hands, depending on your point of view. I kept on going. Upstairs was fifty pounds! Fifty pounds for *me*!

I hurled open the door to the front room and screamed.

There was no letter. There was no fifty pounds.

What greeted me instead was Ruskin. On his arm was an old woman with a missing tooth in front, a thin strand of gray hair, and cheekbones so pronounced they could slice into something.

'O shit!' I said, falling back into the doorway. 'O shit! You've come home.'

9

My mother came back as a ghost. She terrified me.

She floated around our three rooms in a tattered house-coat and slippers bent under at the heels. She stared into space and flicked her tongue in and out of the gap where the missing tooth used to be. She was bone-thin, and her skin had a gray undertone like an English winter sky. She stood in front of the mirror at the small makeshift dressing table Alfred and I had bought at a Salvation Army bazaar and twirled a strand of hair between her fingers. The light was gone from her eyes and death lined them instead.

In the weeks that followed her return home, I'd come upon her pushing at the frown lines on the bridge of her nose as if her face were clay and she could made the anxiety disappear. Sometimes she'd be tapping out a tune on an invisible piano – her fingers moving into chords as if the black and white keys were really there. Mostly she was quiet. Very quiet. Often I'd forget she was in the house until I heard a sound like moaning coming from another room. Eventually it dawned on me that Louise was trying to sing. But someone had stolen my mother's voice, and all that was left behind was grief.

I begged to be sent back to Mrs. Butcher's house.

Alfred and Ruskin were flabbergasted. Ruskin threatened me with bodily harm if I ever mentioned my desires to Louise.

Alfred was distraught. He put his hand on my forehead to see if I had a fever, and asked trick questions to test my state of mind. Some were very easy; others required some thought. 'Two plus two,' he'd say. Then, when I came back with the right answer, he'd ask me to explain the term 'metaphysical' as it applied to George Herbert. He'd stare at me hard when I replied, then look more downcast than ever. I tried to explain to him about Mrs. Butcher and Hubert, how I'd grown fond of them; how routine governed their lives in a way that made me envious. I wanted to explain, but I couldn't do it well. I missed the children I'd helped take care of. I liked telling them Simon's stories, and I'd grown used to Hubert's requests for tea and cupcakies. He and I had formed an unlikely friendship. I could sit with him for hours without feeling compelled to say a word. I practiced my recitations on Hubert. He would repeat what I recited in his usual monotone and that helped me remember the lines. He knew Portia's speech in *The Merchant of Venice*, the first stanza of 'To Autumn,' and the opening of *Pride and Prejudice* by heart. Mrs. Butcher called me 'love' all the time and let me stay up until one or two in the morning if I wanted. She put her arms around me without making a fuss about it, and let me watch television on school nights. But that wasn't the only reason I wanted to go back. The other one was far more serious: I was mortally afraid of the old woman who'd come to live in my house.

I didn't know Louise Buttercup anymore. I hadn't known her since the day she kicked a hole in the wall and tried to strangle me. At night I was petrified. She could come in and hold the pillow over my head in a second – who would know? I began sleeping without pillows before I reasoned that it would be safer to sleep with all of them so that she couldn't get to one easily. I put two between my legs and three under my head. She didn't seem to notice that I'd swiped the pillow from the bedsettee where she slept in the front room. She didn't seem to notice anything at all. It was like living with a shadow that passed through the house darkening the rooms. Alfred couldn't make head nor tail of my behavior. Later it occurred to me that he knew how scared I was, but that even he was afraid to talk about it. It's hard to tell with adults sometimes. They're so secretive. Maybe Alfred was like the rest of us – maybe he didn't know what the hell he should do under the circumstances. Maybe, for once, he didn't have the right answer. Besides, Alfred worshiped my mother. All the men did. She had something in her that was like a spark. Even as a shadow she could set people on fire. It got on my nerves.

Louise Buttercup Moses was old when she came home. About a month after her return, Ruskin took her to the dentist to have a tooth put in where the gap was in front. It looked artificial at first because it was so much whiter than the others. But she didn't smile much, and, on the rare occasions when she talked, she mumbled, so it wasn't too conspicuous. Alfred said she'd lost her own tooth in a fight at the institution. I didn't pursue it. The less I knew about the sordid details of her madness, the happier I'd be. Because she hadn't dyed her hair in months, all the color had grown out. I did my best to avoid her, but I shouldn't have bothered because Louise didn't seem to see me for hours on end. Then she'd look up suddenly and say, 'O, there you are!' as if she'd been looking for me all along. But she hadn't. She was never looking for me. She was looking for someone else who would never, ever come back to Lavender Sweep.

A part of me envied her ability to shut out the world. I'd tried to do that after Alison's death and had failed miserably. People tiptoed around her, and she hardly did any housework. We had to remind her to take a bath. Alfred said she was a 'fragile mechanism.' I was fragile too, I said.

Louise didn't seem to hate me for swearing at her when I saw her the first time. In fact, I don't think she remembered it. She didn't seem to be angry about anything. She was apathetic and passive.

Just as I started to get used to the Shadow Buttercup, everything shifted again. The ground moved underneath me and the scenery changed. It began on a Thursday morning, three or four months after her return home.

I got up at seven as usual, and put the pillows back where they belonged. Another night when I hadn't gone to heaven. If I still believed in God, I would have thanked Him. I climbed the flight of stairs to the kitchen. Worn to a dirty brown, the rusty flippers on the stair carpet didn't resemble themselves any longer. Only a dreamer would ever believe that the paisley pattern had been pretty once. When Simon was alive. When the house sang songs to itself and my mother knew how to smile.

A rhyme I'd made up with Alison came into my head. Alison and I would chant it together, even though she didn't know what I meant by fishes' hands, or that the line referred to the worn stair carpet and the paisley fins dyed into it.

Fishes' hands, paisley swirls
It often stinks to be a girl.

The previous night I'd dreamed I'd sailed away to America. I'd entered it into my diary, detailing the dream so that Alfred and I could analyze it later. A man whose face never looked like a face and whose voice got lost before I could understand the words was there with me on the deck of the ship. Louise saw me off. She waved a long white scarf, longer even than Rapunzel's hair. Then it was caught up by the wind so that it wrapped around her body. 'You're a mummy, Mummy!' I called out over the sea. No one got the joke. Try as I might that morning, sitting up in the chilly bedroom with a pen in my hand, I couldn't remember the rest of the dream. I wanted to know what America was like; but, when I turned the page over, it was blank. I woke up bursting to escape from South London. People were beginning to move to Battersea, saying it was a 'trendy' place to be. But it would never be that for me. Battersea was where Simon died. Battersea was where Maurice slobbered in my mouth. Battersea was where Louise had tried to strangle me. I had to get away. I had to find some excitement to insert into my world and replace the fear that rented a room there. I would leave. Go somewhere. Anywhere, it didn't matter. America, Africa, as long as it wasn't Battersea. All the girls and all the women I knew along the Sweep were waiting for something wonderful to happen to their lives. But if you waited, like Louise had waited for Simon to climb back out of the grave and comfort her, you wasted your life. I wouldn't waste mine. I was going to be some-body. Most of the women I knew were acted upon by men or by the Church. I wanted to *act*. Louise was up in the kitchen wait-ing for the world to love her again. It never would. She'd die miserable and make my life hell too. My mother and I were a piece of a person now that the Man was dead. I thought of the song in *Porgy and Bess* about the man who was gone, and whose footsteps would never be heard again.

It was a song of suffering. All the women I knew sang it. The notes were like knitting needles, and women's hands were working them, working, working, working to make the long notes into nooses for our necks. Louise Buttercup was upstairs growing old waiting for her man's footsteps to join her in the kitchen-in-the-sky. But it was always me. Always only me who came up the stairs.

I reached the top. I opened the door and stepped into the ten-by-twelve-foot kitchen-cum-living room.

Someone had played a trick on me. This wasn't my house. This couldn't be my story. I rubbed my eyes. During the night, Louise Buttercup had died and risen again.

My legs felt weak. I almost screamed. My heart beat like a piston. I grasped the door frame for support.

For there, in front of my eyes, instead of my elderly parent, instead of the grubby kitchen of broken plates and promises, instead of weariness and despair, instead of leftovers from a killed passion, was a table fit for a queen and a mother reinvented.

'Do you like it?' she said.

I opened my mouth. Nothing came out. The room was shining in the sunlight from the window. The lace curtains were white again; the linoleum had a sheen on it as if it had been rubbed with oil; on the table was a white lace tablecloth, flowers in a crystal bowl, new plates, crumpets, jam, napkins, a teapot in a tea cozy, and cleanliness! Cleanliness everywhere!

'It's beautiful,' I whispered. I didn't know how to behave now that I'd stepped into a fairy tale. What do you do when someone sweeps away your suffering and replaces it with dreams? I stood in the doorway with my mouth open.

She told me to sit down. I obeyed.

She told me to close my mouth before a bird made a nest in it. I did that too.

The flower bowl on the table was very pretty. It had gold and crimson flowers on it. It was her nanny's bowl – her mother's mother's bowl. She never used it in case it broke. I was afraid.

'The bowl. Supposing we break it?'

'Don't worry about that. It's not going to break.'

Next to the bowl was a silver spoon, a wedding gift from Mr. Fortesque, a man in publishing who loved my father's work and gave them their most expensive wedding gift. Under the spoon was a napkin with lace around the edges. It was as white as a Colgate smile. On the table was a pale green cloth, creases ironed in, smelling of flowers. The radio was on. The songs I liked. Motown. Diana was telling me to 'Stop! In the name of love . . .' but we'd been doing that for years. Why had we started up again now?

This wasn't my house. I was dreaming.

The woman sitting in front of me looked strange. Like my mother but not like her. What was it? My God! Her hair!

'I bleached it,' she said, catching me staring at her head.

'It's gold! I didn't know dye could look that snazzy.'

'You like it, then? You don't think it's too much, do you? I could always redo it . . .'

'No! Don't touch it! It looks like . . . angel hair. I love it. It's thicker too.'

'It's growing back. It will never be lovely and thick like yours and Simon's, but it is growing back.'

'It's growing back,' I repeated like a fool. The room echoed with the sentence. Everything was growing back. I'd had my legs cut off but the stumps were pushing out like stems. Soon I'd be walking again. A miracle had happened on Lavender Sweep.

'I cleaned up. Do you like it?'

'Yes.'

'You're sure my hair's not too brassy?'

'It's perfect. You look like Princess Grace and Doris Day all in one.' Louise Buttercup Moses smiled. This must be someone else's house. 'What's two plus two?' I asked.

'Four. Why?'

'Just wondered.'

'Do you like the flowers?'

'Yes. They're beautiful.'

'Do you want to stay home from school?'

'Why? Is someone dying?'

'No! Of course not! Whatever gave you that idea? I just thought you'd enjoy it. We could go to the bandstand and get some ice cream. Maybe have lunch in that little cafeteria.' She sounded hesitant, anticipating contradiction.

'Have you won the football pools?' I asked.

She laughed. Louise Buttercup Moses *laughed out loud*!

'No. But I have got a little money. While I was . . . away . . . Alfred was able to draw my pension. There's some money in an account at the Midland. I plan to spend it.'

I nearly launched into a litany of home improvements. I had to stuff a crumpet in my mouth to shut myself up. A few feet away to my right, in the space between the sink and the stove, was the imprint of Louise's foot in the wall. The place where it all began.

'Sorry,' I said.

'For what?'

'O no, I mean . . . I'm glad. That's great.'

She looked over to the window. The sun was shining on the line of clothes she'd hung on a pulley that extended out and down to a post at the end of the back garden. My school shirt was waving in the breeze. The white nylon sleeves looked as if they were clapping. Her nightgown was there too – the one she'd worn in bed when she went mad. The yellowed lace looked white again and the tiny violets stood out against the pale lilac background. She must have been washing all night. Why hadn't I heard her using the kitchen sink? How much time needs to pass for light to enter a mind held in the dark? Who lit my mother up again? Was it the money? Is that all it took? Why hadn't I kept my childhood vow and worked harder to get money for her myself?

'I know it's not been easy since your father died. And then, what with me going away . . . I know it's been hard.'

Damn right. Murderously hard. Louise's hands round my throat. Pressing, pressing in on me. Mother, mother, where have you gone? Who are you now that you've come back?

'I want to start again,' Louise declared in a tone that began emphatically and ended with a question mark.

I bit off more crumpet. There was cereal next. The Kellogg's box was on the table. The red cockerel on the front of the box was crowing. 'Pour a bowl of sunshine' they told us on the adverts. Louise had done just that. How rich were Mr. and Mrs. Kellogg? Rich enough to buy happiness, I should think. Maybe it was Louise's and my turn to buy some too.

But no one changes that fast. This is a trick. Test her. See what happens.

'Okay. Let's go out. But not to the bandstand. To the British Museum. Let's go there. We can eat at the cafeteria and pay for it all by ourselves. And we can ride on the tube instead of the bus even though it costs more. And we can see the mummies. Let's go there.'

'The British Museum,' she said. She seemed puzzled by the notion. I wondered if she remembered where it was. Her fingers twirled the tablecloth. Her movements weren't the staccato gestures of a madwoman; they were as smooth as sanity. 'What a good idea.'

I had to look away. No one should have to endure that much happiness in the space of a few minutes.

'I have to go and ask Alfred something, okay?'

She looked at me and smiled. 'Don't be long. We'll need to get a move on if we want to have enough time for everything.'

I rushed downstairs. Alfred was listening to the radio. His door was open and I barged in.

'Knocking is customary in England, I believe. Even for young ladies.'

'What? O. Sorry.'

Then he noticed how agitated I was. He came up to me and felt my forehead.

'Is anything wrong? Are you sick?'

'No. Neither's Louise. That's the whole point!'

I was talking so fast the words tumbled out on top of each

other. It was as if my words were feet, and I was running for dear life.

'I think she may be on that LTD stuff because she's normal. I mean, normal like we are.' We looked at each other. Alfred raised an eyebrow. They both went up in unison. He couldn't raise one at a time. We'd practiced for hours and never been successful.

'Sit down and tell me what's going on. You're making me nervous. Slow down. What's happened? Would you like a cup of tea?'

'Tea! Tea! Tea doesn't solve the world's ills, you know. It certainly doesn't. All you British people think tea is the answer to everything. Life's not like that, Alfred. It takes more than tea to make things right. I'm telling you, she's so well she's sick! It's that LTD. Didn't they give her all those drugs at that mental asylum?'

'I think you mean LSD, Jacinta. And no, she wasn't taking that. She's not taking anything, as far as I know. Will you please sit down? You're giving me the heebie-jeebies.'

I sat down. My heart was racing. I could see that Alfred was about to test my maths skills. I hurried on with my story.

'I get up in the morning as usual, minding my own business, and I'm thinking it's no fun being a girl and how I want to escape from this place, and then I open the door and –'

'Why don't you want to be a girl?'

'O, I don't mean it like that. Not like you and stuff. I mean, what you said about inhabiting an alien form and all that stuff. Not like that. I just mean . . . well . . . that's not the point. O, Alfred. You've made me lose my thread.'

'Sorry. You were talking about getting up this morning.'

'So I open the door and there she is. Normal! Absolutely normal! No one gets normal that fast, do they? I mean, you could have a hernia or a heart attack normalizing yourself at that speed, couldn't you? Crumpets, jam, tablecloth – it's all absurd! And clean, Alfred. Everything's *clean*! You know Louise *never* cleans *anything* except the dishes. And she leaves egg yolk and stuff on them most of the time so I have to do them all over again. She doesn't see the dirt like we do. And she's changed. Her hair is gold.'

'Really! Is it nice?'

'Yes.'

'Hmm. I've thought about doing that myself but you don't like to cause too much of a stir, do you; and people are so hum-drum, a move like that can elicit unwelcome commentary. Sorry. I'm straying again. So what's your point?'

'What's my *point*!' I was almost screaming with frustration. Adults were too stupid to understand anything. 'My point is that my mother isn't acting like a loon anymore. All of a sudden she's become . . . she's become . . .'

I burst into tears.

'And sh-sh-she wants to take me to the Bri-tish Mu-seum!'

Alfred put his arms around me. He smelled faintly of laven-der. There was lace on the cuffs of his robe. His hands were smooth and motherly.

'There, there,' he said. 'Don't worry, Cinta. It'll be all right. Maybe she's better.'

'People d-don't get better that fast. It's not natural.'

'How do you know what's natural?'

'For God's sake, Alfred! We're not talking about *you* – we're talking about *Louise*!'

'How do you know we're not the same person?'

I blinked. 'Don't do that kind of thing, Alfred. It gives me the willies. What do you mean, anyway?'

'I just think you should remember that we're all more inter-twined than the culture lets us be. You think you begin here,' he tapped me on the head, 'and end here,' he nudged my foot with his slipper, 'and you think you're a coloured girl with a begin-ning and a middle and an end to your story. Well, perhaps it's not like that at all. Perhaps we're all each other's stories. Perhaps we're like rivers – we all run into each other and our identities are not as separate as they try to tell you they are.'

'I don't know what you're babbling about. I know *exactly* who I am. I'm Jacinta Louise Buttercup Moses and I *am* a coloured girl and I *do* live in Battersea and I know *exactly* where the tip of me begins and where the end of me ends. And if you're so mixed up and foolish that you think you begin where Louise does, then you're in deep, deep dog muck, Alfred

Russell-Smythe! That is your name, isn't it? Or is it Alfred Louise?'

Alfred looked away. I'd hurt him. I couldn't stop.

'Okay, if you're so clever, why don't you tell me what the catapult was?'

'The catapult?'

'Yes. The catapult. You know. The thing that made her change.'

'O, you mean the catalyst.'

'That's what I said.'

'Maybe she suddenly realized that life was better than she thought it was. Sometimes older people do that. We'll be anxious and angry at the world for many years; then, quite suddenly, we'll look around and see that the grass is still as green as it was when we lost our joy; that the trees are still as tall as they used to be; that children still remember how to say nursery rhymes and –'

'That's a load of codswallop. No one changes that fast. I think she's as nutty as a fruitcake. I think she's going to snap at any moment. Can you swear to me that she's going to stay sane for more than two minutes? Can you? No! Of course you can't! No one can. She could be eating her feces as we speak.'

'Indeed she could, Jacinta. What a perspicacious observation.'

'Don't be sarcastic. This is serious, Alfred.'

He looked at me, then took my hand in his and squeezed it.

'You're right, little one. She could be temporarily sane. She could turn on you again and say terrible things. Or this could be the first moment in a long series of moments between Louise and the world when a truce has been declared. It could be that she has come to terms with something at last. Supposing you were the catalyst, Cinta. Just you. Your sweetness and your laughter. Supposing she remembered how that sounded and came back to us to hear it?'

'Me? It wasn't me who left us.'

'Wasn't it?'

I stood up quickly and brushed off the front of my school uniform as if it had crumbs on it. 'You talk rubbish sometimes,' I said.

'At least I don't bite my nails.'

I took my fingers out of my mouth. 'I'm on edge. Louise thinks children don't have nerves. She used to say we have to go through wars to have them. Well, I've got them and she gave them to me. And if she thinks for one instant that I'm going to kiss and make up and assume we're all lovey-dovey just because of one trip to see some old mummies she's bloody mistaken.'

There was a long pause.

Alfred's little sitting-dining-bedroom seemed to contract still further under the pressure. A picture of Maurice B. leaped into my mind. He'd stood in front of us like this – not knowing who he was or whether it mattered – angry and excited all at the same time. And I'd laughed at him.

Alfred was speaking. I tried to listen. '. . . a good time. It's important to accept these times, Jacinta. Whenever they present themselves. Life isn't so easy that you can afford to let some of the happy moments go. Don't be afraid of them.'

'I'm not afraid of anything.'

'Good. Then enjoy it. Louise wants to be happy. Be happy with her. Don't worry about tomorrow or the day after that. Just remember what today has been. Then you'll always have that to live by.'

So Louise and I walked down to Clapham Junction, and took the overground train to the underground station. We got on the tube and headed up to Russell Square just like sane people did if they had money and time to spare.

The sun was diluted at first. It came to us weakly, as though it were apologizing for something. But gradually, in the short walk from the tube to the museum, the sun gained confidence. By the time we reached the foot of the massive stone steps leading up to the building, grayness had gone, and Louise's new blond hair sparkled in the light. I told her I liked her hair. It didn't look brassy; it looked classy instead. She returned the compliment. 'If I had hair as black as yours,' she said, 'I'd be in heaven.' She tried to run her fingers through my hair – the first touch in a long time – but, as usual, my hair was all tangled, so she could only pat it and smile.

'Midnight black,' she said softly, almost to herself.

She almost skipped up the stairs to the museum. I told her at the entrance, from within the revolving doors, that her new tooth looked great. 'You'd never know it was a denture,' I reassured her as we made three revolutions inside the doors, just for fun. She laughed.

We knew there were only two things you should never miss in the British Museum. The first was the cafeteria because of the brown sugar that was poured into little crystal sugar bowls and set on the tables. It was more expensive than white sugar, which was why we never had it at home. The second thing you should never miss was the Egyptian collection. It was too early for lunch, so we headed straight for the mummies.

Ruskin worked in the Egyptian room. Not the room exactly, but in a small office near all the dead people. He'd begun as a custodian and had worked his way up. Louise used to say it was a miracle he'd made it to the top considering the fact that he didn't have any paper qualifications. They hated him there. My mother said it was because he wasn't an Old School Tie. I used to imagine all these striped ties working in the museum. It was years before I leaped from ties to people. Ruskin was waiting for us at the entrance to his office. Louise must have called ahead because it was clear that he was expecting us.

When he saw us coming toward him down the long corridor lined with glass cases he began to laugh. A few of the people peering into the cases at the bones of the long dead looked up. One of them said, 'Shh!' Ruskin ignored him.

'Ha, ha! Well, if it isn't the real Louise Buttercup gracing us with a visit at last! Where's the Prince of Monaco?'

I winked at Louise as if to say 'I told you so.'

Ruskin embraced us both, but it was Louise he was enchanted by. He was brimming with happiness. He made us both take his arm, and we went on the grand tour of the museum. Whenever we met someone he knew, he introduced us as Princess Grace and Simone Madagascar. My mother thought he'd made my name up himself – we didn't bother to explain. Each time we met someone new, I'd get the giggles and he'd say, 'Please excuse Miss Madagascar. The museum is a place of such delight for her that she cannot help but snort her way through the rooms, isn't that right, Your Majesty?' Then Louise would giggle too, and the strangers would shake their heads. All except the custodians, who winked at us and told Ruskin he was a very funny fella. Most of them were from India or the West Indies. I thought my father would have felt at home.

That day Ruskin knew everything. He made ancient worlds so fascinating that we tasted Egypt. I stood for a long time in front of the paintings and entered pharaohs' eyes as if I were a camel stepping through the eyes of needles. Everything was possible. The time that separated us from them seemed inconsequential. We had the things that made them. These things could make us. We were the same. Egypt's in Africa, I thought. And Africa's in me. Poor Ruskin and Louise were white; they couldn't be Africa the way I could. I hugged the secret to me like a wish as we raided tombs, and stole skulls, and stumbled across vast treasures. Ruskin told us about the time they pulled one of the mummies from the tomb, unwrapped it, and saw, for a fleeting moment, the full splendor of his face before it dissolved into ash. It brought a song to mind, one we sang in choir. Something about the splendor falling in castle walls. I thought about fallen splendor and wondered if all of us stolen from Africa had a piece of that in our hearts. Was that the burden we carried with us? That memory of how splendid we had been once, before we were taken away?

Ruskin told us stories about archaeologists who had transgressed too far. Many met horrible deaths: eyes gouged out by stalactites, ears gnawed off by rats. Ruskin said one man suffered castration when a coffin lid he'd opened snapped closed before he could remove himself. When Louise scoffed at his story, Ruskin claimed it was well documented, that the man's voice was two octaves higher when he emerged from the tomb. 'Sounded a bit like our friend Alfred,' he said. We were both angry with him, and he had to apologize. Ruskin was the kind of person who would try to get away with murder, if he could. He hated Alfred almost as much as I hated Maurice Beadycap. That kind of hate didn't dissolve on your tongue like a sherbet-lemon when you said you were sorry. Hate like that stayed with you always. I felt sorry for Ruskin. If you had to hate someone, you should hate a person like Maurice. It was more satisfying.

I told Ruskin the museum had a museumy smell. Ruskin asked me what I meant by that, and I said it was the smell of old books in someone's great-grandmother's house. He said it was the scent of knowledge. Louise said it was the scent of death. Ruskin and I changed the subject.

We had lunch in the cafeteria. I ate three spoonfuls of Demerara sugar. Louise never once warned me about cavities. We had tea and digestive biscuits. Then we each had a ham sandwich and a bag of salt-and-vinegar crisps. Ruskin paid for all of it, so I asked Louise in a whisper if we could use our money to buy fish and chips on the way home. She said, 'We'll see,' which always used to mean no. I didn't push my luck.

We spent much of the afternoon with the Vikings, followed by the illuminated manuscripts. Ruskin had to leave us to our own devices because he needed to get back to work. I was glad he had to go. Louise was still excited, and I wanted her to myself. I was trying to live in the moment the way Alfred said I should. It was a hard thing to do well. My mind strayed to tomorrow; it was just the way I was made. Some people, like Louise, for example, looked back. A few, notably myself, looked forward. Today we'd come together in the present. It wouldn't last. I knew that Louise would go off the deep end again and rant and rave about God knows what.

Here were the Viking ships and the helmets. Here were the silver bracelets they wore and the goblets they drank from. A different time. All the ghosts who used them gone. How would I be when I was gone? Which objects would remember me? Ruskin and Louise and I were alive. These people had rotted to dust. I thought about poor Hamlet, dwelling on his own mortality. I didn't want to do that with my life. I wanted to live it fast and high and deep. If my world collapsed because I piled too much stuff into it, so be it. As long as it was full. As long as it was never boring. That's what killed you – boredom. You could stand everything else.

'I'd like to leave something to the world,' I said to Louise as we stared down into a glass display case of Viking artifacts. A helmet stamped with the contours of the smithy's hands shone under the fluorescent lighting.

'What would you leave?'

All day she'd been responding like that. Listening, actually listening to what I had to say, and then coming up with a logical response.

She asked me again. 'What would you like to leave behind?'

'Stories,' I said.

'Like Simon?'

'I suppose. Only they'd be mine instead. Stories or poems or pictures, maybe. Something other people could see so they'd know Jacinta Louise Buttercup Moses was here.'

She looked at me for a long time. I could feel her eyes on my face even though I was looking down into the glass pretending to be absorbed in old things.

'I hope you get your dream. I've a feeling you will. You have the talent and the determination. You're your father's daughter. I don't suppose there'll be much that will defeat you. It's a great thing to want to be some kind of artist. I wanted that once. Hold on to it. Don't ever let it go.'

I wanted to jump up in the air and clap my hands. I wanted to kiss my mother's pretty, worn-down hands because she'd told me it was worth it to try.

'I hope you get your dream too, Mum.'

'I've got it,' she said, taking my hand and kissing it. Such a strange gesture in the strange high light of the museum. 'You are my dream. I want you to be all the things I couldn't be. Then it will all be worthwhile.'

I took a deep breath. I wanted to say something but I was suddenly heavy and my mouth wouldn't open for speech.

On the way out, we stopped at an ice cream van. Louise bought two ice cream cones. Each one had two Cadbury's chocolate Flake bars in it. They stuck out like rude brown fingers. I'd never had two flakes in my ice cream cone before. I ate them slowly, the way poor people can, knowing what they meant.

'I feel like a millionaire,' I said.

'Me too,' said Louise.

'It won't last, will it?'

'No.'

We were strolling along the pavement, casually looking in shop windows. It was close to five; the rush hour was under way. People walked past us in the sunshine, their jackets draped over their arms. British people in a straight line home, foreigners with cameras straying from one monument to the next. Eight million people in a city at the end of the sixties. I wanted to know what it meant – whether it mattered that the Beatles had arrived and flower power was playing in the background like a nursery rhyme; whether it mattered that my hair was darker than my mother's pupils; whether it mattered that someone had knocked out her tooth during her stay in a lunatic asylum; whether it mattered that the sun may not come up tomorrow if the missiles of the world shattered it into brilliant flakes of iridescence; whether it mattered that I was called black and she was called white, and she was my mother – whether that mattered too. I wanted it to matter. I wanted it to matter that people were poorer than we were and that they were waiting for me to help them because otherwise, what was I doing here? I wanted it to matter that I'd known little Alison Bean before the bus ran her over and that we'd played hopscotch in the fading light of Lavender Sweep afternoons. I wanted it to matter that Louise and I were here at this moment in this city together. Like a mother and a daughter. I wanted a daughter of my own, consciously, for the first time. An odd feeling passed over me and made me shiver.

Louise stopped dead in her tracks. She gasped the way you do when you're startled by something.

'What's wrong?' My voice scared me. It was frantic.

'I've had a glorious idea,' she said. Her voice was taut – as if someone had strung it up across the sky like a washing line.

'You have? An idea? What is it?'

She looked at me for a second or two, then shook her head. 'I can't tell you yet. I want it to be a surprise. If it doesn't work, you'll be disappointed.'

I begged her to tell me, but she wouldn't budge. I had to make do with fish and chips at Clapham Junction. I got cod; Louise got haddock; we got plaice for Alfred. We saved it until we got home, then unwrapped the vinegar-soaked paper and poured the fish and chips on to plates. Not since Simon's death had I been happier. We were as rich as kings. The world spun around us clapping its hands. We were us! We were us! We were us!

We sat in Alfred's tiny bedsit. He brought out his Glenn Miller records and a bottle of Sandeman's port. I told him about our day with the mummies, the Vikings, and the illuminated manuscripts. He liked the part about the manuscripts best because he had a kinship with monks, he said. He liked stories about people working in solitude because alone you could see in the dark. I asked him what he meant, but he had a bone stuck in his throat, and by the time we'd dislodged it with vigorous pounding on his back, he was too exhausted to speak. When he recovered he'd forgotten the question – adults always forget the question – but he did go on to talk about the Vikings, whom he called brutish, and the root cause of history's retreat from civility. 'Mass production has ruined artistic endeavor,' he said, leaping to the monks again, in time for my mother to tell him I planned to write a book.

Alfred got very excited about that. If I included a portrait of him in it, he wanted it to be a favorable one. I promised it would be. They made a toast to my anticipated genius, and I made a toast to the secret Louise still refused to share. Alfred said the day would go down in history as one of the best in our lives. Louise said she was glad, so glad we'd gone to the British Museum today.

That night, Louise tucked me in the way she used to before she went mad.

I tried not to let it slip out, but I was afraid. If I lost her again after she'd let me find her, how would I bear it? I grabbed hold of her hand and held it to my cheek.

'Whatever's the matter?' she said.

'Don't go! Don't go yet!'

'Go? You want me to stay here? Are you afraid of the dark?'

'Yes. Yes, that's it. I can't see in the dark. Will you stay?'

'All right. I'll stay until you fall asleep. But mind you close your eyes. No peeking. I'll be right here.'

'Will you stroke my hair?'

She stroked my hair. Her fingers were cold but gentle. Eventually I must have fallen asleep. When I woke up the room was dark. Above me, I heard Louise in the kitchen. Water was running in the sink, and I could hear her humming to herself. Her voice was sweet. The notes ended in a kind of question mark, as if she wasn't quite sure where the melody was going to take her.

I found myself whispering to the dark.

'Don't be afraid, Mum. It's okay. I'm here. We can be strong together.'

I turned over into the pillow.

If all the other days of my life were less than this, it would be okay. My mother had been my mother again. Joy filled me like grief.

The next morning, I tiptoed upstairs to the kitchen. Behind the kitchen door was a devil or an angel: Louise I or Louise II. When Louise II was around, I wasn't a mishap after all; I was a lucky charm. I will never let my daughter think of herself as a mistake, I thought. She's going to know from the start that she's the luckiest thing that ever happened to me.

I looked down at the stairs. What was left of the paisley swirls gathered themselves into fishes' hands. None of them was clapping.

Fishes' hands, paisley swirls
It always stinks to be a girl.

Up the stairs to the kitchen-in-the-sky. Up and up the stairs of the narrow terraced house whose coordinates were Battersea and deprivation. Up to a white woman who could scream down the walls and make me pay for all my past transgressions. Up to penance in the name of the Father and of Simon's Holy Ghost.

Hail Mary, full of grace
The Lord is with thee.
Blessed art thou among women
Make my mother love me.

Inside the door, a woman.

Smiling.

'Good morning,' the woman said.

'Hi.'

'How did you sleep?'

'Fine.'

She's agitated. Don't annoy her. Be good. Otherwise she'll strangle you.

She's pouring me a bowl of sunshine. The Kellogg cockerel is a red clarion on the cornflakes box. She loves me, she loves me not. Her hands are flying around her face like birds. Her eyes are wide open and driven by lack of sleep. She can't stop talking. She's telling me her secret. Listen, you fool. React with care.

'So that's what I want to do. What do you think, Jacinta? Is it ridiculous at my age?'

I haven't heard what she's been saying! I could kick myself! Smile. I smile. She hugs me.

'I knew you'd be a Trojan! I knew it! It will mean some sacrifices, of course.'

I nod. I've said the right thing. A smile comes of its own volition.

'O, Jacinta! I can't believe it! After all these years your mother's going back to school!'

I begin to laugh.

She hugs me again. Then she pulls me up from the chair and spins me round in circles. Her white denture gleams in the morning sun. Her new blond hair looks happy. I begin to believe this isn't dreaming.

At last I begin to believe my mother has come home.

10

I go in to say good-bye to Louise. They are coming for her body, to take it away from us for good. Lady is fast asleep upstairs.

'Alfred?'

'Yes?'

'Do you remember what Vera said about Hubert – about his *becoming* the day rather than just experiencing it?'

'I remember.'

'Sometimes it feels like that, doesn't it? As if there's no separating the experience from who you are. I have to look at Lady to remember I haven't become death too, now that Mum is gone. Do you know what I mean?'

'Yes, I know.'

'We fought, Alfred. Even during these final months. I'm ashamed.' Alfred pats my head in an effort to console me.

I think back to the time when she came to visit me in Virginia. She flew out to see me in her new wig. I combed it for her. It reminded me of my Tressy doll. We moved in and out of accusations as if we were in a courtroom.

After lunch one day, she and I did the dishes in my small kitchen with the pretty view of the Appalachians. I remembered her diary – how for years all she'd wanted to do was lie with a corpse. I was suddenly furious.

'You know something,' I said, shocked by the poison in my voice. 'I don't care what you do anymore. You can give up on yourself if you like and let the cancer eat you up, and I'm not going to try and stop you. You know why? Because I'm sick of being around people who don't want to be alive. You, then Manny, then you again. I'm sick of it. You have to take the rough with the smooth. You can't just give up –'

Before I could finish, she was in my face. We were back again in Lavender Sweep. Only her hands weren't round my neck. She let her words strangle me instead.

'The rough with the smooth, is it? The rough with the smooth!' She threw her head back and laughed the way she did all those years ago. I'd sent her over the edge again! I tried to take her hand. She shoved me away and stormed into the living room. She went over to the window and looked out at the mountains. Her back was filled with rage and her hands were trembling, but I knew it would be all right. She would come back this time. She hated me, but she didn't want to kill me. I was grateful.

'I'm sorry,' I said, realizing I had to push her that far – had to see what she was like when I sent her to the edge. Had to see whether she'd jump into the abyss, the way she did before.

'You're always sorry, Jacinta. But you always want to push and push. Ever since you were little you've been that way.'

'I just don't want you to die, Mum.'

She turned round to face me, making me jump. Her face was bloated with pain. I think, *I did that.*

'You forget everything you don't want to remember, you know that?'

I told her I didn't know what she was talking about.

'The rough with the smooth – all that . . . that crap!' She startled me with the word. One of my words. I wanted to put it back into her mouth and make her swallow it.

'Don't you remember, my girl, what the rough was like? Don't you remember those months after Lady was born? What you were like? How dark it was for all of us? You pushed us away because of some absurd notion you had about beauty. Always looking in the mirror at yourself. Always making me feel as though I was too old, too fat. . . . What right did you have to do that to anyone? What gave you the right to dictate beauty to others? And then your beautiful child came along and what did you do but reject her? Just like you rejected everything you thought was ugly. And all because of some tiny flaw that you –'

'Tiny flaw! Jesus!'

I recovered in time to quiet myself. Lady was upstairs in her room. Beautiful. Alive. I was stupid for a while. I must never send her to the same place this woman sent me. She must be the light I see by, and I must be her light. Just like the moon in Margaret Atwood's poem, able to endure the dark.

'I was sad for a while, but I recovered. It's okay now. It didn't take me years and years. And even when Manny . . . even then I didn't go to pieces.'

'You were always the strong one. Things didn't seem to affect you as much. Always found a way to keep yourself closed off, I suppose. Some people don't feel as much as others. It's a blessing, really –'

'Shut up, you old fool! *Shut up!*'

I was in *her* face this time. She was smaller than I. She who used to be taller had shrunk. When?

I stumbled over to the sofa. I fell down on it and buried my face in the cushions so that Lady wouldn't hear me crying.

My mother was next to me, stroking my hair.

'It's all right, Jassie. I'm sorry. I shouldn't have said those things. I didn't mean them. I was only rambling. I didn't know you felt that way. You poor thing. A life like that – it can make you go mad. I'm sorry. I don't know what's gotten into me. You're right. It's your life and you should deal with it in your own way. You are braver than I was. I think you really can make it on your own.'

'I'm not brave! I'm terrified. Every time Lady looks in the mirror and sees what isn't there, I want to find it for her. My heart is aching. And now you're going to leave us. Please, please don't go, Mum. She's so beautiful. Who will see it?'

'O, Jacinta. Can't you see that everyone sees it? Can't you see that you've loved your child so well that she sees it too? Don't you realize yet how much light you bring into people's lives?

Don't you know it was you who brought me back from hell and kept Alfred laughing all those years? Don't you realize that?'

I sat up. 'Me?'

'Of course. That day – the day before I cleaned the house and we went to the British Museum, remember?'

I nodded. It was the starting point of my faith for nearly twenty-five years.

'The day before you were sitting on the stairs singing a tune from *Porgy and Bess* – that one about the man going and no more footsteps on the stairs, and I was outside in the hallway, listening. And you could only finger out the melody because we'd never had enough money for lessons, and the piano sounded so mournful and hollow and it was horribly out of tune. But your sweet voice rose up above it as if it had wings, and you sang like a woman of forty. And there was pain in your voice – so deep . . . made me think of wells and of water. And then I climbed upstairs to the kitchen and sat down and cried. I cried and cried and cried. And you kept singing that song about the man who'd gone, and I kept crying. And then I woke up. It was just like that. As though I'd been in a deep sleep all those years after Simon's death, and suddenly someone had pinched me. And there I was in the late 1960s, with a daughter and a life to live. And if I wasn't careful, she'd be joining me forever in the place where that song was being sung, and then we'd both be lost. And you were too beautiful to lose, Cinta.

'But it wasn't easy, even after that. And I had to pray harder than I'd ever prayed before. So that night I cleaned the kitchen until it sparkled, after I'd sent Alfred out that afternoon to buy napkins and crumpets, and cleansers and flowers. And every so often I sat down with my rosary and told the beads. All the Our Fathers and Hail Marys and Glory Bes I could muster to get me through. I think I prayed to Simon as much as I prayed to God because I knew that if anyone could break through into this world and help me it was him.

'And then at three A.M. something wonderful happened.

'I must have fallen asleep with the rosary in my hand when I felt a tugging at the beads, and I jumped up thinking it was you. The room was empty, except for a strange shadow on the wall, as if I had a fire lit in the room and a dancer was there in front of it casting his shadow on the wall. And then the shadow gathered itself into your father's face, and there he was – smiling and nodding as if, after all, I'd done the right thing by coming home.

'Because that's what haunted me. The idea that you'd be better off without me. That I was too unstable. That I'd . . . harm you by being there.

'And it was as if I knew then that everything would be all right. Because of your song and his face. And then I woke up again because the first waking up was like the outer envelope of a dream – at least I think that's what it was, I was never really sure. The room was quiet. Nothing was left in it but a kind of fullness. And I knew I wouldn't be empty again because Simon was there in the walls and the floors and in your sweet voice and your gorgeous eyes. I put the rosary beads away and began to clean in earnest. By the time the dawn came, I was singing. When the sun came through the windows, I thought it was you. And when you came into the room that morning, I knew I was right.

'And now you're here in America and I'm here too, and you've written your poetry books and become a professor and done all the things that few people from Lavender Sweep ever have a chance to do. It's funny. After all these years, after all the things that have happened to us, you'd think I'd be ready to die. And sometimes I am, and that's what you heard just now. But you know, the ironic thing is, there's a large part of me that isn't ready to go anywhere. I want to see Lady grow up. I want to remember you as a child when I see her as a child. She is so much like you, Jacinta. So strong. So willful. No one will ever control her for long. And she'll bring light into the world the way you do. I know it and I'd like to witness it. You probably won't believe me, but I'd rather like to stay put, if I could.'

'O, Mum. I'm sorry.'

'Don't be sorry. It's no one's fault. If something happens, I can say I've had a good run for my money. And I'd be lying if I were to say I didn't long to be with your father. I just think there's life in the old gal yet. I want Lady to know me. I'll be a much better grandmother than I was a mother.'

That should have been the last conflict between us because then we would have had closure. But Louise was right: I've never been able to stop pushing. And that's been half the problem.

'Alfred?' I say when all that is left of Louise is a cold indentation in the bed where her small body lay waiting for the reunion with her soul.

'Yes, little one?'

'I'm tired.'

'I know.'

'Mothers should never die. What do you do when you're not someone's child anymore? How do you stand it?'

'Mothers don't die,' he tells me. 'I see mine every day. I talk with her. We tell jokes. People are foolish to believe that death can divorce you from love. You just have to open yourself up to new possibilities, that's all. If you know yourself well enough, and if you're patient, you can do that.'

'Patience isn't my strong point, Alfred. You know that. Alfred?'

'Yes?'

'Africa was the most glorious and the most terrible of times for me. And I never told her about it. I locked her out. A few details about Simon's family – a few comments about Esther and Assieyatu – that was all I shared with her. I didn't let her know me. You were right all those years ago when you said it was me who left us. It was me.'

'No, Jacinta. Don't do that to yourself. Don't you see? You came back. Here you are with your own lovely daughter. Just like sweet Louise, you came back.'

Alfred invites me to sit in his room and listen to his old record player. He pulls out my mother's favorite music – *Carmina Burana*, *Tosca*, *Madama Butterfly*, and everything by Delius. He says he'll see to Lady. I should lie down if I want. He goes out.

Later, between the gorgeous strains of the music, I hear Lady talking up a storm with him in the kitchen. Alfred is old in years now, but he hasn't lost his ability to talk with the young. She is opening up to him. I hear the hum of his consolation, though I cannot make out the words. She loved her Mama Lou and I know I can trust him to find the right words for her to live by. But who will comfort Alfred? The thought makes me feel ashamed again. Guilt creeps up me like rising damp.

Alfred has given me this space in which to grieve. I need to find a way to thank him for this gift. I open myself up to the music. At times I can hardly breathe because so much wells up from the past. I think about Lady and about Africa, about the ride in the Jeep and the ghosts who come back to haunt me, about Simon and what it meant to find his signature upon the land, about Esther Cole and John Turay and the way they swept me up to heaven for a few months before I found out that the night is an overlay of black paper with small holes cut in it for the stars; before I found out that behind that gentle blackness is an infinity of blinding light, the light that lunatics remember. I realize that most people do things out of fear – that's what drives them. They're afraid and then they act that fear out upon the world. That's what tragedy means – the reenacting of fear; and you mustn't judge us too harshly, must you? I mean, how much is our own fault?

Why, at twenty-four, was I so ripe for the plucking? Louise had come back. Life was picking up in Battersea. Why hadn't I grown stronger in a quarter of a century of struggle? If I, with all my advantages, had not been strong, how could I possibly criticize my mother, whose circumstances were always much more trying than my own? Why did I, like so many other women I know, yearn to be saved by a man?

As Puccini takes up the refrain of loss, I think back to midnight mass in St. Vincent de Paul.

O come, O come, Emmanuel,
And ransom captive Israel,
That mourns in lonely exile here
Until the Son of God appear.
Rejoice! Rejoice! Emmanuel
Shall come to thee, O Israel!

Did I meet him then – all those years before when I was a child singing to a God I didn't know at St. Vincent de Paul's

church in Battersea? Was my husband, Emmanuel, the incarna-
tion of the savior who would set me free? Take me away from
one culture and plant me in another? Take me to a New World
of fabulous promises? He was the person with the 'man' in his
name. He was the blond, beautiful American who had been to
all the places I had dreamed about and who loved the Africa in
me more than I did myself. I thought he would set me free. We
wrote together and held out against the rest of the world. Then
the world took a sharp turn to the left, and the night began to
fade into whiteness.

Alfred's words have made me brave. Puccini's music adds to
that courage. My mother's death opens me up to myself and to
a remembrance of what was buried.

At last it's time to remember Easter. Half a dozen years locked
up without a key. I think about Manny, the man who took me to
Paris and made me want to write. I permit myself to think about
the man whose life I ruined and who nearly ruined mine. The
father of my little girl. The man who told me we should kill her.

PART II

THE NEW WORLD

1

By the time I met Emmanuel Fox III, my dreams were turning to ash. I was starting to believe I would never see the Promised Land. In spite of my supposed genius, no editor thought much of the book of poetry I'd compiled at eighteen. The two hundred pages I'd gathered told my parents' lives in sonnet sequences. Alfred loved it; I decided against showing most of the poems to my mother. And, after five years of rewrites and rejections, I filled a pot with water, placed it on the stove, and boiled my manuscript like a piece of ham. There was something pleasurable about watching the pages ball up into pulp. I stirred it every few seconds and cursed the men who'd told me it was worthless, laughing bitterly at my own naiveté. Louise came home while it was on the stove and tried to salvage it when she learned what it was. But it was too late for that. Alfred didn't speak to me for five days when he heard about it. When he was speaking to me again, he admonished me with stories of my father's patience when he too had been faced with rejection.

'I'm not my father,' I said.

'You're certainly not,' he told me, as close to rage as I'd seen him in a long time.

I shrugged. I was tired. I told him to leave me alone.

My yearning for beauty and adventure had not dwindled. I'd

lived away from home when I'd taken my undergraduate degree; but, at twenty-four, I'd stopped being on the alert for miracles and decided to settle for second best. I'd get my teaching certificate. Louise told me I was wise to go into teaching and that she'd never regretted it. She told me I was following in her footsteps. Her words made me shudder. Teaching had changed her from a woman on the edge to a woman who didn't even seem to remember where the edge was. It had rubbed her smooth. She was like other people's mothers, and all she seemed to be able to focus on was the trivia of everyday life.

When Alfred heard I was going to follow my mother into teaching, he told me I should travel instead.

'Only people with vocations should teach,' he said. 'Your mother has a vocation, but I don't sense one in you. Travel for a while. It will be good for you.'

But where would I go? Money was still tight – though Louise's teaching position at an elementary school in Brixton meant we could pay the bills. But the roof needed to be fixed, and the plumbing and wiring in the old house needed repair. After graduation, I worked at a bookstore in the West End. I was like the people I used to despise along the Sweep: exhausted on Fridays, half dead on Saturdays, comatose on Sundays, and depressed on Mondays. I'd been to Europe at nineteen and had fallen in love with Rome, Venice, and the Greek islands. I went again at twenty-two, using up all my savings in the process. After that, it was difficult to save for a trip that could make you comprehend the paucity of your own existence, so I didn't bother. Alfred told me I was spoiled. I had a mother who loved me, he said, a roof over my head, beauty and talent. Sulking about small rooms or a small wardrobe was absurd, what with all the people starving in the world. What I didn't tell Alfred was that I was scared. So scared, in fact, that I was paralyzed. I always thought I'd continue to forge ahead and that education would be the key to everything. But there were too many young women with degrees in English literature – three other women in the bookstore where I worked, for example, all wanting more glamorous careers in publishing or writing, none of them able to escape the shelves of books and the cashier's register. I looked back to the past. When I'd made bold moves before, they'd resulted in tragedy: Louise's madness, the death of Alison Bean. Perhaps it was better not to act at all. Safer anyway. 'The worst is not so long as we can say "This is the worst."' I could still say it. I hadn't gotten there yet. I didn't want to push my luck.

Life had not turned out to be grand after all. The thought of teaching kids who didn't want to learn for the rest of my life made me feel ill. Yet it was better than working at the bookstore and, perhaps, once I got the graduate degree in education, I could teach reasonably well. It had been three years since I'd graduated from Nottingham. I'd done nothing with my life. After I boiled my manuscript, I didn't write a poem for two years. I was finding prematurely gray hairs in my hairbrush. Soon men wouldn't be waiting on the doorstep for me. No one would bring me roses or tell me how beautiful I was. And even though it had transformed itself now that she had found her vocation, my mother's face haunted me. Perhaps, I reasoned, teaching provided a way out; and if it was a slow road to adventure, at least I would be pointed in the right direction.

There were men, of course. Men who said I was exotic. Men who wanted sex. Men who said I was frigid. Men who wanted mothers. Men who claimed I was too clever for my own good. Men who told me I was gorgeous. Men who asked me to lend them money. Men who tried to love me. One or two men I should have loved in return. But Maurice's tongue was still in my mouth. Whoever I loved could not be anything like Maurice. My prejudice against white Englishmen increased as the years went by. I dated West Indians, Africans, Pakistanis, and Irishmen. Alfred said I had courted the United Nations by the time I was twenty-one. He told me to be careful. 'Of course I will,' I said, always in control. I didn't want to love anyone who was as hemmed in by race, class, and circumstance as I was. I longed for someone who could make my head spin the way Little Joe had on *Bonanza*. Louise had been a palpable example of the depth of passion. Even Alfred, with his occasional stories of Lipton and unrequited love, let me know there was something on the other side of reason that could set you on fire and never let you go. I was terrified of it and drawn to it at the same time. I wasn't about to go out and find it, but if it came along, I had a feeling I'd be ready.

I met Emmanuel Fox III in London in February on St. Valentine's Day. We ran into each other at the National Gallery. I went there at lunchtime whenever I could, escaping from the student union at the University of London to find beauty in the high-walled rooms of the gallery. Emmanuel was studying African history at the university too; I'd seen him once or twice in the cafeteria. He was lean and petite, and only a few inches taller than I. I'd noticed him because there was something urgent about his movements that made you believe he had important appointments to keep. As we walked around the gallery looking at Rembrandt and van Gogh, daVinci and Monet, he told me his field was history but his passion was language. A writer from America! I swallowed hard and looked into his eyes. They were a blue-green, and they were oddly empty; they were the kind of eyes you could fill with small kindnesses. Over lunch at the National Gallery, he told me it was love at first sight.

'I'm in love with you,' he said. 'I have been ever since I laid eyes on you in the student union. Didn't you see me staring at you? I asked about you. No one seemed to know much about Jacinta Moses. It was fate that we both came here today. We were destined to be together. We shouldn't fight it.'

I laughed, but inside I was alive with expectation. Supposing it were true, that this small, intense American was in love with me? What would that mean?

'How do you know you're in love?'

He just shook his head.

'You don't know me.'

'So?'

'It doesn't make sense to love someone you don't know.'

'Who said love had to make sense? DaVinci's *Madonna* – does that painting make sense? Think about it. There she is in the middle of what looks like a Gothic nightmare, completely oblivious, bouncing a ninety-pound savior on her lap, surrounded by refugees from Rossetti . . .'

'Rossetti came later.'

'Don't interrupt. I mean, I ask you, does that painting make sense, Jacinta Louise Buttercup Moses? But you love it anyhow, right? Love never makes sense. Period. Never.'

'I never say never. Or not often anyway. It's dangerous.'

'Well, I'm a never kinda guy. I never eat before eight in the morning; I never watch second-rate movies; I never read novels by white males; and I never get tired of looking at the wealth of beauty in your eyes.'

'*You're* a white male.'

'That's my misfortune.'

'Don't you like yourself, then?'

'Jacinta Louise Buttercup Moses, I love myself to death. I think I'm positively gorgeous.'

I looked at him. He was right. His features were perfectly aligned on his classically molded face. His manicured hands moved like dancers. I'd seen women around him, many much taller than he, desperate for him to look at them, to woo them with his soft American accent. I could see the attraction. There was something untamed in this man. His face was full of promises.

'The thing is,' he moved in closer to me as if he were telling me a secret, 'the thing is, no one else seems to have noticed the fact that I'm Superman. What do you think, J.L.B.M.? Am I gorgeous or what?'

His breath was sweet when he was up close. He'd laughed when I told him my full name. He said I was several women all at once. He asked me why no one had cottoned on to that fact. He told me he knew I'd have a name to fit my uniqueness. No one else was like me, he said. I was indescribable.

'Well? Am I gorgeous?' he repeated. 'You can tell me the truth. I can take it.'

I looked down. I didn't want him to know my heart was pounding.

'So!' he continued when it was clear that I wasn't going to respond. 'We've had lunch. I have the whole afternoon before I need to get back to writing the major Western tome of the twentieth century. How about I give you a tour of my estate?'

'You have an estate?'

'You don't believe me, Jacinta Louise, but it's the truth. I'm living in an estate of mind. A darling little habitat off Clapham Common.'

'Clapham Common! That's not far from my house!' I hadn't meant to sound so excited. I'd shown my hand. He moved in closer.

'Well, whadya know! We're meant for each other. Take me home to meet your mother. I'm ready.'

He stood up and brushed himself off. Then he took my hand, kissed it, and bowed low. 'Emmanuel Fox III at your service, madam.'

Just as we were leaving the cafeteria, he took my hand in his again, fell on to one knee, and dramatically wiped a tear from his eye.

'I can't help myself,' he cried, 'I must say it!'

The people looked up over their cups of tea. One woman was obviously offended. The others smiled wanly. The cashier gave me the thumbs-up sign over her head.

'Get up, you idiot! Everyone's looking!'

'Ask me if I care!' he cried. 'This is love. For love you must never hold back. You dare everything. You risk everything. And if it doesn't work, what are you? A mere absurdity. A mere speck in the cosmic wheel of continual misfortune. But still you persevere, and you know why, Jacinta Louise Buttercup Moses?'

I was laughing too much to answer. My heart had just begun to grow wings.

'You persevere because there is WOMAN. And she is where it's at. O, milady. Lovely, lovely Jacinta Louise. When you are old, your hair will be streaked with gray, which men will take for comets flying through the midnight of your hair.' An old man in the corner clapped. 'Bravo, young man!' he said. 'Bravo!'

'O, Jacinta Louise. I've only known you a short time –'

'Thirty-three minutes actually,' I said, glancing at my watch, trying hard to seem unaffected by his hyperbolic declaration of love, hoping he wouldn't feel my fingers trembling.

'But what's in an hour, Jacinta? What's in a second, for that matter? A second is like an egg. As Shakespeare would have said, it's full of meat. I've tasted your beauty, Jacinta, and it has set me afire. Jacinta Louise Buttercup Moses – glorious name – will you marry me?'

The man who had applauded before stood up shakily, brandished his cane in the air, and shouted 'Hurrah!' The offended woman in the hat snorted in disgust. The cashier nodded at me vigorously enough to shake loose one of her plastic pearl earrings.

I looked down at Emmanuel Fox III. For two decades, ever since Simon's death, I'd been waiting for someone to ride into my life, swoop me up and make me into the Potential Jacinta rather than the Actual one. His blond hair, caught in a gash of sun streaming down from the cafeteria's skylights, looked like gold thread. The room sucked itself in like an intake of breath. I remembered the high windows in the hospital where my father died. They'd allowed the light to enter too, scarring the white ward with whiter ways of seeing. My father's hand had waved to me before taking its leave. My mother had walked down the aisle of the ward in her high heels – click, click, click – and I had noticed the mole on her right ankle and the seams in her stockings running a path down her legs. She'd walked toward him and away from me. I'd stood in the doorway and watched love play out to devastation.

Emmanuel looked up at me. Something in the corners of his green-flecked-with-blue eyes said this was important. I'd seen that look before. Alison Bean had it when she asked me if I was her best friend. *Second best*, I'd told her before the bus had come and crumpled her up like a doll in the middle of a road far away from Kingston.

'If you promise to take me to the New World, and if you promise me riches beyond belief, and if you promise to love me past the stars in the midnight sky you see in my hair – yes. I will marry you. If you want me enough.'

The cafeteria broke into spontaneous applause. The cashier behind Emmanuel was crying. The blond stranger in front of me was shaking when he took my hand to go out.

It wasn't until we got outside that we realized neither of us had paid for our food. I told him to go back. He only laughed. 'Let them sell a van Gogh for our lunch!' he cried. 'Banality is not my concern from this day forward. I've found the love of my life! We will populate the earth with beauty and bring the sun up with the sheer force of our joy! No more bills, receipts, or humdrum anything. It's only love from now on!'

He lifted me up and twirled me around. My hair caught the wind and spanned out stiffly behind me. I caught a glimpse of it as it lashed out against the wind. Comets, I thought, and midnight. My tangled African hair changed to poetry. I threw my head back and let him spin me. I'd found a man who could make the world turn faster. I didn't know whether or not I would marry this man. I didn't love him. I barely knew him. But I loved what he represented. He could be the key to the jail. Perhaps we could unlock the door together? Dear God, I prayed, please let him be real.

Alfred didn't like him. From the first time he met Manny, Alfred said he was not what he seemed to be. The feeling was mutual; I put it down to jealousy. I prided myself on my ability to make two men envious of each other. Wasn't that what women with power were supposed to do? When Alfred pulled me aside that day and asked me if it was all a joke, I was taken aback by the urgency in his voice.

'What are you doing?' he hissed. 'This is some kind of prank, isn't it? You don't really plan to marry this man, do you?'

I shrugged. 'Perhaps. I think he's rather remarkable.'

'How long have you known him?'

'Two hours and twenty-two – no, twenty-three minutes precisely. I met him at the National Gallery over daVinci's *Madonna of the Rocks*. He asked me to marry him half an hour later.'

'I rest my case. The man's a complete and utter nincompoop.'

'Why? Because he fell in love with me? Thanks.'

'No! Of course not! For goodness' sake, child, be reasonable. You've only known the man for a few hours. He could be . . . anyone!'

'That's exactly why he intrigues me,' I said.

We were standing off to one side in the front room. My mother no longer slept there. Now, recently repainted white and clean, it was a living room like everyone else's. I was grateful we'd done it in time. With any luck, Manny wouldn't notice how weird we were. He was speaking to my mother about African art over on the other side of the room. She was listening intently. Suddenly it occurred to me that they looked like mother and son.

I turned to face them.

'They look like mother and son,' I said.

Alfred glanced over at them. 'Jacinta, I'm warning you, this is not a good idea.'

'Alfred, I'm telling you to mind your own bloody business.'

I didn't wait to see his face crumple. I didn't care what he thought. He wasn't my father. He wasn't anything. Just a friend of the family. I walked over to Manny and Louise.

It was clear that my mother liked him. She didn't take our engagement seriously, but she had obviously taken a fancy to Manny, and he to her. Over the past few years she'd become increasingly obsessed with her teaching career. Whenever she found anyone who would listen, she spoke for hours, barely taking a breath, about little Gregory Porsino or Lettie Halibut. Sometimes she focused on her headmaster, Mr. Pod, who had a passion for all things potted. 'His office is a greenhouse,' she told Manny, not missing a beat when I came up beside them. 'Of course, he hates the children. When I talked to him about Gregory Porsino's father – the way he looks at those young girls in the playground – and the rumors about his misdemeanors in that respect, all Pod did was giggle and water his nasturtiums. Titter, really. And when I mentioned Lettie's head lice he told me to get a metal comb and get on with it. The man's evil, of course. Quite evil. Wears one of those nylon toupees. You can never trust a man who does that kind of thing, can you? So deceptive.'

I studied my mother. When had she turned into this woman? How was it that someone who had kept her mouth closed for nearly a decade opened it up one day and never closed it again? Why wasn't she who she had once been? I'd become so used to

the new Louise I hardly ever thought about the old one. Louise
the Tragic Lover had become Louise the Dotty Schoolteacher.
She was like everyone else. Ordinary. Perhaps she hadn't loved
my father that much after all. The little primary school in a
blighted part of London had become her main focal point, the
pivot around which she turned. Often she was bitterly angry
with other teachers – an anger that was shocking because of its
force. It came from nowhere and seemed to be premised on
some historical injustice – perhaps my father's death, perhaps
her years of poverty – which her opponents never understood.
Sometimes she decided to take the younger teachers under her
wing. For the few chosen ones, there was nothing but praise.
She became their champion. Until they let her down somehow,
and then she could never forgive them. Yet for all that she loved
the children. All of them. No matter how bad they were, how
snotty, how much they stank, she loved them. When they
picked their noses, she told them that children of seven needed
to behave like ladies and gentlemen. When they scratched their
bottoms, she told them to find work for busy hands. Each and
every one, whatever their learning disability, was able to read by
the time they left her class. Each of them loved her in return.

But right now she was infuriating. On and on and on about
herself and her petty loathing. The room was closing in on me.
This had been my life. Now I made the daily commute from
home, either to the university or to the bookstore. I had stayed
to watch my life leak out from me, one drip at a time.

I took hold of Manny's hand. He seemed surprised at first,
then pleased. 'We need to go, Mum,' I said.

'O stay. Won't you stay for supper? I've got a nice bit of cod –'

'No. We really need to get back to the university. I've got a
study meeting on the philosophy of education and Manny has
something or other on James Joyce. Sorry. Wish we could stay,
Mum, but there you are.' My voice was frantic. Like a claustro-
phobic, I had to get out. Now.

Manny looked at me strangely, then just shrugged. 'She's the
boss,' he said. 'And I sure would hate to miss my class on Joyce.'

Alfred was still standing over in the corner. I think he waved
to us, but I didn't stay around to find out.

On the way downstairs, Manny asked me why I'd lied.

'She can go on for hours about that school. I didn't want to subject you to that.'

'I thought she was pretty fascinating. Gorgeous face. Bet she was a stunner when she was younger.'

'So they say.'

I hurried him down the stairs to the front door. The carpet with the fishes' hands had been replaced a long time ago. We sank into the warm brown tufts of nylon. Yes. The house looked like other people's. I'd done it! I'd actually made a good impression! Alfred had been odd, of course, but then I'd explained to Manny before we'd arrived that he was an actor. Actors are always eccentric, I'd told him.

We were about to escape without incident when I opened the front door. There on the step, in all her glory, was my worst nightmare.

Mary Beadycap was sprawled out on the doorstep with a bottle of wine in her hand. When her family had moved to a council house years ago, Mary had decided to make occasional pilgrimages back to the Sweep to see her 'good mate' Alfred. So, once in a while, Mary would walk the four miles from their terraced council house in Wandsworth to sit, splay-legged on the front step, reminiscing about the good old days. Today of all days! I could have killed her. I blamed Alfred. He encouraged her by giving her cups of tea and ham sandwiches. I pleaded with him not to do it, but he couldn't seem to help himself. He seemed to have forgotten how much she and Maurice had plagued us. He didn't seem to care that she had mocked his masculinity and called me a wog to my face. She was the child who had tried to fill my school hat with vomit, but who had been forced to settle for spit. She was the one who, together with her brother, had brought evil into my life. Her teeth were mustard-yellow and her clothes looked three sizes too small. Her breasts rose above the tight sweater she wore, and she shivered once in a while in the cold. Her nose was red from booze and from the chill. Her hair hung down around her face in long greasy strands.

'Mary! What are you doing here?' I said in horror, staring at

Mary's hunched form and smelling the cheap wine she was guzzling straight from the bottle.

She swiveled around, then swiveled back like a reptile. I tried to step over her as fast as possible. I shouldn't have called attention to myself. Perhaps we could have escaped without notice. Alfred said I should have more sympathy for Mary. But all I could see when I looked at her was a pair of blue knickers in the rigid black fingers of little Alison Bean. Her face echoed her twin brother's. Same eyes. Same nose. I'd worked hard to scoop Maurice out of my memory. Mary wasn't going to insert him again. I needed to get away. Manny had to like me. What if he rejected me now? I tried to leap over Mary's legs but I wasn't swift enough. She grabbed my ankle and held on. Manny thought it was a joke.

'Who's your friend?' he asked.

Mary stood up, wobbled a little, regained her balance, and held out her hand. Manny took it in his and kissed it. I looked on in consternation.

'Well! A proper English gentleman, at last!'

'Alack, not English,' Manny said. 'A mere colonist from the United States of Americky.'

'Well, now, ain't that sweet? And I s'pose you're here courtin' little Jacinta Moses?'

'Yep. That's about right.'

'We should go. It's getting late,' I urged.

'Not so fast, lovey-dove,' Mary warned. 'P'raps I need to let your beau in on a few little details about your former boyfriend, just so's he'll know what he's up against.'

'She's drunk, Manny. Let's go.'

'Because I swear to you, Mister Manny . . . er . . . what was the name?'

Manny began to edge away. Mary's breath was overpowering. 'Emmanuel Fox.'

'Emmanuel Fox from . . . ?'

'Virginia.'

'Virginia! How lovely. I swear to you that my twin brother was truly, as they say, incomparable. The two of them were tight as tight can be. Loved to have him play with her tits, didn't

you, Jacinta?' She reached over and squeezed my breast. Manny
batted her hand away.

'What the hell –' he said.

Mary threw her head back and laughed. Several teeth were
missing. There was an ugly bruise on her throat. 'Loved to play
games with Maurice on Clapham Common, she did. Remember
that time –'

'Let's go, okay?' I said, taking hold of Manny's arm and
pulling him down the front path. Mary continued the conversation, until she was shouting after us.

'He put the screws on that one, O yes he did. HA-HA-HA!'
Her voice did a U-turn into melodrama. 'Then he just went
poof. Off. Just like that! Can you credit it? He was my brother, he
was. And a twin too.' She held up the wine bottle. It had a
Sainsburys supermarket label on it. Burgundy it said. 'Blood
should be thicker than some little bitch's . . . should be thicker
than that. We was kids together. On this street. On Lavender
Sweep. Not her. Too snooty. The convent school tart. Just him
and me. And then gone. Lit out like a light. No light left without
Maurice. The boy was a genius, he was! Me mother's pride and
joy. Not a word. All these years, not a soddin' word!' She swept
herself up and back into accusation. Her voice echoed through
Lavender Sweep like doom.

'It was her fault! Jacinta Moses! She made him do it! And me.
I didn't use to look like this. No, sir. I was beautiful too once.
She'll get hers. She'll pay! Maurice'll find her, you mark my
words. He's still in the background, he is. Remember that, little
Miss Uppity. He'll haunt you yet. Maurice never lets go. I should
know. Once he's got you he gets what he wants and he ain't
never letting go! She and that little wog, they robbed me of my
chas . . . my chas . . . they RAPED ME!'

The charge was so outrageous it hit me in the gut like a bowl-
ing ball. I couldn't turn around to face her. She was several
doors down by now, shouting her filth out over the streets. I
could see the Wall of Cruelty looming in front of us. We had to
get past it, then turn the corner onto Lavender Hill. I ran. 'It's not
true,' I called behind me to Manny, who was running to catch
up. 'She's lying. *She* did it. It was *Mary* who raped *us*. She

killed my friend. So did Maurice. The two of them together. They were the evil ones.'

Alfred must have come out then because I heard his voice in the background imploring Mary to go inside. Then I heard her bawling like a baby. Then the door closed behind them and we were left in the wake of pain.

Manny was gripping me round the waist. I must have stopped dead by the Wall of Cruelty because he had me in his arms and he was holding me up. My voice came out in gulps, as if I were drinking tears at the same time as I was speaking.

'This was where they found him. Right here! By this shitty wall. That's all it amounted to in the end. An ugly wall in Battersea covered in broken glass.'

'Who, Jacinta?' he asked, stroking my hair.

'Simon! Simon!' I cried. 'After that . . . nothing . . . years of grief. This bloody wall has been slicing us up for twenty years! Ugly. I hate Ugly. I dre-dreamed of something . . . grand.'

I hadn't made the right impression. After all my efforts to make us look normal, Mary Beadycap had exploded the myth and I'd seconded the explosion. I'd never see this man again. I'd be stuck in South London in the 1980s teaching secondary school children about a culture I would never be a part of. I'd never be the writer I'd tried to be. I'd be a teacher like Louise. By July I'd have my teaching certificate. My life would never be filled with beauty after all. I'd be just like all the other women who didn't have money or privilege or good luck: disappointed and weary.

I leaned into Manny's small, tight body. His arms were strong. He had a firm grip on me; I couldn't fall.

'You need to sit down. Is there somewhere round here we could go for a drink?'

We found a wine bar at the trendier end of Lavender Hill. We sat in a booth and Manny ordered a bottle of burgundy. Beyond the glass, people hurried by us. Londoners in a hurry to get home. Where did people store their dreams in this country? Up their sleeves? In their back pockets? Under the clock on the mantelpiece? Where did black people go when their dreams came down upon their heads as drizzle? Did the Jamaicans still dream about the turquoise ocean and the extraordinary orange of the mango? Did their fruit taste the same when they bought it in the Northcote Road or in Brixton? Or did its bitterness sting the roofs of their mouths?

I looked at the man opposite. He was beautiful. Petite and perfect like Alison had been. His features were small and his gestures strangely fastidious. What he said didn't appear to be exactly what he meant. But no man knew what he meant – apart from my father, who died, and Alfred, who was, in some ways, as much a woman as he was a man. I drank some more wine and thought briefly about Mary.

We talked, or rather, I talked. He kept filling my glass, and I gave him an edited version of my life with Simon, Louise, Alfred, and Maurice. I said I didn't know what she meant about rape. I'd never hurt anyone. I left out the part about the knickers, the part about Maurice's accusation and his tongue. You don't tell men everything; it was too dangerous. Manny said he believed me, that he could tell I was the good one. 'Who did they kill?' he asked.

'A good friend.'

He didn't pursue it except to say, 'I could be your good friend, Jacinta Moses. Why don't you just lean back? I'll be there to catch you. I've been waiting for a woman like you all my life. I can protect you from those people. I'd never let them hurt you.'

'Why are you saying all this?'

'Listen, Jacinta. There are moments in life when a door is opened up. That's the best way I know to describe it. The door just opens and you can either walk through or close it. If you walk, you could find there are no stairs beyond the door – just a fifty-foot drop, so you hesitate. But if you close the door, then all you have left are what-might-have-beens. And your whole life you spend wondering what the hell was behind door number seventeen. Get it?'

'I'm door number seventeen?'

'No. You're the great treasure behind the door.'

'What do you want from me?'

'The key, Jacinta. That's all. Let me in. It's cold outside. All you need to know about me is that I've been where you are now. Waiting to get out. Waiting for the miracle. That's why I came here. To find the miracle. And to write. I need to write about all this. No American has really done it yet. Passion is too hard to catch hold of. Men are afraid. So they write on the peripheries of experience. I want to break love open like a nut. I want to tell people how crazy and how glorious it can be. I want you to be my subject, Jacinta. Because you're the only woman I've met who I know in my heart would never bore the pants off me. Do you know how rare that is? Please. Please. We can be great together. I know you don't trust me now, why should you? But you will, if you just give me time.'

I let him kiss me. He leaned over the table, knocking over my empty glass, and I tasted the wine he'd been drinking. He'd seen my home; he'd seen Mary; still he wanted me. My spirits rose. I could do this. I could really do this. I could see the country I'd dreamed of saving. I could work with the poor. I could become a millionaire. I could ride horses across the prairie and go to Canada for weekends. I could be free at last, free at last, with this small blond man called Emmanuel.

He sat back in the booth and looked at me.

'Where exactly do you live in America?' I asked.

He smiled.

2

We were married in St Vincent de Paul's Catholic Church in Battersea. I wanted to be married there; it was where I'd first sung about Emmanuel the Savior who had freed His people Israel, so it seemed appropriate. At last, a prayer I'd sent up to God had been answered.

The courtship was a rushed affair. Manny had to go back to the United States by July. We both had to get our degrees by then too, so there wasn't much time to get to know each other. Manny studied every night; I had to prepare to practice teach. We never really made love before the wedding; Manny said he wanted to savor the experience on our honeymoon – a five-day package trip to Paris. I was glad. He could satisfy me in other ways, and I could put off a remembrance of Maurice until later. With other men I'd often had to grit my teeth and pretend I was somewhere else. If that were the case with Manny, I'd rather wait to find it out.

Paris was my mother's gift to us. Simon and she had wanted to go there together, she said, but there wasn't enough time before he died. Her gift moved me. Manny bought her roses and chocolates and took us out to eat at an Indian restaurant in Streatham. He regaled us with stories of his time in Africa as a Peace Corps volunteer. I'd learn later that he'd only stayed for two months, but in the restaurant, listening to him with Louise was like going back to the Red Sea Hour with Simon. Manny made us laugh. He could impersonate people, and he did a wonderful imitation of Alfred. We laughed until we ached. Louise said he should be in the movies. She pointed out that Manny was exactly the same height as Simon had been. She said it was a sign.

Because I needed a visa, we spent much of our time at the embassy, waiting in line. It looked as though I'd have to leave after Manny because there was so much paperwork to be approved; but, when I got a place in the same writing program where Manny had been accepted, they relented and gave us the necessary papers so that we could travel together. I was leaving for America in July! I was to be married two weeks before we were to leave England for good. A calmness came over me. I had done it after all. Nothing could stop me now.

Alfred reconciled himself to our union and agreed to give me away. He wore a dark suit and looked quite dashing after I'd blow-dried his wispy hair and covered it in hair spray.

'I'm a star in the firma*ment*,' he said, impersonating the blond movie star in *Singin' in the Rain*.

'You don't hate him too much, do you, Alfred? He's nice, really. He has high aspirations. He really does. He wants to go back to Africa and help the people there. He was in the Peace Corps, you know. Only he had to drop out for personal reasons. Once we've got our MFAs we'll head back to Africa to teach the children. We've got it all planned. So you mustn't hate him. He's the kind of man I thought you'd want me to marry. He's an idealist like you.'

'I don't hate him, child. If you love him, that's good enough for me. I just have this gnawing feeling in the pit of my stomach. Something tells me there's someone better out there for you, that's all. I always hoped you'd find someone tender, truly tender. Someone who'd put your happiness first.'

'Manny does that all the time! Yesterday he got up at five A.M. and skipped his writing time just so he could get me to college in time for the finals.'

'That's nice.'

'You still don't like him, do you?'

'Jacinta, why do you keep asking me that? You know how I feel. It's not fair.'

'Okay, okay. Don't start bawling, for God's sake. Look, I don't mind. We can't all love everybody. Just don't spoil this for me, okay? I need this day. There. It looks great. I've covered up the bald spot, see?'

'My Lord! How did you accomplish that feat?'

'Mascara. I put it on the hair shafts. Just don't stand out in the rain, okay? It's not waterproof.'

'You're a genius. My own mother wouldn't recognize me.'

I put down the comb and pulled up a chair in front of him. Above us we could hear my mother and Mrs. Butcher vacuuming the rooms in preparation for the reception. Hubert's desolate cry of 'One more lemon cupcakie' echoed through the house.

'Why doesn't she just give the boy a cupcake?' Alfred said. It was unlike him. Usually he had infinite patience with Mrs. Butcher's son. It was a warm summer day and everything in the house had been either washed, starched, bleached, or ironed, including my hair, which Louise had attacked with a hot comb at six-thirty that morning. Alfred said it was too straight now. He liked all the waves, he said. Reminded him of the seaside. I told him I'd wear my hair however I wanted. He said he would do the same thing. I had to relent then and wash it all over again. Under my veil, it was as wild as ever. Alfred called me Titania when he saw me in my veil. 'You're a midsummer night's dream,' he said. 'He doesn't deserve you.'

I took his hand in mine and looked at his long fingers.

'You've been biting your nails again, Alfred. I thought you were going to try to let them look halfway decent for the wedding.'

'I'm all nerves.' He absentmindedly put his fingers in his mouth and began to chew.

'Look, Alfred, you don't have to be nervous. You don't have to say much. Only two words. When the priest says, "Who gives this woman," etc., you say, "I do." It's easy.'

'Should we practice the walk again?'

'We've practiced it a million times. Okay, okay, we'll practice it.'

So I took his arm and we pigeon-stepped the wedding march

in his tiny room. He stood up straight and walked like an automaton. I could feel him trembling through his sleeve. I squeezed his arm and told him he was doing fine. We sang the wedding march in unison, and I was momentarily afraid that he'd do that during the ceremony. I caught a glimpse of his enormous nose in profile. There were four or five hairs protruding from his left nostril.

'Alfred, I think you need to pluck your nose.'

'O dear, not again!' he cried. 'I did that only last week. What is going on in my orifices?'

I didn't want to touch that one, so we continued to practice for another few minutes. When we sat down again, Alfred said he felt much better about the whole thing. 'I've got the rhythm now,' he said. 'I'll be fine.'

He leaned back into the bedsettee and closed his eyes: 'I wish the Chief could see you now. He'd be so proud of you.'

'Even though I'm marrying the wrong man?'

'Hush. I didn't say that. I'm just an old man with particular preferences, that's all. Look. I've written something down for you.'

He handed me a card with a dried flower pressed on to the front. Inside, in Alfred's handwriting were these words:

> *No one knows anything about the future, Jacinta. Not really. We think we do, but we don't. The few brave ones make a small space for themselves and for the ones they love; then they fill the space with treasures. I'm not talking about hoarding jewels or mansions or things like that. I'm talking about real treasures – the look a mother can give her child when she knows he's not who she thought he'd be and still she loves him; the snippet of sky a man sees from his small tenement window that tells him there is beauty in the world. I'm talking about treasures like friendship in the face of tragedy and kindness in the face of death. I'm talking about things – gestures – that stay with you and give you peace. It's those you keep in your chest of drawers. You keep them hidden and take them out in times of need. And these*

are the treasures that help you get through life. Because
sometimes life is hell on earth. It can chew you up so
badly that the only thing left of you is a hungry mouth
and empty hands. It can make you feel worthless. And
that's a terrible feeling. Don't let anyone, not anyone,
make you feel that way. You are an extraordinary
woman. If anyone tells you you're not, spit in their eye!

I love you, Cinta. You are the child I always wanted,
and the best friend I have. May you be blessed forever.
And may you live wisely and generously and be a credit
to your sainted father and your beloved mother. May
people see in you that racial differences can be
reconciled into beauty, and that black and white are not
opposites but complementary shades of the same spirit.

> *Love always,*
> *Alfred*

'Thank you,' I said, embracing his thin body. And then I couldn't speak, so Alfred covered for me.

'Fair enough. And now, for the gift,' he said.

He stood up and walked over to the bedsettee. He pulled it out gently and reached down behind it. The package he pulled out was small. Wrapped in silver paper with a large white bow, it was obvious he'd wrapped it himself.

'Alfred! You didn't need to get us anything. You know that.'

'Of course I did. It's your wedding day! You'll only have one, I hope. Besides, it's for you, not him. You know what I mean.'

He handed me the package and I undid the bow. The paper was hard to unwrap. Alfred said he'd used half a roll of tape because the paper refused to behave itself.

Inside was a box. Inside the box was another box on top of which was a note. It read:

When we're apart, you'll have my heart.

'Alfred, this is lovely! Your handwriting is beautiful!'

'It took me forty-five minutes to get it right. You know how bad my handwriting usually is. Even I can't read it.'

'It's lovely.'

'Go on. Open it.'

I carefully opened the lid. On a tiny white satin cushion lay a gold key.

'My God, Alfred! This is real gold, isn't it?'

'Eighteen carat. Nothing but the best for you. Well? Do you understand the symbolism? It's the key. The key to my heart, Jacinta. One of the treasures for your chest of drawers. Whenever you're lonely or sad, take it out and hold it to your heart. I've held it to mine for a long time so my love is . . . fused . . . fused to it now. Then I can be there for you even when I'm not. Do you understand? Don't cry. I'll look after your mother. Don't cry.'

'Who'll look after you?'

'She will.'

'You're such a twit, Alfred. But I thank you from the bottom of my heart for the gift and for the card. I'll never get anything more precious than this.'

We tied the key on a blue ribbon and I wore it round my neck – something new, something blue. My mother had given me a tiny photograph of my father as a boy with his parents. I wore that up my sleeve – that was the something old. Something borrowed were the pearls Vera Butcher let me wear. Her husband had given her those on her wedding day some forty years before, the day after some major World War II victory. The pearls had an antique sheen to them. They put me in mind of the depths of the sea.

There weren't many people at our wedding. Probably thirty, forty tops. When I entered with Alfred I was taken aback by the empty pews. Surely I have more friends than this, I thought. Why didn't I invite them? The answer upset me: I didn't have many friends. I shoved the realization into the background. Who needed friends when I had Manny? But then I banished those regrets because Manny had no one at the wedding at all. Later I learned he hadn't even told his family he was getting married. He stood there at the altar alone. No best man. No mother or father. Vera Butcher and my mother took him under their wing. They claimed him as their own and made a point of telling him how handsome he looked. Even Alfred must have felt sorry for him. He placed Manny's hand in mine when we reached the altar and squeezed our hands together to stop Manny's trembling.

Things speeded up after that. Manny took me, Jacinta Louise Buttercup Moses, to be his lawful wedded wife. I took Emmanuel Robert Fox III to be my lawful wedded husband. We signed the register, we sang hymns, and I received communion with those guests who were Catholic and a few who weren't who didn't know any better. Hubert sounded off about cupcakies until Vera had to remove him from the church. She boxed her middle-aged son's ears on the way out, and the slap resounded round the church just as Father Moth blessed us and wished us peace.

When we turned round to walk down the aisle, I noticed that my mother wasn't crying. Brides' mothers are supposed to cry. I wanted to ask her why she wasn't, but then I caught sight of Alfred. He had a huge polka-dot handkerchief scrunched up to his nose and his shoulders were heaving. The people in the rows behind him were laughing. He'd been complaining about gas for several weeks, ever since we'd finalized the date of the wedding. As he tried to stifle his tears, he went off like a small firework. The children sitting behind him covered their noses. I tried to restore order. This was my wedding; I was married now to the man of my dreams. Look at me! I've done it! I've found the one I was looking for! But it was too late. Even my mother was beginning to titter. I shoved my train back with my left foot, fervently wishing I'd had the sense to include bridesmaids. But who would I have chosen? I never saw the girls from school anymore; I didn't like them much anyway. Alison was dead and the women at college hadn't impressed me. I looked down. All over the train were footprints. It was easy to tell whose feet they were. When I got home, I'd kill Alfred.

The reception was subdued. Apart from Hubert Butcher, who brought his single roller skate into the house in an attempt to freewheel it down the stairs, everyone else adopted a British reserve. My mother wore her funereal face – which meant that she sucked her cheeks in as though she had lemon peel in her mouth and tried to smile. I overheard Ruskin asking her if she had constipation.

We hadn't seen Ruskin Garland for a while. He said he'd been busy with the latest book on Mayan archaeological findings. He said he liked the wedding and the 'boy' I'd married. Manny got on well with Ruskin. They spent much of the reception huddled together in a corner talking about Africa. I came upon them in mid-conversation trying to decide whether African or Western art was more nihilistic. Ruskin said African art deified nihilism. Manny said it was Western art that had made a fetish of negativity. I found the whole conversation unsuitable for a wedding reception. Manny patted my bottom when I came up to greet them. Ruskin said he was a lucky man to be able to take such liberties with a woman like me. I glared at the old man so hard that he began to stutter. When I left them, they'd returned to their argument.

I went upstairs to the kitchen in the sky and plopped down in the rocking chair we'd bought so that the place would look charming. It wasn't really a kitchen now that we had the Beadycap rooms too, but we'd kept the sink in there and the stove and tried to give it a festive air. Bedsits were all the rage, and I'd tried to persuade Louise to turn the whole room into an attic bed-sitting room for me. But she steadfastly refused, saying there'd be no beds in her kitchen. I backed off; there was a small part of me that was still fearful of her temper. So we left it pretty much as it had been when it was first built over a hundred years before. People at the reception liked it; they called it 'quaint.' Things were quaint when you didn't live in them. Quaint went down the tubes when it had to be endured on a daily basis.

I tore off my veil and flung it on the floor. This wasn't what I'd hoped it would be. I hadn't orchestrated it correctly. In the back of my mind a voice said, 'It'll be better next time.' I was shocked. There wouldn't be a next time. This was it. I was married now. A sacred vow. No going back.

I went to the window and looked down over the back. The line extending down via pulleys into the back garden was empty. For weeks it had been heavy with curtains and tablecloths. But

now the festivities were almost over. The frantic wash was done.
The minuscule garden was flanked by other people's tiny plots.
The concrete air-raid shelter was still intact. It ruined the efforts
Louise and Alfred had made to prettify the view. Louise had
bought two dozen potted plants – some from her headmaster,
who'd told her he'd let her have them at a discount. She stuck
them in the ground, not bothering to check to see whether they'd
endure outdoors. Some of them wilted that afternoon. Our neighbors, in typical British fashion, had walled themselves off from
each other. KEEP OUT! said the walls and fences and privet
hedges. Strange to think that there was so little beauty in this city
that people were migrating to Battersea in hordes.

'What would your father say?'

It was Louise. She'd come into the room without my noticing.

'O, Cinta! What would your father say about you? Pretty as a
picture standing there by the window all grown up.'

I shrugged.

'What are you doing up here, anyway?'

'It was hot down there, and the silly veil was getting on my
nerves. I'll go down and change.'

She stopped me at the door.

'You are happy, aren't you?' she said, her hand on my arm,
her tone full of concern.

'Of course!'

It was what she wanted to hear – the only thing she would
accept. She sank back into platitudes.

'He's such a nice boy, isn't he?'

'He's great. And he's a man. He's nearly thirty, you know.'

'It's such a shame his family couldn't be here.'

'Too expensive.'

'You are happy, Cinta, aren't you?'

'Of course.'

She let go of my arm and moved over to the chair. She sat
down heavily and kicked off her shoes.

'I remember when your father and I got married. Auntie paid
for the wedding. It cost two pounds altogether. I wore one of her
old dresses. I jazzed it up with flowers and a pretty belt. I borrowed a hat from my friend Cynthia Huggett, and I bought a pair

of shoes for two and sixpence from Woolworth's. Your father said I looked like an angel.' She giggled like a girl. (Manny hadn't said anything about my gown. He was downstairs talking about nihilism with the dirty old man who'd tried to molest me.) 'We had bacon sandwiches. I wanted a nice bit of back bacon but your great-aunt Jessie said streaky was fine for a wedding. No need to make a fuss. So we had streaky. Your father said the sandwiches were the best he'd ever tasted. Someone brought a bottle of champagne with them. We shared it out between twelve guests. That was a good bottle of champagne. I never thought I'd see my own daughter having such a fancy wedding. Yet here we are. You know what your father would say? He'd say "Swap me for a piece of cheese!" because he always said that if he was shocked by something.'

'So you've told me. About a million times.'

'What is the matter with you?'

'Nothing. Look, I need to go downstairs and check on people.'

'Most people have left. Ruskin, Alfred, of course, Vera, and a few others are still here, but most of them have gone.'

'Great. We didn't throw the bouquet or the garter.'

'Shall I get them?'

'Mum, what is the *point*? Everyone's gone. Who'll catch the garter? Hubert? Alfred? Give me a break.'

'All right, young lady, why don't you tell me what's bothering you?'

'Okay. You want to know what's bothering me? I'll tell you, then. I'll go ahead and tell you.' And I almost did. I almost stood there and told her I had a terrible feeling in the pit of my stomach, just like Alfred did. I almost told her that I'd married the American downstairs to escape the terror of a racist island filled with Beadycaps and squalor. I almost told her that she was the one to blame for whatever I did next. Her insanity had left me with a big hole in my chest and someone had to fill it. Someone who would take me far away and make me forget what it was like to be me. But behind me the filled-in hole in the wall announced itself, reminding me of how far we had come. The woman in front of me needed to believe it had turned out all right in the end. If she wanted to believe that, I should let her.

What right did I have to take her single dream away? Alfred's voice in my head, the best conscience I knew, told me I had no right.

I decided to blurt out the first thing that occurred to me.

'I suppose I'm just a bit upset that no one seems to give a damn that I probably won't ever set foot on this stinking island again. You seem to be quite happy to be rid of me and –'

'Jacinta, sometimes, my girl, you're an absolute fool. It's about time you grew up. The moon doesn't follow you, Jacinta Moses. You have a lot to be thankful for – much more than most. You have a husband who loves you, a wonderful degree from one of the best universities, your health, what else do you want?'

I looked over at her. 'I'd like a guarantee,' I said.

'A what?'

'A guarantee.'

'Of what?'

'Of fidelity. Of health and happiness. A warranty that would let me return him if it didn't work out.'

'Well, my lady, there's no such thing, so you'd better get that notion out of your head. It'll work if you make it work. It's up to the woman to see that the home is a happy one. I always had a nice dinner ready for your father when he –'

'What about the man? What is *he* supposed to do?'

'If you're lucky, Manny will be a good father and a kind husband. He won't do much around the house. In spite of all this women's lib nonsense, men are much the same. They do as they please because they can. They don't bear the children or cook the meals. Even your father wasn't much good around the house. That was my job. But he loved us both with all his heart. You can't ask for any more than that.'

'Yes I can, Mum. I'm not putting up with that male rubbish. I'm not. You can suck on that lemon if you like, but it won't change a thing. Times have changed. Women don't put up with that kind of treatment anymore. We'll both work at this marriage; we'll both do the housework. Manny's nothing like the men you describe. He keeps his own place spotless; he'll do the same thing now that we're married. We'll share the housework and the child rearing. And if we don't . . . Well, we're married and that's that, but I tell you, there will be hell to pay!'

'We'll see, young lady. In a few years with a few toddlers round your ankles, you'll be singing a different tune.'

There was bitterness in her voice. It struck me for the first time that perhaps marital bliss had been more elusive for her than I'd been led to believe.

'Would you and Daddy still be married?'

It had slipped out. I hadn't meant to say it aloud.

Instead of pouncing, my mother looked out of the window and sighed.

'Who knows?' she said. 'Simon Moses was the most wonderful man I've ever met. But people change. And emotions . . . emotions change too. Don't expect too much from life, Cinta. It will crush you if you hope for too much.'

'I'm going to hope for whatever I want. People have to have dreams. They have to.'

She shrugged. The conversation was ended. That was all she had to tell me. On the way out, she started up again.

'And do you know that Mr. Pod is thinking of making all the teachers do double lunch duty. Can you believe it? I told him it would be over my dead body. The man's positively evil . . .'

Ruskin drove us to the train station. It was slow going because Ruskin's reactions weren't what they used to be, and so he drove like a snail to compensate for errors. Manny talked to him about digs the whole way there. By the time Ruskin let us out at Victoria, I was ready to burst. I didn't speak to Manny all the way to Dover. On the ferry, he realized something was up. By the time we got to Calais, though, he'd made me laugh. When we pulled into the Gare du Nord in Paris, he'd made me forget all about our sad little wedding – something about him during the early days took all the pain away and made things whole. When Manny was in the mood, he could make me believe that life with him could be a storybook. America rang in my head like a song of celebration. We'd be going there soon. Back to Virginia. Back to where he lived. I'd meet his family; we'd study writing together at the university. We'd be happy. Just the two of us.

That night in the hotel room not far from the Sacré-Coeur, we made love. It was like making love to an idea. Manny wasn't the man on top of me; he was more like a projection of something we both wanted. He'd rest for an hour or two and then he'd start again. And I'd let him because I'd never been caressed in that way before. Sometimes it seemed to me that he didn't really want to do it – he was compelled, addicted. He couldn't help himself. Sometimes he seemed to have found in me all the keys he'd been searching for; at other times, he couldn't even find the door.

The white sheets became damp with sweat in the heat of the summer night. My breasts were sore and between my legs was a burning sensation, but still we made love. He called me by my names; he nibbled my ears and stroked my thighs. He said I was all women at once. He carried me to the bathroom and told me to step into the bathtub. He filled the tub with water and washed me with a special perfumed soap he'd packed in his suitcase. He rubbed and rubbed until the soap-suds turned to cream in his palms, and the water clouded up to opaqueness. He poured wine into plastic cups and we drank until I was dizzy with it. The warm water lapped me up. I dissolved into it like bath crystals and opened myself wide to his hands. At one point, I opened my eyes to find him looking at his hands, an expression of what amounted to anger on his face. When I asked him what was wrong, he smiled, but only with his mouth. He took his glass of wine and poured it into the bath. The water turned a pale red. 'You're bleeding,' he said. He bent down to taste me.

'This is your body.' He ran his finger from my neck down to my navel.

'This is your blood.' He scooped up the rosy water and poured it over my head in a kind of baptism.

Then his hands were everywhere. My body gathered itself up to a crescendo. I was ringing with the feel of him. I didn't know where he began and where I ended. We were one note sounding out into the dark.

Later he helped me out of the bath and patted me dry. His gentleness reminded me of my father; he'd dried me off after a bath once. I could only have been three or four. I had a rash.

Louise and Simon soaked me in a tin tub we kept behind the curtain under the sink. They'd made a fuss of me late at night, and my father had dried me off while my mother made me some cocoa. I relaxed into contentment as the soft towel turned the palest pink. 'I love you, Emmanuel Fox III,' I murmured, and it was the truth.

'I know,' he said.

We went back to bed and listened to the faint sounds of the night-time. I had no desire left. Everything was appeased. Manny fell into a deep sleep. Once he called out: 'No! Help me, Jesus!' I held him tighter until he was quiet again. Who was the man who had taken me to the other side of my body and left me there? I hardly knew him. He could be anybody. I had given myself over to him without saving a part of me for later. No going back now, even if I wanted to.

No one had ever made me feel the way Manny did. At the intersection between passion, hope, fear, and pain, he'd emptied me out like a cup. There was nothing between me and consciousness. The outline of my body had been taken up by shadow. I merged into him and into the night. I didn't know whether I was blissful or terrified. Whatever this man had, he was going to give it to me. I didn't know whether courage or foolishness had led me to him. I did know I'd fallen in love on the first night of our honeymoon in Paris. At some time, that love would cost me. Alfred was right. In the perfumed hotel room in France, I knew he had been right to be wary, yet I had to know what drove this man to frenzy. I had to find out what it was so that it could always be me who satiated him.

Manny woke up with a start and began to fondle me again. When I said no, he covered my mouth with kisses and made me forget the objections I'd had. I kept thinking there was something I was forgetting – a clue of some kind. But then his will became mine, and there was nothing left to do but relinquish my hold on who I was and give my names over for Manny to claim them.

At nine A.M. there was a knock on the door followed by footsteps. A maid dressed in a black skirt and blouse stood at the end of our bed. She must have been close to my age. Manny and

I were uncovered. His leg was clamped over mine and his pretty blond hair was damp to the touch. My skin looked even darker against the whiteness of his arm. He was sleeping again – breathing softly into my ear. The nightmares were over. He was finally satisfied. The woman at the end of the bed stared down at us. She ran her eyes over each part of our bodies and smiled. Then she said something in French about black and white. Then she smiled again. She placed new towels at our feet and left us. For all I knew, I could have dreamed it.

The next night was a repeat of the night before. For three nights in a row, Manny fought with me as if he were on fire. Sandwiched in between those nights were oddly innocent days of museum visits and church tours. Paris became a blur. It existed on the hems of our bodies. It was far less real than we were. Paris was the negative space in the background of our passion. It only existed because we allowed it to. No one mattered but we two. The night opened up around our play like curtains. Each morning while we were still in bed, the maid came to look at us. I didn't wake Manny up. I liked her there at the foot of the bed with the warm towels in her hand. Sometimes I fancied she was Death come to claim us. Had I died then, I would have been happy to let go of the world – not because I didn't love it, but because, finally, it had given me all I wanted.

On our last morning, I tried to ask her, softly so that Manny wouldn't hear us, whether she was real. But my French was terrible, and I must have said something funny because she began to giggle. Then she chatted away in French, softly interrupting herself with laughter. I laughed too, and Manny turned over and began to wake up. When I turned back to the foot of the bed, she'd left.

'She's gone,' I said.

'Who?' Manny asked, yawning.

'The woman in black.'

'Mmm,' he mumbled, and went back to sleep.

I tried to remember what she'd said. My convent schoolgirl French was terrible. Something about men. Something about angels. Was she saying Manny was an angel? He was beautiful

enough to be one. Is that what she'd meant? She'd said something about black and white too, just as she had before. And I
could have sworn she talked about children – though the word
I kept coming up with in translation was 'woman' or 'lady' or
something. How could a baby be a woman? Did she mean girl?
Perhaps Manny and I would make an angel child – a girl. With
blond hair and dark skin. A face that featured Louise and
Manny and Simon and me. I reached over and stroked Manny's
cheek. He woke up smiling. He took my thumb and put it in his
mouth. We'd both found Beauty. We would never let it go.

3

A short time after we returned from Paris, we were at Gatwick Airport, ready to board a plane for America. I'd flown only once before – the second time I went to Europe. My heart fluttered in my chest, and I kept opening and closing hand luggage to check to see that we had all the things we'd need if our bags were forever lost.

Louise, Alfred, and Ruskin all came to see us off. Luckily, we'd been able to take the train to Gatwick so we didn't have to endure Ruskin's driving. We said we had too much luggage for his car. He seemed relieved.

Manny was in a bad mood. His brows hung over his eyes like a cloud, and he stuffed his hands in his pockets like a man trying to hold himself back from killing something.

My mother kept telling me to be good. I told her I had no intention of being good and winked at Manny. Manny pretended he hadn't seen it. Alfred had bought five different sets of notelets so that I would write to him. He asked me every ten minutes whether or not I'd packed them all. Ruskin was barely there. The journey had been rough for him. He held on to my mother's arm and leaned into her with age. Spider veins clustered round his nose and cheeks; the remnants of his hair fluttered like wisps of smoke even inside the airport. There must have been a moment when Ruskin Garland finally relinquished any claims to being a dashing, middle-aged warlock to stand forever in the company of selfish old men. Perhaps it had passed by unnoticed; or perhaps he knew it every morning when he looked in the mirror and saw what had become of him. It occurred to me that I would never see Ruskin again. I wondered how it felt being old. It was a brief thought. Old age couldn't touch Manny and me. Not for a long time.

I was in a hurry to leave; Alfred was desperate to keep me there.

'You could still change to another plane, you know,' he said. 'It's not too late. You could fly tomorrow. The thirteenth isn't the best day to take to the sky, you know. Did you hear about that awful crash in Siberia?'

My mother told him to be quiet. He gulped back his words and looked down at the floor. The top of his head was huge – a giant baby head. I took his hand.

'You know I love you, don't you, Alfred? And you know you've been a father to me since Daddy died, don't you? Our house is your house, okay? Even when we're miles from here it will be the same. You and me. I have the gold key now, remember.'

My mother held us both for a long time.

'Be good to each other,' she said, which was a distinct improvement over imploring me to behave.

'Jacinta, don't forget to . . .' She stopped in mid-sentence. 'O dear. I've forgotten what it is you're supposed to remember.'

We all laughed except for Manny, who had moved off already and was gesturing to me to follow.

Ruskin had brought a camera. 'One last photo,' he said.

So we all stood there together and had our picture taken by a kind Japanese man who happened to be passing by.

Then it was time to leave.

After I passed through security, I looked back at the three of them. My mother was in the middle, Alfred was waving his polka-dot handkerchief, and Ruskin had lifted his cane into the air and was in danger of knocking himself out with it. My mother blew me a kiss. I pretended it hit me on the head and almost knocked me over. Manny called to me to hurry up, for

God's sake. So I picked up my hand luggage with the five sets of
notelets in it from Alfred and walked away from England and
everything I'd known for twenty-five years.

We sat in row twenty-three, seats A and B. I sat by the
window. Manny said he didn't want to look at London. It's one
of the ugliest cities in the world, he said. Thank God we're leaving. Though it was the kind of thing I would have said, it didn't
sound good coming from him. I opened my mouth to defend it,
looked at the solidity of his expression, and closed it again. The
engines on the jumbo jet began to churn; the huge machine
began to move. I must have squealed with delight, but Manny
told me to be quiet.

It began to rain outside. Drizzle at first, then a heavy down-
pour.

'Can we still take off?' I asked.

'Sure.'

'Won't it be too slippery?'

'What? In the air? I don't think so.' His voice was mocking. I
decided not to speak to him at all until he could be civil.

I put my nose up against the window to try to see into the airport itself. My mother had said she'd stay there until the plane
took off. I thought I caught sight of a polka-dotted handkerchief
once; but then the rain washed the image away, and we'd trun-
dled on to another part of the runway by the time it eased up a
little.

Taking off terrified me.

I sat back in my economy class seat and felt my back boring
a hole into the fabric. Up, up, up. A steep incline up a hill that
wasn't there. I was in the belly of a winged whale. I'd never
been good at science. As far as I was concerned, there was no
logical explanation for what was happening. I gripped the arms
of the chair and accidentally pressed the button that reclined
the seat. I screamed as my head jerked back.

'What are you doing? Look, we had two hours of sleep last
night by the time Alfred had finished with his damn stories,' he
said, helping me straighten the seat.

'I like Alfred's stories.'

'Maybe they're okay, but not at three in the morning when

you've heard them all before and you have a plane to catch in the morning. I need to get some sleep, okay?'

'Sorry. Manny?'

'What now?'

'Aren't you just a bit sad to be leaving? I mean, won't you miss anyone in England? You've lived here for two years. Won't it make you sad never to see them again?'

'I guess.'

Soon after that he was fast asleep. I didn't wake him when they came around with a snack. I just ate his too. I used his stereo headset and mine so that I could check on some of the music channels while listening to the movie. I got wine and spirits with my lunch and, once again, ate Manny's because he was still snoring and I didn't like him very much at the time.

When he woke up, we still had an hour and a half of flight time left.

'That felt good,' he said, yawning all over everyone. 'Where's the food?'

'I ate it.'

'What the hell for?'

'I was hungry. Glad you're awake. I need to pee. 'Scuse me.'

He didn't speak to me again until we reached Washington, D.C. But I didn't care. I was landing in America. I'd been given a chance to start all over. I'd never have to see South London again if I didn't want to. I'd flown away.

I turned to Manny as the wheels hit the runway.

'Yippee!' I said. 'We made it!'

'Look, did you bring any money? We've got time for lunch in D.C. before the next flight.'

'I thought you had the travelers' checks.'

'Yeah, but we need to hold on to those. Money's going to be real tight for a while. Grad assistants don't get much, you know.'

I handed him a twenty-dollar bill. My mother had given me several hundred pounds from her savings. I'd changed some of it into American dollars last week.

He didn't thank me. What was mine was his. He stuffed it into his pocket.

We went through customs, ate in D.C., and passed the time looking at all the people in the airport.

'I'm in D.C.! I'm in D.C.!' I cried.

Manny warmed up to my excitement. He squeezed my elbow and told me I was the best thing to hit America since pizza.

The next plane we boarded was the size of a poor woman's bank account. It bounced up and down on the air currents and made Manny feel sick. I spent the time watching out for flocks of birds in case they got stuck in the propellers. I would shout out 'Flock ahoy' if I saw any approaching. (The pilot would certainly hear me as what separated the twelve passengers from the cockpit was eighteen inches and a shower curtain.) In spite of my fear, I was excited. I was flying over the New World with my new husband! My story would not be the same as my mother's. I had escaped.

Mrs. Fox was there to meet us at the airport. His parents were divorced. He wouldn't say much about his father, and I didn't pursue it. I had felt abandoned by parents too, and there was nothing more devastating. Mrs. Fox was friendly enough, though she was quiet, and she seemed to be somewhat afraid of her son. She did everything to please him, including carrying one of his heavy bags. She invited me to call her 'Mom,' but it seemed like a betrayal to do so, so I tried to avoid calling her by name at all. She didn't live in the college town where we'd be living, but she'd made the two-hundred-mile drive up from southwest Virginia because Manny had told her to find us an apartment. She'd found one three blocks from the university, she said. When Manny seemed pleased, she brightened up considerably. Lydia Fox's chatter was nervous, and her eyes were fixed on Manny's face when he wasn't looking and averted from him when he glanced over at her. Like Manny, she didn't talk about his father. As for the racial difference between us, she told us that if Manny loved me, that was all that mattered. But her tone when she said it was mournful, and I got the sense that she would have preferred a pale English rose to the African wildflower she'd gotten. I didn't much care. Manny and I would make a world of our own. What happened outside it would not affect us.

The distractions in America soon made me forget about
Lydia's misgivings. The next few weeks came and went too fast.
I was interested in everything. I wanted to travel around the
U.S., I wanted to learn to drive. I wanted to watch every movie
on at the mall; I wanted to eat tacos and burgers, ice cream and
pizzas. I gained twelve pounds. After we made love one night,
Manny told me I was getting fat. '*You're* getting bloody rude,' I
said, turned over, and didn't let him see that I was crying. The
following day, I began dieting.

I'd never seen anything like America before. For a claustro-
phobic like myself, it was heaven. I couldn't believe how much
space there was to roam around in: houses had dozens, sometimes hundreds of feet between them; rooms even in apartments
allowed for generous pathways between furniture; cars were
able to do U-turns, and parallel parking was the exception rather
than the rule; trees edged the skylines and the skylines ran for
miles uninterrupted by buildings. I could see the moon! At
night I'd go out on to the balcony and watch it come up. I hadn't
known it could vary as much as it did, nor that it could deter-
mine someone's mood. Mine changed whenever the moon was
full. Manny said I was imagining things, that the moon's influence on women was a myth. In his dismissal of the
supernatural, he reminded me of Theseus in *A Midsummer
Night's Dream*. When I told him that, he mumbled something
about me and Bottom. When the moon appeared as a pale
lemon-yellow plate, and when shadow pools gathered in its
face, or puddles of light etched a pattern across a disk of lumi-
nescent white, I knew that Beauty could be purchased cheaply
in America, for it was everywhere. Parks were not ten or twelve
acres, they were two thousand or more. National forests were
the size of small countries! I tacked a map of the United States
to our bedroom wall and stuck flags in all the national parks. I
told Manny we'd visit every one. He said it would take us centuries to do that. I told him we'd choose the biggest and work
down from there. The university was huge too, and it made me
laugh when students complained about being overcrowded.
Americans were spoiled. They took everything for granted. I
wrote poems about their selfishness and showed them to the

few students we met before classes began. They accepted the criticism with such good grace that I was taken aback. Much less sensitive than the British people I'd grown up with, the young Americans I met were confident enough to delight in occasional castigation. I began to think that perhaps Americans were not as bad as Manny made out. Some of them expressed a desire for all things alien. They adopted me as proof positive of their lack of prejudice. They spoke in eulogies about Martin Luther King and Rosa Parks. They wrote about their travels to India and mocked the middle-class homes that had produced them. When they heard about my father, they tried to find copies of his work. They called him a master of deliberate naiveté. They complimented the rhythm in his sentences. I told them he was a great dancer too and that he munched daily on watermelons and fried chicken. 'You're a riot,' they said.

Manny didn't like Americans even though he was one. He said they were vulgar. He said he was an American by accident of birth, not by inclination. He claimed to have an African spirit. 'We'll go back there after we finish up here. You'll love it.'

'But I only just got to the United States. There's so much to see.'

'Don't you want to learn about your heritage?'

'Yes, of course. But –'

'Don't worry. You'll love Africa. I promise.'

'I know. I know I will, Manny. I've always wanted to see where my father grew up. But I'm excited about this country too. About your country. About writing. We're going to learn how to write in this MFA program. Aren't you excited about that?'

'You poor, deluded girl,' he said, stroking my cheek. 'No one can teach anyone how to write. You're either born with it or you're not. Most of the guys in this program can't write themselves out of a paper bag.'

'What are we doing here, then?'

'Playing the system for all it's worth. Networking. Making the right contacts. After I've been introduced to editors and agents, we'll be free to go back to Africa and be ourselves.'

'What about me? Won't I meet them too?'

'O yeah. Sure, honey. But it's different with poets. Not likely you'll be making much writing sonnets. Fiction's where the money is. But don't worry. I'll be generous. When they turn my novels into movies, I'll take you anywhere you want to go. You can see this whole damn country, if you want. We'll pile the bambinos into the station wagon, and head out West.' Manny never expected me to take the program seriously. It was true – I'd applied on a whim, just because he was going there. I knew nothing about MFA programs or what it would mean to the rest of my life if I took writing seriously. I knew nothing.

When Manny made comments I found disturbing, I convinced myself he was being ironic. I had to be right about Manny because it was too late to be wrong.

We enrolled in the MFA program so that my husband could network. I didn't understand exactly what networking meant, but Manny said it was what America was all about: self-promotion. I caught on quickly. It was easy. I watched Manny and copied him. He was very pleased with me. We had quite a routine going. When Manny was asked by other students how much he'd published, he'd say, 'A little. Here and there, you know. Nothing big.' Nobody asked him to be more specific; they were intimidated by him. He'd read everything and wasn't shy about letting you know it. Even though he was small in stature, tall men backed away from him and gave him room, as if the very breadth of his knowledge required breathing space. I didn't say anything about publishing because I hadn't published a darn thing. Manny advised me that there was no need to mention my old manuscript and how often it had been rejected. 'Let's keep that little morsel under wraps,' he said. I wrote sonnets again and strange little allegories in rhyming quatrains and fourteeners. The professors we met with during orientation said they'd been delighted by my application. They seemed to think I was charmingly eccentric. No one paid that much attention to me until I began speaking about Africa, then they all listened intently, knowing that, as writers, they were supposed to appreciate the divinity of the primitive. I didn't mention the fact that I'd never set foot on the continent; Manny hinted that it wouldn't be in my best interests to admit it. When they asked me about Africa, I implied that I had been very young when we left. They seemed satisfied. Lying began to come easily. Manny said that as long as the lies weren't whoppers, they were a good way for writers to stretch their imaginations. I didn't think Alfred would agree, but his voice was waning in my conscience. Manny's was taking over.

The night before Mrs. Fox left for the tiny southwest Virginia town where Manny was raised, she cooked a pot roast. I'd never had an American pot roast before, and I wanted to sample one. All three of us were sick of being cramped up together in the tiny apartment for the summer. I don't know why she stayed for so long. She often seemed listless, and Manny made her jump whenever he spoke. Money was tight and feeding three was hard. Manny assured me he didn't have a penny to his name; and Mrs. Fox had taken an unpaid vacation from her secretarial position to 'help us move,' so it fell upon me to use my mother's savings until we began as GTAs at the end of August. In fact, I'd been surprised by Manny's circumstances. I had assumed he was fairly wealthy and that's how he'd had the money to study in England; but it turned out that a scholarship had afforded him the opportunity to go abroad. His family fortune was as small as my own. But I wasn't resentful about it. In this country, if you worked hard, and had a little luck, you would be successful. We would be wealthy soon enough. Manny told me he'd give me the moon when his writing took off. I would give myself the moon too, I thought. Two moons for the Jacinta-in-the-Story. Not bad.

After we'd eaten the pot roast, Manny told stories about Africa. He was his old self – the man I'd fallen in love with in Paris. The man with the dreams as large as my own. He was very relaxed, very much in control. He reminded me of Simon, although he didn't try to make a pattern out of anything he'd seen the way my father had. Manny's gift was journalistic; he could make you see details as though you were watching a documentary on the BBC. We saw the bread men carrying their loaves of bread in huge wooden trays on their heads; the kerosene boys in their tattered clothes singing out their poignant call to the evening – 'Kerosene! Ten cent for de pint, kerosene!'

We saw the 'gara' fabric worn by the dark-skinned women, the poda-poda vans that carried passengers along roads alive with potholes. We saw Manny in the light of the kerosene lamp as a young Peace Corps volunteer from a town near Martinsville. We heard about his bucket shower, the ant-infested outhouse, the snakes, the banana trees, the rice field, and the invasion of a horde of rats.

When Manny spoke about Africa, there was something in his tone that said it could all be so much better if only the guys over there would get their acts together. He talked about going back to 'fix things.' I wanted to go too. Not to fix anything. Just to see this land that had been in my father's bones and that was lighting up my husband's eyes.

'There's so little perfect beauty there,' he said. 'I mean, it's gorgeous, don't get me wrong. But it's full of contradictions. One minute you think you're in paradise, the next you're sure you're in hell. Lithe, beautiful women, magnificent landscapes, all flanked by squalor, leprosy, cholera. You don't have time to filter any of it. You can't. If you try doing that you go mad. The smart thing is to immerse yourself in it – forget about your own criteria for beauty and just let Africa exist in her own right. . . .'

Even in the light cast by the ugly yellow lamp we'd picked up the day before at my first yard sale, I thought he looked beautiful sprawled out on the green vinyl sofa that had come with the apartment – too beautiful, in fact, to disagree with. So I kept my thoughts to myself and listened to Manny's version of Africa that was so different from my father's.

I caught myself wondering about the kind of children we'd have. How could they not be beautiful, looking at Manny's exquisite features? I felt the ache rise in me – the ache to make replicas of us and watch them grow. I wanted to make amends for my own childhood, to raise a child who would shine in the certainty of her own beauty. A nagging sense that there wasn't much time told me that we had to move fast if we were to keep up with our dreams and make our future perfect. If I had a child, I would never be lonely again. Even if Manny turned away from me, the child would be there, loving me the way I'd yearned to be loved by Louise. Manny made it clear he didn't want children yet, but I knew he'd love them once they came along. You saw that all the time. Early on in our marriage, I began to think of ways to catch him by surprise before he could remind me about my diaphragm.

I was planning a strategy as Manny finished his narrative and stood up. Our audience with him was over.

'The page awaits,' he said.

I was dismayed. 'You're not writing tonight, are you? It's your mother's last night, for God's sake! I thought we could go out for a walk, or get some ice cream or something.'

Manny's mother stood up quickly and ran her nervous hands up and down the apron she was wearing. She was real content, *real* content, she said, just to spend time with me that evening. She suggested we do the dishes while Manny wrote.

'Writers work on a different schedule than the rest of us,' she said. When I reminded her that I was hoping to be a writer too, she pretended not to hear me.

I did the dishes because it was her last night, and I didn't want to argue with anyone. We couldn't drive anywhere because Manny had only found time to give me two driving lessons so far, and Lydia never drove 'after the sun had set in the west.' I'd asked her once what happened if it set in the east. She'd blinked a few times and then changed the subject.

We sat down to play cards after we'd finished the dishes, but the furnished apartment had a dismal atmosphere, and Manny's typing grated on my nerves. My father had typed well into the night, and the tapping had acted as a lullaby. Now, however, it didn't soothe me at all.

'Let's go for a walk,' I said to Manny's mother. Obediently, she put on her walking shoes and we stepped out into the evening.

Something about the Virginia summer night cheered me. We walked down to the north end of the campus. It was still hot – close to eighty degrees. I felt warm in my T-shirt. Mrs. Fox, in her hose and heavy walking shoes, must have been very uncomfortable, but she didn't complain. I felt as though I were taking a pet for a walk. She stayed at my heels and waited for small favors.

'Let's sit here,' I said, taking pity on my mother-in-law, who would probably have walked ten miles if I'd made her.

I wanted to love my mother-in-law, but it wasn't going to happen. I'd grown up with Alfred and Louise. They saw the world the way poets do – at least Louise had before she'd found Mr. Pod and her classroom. Lydia, however, was an ordinary woman. At that time in my life, I didn't have patience with the ordinary; I failed to understand that the ordinary could yield something extraordinary if only you gave it some space in which to perform. Lydia's disdain for our way of life was clear, even though she never made it explicit. A slight incline of her head, a barely imperceptible furrowing of her brow, and I knew that she was infuriated by our behavior on Sunday morning. People went to church on Sunday; they didn't laze around in bed, or watch television shows. Lydia sighed when she sat down. She wiped her forehead with a Kleenex.

We sat on a bench under a tree. Ahead of us were some stately university classroom buildings and a high stone wall that enclosed one of the old gardens. The lawns were perfectly manicured and the late summer blooms punctuated the earth with color. I leaned back in the bench and closed my eyes. The first few months hadn't been easy, but soon Manny and I would be alone at last. We'd have time to live as a couple and get acquainted with each other. I couldn't wait for Lydia Fox to leave.

Lydia began speaking. Perhaps it was being away from her son that made her bold, or perhaps it was the calmness of the evening. She spoke like a woman who'd been wound up with a key, but not allowed to unwind until now. She spoke quickly and furtively, looking around to see whether we were being overheard.

'He's a genius,' she began, glancing over her shoulder. 'Like his father.' Another glance to the right. A handful of students, one or two professors strolled by. The students were laughing. Their American accents made me happy. In their pronunciation were the wide, bright spaces of their country. My country now.

'What's his father like? I mean, Manny never talks about –'

'From the beginning, that's the way he was. A genius, like his father. Always artistic. His father is too – *very* artistic. Thought he'd paint. We both did. Never without a paint box. Watercolors. Then there was that episode with Sophie and . . .' Mrs. Fox put a hand over her mouth. 'Slipped out,' she said. 'Don't tell him.'

'Don't tell him what?'

'About Sophie.'

'What about Sophie? Was she a girlfriend?'

Mrs. Fox began to giggle. It was the first time I'd seen her do that. Her face was suddenly girlish and I could see traces of her son's energy in its expression. I warmed to her. We were bonding at last. 'No,' she said, still giggling, 'Sophie was his pet.'

'So Manny had a dog?' I suggested.

'No. A fish.'

'A goldfish?' I was disappointed. I'd already pictured him leaping over the green Virginia fields with Lassie.

'Not exactly.' She seemed afraid.

'What then?'

'She wasn't a goldfish,' she said. 'O no. She was huge. Much bigger than that. A beautiful fish. I can't remember what those fish are called now, but she was big. Not one of those tiny fish. Big as your fist.' She made a fist. Even in the gathering dark, I could see the veins in her hand.

'What happened?' I asked, trying to stifle a yawn. It was the only cue she needed.

'I got back from work one day. Not long after his dad left us. We have a small house. Real small. Soon as I came in I could hear him. Swearing.'

'How old was he?'

'Ten. But he didn't act ten. He acted like a little man. Like he was all grown up. He came out of the womb like that. Childhood didn't interest him. Being a genius was hard, I guess. But I could hear him. Swearing and cussing up a storm. I peeked round the door and he was splayed out on the carpet with a pad and pencil and he was drawing like a child on fire.'

'Drawing?'

'Circles and swirls and fins and gills. Looking up at the tank and cussing at poor Sophie. He got up and jiggled the tank and

made the water swish like this.' She moved her hands to show
the effect of the water. 'I wanted to go in and stop him, but I
knew I couldn't. He's like his dad. He does what he pleases and
you don't cross him. He kept on drawing. And he'd bang on the
floor with his hand and stamp with his foot and say, "Sophie,
you damn fool! What is wrong with you?" But Sophie wasn't
the one drawing, was she? So it struck me that perhaps the boy
had a fever. But I bided my time and kept on peeking. And by
now he was pressing down hard on the paper and going right on
through to the carpet! And I didn't know what to do. His father
would have beat him. But I never did believe in beatings. So I
just kept on peeking and hoped for the best.

'Now you have to understand about that fish. It wasn't an
ordinary fish. No, ma'am. It was a special tropical fish. Real
expensive. Cost me most of the savings I'd put away for his
microscope. But he wanted it when he saw it in the pet store.
And there was no crossing him. If Manny took a liking to something, you got out of his way. And he loved that fish. Adored it.
Kissed the side of the tank each night before he got into bed.
Prayed for Sophie too. "Dear God, bless all those I love.
Especially my beloved Sophie." He made that up at nine years
old. Anyhow, he loved that big old fat fish. And so did I. She
wasn't green and she wasn't gold. She wasn't copper and she
wasn't red. It was like she was every color of the fall with a
shimmer added. And you'd look at her one large eye and see . . .
see . . . what things must have been like before we came along to
spoil everything. So I couldn't believe it when Manny stormed
over to the tank again and reached his hand in. She didn't want
to leave. Sophie knew what he was planning and she didn't
want to leave. You'll think I'm crazy, but I thought I heard her
scream. It was a wail. Soft and far away. Like one of the whale
songs you hear when you watch those underwater movies about
the sea and how we're destroying it. I froze. Manny's hand was
in the tank grabbing for Sophie. Water was sloshing over the
side onto the carpet. It sounded like the splat of vomit when she
landed on the floor. Splat. Then he had her in his hand and she
was still in her death throes. He watched her die. He stood there
and watched her die in his hand. Then he carried her back to his

place on the floor and laid her at the top of his drawing pad. "There," he said. "Now you'll be good and still."

'Then he began to draw her. Like nothing had happened. Like she'd always been as dead as a doorpost. And then I crept away. Because there's some things about your children you shouldn't know. And I'd seen them.'

I swallowed hard. I didn't know this woman. Maybe she was trying to frighten me – make me as pathetic as she was. Perhaps she was jealous of her son's love for me and was trying to turn me against him. She began to talk again.

'Forty minutes later he came out with this picture in his hand. It was Sophie and she looked just like herself. He showed it to me with pride. I pretended I hadn't seen a thing. "How did you get her to keep still?" I asked. "I killed her," he said, calm as you please.

'I asked him why.

'"She wouldn't keep still, Mom."

'I told him she was a fish. Fish don't know when their portraits are being drawn. He just shrugged and asked me to throw Sophie out. "She's getting stinky," he said.

'I flushed the poor old fish down the toilet. She left this trail of glitter gold round the bowl. Broke my heart. Then the toilet got plugged up and I had to call a plumber out. Cost me a fortune.'

We sat in silence for a while. I was angry. She shouldn't have told me that story. It was deliberately cruel. What did she want me to do with it, anyway? I was married to the man, for God's sake. She answered before I had a chance to ask the question.

'I told you because I want you to be careful.'

'How do you mean?'

'I want you to be careful,' she said again, whispering this time. 'He's dangerous.'

'O for goodness' sake! He was a child.'

'And now he's a man,' she said.

She stood up the way her son had earlier, indicating that my audience with her was over. I stood up too and we walked back to the house in silence. I thought about the fact that I'd married a man I barely knew. Don't let Manny be Maurice! I couldn't live with a man who was violent. But Manny wasn't like that. Joy lit up his face when he swung me around outside the museum. I was the treasure behind the door. I saw a side to Manny that Lydia could only guess at. What did she know, this ordinary woman from rural Virginia?

When we got home, Manny had his feet up in front of the television. A beer was in his hand.

He ran over to us and embraced us both.

'The muse was awake!' he exclaimed, laughing at himself. 'The story is finished.'

'May I read it?'

'Not yet, Jacinta. I need to rework a few things. Soon. Soon. How was your walk?'

'Fascinating,' I said. His mother blanched.

'Mom tell all kinds of stories on me, did she? Always does. Most aren't too flattering, are they, Mommy dearest?'

Mrs. Fox tried to laugh.

'I'll go on to bed,' I said. 'I'm tired.'

'It's too early. How about a game of cards? It's Mom's last night.'

We played cards until well past midnight. Manny was happy. He won almost every hand. I could see the boy in him as he slapped his thigh and laughed with his mouth wide open. If her story was true, it could still have a happy ending. I'd been lonely too as a child – lonely and desperate. Perhaps that's what brought us together. Manny's mother, Alfred, they were both jealous – both trying to ruin things for me. But he was the man who had said that gray would streak my hair like comets; he was the man who had bathed me in wine in Paris and made the woman in black say we would have an angel-child. He was Emmanuel. He was the child his father had beaten. I was the child my mother had tried to kill. We could save each other. I smiled up at him; he blew me a kiss.

'Isn't she gorgeous?' he said.

His mother pretended not to hear. She screwed up her mouth until it was zipper tight and dealt us our cards.

Manny made love to me that night. I didn't try to be quiet; I wanted his mother to hear us. She needed to know that her son had moved on; that she couldn't try to control us with her stories.

He rolled off of me and fell into a deep sleep. His profile in the relative darkness looked boyish, innocent. He could be anyone. I shivered. Yet didn't I know all I needed to know? I knew he loved me enough to die for me. He said so, and I believed him. I knew his name. I knew he was a writer. I knew he had a large mole on his left shoulder, a fear of lightning, and a greater fear of drowning. I knew he thought Faulkner and Joyce were the only writers worth emulating. I knew he'd begged me to marry him and bathed me in wine in Paris. I knew he would be the father of my beautiful children. I knew I could touch him; I knew he was real. I knew he'd never let me go.

I was sore. Manny had been in a hurry. I hadn't been ready, but I forgave him. It didn't matter that his father had been white and mine black. It didn't matter that we'd grown up on different continents if we had the same dreams.

I wanted him to make love to me again, not because of desire but because of need. I decided against waking him; instead, I lay in the dark and imagined what his sperm looked like on their long journey inside my vagina. Were they tired by now? How many thousands upon thousands of them were already dead? I imagined the congestion around the cervix. The pushing, the shoving. Only the rude would survive. I pictured them marching on relentlessly – tadpoles in hard hats and work boots with a few strands of blond hair and dimples where their chins would be if they'd had them. I thought about the miracle of childbirth. I imagined Manny holding my hand, breathing with me, telling me it would be okay, crying when he saw how beautiful the baby was. We wouldn't be like our parents. We would give our children room to be happy in.

I smiled. He hadn't remembered about the diaphragm.

Everything was going to be much easier than I'd thought.

4

I didn't get pregnant, and Manny cursed himself the next day for forgetting about protection. He said we had other things to think about right now; we didn't need some bambino weighing us down. So I stopped thinking about it for a while and let the writing program and the teaching of freshman English consume our lives.

It wasn't long before writing became torture: as criticism of our work grew, Manny and I huddled together for comfort. We identified the 'enemy' as Professor Brandon and the other fools in the program who failed to recognize talent. No one seemed to like our work very much, and I wondered why we'd been accepted into the program in the first place. We made up names for the professors and speculated about the absurdity of their sex lives. I began to sound more and more like Manny. When Alfred called from England on my birthday, he said I sounded just like my husband. 'Good,' I said. 'He's the man I most admire in the whole world.' When Alfred asked why we stayed in the program if we found it so disappointing, I told him he'd missed the point. 'We're in the program to network, Alfred. That's what matters over here. Networking.' Alfred said I sounded like a nincompoop, which I thought was very rude considering it was my birthday. He gave me a long lecture about value systems and how people need to hang on to them in order to be happy. 'I *am* happy,' I said. 'Happier than I ever was in that stinking hole of a country.' Alfred just sighed and told me he'd call again soon, which was a lie, of course, because he didn't have any money. Then he put my mother on the phone.

Louise was Louise. She spoke with loathing for ten minutes, non-stop, about Mr. Pod and his misanthropy. It was almost funny. Then, in typical Louise-the-Dotty-Schoolteacher fashion, she skidded off to the outer banks of the conversation and told me that Ruskin was dying. She said it with surprising calmness, almost callousness.

'How?' I asked.

'Cancer,' she said. 'It's everywhere.'

'Does he know how bad it is?'

'O yes. I think he's quite relieved, really. It's hard to keep your spirits up when you're in pain like that. Everything's eating at him. He rants and raves about all kinds of strange things – warlock rituals, Mayan ruins, African tribes, sex, of course. And his arthritis is terrible.'

'Won't you miss him?'

'O yes. Of course we will.' By 'we,' I gathered she meant she and Alfred, which I knew was ridiculous. Alfred thought Ruskin was a sham. I began to ask Louise who was taking care of Ruskin, but I was caught in the echo of long-distance phone calls that sends words back at you before you've finished uttering them, and she didn't hear me.

'We all have our time,' she was saying. 'And if I'd had a life like Ruskin, traveled all over the world, written books, danced naked around trees, I'd be pretty happy about my lot. No sense complaining.'

'"Do not go gentle into that good night,"' I said.

'What? What did you say? The line's awful.'

'Nothing. Just, I'd thought he'd be more reluctant to leave. I thought he liked it here.'

It was a childish comment, I know, but I was strangely offended. For some reason, Ruskin Garland's witnessing my success had been important to me. Now he would never know how much I'd achieved. He'd die thinking I was still Jacinta

Louise Buttercup Moses – the girl whose thigh he'd fondled in a car in Clapham – so he wouldn't know me as a great poet. I could never be more to him than I already had been.

'He smokes. No wonder he got cancer,' I said with vengeance leaping across my voice like a stepping stone. 'If you smoke, you're bound to come down with it sometime. God, you'd think he would've known better.'

'He's in excruciating pain,' my mother said.

I felt chastised, although my mother didn't seem to be directing any criticism at me. She was simply relaying a fact. I imagined Ruskin Garland reaching for the painkillers, trying to come to terms with what his body was doing to him. Was he afraid of pain like the rest of us? Did his being a warlock mean he had a store of magic tricks to get him to the other side of suffering?

'Only morons smoke,' I muttered before guilt made me ashamed.

'What, dear?'

'Nothing. We're going out to eat for my birthday. A small Italian place. Great value, lots of atmosphere, and it's open tonight. Most places are closed, what with it's being Christmas. Manny's buying me whatever I want to eat.'

My mother hadn't mentioned the fact that it was my birthday. She hadn't said 'happy Christmas' either.

'O good,' she said, then launched into another tirade against her headmaster.

When I got off the phone, Manny asked me who was dying.

'Ruskin Garland. Remember?'

'O yeah. The fat old guy who drove like a snail.'

I turned away. Ruskin Garland had been more than that.

'He has an extraordinary mind. You seemed quite taken with him at our wedding.'

'Wasn't much to choose from.'

'I'm going for a walk.'

'It's snowing.'

'Then it will be very pretty.'

'Suit yourself.'

Outside the air was as crisp as a wafer. My breath billowed

out in front of me and my fingers were cold before I'd turned left on to the road.

Ruskin was dying.

By the time the new year came in, he'd probably be gone.

For years he'd loved my mother, and she had talked about him as if he were a sidebar in a story she wasn't very interested in. He'd been a writer; he'd been a warlock. He'd gone to nudist camps and sat in bars with famous artists in Paris. He was known by people who knew about archaeology. He was a scholar, if not a gentleman. He was from the wrong class. Most of the other 'authorities' in England would ignore his death, snub him at his funeral. He'd taken me from the foster home to Mrs. Butcher's – unwittingly doing me one of the great favors of my lifetime. Without Vera Butcher, there wouldn't have been an end to Simone Madagascar. Vera had given me evenings with the other lost children who wanted stories like some people want drugs. It was there I'd learned to tell stories the way black people need to tell them: to save our own lives. I'd found my voice in that house. And if Ruskin had transgressed as he drove me to Mrs. Butcher – if he'd allowed his hand to wander too far from where he'd promised my mother it would remain, then what he'd done in comparison to the gift he'd given me was not as bad as I used to think. He hadn't gone farther; he'd stopped himself. He hadn't permitted me to live with him, thank God. In his own, limited way, he'd loved me.

For the first time since I'd arrived in America, England seemed too far away. A woman hurried past me with a hat pulled down over her eyes. Something about her reminded me of British women. 'Hi,' I said. She looked me up and down, then hurried on into the clouds her breath made ahead of her. She didn't reply, though she must have heard my greeting. I felt rejected. Had she ignored me because of my color, or was I just imagining things? I closed my mouth. I'd been smiling at the stranger, and my teeth were freezing. 'Bitch!' I said, a hatred for the stranger taking me by storm. 'Bitch, bitch, bitch!' I was rocking with rage. I found myself kicking the low stone wall surrounding the campus. What was wrong with me? If I was caught vandalizing this sacrosanct campus, I'd be summarily dismissed. People here were conservative; they loved their history and revered the few monuments they had to a past that didn't go back very far. I sat down for a minute and tried to calm down. I took a deep breath. The bitterly cold air hit my front teeth again and made them chatter.

I wanted things to add up to something grand, but they rarely did. The sum of a life was a pair of soiled knickers exposed to the public on a road in Battersea; it was a sad wave from a man in striped pajamas who would never see his wild and tropical country again. I'd come to America wanting to write, but it was a half-hearted desire, perhaps because of all the earlier rejections I'd faced from editors in London. I didn't live for words the way Manny did, which resulted in a certain jealousy on my part when I'd see him breathless with excitement because the paragraph was finally right. If death were to find me now, would I have done the great things I'd planned on Lavender Sweep? 'Ripeness is all.' The words from *King Lear* resounded in my ears. It was true. Was I ripe for dying? I was in my twenties, but I wouldn't be there for long. I had left the country I grew up in. I was following my dreams, but there was still a gap inside me. I had never been to Africa. I didn't know who my father was. I had to find him in the contours of his own continent. I needed to find him in a place where blackness was a given cause for celebration. The African Americans in this country fascinated me because they took this land as their own. Black Britons didn't do that in the same way. We were always aliens; in the corners of our eyes was the fear of repatriation. I wanted to find a home like the Africa of Simon's stories – a place where no one would question my right to put down roots. I wanted that for our children. Somehow, they had to have a happier childhood than I had had. How else would they grow up to celebrate the glory of the world?

And now, one of the people who introduced me to that glory was dying. I'd looked at the Egyptian kings with Ruskin Garland and read about unpronounceable gods from Mexico's ancient history. He'd shown me the only wildness left in Britain – the legacy of Celts and the blue men of the north who'd terrorized the Romans. Indirectly, he'd helped me understand Emily Brontë's savage love story in *Wuthering Heights* and Thomas Hardy's mournful quests in *Tess* and *Jude*. He and my mother, and Alfred too, were not afraid to remember the rim of the chasm – the place where storms met and the polite veneer of British etiquette was ripped away like skin. What was underneath was blood and romance. It could kill you. It could make you large. Better to have loved and lost than never to have loved at all – that's what my mother quoted in her diary. But at what price? And at the end of all that passion and all that pain, there was a period – not even ellipses, just a full stop. When I died I wanted my life to reverberate through the centuries. I wanted people to miss me enough to commit suicide at my leaving. Would Manny do that? Would he be so overcome with sorrow that he would sharpen the knife we used for cutting bread, roll up his sleeves, and draw the knife across his small, white wrists in a clean sweep of despair? Perhaps. Manny was dramatic enough to attempt it. But somehow I knew he'd be found by one of the many women in the writing program who had a crush on him.

I stopped myself. What was I doing? I loved Manny. Of course he'd be lost without me. But I wasn't selfish enough to want him to kill himself if I were killed. I needed to give him something to make life worth living. Someone to look after. Someone he would want to live for more than anyone else. Writing alone would never be enough for me; I needed to live beyond words if I were to live at all. I needed to pass myself on somehow and become part of a longer journey. I wanted to make things right by being the mother my mother never was. I hurried home to make a baby.

When I stepped through the door, I heard the stiletto keys of Manny's old typewriter.

'I'm home,' I called.

'Mmm.'

'Come on out and sit with me for a while. I'd like to talk –'

'Shhh! O shit! I've lost it now.'

My child would not be conceived on Christmas Eve. I turned

on the television and watched a special with Julie Andrews, whose breasts were as perky as ever and whose smile left a streak across the screen the way headlights do in those night photographs.

Later, Manny came out to join me. He was in a better mood; things were going well. He'd have the novel finished by the summer, he was sure of it.

I snuggled up to him. In the United States of America, he was the only human being I could do that to. For the second time, England seemed a long way away.

He spoke about his writing. He was passionate about words, and his excitement sparked my own. He wouldn't tell me the title; I sometimes thought he was scared I'd steal it. Eventually, however, after I'd tickled him for two or three minutes, he gave in.

'Okay, okay,' he said, snorting with laughter. 'It's called "Sophie."'

'"Sophie"?'

'Yeah. You don't like it. I knew you wouldn't.'

'No. I like it. I do. Where does the name come from?'

'Just picked it out of the air. Fits, though.'

'Is it a sad story? Does anyone die?'

'Someone *always* dies, Jazz! You kill me. How can you have a novel without death in it somewhere? That's the way things are. You live a little, then you die a lot. 'Tis the way of all flesh to rot.'

'How does she die?'

'Who?'

'Sophie.'

'Now that would be telling, my little brown sugar dumpling. And I ain't about to tell.'

'Is she murdered?'

'I'm not telling,' Manny said, covering my face with a cushion, tickling my stomach until I screamed for mercy. He was going to kill me if he didn't stop, I said when I got my breath back.

'Then it would be a crime of passion,' he warned.

'That's a man's poor excuse for murder, if ever I heard one,'

I told him, but he wasn't looking; already he'd retreated into fiction. Soon he was pecking me on the cheek, wishing me a quick happy birthday and asking if I'd care if we didn't go out tonight after all.

'S'going well, Jazz. It really is. I hate to leave myself in mid-sentence. I know it's your birthday. I'll make it up to you. Promise.'

That night he came to bed a little after three A.M. I heard him climb in next to me. I heard him lean back into the pillows and sigh.

'What happens to Sophie?' I asked, surprising him.

'Hell, you made me jump! Thought you'd be sleeping by now. What's the time anyway?'

'What happens to her?'

'Okay, okay. I can see I'm not going to get any sleep unless I tell you. But now listen, Jazz, and I mean this, don't go repeating this to any of the nerds in the program. They steal ideas before you've even thought of them. Okay?'

'Yes. Okay. I promise.'

'Well, the thing is, Sophie's an actress and a model. She meets this guy whose story this is. He's ambitious. A painter. He paints her and it's the story of their love. She's his subject, you see.'

'That's what you said I was, remember?'

'When did I say that, for Christ's sake! I don't know where you get your ideas from. I'm not some chauvinist, Jazz. You're not my *subject*, for Christ's sake! You're my *wife*.'

'So this guy's chauvinistic, then?'

'God, yes. But good. A genius, really. And the girl, she's okay. She has a kind of instinctive, animal quality about her. Something raw. And he sees that in her and he paints it.'

'Then what happens?'

'Love. Love happens. Passion. Violence. Everything happens.'

'What kind of violence?'

'Don't know yet. Don't give me that look, I don't! God, even in the dark you could kill someone with a look like that. All I know is that it's not going to be some dumb, happy ending.

Some Hallmark card. It's going to be thrilling and tragic. A grand passion laced with blood.'

'Sounds sick.'

Manny didn't say a word. I began to apologize. He told me to shut up. His voice seemed to be coming out of a paper bag.

'You asked me what the fuck I was writing about and I told you. I really don't give a damn whether you approve or not. It's my story, not yours. Get it?'

Then he rolled over and went to sleep. I thought he'd be too angry to sleep, but he wasn't. He was snoring before I had time to make up a suitable apology. I knew he wouldn't talk to me about 'Sophie' again for a long time. He'd sworn at me. He hated me. I cursed his mother, who'd made the whole thing happen by poisoning my mind against her son. I cursed my mother for making me believe that people you love can stop loving you in an instant and take years to find their way back. Hell, what did it matter if he'd killed a fish when he was ten? Hadn't I done much worse? I'd sent my own mother to a mental asylum and been party to the death of my best friend. 'God help us all,' I said, remembering Manny and me and Ruskin, putting my arm around the only man I knew who had told me I was Africa, who had lifted me out of South London, who had made me laugh until my throat ached, and who had loved me with a passion as red as the wine he'd poured into the bathtub in Paris to baptize me with.

I resolved to begin saying the right thing. I was making too many errors, just the way I had with Louise. Was I a person who would never be satisfied? Louise and Alfred had suggested as much. My tongue would be the death of me if I wasn't careful. When we made love in future, I'd moan a little louder. Because Emmanuel Fox III could never leave me. I'd given everything I had to him. If he were to leave, what would I do in this strange country? Would the authorities send me home again? The thought terrified me. I reached over and stroked Manny's hair. In his sleep he caught hold of my hand and held it gently. I knew that 'Sophie' had better be a success – more than Manny's ego was riding on this book. I'd give him space to write it. Once he had a novel under his belt, he'd be happy, I told myself, thinking about what I could do over the next few days to please him.

I spent the first year in America falling in love with the land and trying to make sure that Manny stayed in love with me. I was careful with my words. I cooked and cleaned and didn't demand too much of his time. I made friends with other students and learned how to drive. We moved to a duplex at the end of the first year. It was a modest place on the edge of town, but the rooms were spacious and there was a pretty view. Unlike our first apartment, the duplex was light and airy. When Lydia, on a weekend visit, stepped through the door and clapped her hands – a strange gesture for a woman of her age – then told Manny he was a genius to find a place like this, I didn't let her know how many months I'd spent looking for a larger place with a rent we could afford. It was important that Manny remain happy because, as I now understood, he was hell to live with if he wasn't.

I made curtains with bedspreads to match. I grew thin. He liked it. I grew thinner. He liked it better. Sometimes I thought he'd like it most of all if I disappeared altogether, or got so frail he'd have to do things for me. I didn't care. He loved me. There was little doubt in my mind about that. He would die for me. The only other thing I wanted was a baby.

I tried not to let Manny know how much I was falling in love with the country he despised. His dream was always to live in Africa. Gradually, I began to see Africa as a place we'd visit and America as our home. When I mentioned becoming an American citizen, he almost spat at me. I wouldn't back down, however. Eventually, he gave up. All he could concentrate on was 'Sophie' and it was not going well. He hadn't finished it during the summer after all. He bit his nails and picked at his skin. 'Goddamn the woman!' he'd cry, tearing up chapters into tiny fragments and launching them toward the wastebasket. He was beside himself with rage when he found out there was a novel by Styron called *Sophie's Choice*. 'Why didn't they tell me?' he wailed. I said I thought he knew. I thought everyone knew. That wasn't the right response. He laughed bitterly and told me I was naive.

The basketball game was my idea. I thought it would take his mind off things. They'd trashed his story in the workshop again and called it maudlin and melodramatic. Tom Brandon, the director of the program, had asked him why he'd devoted his time to writing about characters whose lives were boring. 'No one wants to read this shit,' he'd said, flinging his copy of the story down on the table. Manny had come home, locked himself in the bathroom, and wept. Outside, the sound of his sobbing tore a hole in my heart. I asked around about entertainment and a friend recommended watching sports. I stood in line for three hours in order to get tickets for the game.

Unfortunately, basketball wasn't a game Manny liked. In fact, he told me, when I handed him a ticket, he hated it. But I took him anyway because it was the only solution I could come up with, and we needed to get out of the duplex for one night at least. I pried his fingers from the typewriter keys, then pleaded and cajoled until he agreed to come.

We sat near the front, and I was amazed by the physical size of the players. I had never before seen men that big. A few rows up from us, as luck would have it, was Tom Brandon with his poor, long-suffering spouse. Manny almost threw up when he caught sight of him, and spent the rest of the game talking about Tom's impotence. 'It's a well-known fact,' he said. 'Alcoholism has robbed him of his virility. He won't go to the bathroom when anyone's in there. Dick's too small.'

I looked over at Manny. He could be mistaken for a teenager, especially from the back. A petite, blond, American boy. If he lost his blond waves, his emerging skull would seem strange. He had a hollow face – enormously pretty, but hollow. There was something cadaverous about it when he was tired. I prayed he wouldn't lose his hair all at once. I knew I'd need a period of adjustment. Was it only his hair I'd fallen in love with? What did that make me? I needed to love him for his inner self. 'Dick's the size of a wiener,' Manny said. I tried not to hear him. I still had one of the first hairs I'd retrieved from his pillow in Paris and tucked away in a matchbox. I used it once to floss my teeth. I liked the feel of his blond hair in my mouth. When I told him about it, he thought I was joking. Did I love him in the same way after a year and a half of watching him eat and work and sleep with me? I haven't been tested yet, I thought, surprising myself.

'It was like rape,' Manny was saying. 'There was something so damn sordid about it. And the thing is, you know, it's damn good. Damn good. Chapter three of the novel. I know it's damn good. Hell, *The Atlantic* nearly took it a couple'a months ago . . .'

Manny stood up. The play was about to begin.

'Got any change?' he asked.

'For what?'

'Popcorn.'

'But the game's just beginning. . . . Okay, okay.'

Manny hurried off with the money. He looked young from the back, like a freshman. It was only his eyes that betrayed his age. As I sat waiting for the buzzer to sound announcing the start of the game, I thought about our lives. Being a writer would never be glamorous, and there was a large part of me that couldn't give a damn about it, especially when I saw what it did to the rest of them. Living with a writer was pain – a tapping out of signals in the Morse code of ambition – publishing three books by the time you were forty. Writers never saw much of anything – only what they could easily translate into narrative. The rest was thrown out as garbage. People around you became negative space. You were doomed to keep riding those type-writer keys once you had boarded the train. Faster, faster and faster. Let me win, Lord! Let me win the Big Prize! When did satisfaction come? When did we find out whether or not we'd won? How had our lives sped downhill so fast? We used to ache to get each other's clothes off; we used to be tender with one another and find a way to soothe each other's pain. And there were still good times when we relished one another in spite of Manny's desperate quest for words, but those times were becoming less and less frequent.

I didn't even notice when Manny returned with his Coke and his popcorn. By the time they began playing the second quarter,

I was so engrossed that he receded into the background completely. Something was happening. Something beyond belief. I realized I was witness to a miracle.

The miracle came in the form of a black player on the team named Lawrence Helios. The crowd called out his name and I saw that he was darker than the sun was bright, and it made me happy. He was from North Carolina, they said, and the Tar Heels had almost snatched him up. We'd tempted him away from his state and now he was making us win. When he'd stepped out on to the court, the place had erupted and I'd looked up at the beams that held the arena together, certain I'd see stress fractures.

All those white people gathered in a Southern state to marvel at a black boy who played their dreams like a dancer. Helios, the tall black senior, *was* the game. It was he who controlled the tempo, he to whom the other players, black and white, looked for direction. He bounced the ball as though it were attached to his palms by an invisible rubber band. The other team began to get frustrated. One of them fouled Helios. The crowd jeered. I was on my feet shouting for him. I wanted Helios to slaughter them.

As the game went on, the margin between the teams grew. Helios was on fire. Even Manny began to be caught up in the scoring. I watched the way the African American lengthened and widened the court until it was bigger than a wish made by a hungry man. His arms and legs were sweat: they shone in the bright lights of the court, highlights slashing his dark limbs. The hair on his head was close-cut. His profile looked familiar to me. And then I noticed the resemblance. My father had looked like that. Helios must have come from West Africa. His ancestry was mine. I wondered what other people were seeing – whether the blond sorority girls could recognize in the black man's forearms the arc of inevitability that guided the game; whether the parents from Giles County were thinking that their boy could leap that high given the right coach; or whether they knew that there was something black in the leaping that could never be taught. The young man whose parents' parents' grandparents had been stolen away from where they should have been was making up for lost time by claiming his own space in the wide bright arena in Virginia.

We won. Of course.

Manny and I were both subdued when we got home. We stepped inside the door and stood there for a moment without saying anything.

'That was genius,' Manny said, a strange sorrow in his voice.

He sat down on the hideous black and white sofa bed we'd bought from a fellow grad student with appalling taste. Manny put his head in his hands as if it were too heavy for his neck to hold up. I sat down next to him. I didn't feel much of anything except a familiar desperation that told me to make something happen if any of this was to be salvaged. I could feel things slipping away from me. If I didn't act soon, it would be too late. Then, as if the sun suddenly showed itself from behind dense cloud, Manny looked up at me and said, with utter sincerity, 'I'm sorry, Jazz.'

'For what?' I replied, fearing I'd misheard him.

'For everything. My moodiness. The damn novel. Everything. Thing is, I'm shit scared, if you want to know the truth. I'm thirty-one and I'm no farther along than some of the kids who are twenty-two and -three. I work so damn hard, and sometimes it seems as though I'll never be able to do with words what that black kid Helios did tonight with the ball. I used to be on fire too, Jazz. But I feel myself getting so goddamn weary. And then I take it out on you. It's not right.'

'It's okay,' I said, not knowing how else to respond to his confession.

'No. It's not. And things are going to change, I promise you that. I haven't been fair to you. It must be real strange, living in a foreign country, far away from people you care about. I've been there too. It's the pits. Look, you know how much I love you, don't you?'

'I know.'

'Well, I guess what I'm asking for is your patience. The book's good, Jazz. I swear it. We can do this. You with your poems – damn fine poems too – and me with my novel. We're a team. We can make the world fly, just like Helios. I know we can. And when we're together, sweet, sweet, Jacinta Louise, we'll find the Promised Land the other Moses only viewed from a distance.' He smiled. 'I promise.'

He took both my hands in his and his touch was as gentle as a child's.

'I love you, my angel wife,' he said. 'Only death will be able to tear me from you. I swear it. You'll never be rid of me until then. You are the best thing that ever happened to me. If I don't always show it, you must forgive me. We grow up a certain way and then it gets so damn difficult to say what we mean, you know? I will try harder to be a good husband. Together we can get through this crappy writing program. I know it.'

I told Manny I loved him too. I meant it. His confession had revived in me emotions I had assumed were dead. I could meet him halfway, if that's what he was asking – I could do it.

When we held each other, I could feel his heart pounding against my chest like a bird trying to beat its way out of a cage. I thought of the phrase from the Dunbar poem we'd read in Tom Brandon's class the other day: 'I Know Why the Caged Bird Sings.' If, up until now, Manny's song had been an elegy, it could change to a song of victory if we dared to dream large enough to achieve transcendence.

'Come upstairs,' I said, undoing the buttons on his shirt and bending down to kiss the honey-colored curls on his chest.

We never got upstairs. He put his arms around me and wouldn't let me go. I closed my eyes and thought about the game. The push to win, the sweat, the energy of men desperate to reach the end, triumphant. Manny called out my name and buried his head between my breasts. I stroked the shock of blond hair curling up around his ears and wished for nothing except a permanent end to loneliness.

'I want you more than life, Jazz! I want you, baby!'

He took me to the edge and let me look over it. He brought me back, took me out again. I had to stop myself from uttering Helios' name because, in spite of myself, it was the basketball player I saw above me. The Black Son. The man from Africa. 'Yes, yes,' I said, giving way, giving in again.

We slept on the rug in the living room. The next morning we laughed at ourselves. As I made a pot of Twining's English Breakfast tea I sent a prayer up to Simon: *Yes! At last! Thank you!* Because I knew what had happened. Our child was made. Her beauty would crown our love.

The real game of luck and grace and fortitude was about to begin.

5

Manny's first reaction to the pregnancy was one of profound depression. The world wasn't clean enough for a child, he said. He wouldn't be a good parent. His own parents had been lousy. He needed more time. When I asked what he meant by clean, he just blew air out from his mouth in a sound reminiscent of the snorts of horses and turned away from me. In his eyes was a pain so deep that I regretted not using protection. I didn't know much about parenting either. Maybe this was a bad idea. Manny's depression became the catalyst for my own. For three weeks we could barely look at each other.

Gradually, however, Manny began to question his own assumptions. After a lengthy phone conversation with his mother, he came down the stairs and sat down on the black and white atrocity we called a sofa. 'Perhaps we could raise it well,' he said, seemingly thinking out loud.

Five weeks after my period had failed to make an appearance, Manny came home from teaching second-semester English, flung his book bag on the table, and picked me up and spun me around.

'I've found a solution!' he cried, putting me down gently. His eyes were wide open and he was breathing hard and fast, like a sprinter. I gathered he'd run the three miles home with this news.

'What's that?' I said, fearful and fascinated all at once.

'Africa!' he declared, then laughed out loud. I wondered whether he'd been drinking. After three or four glasses of beer he sometimes displayed the same kind of behavior. When I'd seen him smoke pot once, he'd shown the same euphoria and spoken with a similar breathlessness.

'Africa?' I said warily.

'Yep.'

'What do you mean?'

'Look, Jazz,' he said, drawing me to the sofa and guiding me on to his lap. At first I thought he planned to have sex, but soon it was clear he only wanted to hold me. He began speaking. He sounded calmer and I relaxed into him, letting go of some of the weight I'd been carrying.

'The thought of having a kid scared the living daylights out of me. America stinks. It's depraved, if you want to know the truth. It's commercialism taken to absurd extremes. It sucks people up and spits them out like garbage. None of the big publishing houses represent artists these days. They want celebrities. It's pathetic. If you have integrity, you may as well forget it. Anyhow, what I'm saying is we could go back to West Africa. You'd love it there. We could go to your dad's homeland. It would be sort of like a pilgrimage. And the kid could grow up where it's natural. It was hard the first time round, being young and all, not having an in to the place. But this time will be different. We can explore together. You, me, and the bambino. You have no idea how . . . how glorious it can be there, Jazz. No idea. Hell, we may never leave.'

He didn't ask me what I thought, and he wouldn't have heard me if I'd spoken because he was speaking to himself. So we left it there: Manny determined we were going to raise the child in Africa, me determined to remain in the land I'd grown to love. Yet still I was happy – happier than I could recall being in a long time. We both wanted the same thing: a child who would bless the world with its wisdom and beauty. It would be easy to love our baby, I thought, suspecting that the most difficult part for both of us would be not loving it too much.

When I told Lydia that Manny was becoming more and more excited about the child, she sounded relieved.

'Now perhaps he can rest in peace,' she told me over the phone.

'Who?' I asked, thinking she must be referring to someone long since dead.

'Manny. He can rest easier, put some of the nightmares behind him and get on with his life. Let go of the revenge. It isn't healthy.'

I didn't ask her to elaborate in case it resulted in another Sophie saga. Besides, Manny wasn't vengeful, just afraid. I put Lydia's comments down to envy and began to wait in eager anticipation for the birth of a baby who would enable Manny to find joy.

In the morning, Manny would touch my stomach and say, 'I hope she's as beautiful as you are, Jazz. The world is short on beauty.'

And I'd picture a little girl running through the Virginia countryside, her skin tanned, her brown hair streaked with gold. We'd find baby pictures in magazines and I'd cut them out, making a scrapbook to the child I had yet to see. Like my earlier obsession with home improvement, this desire overwhelmed me. I told Alfred over the phone I didn't think I'd be able to wait another seven months.

'Savor the present,' he advised me, 'your child will arrive soon enough.'

Manny and I knew it would be a girl, though we didn't opt for ultrasound. I'd read somewhere that it could be risky, and I wanted this birth to be as natural as possible.

Some of the more ambitious students in the writing program obviously couldn't understand why we hadn't aborted. 'I'd resent the baby,' one particularly bad fiction writer told me. 'I need space to write. Art doesn't happen between diaper changes.' 'Sometimes it doesn't happen at all, does it, Muriel, baby or not,' I said. The teaching assistants with children were happier for us, but even they talked about the good old days when time was their friend. I didn't care what they said. It was our baby. We could exist in isolation if we wanted to. When

Manny said the baby would be over a year old when we went to Africa, and so could have the necessary vaccinations, I ignored him. He continued planning our time in Africa as if we were definitely going. His experience there before and his first degree in agriculture would make it easy for him to get contract work, he said. I could teach. There was plenty of work for English teachers over there, he assured me. We'd go to West Africa – try to find my father's family, the aunt I was named after. I said I thought she was dead. He said we could be lucky; she could be living in some convent or something. I said my aunt Jacinta hated the nuns; he said people changed as they got older. Nothing could discourage him. He was determined to find my roots. I began to believe they were his roots too. I was the ideal family he'd wanted ever since he'd been fascinated by Africa as a boy. I would legitimate his claim to difference, and explain his inability to fit into the country that had created him.

As the months went by, I developed an odd fascination. Manny said it was unhealthy, and I could see his point, but I was drawn to the place anyway.

About an hour's drive away, in the middle of nowhere, was Quasar Hicks's Drive-In Funeral Home – the most ludicrous monument to bad taste I'd ever seen. I loved it. About once a month I'd make the drive out there, down through the heart of the state, along two-lane highways barely wide enough for two cars. Sometimes I took a picnic lunch and sat in the driveway staring at the corpse-of-the-day. It was always laid out in style in the large picture window. There was a neon sign above the drive-in lane that said OPEN FOR VIEWING and then the name of the deceased.

The first time I visited was by accident. Manny and I had gone for a drive in the country and we caught sight of the billboard sign saying DRIVE-IN NEXT RIGHT. We thought we were going to see a movie. It was dark; and when we realized what we were looking at, we both screamed. The corpse we saw that day belonged to Jonathan Jeremiah Linkous – J.J. – a large man of about sixty. Quasar had forgotten to draw the curtains after closing, a practice he'd adopted, I later learned, in order to discourage hooligans from making fun of the dead. Manny was horrified. He tore out of there like a man on fire. When I said I'd like to go back, just to see if it was real, he said I was sick. So I convinced a friend of mine, Barbara Simpson, to come with me. She was a poet too so I knew she'd appreciate the absurd.

That was the day we met Quasar Hicks, the owner. He was very kind to us, thinking we knew the new corpse, Mary Ellen Brody, though of course we'd never set eyes on her in our lives. When I kept coming, he realized I was just a sightseer and began to shoo me away. On my fourth visit, he could tell I was pregnant. His office was just near the viewing window, so he saw people when they drove up. He came out twitching with anger and asked me what I thought I was doing. Barbara wasn't with me this time; she'd had a class to teach.

'I'm only looking,' I said.

'Why?'

'It's fascinating.'

'Why?'

'Because they're dead. I like the dead.'

He warmed up to me after that. Said there weren't many people who could appreciate a corpse. He showed me round the facilities the next time I came; and when he learned I was in the writing program at the university, he asked me to write a poem about them, if I ever had time. I promised I would.

And so began the sequence of poems that launched my writing career and resulted in my first four publications. They were called 'The Drive-In' and they were a series of poems on rural America. I even used Quasar's name in a few. He'd never know, I reasoned. When the first of the series was lauded in a workshop and summarily accepted for publication by a prestigious journal out of the Midwest, I was ecstatic. Manny was taken aback when I showed him the acceptance letter. He swallowed hard, then, to his credit, took me out to dinner to celebrate. 'A poet for real,' he said. 'A real poet. My little Jacinta's a poet.' His surprise was something of an insult, but I chose not to think about it. 'Poetry's easier to publish than fiction, of course,' he said. He was still fielding rejections. I knew he was struggling with 'Sophie.' I tried to be magnanimous in triumph. 'It's only a matter of time, Manny. They'll recognize your talent in the end.'

For my part, I was delighted – and even Alfred's comments couldn't dampen my spirits.

'The series is condescending,' he told me, criticizing my writing for the first time. 'You sound like a snob.' His criticism stung. These were satires. All satires were inherently patronizing. It wasn't a question of class; it was a question of good taste. Quasar and people like him, I reasoned, lacked it. They were like Maurice and the other Beadycaps, I told myself, linking bad taste to immorality and tying it up with an artistic flourish of the pen.

Louise was happy for me in spite of Alfred. She didn't see what the fuss was about. 'They're magnificent poems,' she told me in her high-pitched, long-distance-phone-call voice. 'I could just see the place! What a name! Quasar! Published – my little girl! And pregnant to boot!' she cried, as if they were somehow related.

Then I went to the funeral home one last time and that changed everything.

Previously I'd found the whole thing ridiculous, and the tone of the poems had been a reflection of that. Here I was in podunk Virginia at Quasar Hicks's Drive-In Funeral Home. Lordy! How could anyone named after a TV and a redneck be taken seriously? What kind of culture allowed for the commercialization of their dead? Like Joan Didion in Las Vegas, I was outraged. The editors at the journals where the poems had been taken wrote complimentary letters about my use of irony. Even Tom Brandon said the poems were quite good. So I never expected to be moved during my last visit. But then I'd never expected to find Leonora.

The new corpse lying in the picture window was shocking. The name in neon was Leonora Hicks. She had red hair and freckles. She must have been four or five years old. She was wearing a dress of red polka dots edged with lace. In her hair were red ribbons.

Quasar came out to meet me.

'I'm sorry,' was all I could say.

He was hunched over and his eyes were red. It was his second cousin's child, he said. He'd wanted everyone to see how beautiful she'd been.

As we talked a half-dozen cars went through the drive-through. Each person sat in the privacy of his or her own grief. Each person drove away more slowly than they'd arrived.

'How?' I asked him.

'Drowned,' he told me. 'Swimming with some friends. They seen her go down. They called. She waved back at them. Kids thought she was just playacting.'

'There's a poem about that,' I told him. 'It's about someone who wasn't waving. Just like Leonora. Only no one knew.'

'Could be we're all waving like that,' Quasar said. 'And the lousy part about it is no one ever knows – not even the ones who's doing the waving.'

I swallowed hard. It was too deep a thought to come from a man I'd converted to caricature. I shifted uncomfortably in the front seat. I had the window rolled down, and the sun was full on my face. Quasar stood over me in silhouette. Heat permed everything – waves everywhere – as if we too were underwater.

'She doesn't look as if she drowned,' I said.

'No. She sure don't. Strange, ain't it?'

I drove through once more after the other cars had left and I'd said good-bye to Quasar. I'd brought Kentucky Fried Chicken for my lunch, but I couldn't eat it. Leonora Hicks was sleeping. A beautiful little girl. Hair as red as sunsets. How her mother must have deemed herself blessed as the child grew in beauty and transformed the world with the sheer magic of her face. In her sweet, innocent beauty, Leonora struck in me a chord that had been silent. Alfred once accused me of 'aesthetic tyranny.' 'It will catch up with you one day, my girl,' he'd told me when I'd commented on Mary Beadycap's unattractiveness. Yet still, perfection drove me. My poems, my body, my baby, Manny – all needed to look as close to perfect as nature would allow. And the world I lived in reinforced my yearnings. Didn't we all worship at the shrine of perfection, each in our own way? What was Lawrence Helios but a manifestation of that lust for the perfect man with the perfect athleticism and the perfect face carved from black marble? In America, more than in England, people made a fetish of beauty.

I looked at Leonora Hicks. The tragedy of her going was the recurring tragedy of transience. What was most beautiful in bloom was most likely to die young. It was as if her beauty existed outside her, and that she walked within it, like we walk inside a garden – her beauty a manifestation of the spirit we could all have with just a little good fortune. Poor Leonora. Someone's daughter. I began to cry. I had a daughter now. If I were to lose her the way this mother had lost Leonora, there would be no bearing it.

Suffering was the same wherever you happened to be. It could fool you at first – make you think it was a different creature altogether, because of an accent, or a way of dressing, or a gesture confined to a particular class. But it was the same. Alfred had tried to teach me that. He'd tried to show me suffering in relation to Mary Beadycap, in relation to her twin, Maurice. I hadn't listened because it was easier to believe that certain privileges were earned rather than randomly given.

Leonora had drowned. She'd felt the water fill her lungs and she'd probably screamed out loud. She'd gone back through time to bubbles and gills; but her consciousness had failed to make the journey. Her face was composed. What had she seen down there in that Virginia riverbed? Was it something so fascinating that she had been eager to relinquish her hold on this world? My daughter was alive in water right now. Floating in the womb. That same suspension Leonora returned to. My daughter's name would begin with 'L' just like Leonora's. Manny wanted her to be named after his mother. She would be Lydia Moses Fox. She would wear red ribbons in her hair and laugh up at the sun the way Leonora Hicks had laughed.

I rolled up the window and drove on. I gripped the wheel, praying harder than I'd prayed in years. Just don't let her die, Jesus. Please. Don't let her die. I can bear anything else. I drove on and the rain came down as a deluge. Water, water everywhere. Streams I'd never noticed before flanked the road; and the rain kept coming – shocking, insistent, hammering down on the windscreen. The road curved into question marks. Yellow signs, DEAD END, breathing in the rain. The tires carved through channels of water. I was driving through an ocean! The sky had gone! The grays that had raised me in England came down upon my head. There was no escape after all. You thought you were safe, but it was a trick. The rain caught up with you in the end. At some point we all drowned, our eyes wide open like fish eyes. We saw the inexpressible and our mouths clamped shut forever. The rain came down harder. I pulled over to the side of the road. A truck barreled past me, going fifty or sixty. The bulk of it swayed back and forth like an elephant. We were inside the floods of the Old Testament. The car was nudged off to the right. I pulled over. God was mad. The bully raindrops turned into lances. The universe was sinking. Inside me, Lydia kicked. *Let me out! Let me out now!* I put my hand on her and told her to be still. She wouldn't listen. *Let me out! Let me out now!* What did she hear inside the cave? Inside water, what can you know of water? Inside life, what can you know of death?

Leonora has a secret. Yes. That was what her face said. A secret. She'd found out something down there in the dark of the river. But she wasn't telling. No one ever told. And babies forgot. As soon as they were out, they forgot. Whatever the secret was, it had to have something to do with rhythm. In *Out of Africa*, children tell Dinesen when she recites some poetry that it sounds like rain. And she knows what they mean because we all know what they mean. Poetry and rain. The beat of water. The rhythms of the drowned. Lydia kicked again. This time it was furious. And then there was water in the car. Water in the car! Dear God! Was it me? Had I burst? It was too soon! Jesus! She'd die! We'd both die out here in the rain!

I cried out. My teeth were chattering although it was steamy outside. My water! My water! Lydia would drown in the air. She was still a fish. She hadn't evolved yet. Birth was the evolution. Too early! Manny! Alfred! Louise! I started the ignition. I leaned forward to peer through the rain.

I don't remember the journey back. All I know is, when I pulled up in front of the duplex, the sun was bright in the sky, and the car was dry.

Manny was waiting in the doorway. He was angry until he

saw my face. Barbara had broken down when I was late and had told him where I was going. But he closed his mouth when he saw me and carried me inside because I could hardly walk.

When I told him I thought my water had broken, he panicked. He reached down inside my panties to check, and I was too exhausted to be embarrassed.

'Don't feel anything. I think you're okay.'

'The car was wet, Manny! I was all wet! I think she's drowned!'

'Who?'

'The baby! Little Lydia! I think she's drowned!'

Manny panicked a second time. He thought I'd had the baby out in the storm. 'It's in there,' he cried. 'I'm sure it is. I can feel it.'

But I kept saying she'd drowned. In the end he called our next-door neighbor in to see whether I'd had the baby or not. Debbie listened to both of us and then began to roar with laughter. She laughed until her face turned red.

'If you've had that baby, I'm a monkey's uncle,' she said. She went out to the car and came back laughing as much as before.

'One of the windows was open a crack,' she said. 'The rain must have come in. The window's down a crack in the car, okay? You're intact. No leakage yet. You're fine, Jacinta. So's the kid. Believe me, I've had four of 'em. I should know.'

'The window wasn't up all the way, Jazz. It's not your water. Just the rain,' Manny repeated because I was too stupid to get it the first time. Debbie stayed for a while and made me hot tea. Manny calmed down until he remembered he was angry.

'It's sick, Jazz! They're corpses, for Christ's sake! I didn't know where you were. The storm came from nowhere. I know how much you hate storms. I was shit scared, Jazz. What would I do if I lost you in some storm, for Christ's sake! You're everything to me. You could've been killed driving in rain like that. You know you're not great driving in the rain, and the tires are shitty. You know that.'

'I know. You're right. I'm sorry. It was horrible this time. You were right. I shouldn't have kept going back. I don't know what got into me.'

Manny's point had been made. He'd won. The argument was over. He was generous in victory.

'Hormones. I bet that's what it is. Women when they're pregnant are neither sex, did you know that? Not male or female. They exist in a kind of hormonal limbo. That's probably it. But I don't want you risking my child's life on these crazy excursions to Hicksville, okay?'

I wanted to explain to him what had happened. I wanted to tear up my patronizing sequence of poems and start all over again, this time from a more modest place. But I knew he wouldn't understand. So I nodded and fell asleep. I dreamed of little girls floating up through the water. I was at a strange angle. I must have been viewing the scene from a position on the riverbed, which meant, of course, that I was a ghost myself. In my dream, death didn't bother me; what I felt was relief. I'd passed through the final frontier, just like Captain Kirk, and it was okay. Nothing bad had happened after all. The only fear was fear itself.

I went into labor early. First pregnancies were meant to be late, so we were worried when my water broke. It was around one in the morning, and the bed was damp when I woke Manny up. He was confused at first. He called me 'Mom' and kept apologizing for wetting the bed. It took a good minute to convince him he hadn't done it. When he caught on, he stood up like a robot, too suddenly awake, and rushed me to the hospital. The nurses took over with their we're-professionals-and-you-don't-know-a-thing voices, and told us everything was normal, so Manny should get himself some coffee. They strapped monitors to my stomach and told me to breathe the way I'd been taught.

Manny worried about health insurance. He kept asking people whether this or that procedure was covered. I hated him when he did that.

'What do you want them to do if it's not covered, Manny? Not treat me?'

'No. Of course not!'

'Why ask, then?'

He waited to see that the nurse had closed the door behind her.

'Because these people try to screw you for everything they can get, that's why. If I keep a record of what's been done to you, they can't try to charge us forty bucks for an aspirin.'

'Jesus, Manny, you're such a bloody Scrooge.'

'Thanks a lot, Jazz. I'm glad you appreciate the way I look out for our money.'

'*Our* money! Since when have we ever spent *our* money! Listen, Manny, I'd like to make one thing clear. After this kid pops out, there'll be no more handouts. You make as much as I do. You pay your own way, Emmanuel Fox. No more free rides.'

If I hadn't had a major contraction just then, I think Manny would have slapped me. He recovered himself in time, though, and breathed me through it.

For hours we kept doing the things they'd taught us in Lamaze classes. After four hours, his mother arrived. She took over for a while and was much better at it than I thought she'd be. She had quiet hands. She held one to my forehead and one to my wrist. During the terrible moments, she was next to me like a mother.

After fourteen hours of labor, I was four centimeters dilated.

'Something's not happening,' the doctor said.

I asked him why it had taken him fourteen hours to realize that. He ignored me.

I was prepped for a C-section. Manny was going nuts.

'She has rare blood, okay? Don't cut her. I mean, not much. She has very rare blood!'

When they gave me the epidural I thought I'd died and gone to heaven. Nothing from the waist down. Nothing. They could have sawed me in half and I wouldn't have noticed. I told them all they were angels. I told them to come to my house so that we could have baked Alaska and steamed crab. I said they were the kindest, gentlest people in the whole world. I would always be grateful to them. I asked to kiss their feet.

They gave me other things too. I don't know what they were, but I wanted everything and asked for seconds. They made me count. I wondered why they all had shower caps on. It must be raining.

I talked to everyone. 'Howdy,' I said. 'Have you been to Quasar Hicks's Drive-In Funeral Home? It's a real treat.'

People smiled at me. I could tell, even though they all had green mouths.

'Have you heard the one about the wide-mouthed frog?' I said. No one thought I was funny.

There was a sucking sound like a plunger over a drain or a giant's mouth on a lollipop. I looked up at the mirror. Something blue. They've taken her out! My intestines follow. Fascinating. Sudden quiet. They are letting me sleep. Baby cries. Let me hold her. 'My God, my God!' – Manny's voice. Full of emotion. Just like the men who become daddies on *All My Children*. I always knew it would be like this. I'd given him a baby. Silence.

There is a man speaking down at me. He has a white coat on. There is a woman too, also in a white coat. She is holding my hand. There is a priest in the corner. Manny has disappeared. There is a bundle of clothes over there on the other bed. No. It's Manny grown shorter. 'Stand up,' I tell him. 'I am standing,' he says.

Manny's eyes look funny. The doctor is telling me something. Something about priestesses. I tell him to hush. There's a Catholic priest in the room. We can talk later.

When at last I understand, I tell them to bring her in to me. They say I can wait until I'm stronger if I want. I swear at them. They bring her in to me.

The nurse who puts her into my arms is the one who told me for fourteen hours that everything was normal. She is crying. They watch as I unwrap my child.

I've unwrapped my baby twelve times now. I've been counting. This will be the thirteenth time I've gently pulled back the blanket stamped with the hospital's initials and seen their mistake.

Right leg: Good.

Left leg: Fine.

One, two, three, four, five, six, seven, eight, nine, ten toes. That's right. Torso: Excellent.

Right arm: Lovely.

Fingers now – one, two, three, four, five. Once I caught a fish – no, no. Don't sing that.

Left arm . . .

Left arm . . .

Left?

Someone has made a terrible mistake.

I'll have to make sure I tell Manny.

Some fool has swapped my baby's arm for a fish's fin.

They'll be frantic when they find out. They'll have to search until they find the culprit swimming around with an infant's arm where its fin should be.

I'll tell them in a moment, when Manny stops crying. They'll pay for this. It isn't right to frighten me this way.

I begin the ritual again, pulling the blanket aside with a flourish this time, the way a magician would when he wants to alter what your eyes have been witness to.

The clock in the private room ticks as loudly as time past. The hands move round to the right the way they always do. Through the window, the hills change from brown to purple to black. Mostly they let me keep it. Sometimes they take it away. It always comes back the same, so I wait patiently for them to find the rest of it.

Manny sits in a chair beside me. Sometimes he is a picture. Sometimes the picture blinks.

Somewhere in the back of my mind, I feel the word 'luck' pushing itself to the surface. Luck had something to do with this. Blind, dumb luck. I see the great basketball player Lawrence Helios hurl a ball through the expectant air of the arena. If he'd had a little less luck, could I have had a little more? I hear the people clapping.

What is the sound of one hand clapping?

No sound.

Silence.

6

Two days after the baby was born, Manny left.

No one could find him. His mother showed more anger than I'd imagined she was capable of. She spoke of him with derision, saying that he needed to start growing up if he was ever to function in this world, and held her grandchild to her breast with a kind of savagery that seemed to surprise even her.

I asked her to find out whether there could have been some mistake. 'Maybe it's someone else's,' I said. Lydia patted my hand.

When there was a knock on the door late in the evening, I was sure it was Manny. I sat up quickly with the baby in my arms, forgetting how painful sudden movements are after C-sections.

It wasn't Manny. It was Alfred and Louise.

I stared at them as though they were ghosts. They rushed up to the bed and stood gazing down at me and my child.

'She's beautiful,' Alfred said.

'She certainly is,' my mother echoed.

'But look . . . look,' I said, pushing the blanket aside. 'Something went wrong, Mum, Alfred . . . Something very . . . fishy.' The word leaped out before I could stop it. I saw the worn stair carpet at Lavender Sweep come back to haunt me, swathed in a long band of ugliness that had followed us from the Sweep. It wasn't just the worn stair carpet, it was also the taunts and racial slurs, the patched-together lives of our neighbors, and a damp house that sheltered a tragic, futile love. 'Look!' I said, pulling the blanket aside, half-believing that, if I tried hard enough, I could magic the abnormality away.

'We know,' they said. 'Lydia called us.'

'Something went wrong,' I said, showing them again. 'Can you make it better?'

Alfred and Louise stayed for two weeks. They would have stayed longer if I hadn't shut them out. What I didn't tell them was that I was deeply ashamed. If I'd had the ultrasound we would have been forewarned and the tragedy could have been avoided. On top of that, I carried a nagging secret. When I was two months pregnant, I'd taken extra-strength painkillers, forgetting about the fetus altogether. It was my fault the baby was malformed. When, after three days, Manny came back with a distant expression on his face and a new habit of scanning the floor, he asked them and Lydia to leave.

'You won't find her arm under the bed, Manny,' Lydia said, shocking us all. 'So why don't you stop looking for it and start loving your baby.'

He told her he didn't know what she was talking about. Alfred followed him when he stormed out of the hospital room.

'Sometimes I despise him,' Lydia said, placing the baby in my arms. 'His father was the same. Made the boy feel wretched because he wasn't tall enough. "No son of mine is going to be five foot two! That's a girl's height!" That was the way he was. A damn fool. Measured the boy every week. Gave him a complex. Beat him every other week if he was drunk enough. Jack Daniels. Loved his Jack Daniels. He could be charming without the booze, but with it he was the devil himself. Broke the boy's arm once. Man was a fool. Best thing I ever did was divorce him, in spite of what the reverend said. The church can ruin the lives of women, you know? But look at this child! She's a little piece of heaven and he can't see it because my son is a jerk. Like father, like son.' She set her face in a scowl, then reached over and took the baby back from me. Her expression softened each time she held the child in her arms. I envied her the peace she found in her adoption of motherhood. I wished Manny had let me know about his father. I wished it because I never would have married him had I known about the demons he carried.

Alfred tried to talk to Manny but he didn't have any luck. He gave up in the end and sat with me instead. He read me Simon's stories and my own poems, which he'd bound in a volume he'd covered in dried flowers and plastic. 'JACINTA'S POEMS' was the handwritten title on the cover. He said Louise had helped by gathering the wildflowers. They made a special trip to the New Forest to find some, he said. The poems I'd sent them over the past two years were pasted to the pages of the scrapbook. Next to them were photos of me as a child and excerpts from my father's stories. Alfred had grouped them thematically. He said Simon and I wrote from the same convictions. I didn't say anything.

Alfred and the baby became inseparable soon after he arrived. Lydia was jealous at first, then she let him have it. The baby was quiet with Alfred; she even seemed to smile.

I came down with a case of the flu so they kept me in the hospital for a few more days. I enjoyed being sick; it meant I didn't have to do anything. I watched *All My Children* and imagined I was Erica Kane because she escaped from her nightmares. When they tried to usurp her, she found a way out; if they came along to bankrupt her, she was a millionaire again in a month or two. Erica conquered the world with cunning and coy artifice. I didn't care that it was ridiculous. Anything was better than Manny's face.

I didn't hold the baby much; I couldn't hold it without unwrapping the blanket to see if anyone had found the other part yet. It got on Alfred's nerves when I did that. Once he snatched it away from me and told me I was becoming as big a nincompoop as my husband.

'Look, Cinta! Look at her! No, don't turn away. Don't you see, child? She's beautiful. You have a beautiful little girl. I'll tell you something. Don't look away! If you can learn to look at her without thinking about what's not there, she will grow up to be a strong woman. My mum did that for me. She looked at me when I was a teenager, and at first you could tell I wasn't what she'd hoped for. But she overcame it. She took me in her arms and she said, "Alf, your father thinks you're a queer and he hates you for it. The boys at school beat you up every week because you're not like boys are supposed to be. And now you say you want to be an actor so I suppose there's no hope you'll be changing any time soon. So I just want you to know you've got one ally in this bleedin' awful life who'll stick by you no matter what. And that's me. And I may not be much but I love you enough for twenty dads and a thousand friends. And you and I can see most things through if we stick together." And we did until she died. We stuck together against all the rest.

'I don't know how to let you know what that means. All I can say is that you die without that kind of unconditional love from somewhere, otherwise you look as if you're alive, but you're not. If you only do one thing in your life, love your baby with all your heart. Please. You ruled the roost on Lavender Sweep. You did it since you were a baby. It spoiled you, in a way. You go whichever way you choose and you don't think about other people. You're not evil, Cinta, just a little dangerous. But now it's time to think about others. It's time to grow up. It's time to love your baby because it's either that or torment. There's nothing in between. It's time to love someone more than you love yourself. It's time.'

He put the baby into my arms and left us alone.

I must have sat quite still for a long time. Then the baby stirred and began to whimper. I'd been bottle feeding. I hadn't wanted to nurse. Besides, I'd been sick. But I was over the worst. I undid my nightdress and let the baby find my nipple. There wasn't much milk there – probably nothing at all – but it comforted the baby. The crying stopped. As the baby sucked it pulled on its ear and patted my breast as if it were trying to comfort me.

'O, girl-baby,' I whispered. 'O, baby, baby, baby.'

I reached down and drew aside the hospital blanket she was swaddled in. I looked long and hard at the flesh shaped like a flipper on her left shoulder. If you weren't expecting something else, it had a kind of cuteness to it. It wasn't grotesque – just tiny.

The baby opened her eyes, looking for an ally in this bleeding world who would love her enough for twenty dads and a thousand friends. She fell asleep sucking. I lifted her up gently and kissed the bud that grew from her left shoulder.

That was the beginning of a pact between us. Between the baby and me. As we lay there together, something rose up inside me and made me begin to recognize the splendor of my child. Holding her in my arms, I realized she was mine to love or to leave. Manny had left us. Even though he had come back, he was still gone. I held the baby tightly to my breast. I'd be damned if I would treat her the same way he had.

Louise and Alfred enjoyed their visit, in spite of me. They visited the campus and saw a bus trip advertised in the student union that they bought tickets for. The trip was to Busch Gardens, all-inclusive. They traveled in a bus with thirty students from the university and caused quite a stir. I was hurt that they were having a vacation while I was languishing in the hospital; but there were days when I wouldn't speak to them at all, and I suppose they finally took the hint when I told them to go away. Alfred came back raving about the rides he'd been on. 'We could see the whole world from the top of the roller coaster; your mother was quite sick. It was *wonderful*.' Louise talked about the European feel of the place. 'It's all plastic,' I said. 'Yes,' she told me, completely misunderstanding what I was trying to tell her. 'I don't know how they do it. It looks so real! And America is so clean, isn't it? That's what I like, the cleanliness. You just don't see that kind of cleanliness in London. Everything's covered in graffiti there.' Alfred joined in: 'And I've seen people with those nice shovels and pans they use to scoop up the dog doo-doo. That's a nice touch.'

'The baby's sick,' I said, furious with both of them.

'Why didn't you say something? What's wrong with her?' they cried.

I shrugged. 'Could be anything. Her breathing isn't right. They're doing tests today.'

'Poor little thing,' Louise said.

Alfred was pale. 'Is it . . . ? How serious? . . . I mean . . .'

I shrugged again, then gazed out of the window.

They stayed close by after that. No more trips to theme parks. Louise did go to the mall once, but it was a quick visit. The rest of the time they stayed with me and the baby. They probably realized I'd been melodramatic about a slight cough the baby had. But neither of them said anything.

Now that I'd begun to love the baby, Manny became the root of my pain. Angry at him, I filled his absence with irritation directed at Alfred and Louise because they were there. I had to be angry with someone.

Alfred still got on my nerves because he wouldn't shut up about his excursion to Busch Gardens. Every few minutes it was Busch Gardens this or Busch Gardens that. When he realized the park was owned by the beer company, he bought a six-pack and toasted roller coasters. My mother was just as bad. If I heard how clean things were in the United States one more time I'd barf. I told her so. She said, 'Why do you need a bath? I thought you took a shower earlier today.' It was useless. I tried to explain how violent most American cities were. They both listened with their ears closed, and then told me what was incredible about the funnel cakes at Busch Gardens was the light dusting of confectioner's sugar on the top. I told them that a child was shot in America every ten seconds. (I didn't know whether that was accurate, but I thought it would carry some weight.) They said that was a terrible shame, and wasn't there a gondola of some kind in the Italian section of the park, or was it over there by the theater?

I'd never been to Busch Gardens. Manny had said theme parks were a waste of money. And now, were I to go with the baby, everyone would stare. I'd stared. Each time I'd seen a family with a child like the one I'd had I would send up a silent prayer and be glad it wasn't me. And now it was me. I could never go unnoticed to a public place. There would always be curious onlookers hoping for a quick rise from someone else's misery. Well, tough shit, I thought. If anyone stares at my child, I'll gouge their eyes out. Vengeance comforted me. No one would hurt my child.

'I think Manny was right,' I said the day before I was due to be discharged. Alfred was cooing to the baby in his arms; Louise was looking out of the window at the remarkable cleanliness of the street below. 'I think you should both go home. The show's over.'

'Now, Jacinta. That's no way to speak to your mother. She's come a long way to be here and –'

'That's all right, Alfred. I think Jacinta's tired.'

'Damn right I'm tired, you old fool! I'm tired of you telling me how clean everything is when everything is soiled now. Soiled, soiled, *soiled*! I hate him! I hate the bastard! And you are getting on my nerves, do you understand? So chirpy all the time. It's nauseating. Where's a person supposed to get some peace around here? You think it's easy listening to you go on and on about your fabulous day trip to some shitty theme park? You think I don't know how glad you were to get away from us?'

'Jacinta!' Louise cried. 'We would never have left if you hadn't told us to leave. We thought you wanted some time alone.'

'I hate him,' I said softly. 'I wish he was dead.'

Alfred held the baby close to his chest and looked down. He knew I was sincere. My anger bled into the room until it was soaked in venom. No one knew what to say.

'I want to kill him,' I said at last. 'He left us just like you did, Louise. Just like you.' My mother sat down in a chair like someone who had had all the air let out of her. 'I want you two to leave now. Both of you. Now. Give her to me.'

I reached out to take the baby.

'Give her to me.'

Alfred didn't want to do it. He held on to the baby until Louise told him to hand it over. She was crying. I didn't care. The only thing I wanted was for them to leave. When they walked out I began humming a tune from *Porgy and Bess*. 'I Got Plenty o' Nuthin'.' I hummed myself into a frenzy and then fell asleep, the baby still cradled in my arms.

The next morning, as I was being prepped for the trip home with a man I'd grown to hate, Alfred and Louise came into the room dressed for a trip.

'We came to say good-bye,' they said.

'Good-bye.'

'May we see Lydia?'

'She's down in the cafeteria.'

'No. The baby. Little Lydia. May we see her before we go?'

I shrugged.

'We love you,' Alfred said.

My mother kissed me. 'We can still stay, if you want. The people at the airline have been very sweet. They said we could change our plans if we needed to. We explained the situation and –'

'What "situation" is that? The baby with one arm? The mother on the brink of a breakdown? The father who is too damn cowardly to love his child? Which situation are you referring to, Mother?'

Louise bowed her head. I'd conquered her.

'You're acting like a spoiled child,' Alfred said as he patted my mother's hand.

'Am I? So what?'

'Remember what I told you.'

'Sure. I'll remember it.'

Alfred shook his head and then they were gone.

They stopped by the nursery after they left my room. The nurse told me Alfred had wept over the baby and asked if the hospital would call if things didn't improve. I told her I'd sue if they so much as thought about calling anyone. She wouldn't talk to me after that.

An hour later, however, the baby's breathing got worse. The doctor said I could stay for a while, wait until the afternoon to be discharged. By late morning, the baby was sick. By the afternoon, she was very sick. The doctors came and told Manny and me the baby needed surgery – she was messed up on the inside too, apparently, though none of what he told us made any sense to me. If she didn't have the surgery, she would die.

Manny and I were left alone.

'It's for the best, Jazz,' he said, taking my hand in his. He hadn't touched me since the baby had been born. His hands were cold and clammy.

'What do you mean?' I asked him.

'I mean . . . if things don't work out with the surgery. . . . It would never be normal. It wouldn't be fair –'

'Fair for whom, my sweet? For you, that's who! Christ, you're even worse than I thought.'

'Don't you try it, Jazz. I'm warning you.'

'Try what?'

'The holier-than-thou shit. I know what you've been saying to people. I know you want the problem to go away as much as I do. We didn't make this happen. We don't have to let it suffer and suffer ourselves. I'm not saying . . . I'm just saying we should ask if . . . if we don't opt for surgery –'

'*Opt* for it! Did you hear what the doctor said? Without it she'll probably die. We don't have an option! We may have had a choice once, before she was born, but it's gone now. She's ours. It's too late.'

'It's not, Jazz. Don't say that. I can talk to the doctor. He'll understand. You should have seen his face when it came out. He felt like we did. We can be like we were in the old days. We can laugh and joke and love each other. Next time we'll do it right. We'll have the ultrasound. We'll do it right.'

'No, Manny. It's too late. He wasn't giving us a choice. It would be murder. We'd be killing our baby. It's not like she has something major wrong with her. She's not one of those babies with no brains or anything. She may be brilliant for all we know. She may –'

'It's not too late. It's our *choice*. We can say no. It may die anyway, even with the surgery. There's no guarantee. Why put the poor little thing through that hell? We don't have to do it, Jazz.'

His face was red and he was gesticulating wildly to get his point across.

Just then, they brought the baby in.

The nurse handed her to me without saying a word and then walked out. The baby was very quiet. She looked weak.

'Why'd she do that, for Christ's sake?' Manny said. 'Don't these people communicate with each other, for Christ's sake? It should be in the nursery, for Christ's sake! We have a decision to make here.'

I held the baby in my arms.

'She's burning up,' I said.

'Why'd they do that, for Christ's sake? We have a decision to make.'

'I think she has a fever.'

'They need to take it back. I'll call them and tell them to take it back.'

I grabbed Manny's wrist and held it so tightly he had to wrench it out of my hand.

'What the hell are you doing, Jazz? What's the matter with you? Let me take it back to –'

'Her. She's a "her," not an "it."'

'What?'

'She's a *girl*. She's our little girl. You keep calling her an "it."'

'Okay, okay. I'm sorry, okay? Now let me take . . . her, okay?'

'Just try it.'

'Jacinta, you're not thinking straight. Let me –'

'If you touch a hair on her head, I'll kill you.'

'Jacinta, you're tired. You don't know what you're saying. We need to talk –'

'We have nothing to talk about. You're not touching her. You're going to go and find the doctor and tell him we're ready. Do you understand, Manny? You're going to go and find the doctor right now and tell him we're ready to go ahead with the surgery.'

Manny's bottom lip began to tremble. Then it spread to his whole face. He looked as if he were about to have a fit.

'I can't do this, Jazz!' he blurted out. 'I'm no good with handicapped people. I'm no good. We can put it up for adoption. That's one of the reasons I couldn't take Africa, if you want to know the truth. Those lepers. Those stubs for arms and legs. Outside the goddamn grocery store, for God's sake! Reaching out to you. Grabbing you. No noses. The filth . . . I couldn't take it.'

'I thought Africa was paradise. I thought that's where we'd be taking our beautiful little girl.'

Manny looked away.

'You never really intended to go back, did you, Manny? All of this, the whole thing, was just a farce, wasn't it? Your daydream.

God, I despise you. You're pathetic. Now listen carefully when I say this. It's too late to give her up even if we had the choice.'

'Why?'

'Because I love her.'

He sat down hard in the chair by the bed and put his head in his hands.

We grieved in silence.

Then the nurse came back to take the baby. Manny left soon afterward. I called the doctor and told him we were ready to sign the papers. He told me again it would be a complicated procedure but that the success rate was excellent. I signed the papers saying I wouldn't sue them if they failed. Manny couldn't be found until several hours after the surgery began.

He came in and joined me in the waiting room near the OR. We sat in silence until the doctor entered and told us everything had gone well. Manny looked down when the doctor delivered the news. I walked out then. Out of that room where he was and into the corridor. I walked slowly because I was still sore. I found the chapel and stepped inside. I knelt down and joined my hands together. I wanted to pray, but all I could find were two words to repeat over and over again: 'Thank you, thank you, thank you.'

I had wished her perfect and wished her gone; neither of those wishes had been granted. I had a daughter. She would be mine the way Alfred had described. And if Manny could never bring himself to see what was there for the fact of what wasn't, then I would love her twice as much, five times as truly as any father would. She was mine now; he'd given her over to me when he'd made the decision to lose her.

I turned around; he was standing at the back of the chapel.

'You got what you wanted,' he said. 'Looks as though it's here to stay. I'm going now. I'll pick you up tomorrow. They say you can stay an extra day courtesy of the hospital. So damn scared of being sued they'll do anything to make you comfortable. Should sue them anyway. It's their fault she's deformed. It's their fault. Then there are all the other expenses. God knows what the co-payments will amount to.'

'We're covered, aren't we?'

'Only ninety percent. I'll pick you up at nine. Doctor should have okayed it by then.' I could hardly believe we were arguing about money again. It was almost funny.

'I want to call her Lady,' I said.

'Who?'

'The baby. Who do you think?'

'It's a dog's name.'

'Lady Moses.'

Manny looked at me. There was nothing tender in his expression. 'Whatever,' he said.

'I like your mother's name, but I think Lady's more —'

'I don't give a damn what you call it, okay? I'll be here tomorrow morning.'

I raised myself from the kneeling position and sat down on the pew behind me. The door swung slowly on its hinges in the wake of Manny's exit.

I'd given Lady her name. I'd claimed her as mine. Manny didn't want her. He'd given up all claim to her as easily as someone discards an idea. She was supposed to be his idea of perfection, but she hadn't passed the test. If she were to grow up to be vain and selfish, he would have been proud of her. 'Look at my lovely daughter,' he would have boasted. 'See how many hearts she breaks.' For all we knew, Lady could be a genius. She could be the next great artist of the Western hemisphere. She could sing like Leontyne Price or dance like Margot Fonteyn. She could write music like Beethoven or paint pictures like Georgia O'Keeffe. Or she could have the rarest gift of all: she could recreate happiness and bestow it freely on people she met. And still her father would be looking for the missing part, wondering at his own misfortune. The act of despising my husband relieved me of my own guilt. Next to him, I looked pretty wonderful.

'Lady Moses,' I mumbled, to no one in particular. 'Lady Moses. My daughter. You came back. And this time I was ready.'

Perhaps we'd go to Africa after all. Perhaps that would help. I could take my daughter back to where my father came from. We would be happy there, in his land, among his people. Maybe Manny could . . . No. Don't do that to yourself. Manny was dead now. He'd chosen a different path. Even if we went there together, Lady and I would be on our own.

But I wasn't afraid. I didn't think I'd ever be really afraid for myself anymore. Something larger had replaced that fear.

Later, when I went to intensive care and held her tiny hand, I brought each one of her fingers to my mouth and kissed them. She smelled of milk combined with something else. What was it? I couldn't say exactly; but it reminded me of a time I'd spent at Brighton once with my parents, just before my father had his heart attack. It was the smell of the wind brushed over the waves; it was the smell of sunlight on water. I thought about the mother of Leonora Hicks, the little girl at the drive-in funeral home who had drowned. My daughter had not drowned. She was still with us; I'd been allowed to keep her. Luck took many different forms. Sometimes it masqueraded as tragedy; sometimes it closed all the doors of the world. Luck gave me Lady. Lady Luck could take her back. Five pounds of flesh had just begun to alter things.

When Manny came the next day to pick me up, I told him Lady would be ready to come home with us in about a week, if all went well. I told him if he ever tried to harm her I'd have him put in prison. And I told him to look into finding contract work in West Africa so that we could go there once we'd graduated from the writing program. 'Lady will be around two by then,' I said. 'Everything's changed. I didn't want to go before but now I do.'

'Do *I* have any say in this or will it be Your Highness's decision?'

His sarcasm slid off me like baby oil.

'Lady and I are going to Africa once I've graduated from the program. You can come too, if you like. If you don't want to come with us, that's fine. No one's going to beg you.'

He flung my suitcase into the trunk and I had to scoot out of the wheelchair and into the car on my own. I didn't care. We didn't need him anymore.

'I don't plan on going to some Third World country with some handicapped kid. Who's going to pay the medical bills when she gets sick again?'

'I'm sure it won't be you, will it, Manny?'

He set his face to the road and followed the exit signs out of the parking lot.

'We're going to West Africa whether you like it or not. The offer will be there if you want to come with us. That's all we need to say to each other right now. I despise you and you hate me. And there's an end to it. One day we may feel differently, who knows? But right now I haven't got the energy to care about what happens to you. I need to visit the country my father grew up in.'

'You're the most selfish person I've ever met,' he said.

I sighed. He hadn't said he wouldn't come with us. When you're Catholic you stay married against all the odds because there's always the chance miracles can happen – at least that's what I'd been raised to believe. But I'd never been as devout as I'd once hoped I'd be. Skepticism and irony crept into my faith and curled up the Bible pages and smudged the print. If Manny remained as pathetic as he was right now, sooner or later I'd leave him.

On the drive home from the hospital, I dozed off. My head was filled with pictures of red-ribboned children floating to the surface of something strange; and fish, leaping like commas of silver sunlight high above the waves that had held them in the dark for much too long. And propelling the visions was Africa – rich and lovely dark – waiting for us to come home.

7

The night before the funeral, I sit with Alfred and Lady and prepare the lecture I plan to give when I return to teach in Virginia. I don't teach at the place where Manny and I received our degrees, but at a much more modest institution in the western corner of the state. When I went back there after Africa, I found friendship and peace. The mountains nurtured me, and I found the space I needed in order to watch Lady grow.

I write the lecture because, now that Louise has gone, I need to find a way to get things in focus. Lady sits beside me on the pretty sofa Louise bought with her teaching salary long after I left for the New World. Alfred sits across from us in an easy chair. He looks old. He is old – well past seventy now. I smile at him. He smiles back. Jane, a good friend of mine at the college, has taken over the class in my absence, but I am scheduled to teach *Philadelphia Fire*, Wideman's novel about urban chaos and the repercussions of racism, when I get back. I don't know whether I will be able to do it. It is too close to the pain I have known.

The graduate students in the class sent a large bouquet of red roses for me and Lady and a wreath for my mother. They arrived this afternoon. Lady squeals in delight when they are dropped off. 'My first bouquet!' she cries, making Alfred and me laugh. Earlier in the day, Lady posed in front of the mirror, trying to decide whether or not to wear her prosthesis for the funeral. In the end, she decided against it. Alfred and I agreed to pin up the sleeve on her black velvet dress using one of the beautiful red roses from the bouquet.

'Am I beautiful like you and Mama Lou?' she asks me while we experiment with the corsage.

'What do you think?' I ask her.

'I think yes,' she answers, 'on some days. Not on other days. When I have a bad hair day, for example, then I look pretty gross.'

'Bad hair days,' Alfred commiserates. 'Those are, as you say in America, the pits. Your mother had to save me from many of those with a judicious application of mascara and hair spray.'

Later we hear Lady out on the doorstep, which is still red, painted a dull crimson by Alfred rather than polished to a shining ruby by Lily Beadycap. She is looking out at the rain, which has been coming down heavily since noon. At first we can't hear what she's saying as we peek out at her through the net curtains, then we both fathom it at once. 'Cease! Cease!' my little girl cries, commanding the rain to stop.

'She will be one to reckon with, I reckon,' Alfred says, in an atrocious impersonation of an American accent.

'Like mother, like daughter,' I reply.

Cease. Cease. It would be a great gift if the demons of the world would cease their rioting and let us all live in peace. As I sit and work on the lecture, I try to find comfort in causality – but it escapes me again, and what is left is a remembrance of evil and its strange intersection with glory.

I write down some thoughts. I'll hone them into something more coherent when I get back to America. I try the lecture's introduction out on Alfred and Lady as we sit in the pretty room Louise had to decorate without me.

'Some people may wonder why Wideman would write a book like this. It's relentless. There is pain everywhere. Characters wander around looking for clues, trying to find the way back. Some are going back to Africa; some to a time before the storm; some to a bright circle of peace that can exist on a basketball court or in a woman's hair. We could write some fine

essays about this book – about the persistent metaphor of the
tempest that controls the mood of the prose – about the savage
disillusionment of the main character. We could even pretend
this was a novel. But it's not. And sometimes I wonder whether
art takes us farther away rather than closer to where we should
be. We've read it; and now we think we understand something.
But we can never understand racism or tragedy or pain unless
we suffer them. And within the walls that surround our privileged campus, suffering is, by definition, once removed.

'Some people wonder why Wideman wrote a book like this.
I think perhaps it was because he had to tell the story – the way
Holocaust survivors are forced to bear witness to the unbearable
heaviness of being. And because he knew he could. Some of his
readers will know how to read this book. The fire inside them
will connect to the flaming pages, and they'll have to keep
putting it down and taking deep breaths because burning and
drowning are the same thing; and they'll say, "How did he know
what I've seen?" And they'll shake their heads at the awful
grandeur of the world.

'I knew a woman in Africa who could sing the way
Wideman writes. When she put her voice down on the table in
front of you, just next to your screwdriver or your beer, you put
your hand over your mouth, thinking the voice arose from your
own throat. She had a rare talent: she could take your pain and
fashion it into her beauty and hand it back to you as a recog-
nizable thing. She could create spaces in her voice, pauses for
you to lie down inside and dream. She could make you wish
you were dead and make you thrilled by the glories of life all
at the same time. And when the fire came the next time, you
were ready. Because of that woman's voice and the wings it
had given you.

'At some time you will suffer. Some of you have already. And
at some time nothing will be there to comfort you. If this book
has worked, you'll think about Wideman and his Philadelphia
fire. You'll think about the firestorms and what they take from
you. And, if you're very lucky, you'll emerge through them to
discover what it is they give back.'

Alfred nods his head. Lady, although I don't believe she has understood much of what I've read, applauds by banging on the arm of the sofa and stomping her feet on the floor.

'I like it!' she says. 'I remember Africa already!'

Alfred wants to meet the woman I've written about, the singer. He says when you meet someone like that it's like having a good mother – a blessing that continues throughout your life.

Later that evening I find myself in Louise's room – the room that, during my time, was mildewed and uninhabitable. Now it is full of small treasures. She kept every item she ever collected in her visits with us, and squirreled them away to look at later: photographs of the three of us together, postcards from Natural Bridge and D.C., stamps, dinner menus, napkins from KFC. . . . They are in the drawers beside her bed. Underneath these mementos is the Dream Book I made for her birthday and a very early black-and-white photo of my father standing against a backdrop of palm trees. He is laughing. I see my eyes in his, and the barest hint of Lady's mouth there in his smile. The photo carries me back across the ocean in which so many of our snatched bones are buried.

I find a pen and a few sheets of paper. Time to climb on to the shoulders of the elephant again and begin the long journey across the ocean floor – back to the place where love reclaimed me, and death made one last, grand attempt to kidnap us all.

PART III

L U N A M A

1

We went to Africa when Lady was two years old. It was like entering one of Simon's stories. It made me believe in God.

Africa was Light. Objects came at me all at once before I had a chance to put them in order. Shadows at midday were a deeper black. Objects in shadow became voids, they lost the essence of what they were in sunlight and turned inside out into their opposites. There were trees and not-trees, men and not-men, snakes and not-snakes, things were lost altogether in the intensity of light and dark. Water shone there – not like a series of light particles, not in fragments, but in slabs of iridescence. In England, if light could cry out it would sound like an infant's wail. In Africa, the sound of light would be the shriek of a grown woman – the shriek of a prophet or the damned. Africa was never dark; they got it wrong. But Simon wrote that it stirred the darkness in white men who wanted to triumph over its gorgeousness and majesty.

In the early morning, a certain light rose from the earth – not the throwing on of light from above like a cape, but a rising from below, as if somewhere nearby the crust of the earth had split open, and lava had risen up, spreading itself and its gaseous light across the land. Things changed then, by magic. The faces of men on their mats bowing toward Mecca were suddenly lit from within; their skin turned to burnt copper and their clothes turned from cloth to clay as the light of dawn made everything malleable. It wasn't simply a world waking from sleep; it was a world shaking off the chains of mortality – at least that's the way it seemed to me because the contrast was so extreme.

By midday, the light changed into a glaring opaqueness, a thick wall. Walking in the noonday sun of tropical West Africa is a pushing through heat toward heat. People's block-dyed clothes are so bright that reds, greens, yellows, and blues don't look like themselves; they're hyperboles on cotton and linen. The people themselves seemed to absorb the light so that the dark skins of the nearly black became the color of their pupils, and the light skins of the lighter black became what dark should be. Things weren't lightened by the sun, they were deepened by it. At midday, the palm trees took on a bluey-greenness, the shade of the sea in a storm. If there was no breeze, the fronds were hard against the hot blue-white of the sky. Sometimes I'd imagine that part of the sky had been cut out to fit the shapes of the trees, the palms looked so bold lined up against the sky.

Then, when dusk descended, it was difficult to remember the way the sun had been before. People who looked old a few hours earlier were complimented on their good health; trees that seemed withered and grass that seemed brown at noon had a healthy sheen to them; and houses whose rusted tin roofs and bowed walls seemed ugly before glowed orange-white in the gentle light that covered the land.

At dusk, I often caught the shimmer of a black or green snake in the backyard. I wrote poems about elephants, and animals who used to roam across the land. Often I wrote about things that were not quite themselves, so a black snake in a poem became its logical, expanding jaw, and a banana tree became a series of yellows and earlobe greens, until I hardly knew what the images represented – shape and color were the same thing.

In West Africa, the word 'because' made a mockery of logic. The year we arrived Christmas had been canceled because the president decreed it; several thousand young men of a particular tribe disappeared within the space of a few weeks because it happened to be the time for tribal warfare; the usual number of women died in childbirth because they always did; a cow, a donkey, and a boy were buried alive by the paramount chief of the northern province because of a dream he had that told him doing this would restore his virility; and cholera vaccine that had been sent free from the U.S. was sold to the people because self-help was a government motto taken very literally by cabinet ministers who helped themselves. But I loved it just the same. And Lady and I grew whole again in its light.

Manny worked on a number of different agricultural projects, but I never learned much about them. He hadn't wanted to return to Africa after all. It had been a dream he'd held on to, never meaning to do anything about it. When he talked about the World Bank and IMF, the rice shortage or appropriate technology, I'd try to listen. But invariably my mind would wander and I'd end up focusing on Lady or on the view of the ocean we had from the dining room window. He rarely held Lady at that time. Rarely changed or bathed or fed her. It was understood that she was mine. I'd made her happen because I'd chosen to keep her. I had to pay.

I taught part-time at a girls' convent school in the city, just for something to do. Manny got a good salary, but I didn't see much of it. He'd pay the bills grudgingly, and I'd find money for 'extras' like Lady's clothes. I taught the girls on Monday, Wednesday, and Friday from noon to three. It was the hottest part of the day and the school, like all the others in the city, was without air-conditioning. The only unit they had hummed away in the principal's office. Sometimes I'd invent a problem just so I could go and sit in there and enjoy the artificial coolness. I'd leave Lady with Assieyatu, a young woman I'd met through another expatriate. She cleaned for a woman named Hilary Masters on the days when she wasn't looking after Lady. When they discovered I was paying her wages on an American scale, the Americans and Brits scolded me for encouraging indolence. 'They're not used to that kind of money,' they said. 'You'll spoil her.' I told them to bugger off and gained a reputation for crudeness that was somewhat thrilling. Assieyatu left Hilary's employ and came to work for me full-time. It took almost all the money I earned to pay her a decent wage, but it was worth it. We became friends. Soon we were going to the beach together with our children – she had a boy named Michael who stayed with her when he wasn't with her mother or her aunt. She would tell me stories about Temnes and Mendes, Creoles and Hausas, and I would listen because there was so much to learn, and even then I knew there wouldn't be much time.

In those first eight weeks, the beach times with Lady, Assie, and Michael were my main source of solace. Teaching was making me sick – literally and figuratively. Gradually I decreased my hours, supplementing my income with a little freelance editing so that I could pay Assie. The girls had no money for books or clothing. Their poverty threw me into depression. How could I change things simply by teaching a few girls about Shakespeare? Even if we read Achebe together, what difference did reading a Nigerian male make to their lives? There were no African women writers on the syllabus. There were no voices like their own. Those from Temne or Mende country spoke through the veils of three languages – their tribal language, then Krio, then English. We could hardly begin to know each other. My problems with air-conditioning or boredom were as remote from them as theirs were from me. We lived on parallel planes. When we intersected with each other, it was an illusion. But on the beach, I could pretend I had come home. On the beach we played together as children. Assie was only nineteen. Her son was four. She was raising him with the help of a mother and an aunt. Her home was upcountry, in a place called Lunama. She told me about her town as we sat on the beach. I made her describe it in detail, and she would laugh, not understanding the need I had to know the country. She was happy when I told her my father had come from there. 'You are African too, Jassie,' she said. 'Jassie and Assie. Two African women together.' Then we twirled around in a circle with the children in the middle nearly tripping us up. I told her we'd go to Lunama together soon. She clicked her tongue in her mouth and shrugged. I asked her if there was something there she didn't want to see again. She said the town was dying; it was the city she loved. The city was full of liveliness. 'The city is my kind of town,' she said, making me laugh again.

On the beach, Lady was wild. She knew how to swim before I put her in the water. 'She is a fish!' Assie cried, and I felt my heart contract. Then I looked at my daughter. She was the most beautiful thing I had ever seen. She moved through the water bent slightly to one side to compensate for the lost limb; and her tiny strokes were more graceful than children's doggy paddles. She smiled when a wave came down on her head and smiled when water got in her eyes. Her skin was as brown as mine. She was my child. I forgot Manny had anything to do with her. Assie told me Lady was special. 'She is not like other children,' she said as we sat at the edge of the water and watched the children play in the sand. 'How do you mean?' I said, bracing myself for insult. 'She is not like a two. She is like a four or a five. Michael is a smart boy, but Lady is a smarter girl. She can count and sing and dance. She can swim too. She is speaking Temne before I teach her. I think tomorrow she will read. You have a smart, smart one.' I thanked her. I would tell Manny about this. No. I wouldn't. He'd wanted her dead. She was mine. He could go to hell thinking his daughter was a mistake. I wouldn't tell him a bloody thing.

On the beach Africa was kind. The sand sparkled in the sun and the waves were turquoise or emerald green. We steered clear of most tourists and ex-pats. We mixed with Assie's friends – the waiters, the fishermen, the market women. We bought mangoes and pawpaws and ate them in the water so that the flies wouldn't get us. Lady took to swimming under-water. I'd watch for her for several seconds swimming just below the surface, then I'd reach down and pull her up. She didn't want to come. She'd get angry. Her little forehead would scrunch up and her mouth would be puckered into a sulk. I'd kiss her then and she would push me away. Then I'd tickle her and she'd laugh in waves and waves of childhood, and I'd be glad, so glad we were here in my father's country, she and I together.

When the rain came in brief, heavy downpours, we ran for shelter. We sat in the bar run by an old Irishman named Murphy. Assie drank Coke and I drank Star beer. The children played in the rain. We became beach bums. We were happy.

Although I fell in love with Africa, she wasn't an easy lover. She was capricious and occasionally insane. I must have lost my temper a hundred times within the first two months. When we lost the air-conditioning for three days, Lady developed a painful case of diaper rash. When the electricity went out for forty-eight hours, we spent two days on the beach just to avoid the stale air in the house. When I went to the market, I was penalized for being a 'Piss Corps,' which of course I wasn't. They told me all white people were Piss Corps. I said I wasn't white. The women in the market laughed hard at this. 'Black American, white American,' they said, 'what is different?' When I got angry, they laughed all the more. When I brought boxes of cereal home, they were filled with mealybugs. When I turned on the light in the kitchen, cockroaches scuttled off to hide. When we walked through the yard, Lady would cry out 'Sake!' and I would grab her in terror and run inside. For two months, I was angry, angry, angry. And then it all went away.

It's not supposed to happen like that. Change is meant to be a gradual thing. You adapt slowly, so they told us in orientation. Wives of contract workers often didn't adapt at all. They were psycho-vacked – a Peace Corps term invented by a doctor with a sense of humor – back home to recover from nervous break-downs. But that didn't happen to me. Instead I woke up one day to find I'd shed my anger the way a snake sheds its skin. In its place was an abiding curiosity, and a willingness to accept the land and the people on their own terms. I'd like to take credit for it, but some of that belongs to Esther Cole.

Assieyatu and Esther were friends. They had been lovers once, but they didn't refer to each other in that way because of course you loved your best girlfriends and of course you wanted to make them feel good. Sex was different for Assie. Sex was what you did when you felt like it without making too much of a fuss about the whole business. She would complain about Western views of lovemaking: 'Americans like to think about sex all the time. It is very puzzling. Then when they do it, they like to think about it again. I was with one man once, a Peace Corps. After we did it, he is sitting up in bed saying we did it. Now I know we did it because, Jacinta Louise Moses, I am there,

isn't it? But this man is telling me we did it as if it is a surprise
of some kind. Then he wanted to know if I liked it. Now why
would I do it if I did not like it? Am I mad? Am I a fool? I tell
him this. He is disappointed. Americans are always disappointed. They expect too much. They want everything
now. They want everything better. Americans do not know
how to wait for a bus. They do not know how to wait for a
fever to go down. They take pills or they ride in cars. Americans
are stupid.'

I found myself in the uncomfortable position of defending a
country and a people I had known only briefly. I tried to tell
Assie that people were much the same. Circumstances changed
them, but only cosmetically. Yet even I knew my argument was
weak. If you grow up without cars, electricity, running water,
televisions, shoes, if you grow up without enough rice, how
could you be the same as those of us who have all these things?
I'd grown up poor in London, very poor, but I was rich in comparison with most of the people here. We were not all the same;
privilege was the most successful form of segregation.

'You meet Esther,' Assie told me one day as we ran inside
Murphy's bar to shelter from the rain.

'Who's Esther?'

'Esther Cole,' Assie said with finality.

'Who's Esther Cole?'

'My girlfriend.'

'O. Why should I meet her? Does she live here in the city?'

'Yes. Most of the time. Sometimes not.'

'What does she do?'

'She is Esther Cole. She sings.'

'A singer.'

'Uh-huh.'

'Where?'

'Everywhere. Big hotels. Everywhere. You do not know her, is
it so?'

'No. I don't. I never go anywhere. How could I know her?'

'You go to the beach.'

'Does she sing on the beach?'

'You go to the market.'

'Does she sing in the market?'

'Everybody knows Esther Cole. She is too famous.'

'When do I meet her, then?'

'Tonight. She sings at the Kimani. Come with me. Only twenty dollars for a ticket.'

'Twenty dollars! Assie, I don't have it. You know what Manny's like with money.'

'I know you do not have it. You give it to me. Now I give it back. My treat. We go tonight.'

'Who'll look after Lady?' We both knew Manny was out of the question.

'My aunt,' Assie said.

She took my hand.

'Come on, girlfriend.' Her pretty eyes were wide and bright. 'All the people will see us. Two African women going to party at the Kimani. We will meet some fine people there. Very fine. They will buy us drinks.'

I shook my head.

'Okay, okay. They will buy me, Assieyatu, drinks and I will share them with my girlfriend. And then you will meet my Esther.'

'What's so special about this Esther Cole?'

'You will see,' she called over her shoulder as she ran back to the sea. 'You will see you are the same one.'

'The same what?' I called after her. But she was already in the water, too far away to hear what I'd said.

The hotel where Esther sang was new. The guests were European and American – businessmen and tourists accustomed to being entertained on demand. A few Indians and a few Lebanese stayed in the well-appointed rooms overlooking the beach, but most of the people who could afford to pay the Kimani's rates were white. They were served by Africans dressed in white jackets and black ties. I wondered how long it had taken them or their women to press these jackets with irons filled with hot coals. I'd tried it once and burned three of Manny's shirts. Assie had laughed so hard she had fallen over.

She said people from the West could not manage without electricity. She said she felt sorry for us.

The guests at the Kimani were not made up of local people, but everyone came to hear Esther sing. At least half of the audience in the ballroom was African. They stood up and cheered when she came onstage in her red African gown, embroidered with white thread. She was tall and strong. She weighed as much as most of the men in the audience. Her nose was generous, her lips full and dark. We sat toward the front. Assie's eyes were sparkling. 'Look!' she cried. 'Look at my Esther! See how they love her! She is a great one indeed, is it not so?' And I nodded because there was something of greatness in the way she inclined her head to the applause and in the way she looked out over the heads of the audience as if she were aiming for a place above us, as if she knew how to lead us there.

Later that night I wrote a poem about her. It was a sonnet and it began

When Esther sings, the world takes off its clothes.

And it was true. Because we did. She knew us – black, white, mixed, it didn't matter. She knew us. Esther had been where we had been and she had seen it with us. She'd seen my daughter's lost arm, swimming with the fish; she'd seen it in the paisley swirls of the stair carpet at Lavender Sweep; she'd seen Manny scanning the floor under the hospital bed, looking for it in the days after Lady was born; she'd seen my father in London saying good-bye to the woman he loved in a high-windowed ward made of British ice and indifference; she'd seen little Alison Bean cradled in her father's arms after the slaughter; she'd seen Leonora Hicks finding her way in the dark of drowning in Virginia; she'd seen Maurice Beadycap and his twin sister, Mary, as they groped for answers to questions they didn't know how to ask; and she'd seen my mother bury my father in a grave that was never large enough to hold him. She'd seen us all. We were in the quilt she made with her voice. She threaded us together and we were joined. There was no difference between us. Like Vera Butcher's Hubert, we didn't know where we began and where we ended. Outlines had disappeared. Everything was inside where we were.

I can't remember what Esther sang about that night, but I thought it had something to do with peace. In the West we call it inner peace, but for me in Africa it was stillness. It is standing in the heart of the bush and feeling its pulse and calling it home. It is the woman with wood balanced on her head turning toward you and saying, 'Kusheh, kusheh-ya' in slow motion. It is you not knowing where that woman begins and where she finishes because she is the bush — her skin the color of tree limbs, her clothes the colors of the earth. In the West we comfort by forgetting; we are always trying to escape. In Esther's songs, escape was not possible. Comfort was housed in remembrance. If you remembered what was lost, you were made strong. In the act of remembering was triumph. You cried and were washed clean. The key was always recognition.

I didn't fall in love with Esther that night because she did all she could to push me away. She came up to our table after she had finished singing and began to mock me. Esther liked to mock; it was her forte. She liked to take you and string you up on a pole and show you how foolish you were. When she spoke to you one-on-one, she was the antithesis of what she had been onstage. She wanted to make you suffer. Comfort was the farthest thing from her mind.

'Jacinta Louise Buttercup Moses,' she repeated after she had learned my names from Assie. 'Jacinta Louise Buttercup Moses.' She uttered my names with derision. Her accent and idioms were a strange mixture of Africa, Britain, and America. She tilted her head up so that she was looking down her broad nose at me. Assie thought it was all very funny.

'So you want to be an African like your daddy. How quaint. And you have come to learn about the culture by hearing Esther Cole sing. And what did you think, pretty little Jacinta Louise Buttercup Moses, of my performance?'

'You were stunning,' I said truthfully.

'Yes, I was. You are right. Stunning. I was stunning. I always stun. That's what I do best. Look around this room, Jacinta Louise Buttercup Moses, and you will see there are some men here who think I am a god; some women who would agree. Many of them have slept with me. I sleep with them once only. You know why?'

I tried to look indifferent.

'I sleep with them once because they bore me.'

Assie giggled. Esther let herself smile. There was a gap between her two front teeth. Enough space for a tongue to slip inside if it were turned sideways. She caught me looking at her mouth.

'Assie is my friend. We love each other. Assie says she loves you too. Is that so?' Esther asked.

'We're friends,' I said. I felt awkward, defensive.

'And what of you? Do you love her too, or will you do what all Americans do – take and then leave? I have seen many like you. Black Americans, black Europeans, coming here to claim the land. They sit on top of it like a chicken on a borrowed egg. They see nothing. Hear nothing. They go away thinking they are African because they have bought some gara fabric and a mask. And they use our people to look after their spoiled babies and do their yard work.'

She looked at me and laughed: 'But I am in hell already, Jacinta Moses. Didn't you know that from my singing?'

'I didn't say . . . I didn't –'

'You didn't have to *say* it, Jacinta Moses. Your eyes speak for you. You should be careful of eyes like that. They will betray you every time. They are not a politician's eyes. One day they could get you into serious trouble, isn't it so?'

'Why are you so rude?' I asked her.

'Rude? Rude? I am not rude, Jacinta Moses. I am Esther Cole. I say what I please when it pleases me to say it.'

'Sometimes you should learn to keep your mouth shut.'

She laughed again, much more loudly this time. Her laugh was broad. People stopped talking to hear it. The laughter spread out across the table between us like someone's hand.

'Ha, ha! So! Assie was right. We are the same,' she said.

Before I could think of anything to say in reply, Esther had stood up and was heading back toward the stage to begin singing again.

I told Assie we had to leave; it was getting late. Assie went crazy. She didn't want to go yet. This would be the best part. Esther would sing the water carrier song. She'd paid twenty dollars each for the tickets. It would be too sorrowful if we left now. There were tears in Assie's eyes. I took a deep breath and made my mouth smile in acquiescence.

I tried to turn my ears off to Esther's singing, but I couldn't. She seduced me again. I resisted at first – then there was no point. She was taking me to a beautiful place where the air was cool. A breeze was blowing in from the ocean and the moon hung in the sky like a clean wish. There was time to think. I let my mind go back to where Manny was sitting at home banging stories out on his old typewriter. *Bang, bang, bang.* Words and full stops – a man's way of seeing. Manny changed into my father, Simon. He was a man too and yet his words had wings with soft feathers on them. They brushed you quiet. Alfred was in the picture too, and Louise, saying she was sorry. Suddenly I wanted to go back to London, to the place I thought I would never want to see again. I wanted the house on Lavender Sweep and the narrow rooms. I thought there had been weeping in that house and I was right. But I'd forgotten the most important thing: there had also been love. Why had it taken me so long to remember that? Alfred's sweet and feminine face shone through the dark. As ugly as it was beautiful. Esther was taking me there. Esther Cole was taking me home.

When she'd finished singing, she snubbed us. She swept over to another table nearby and sat talking with a group of British tourists until we stood up to leave. Then she toasted us with the Bloody Mary in her hand. 'To blood,' she called out to us as we left.

'What did she mean?' I asked Assie as we unlocked the Jeep. 'What blood is she talking about?'

'It is her song – her famous one. It is called "Blood and" . . . "Blood and" . . . how can I forget? I am indeed a silly-Billy! It is about her own daughter, and it is about when she died. She sang it, Jassie, you remember? The song about the water carrier. I do not think you were listening, girlfriend.'

'She lost a child?'

'Of course!' Assie said, shaking her head at my stupidity. 'All night she was singing to us about that thing. Were you not listening to her? Didn't you hear what she was telling us?'

We got into the Jeep. Assie was excited. She was sitting in the front. It always made her happy.

'When I go to the United States, I will be driving around in Jeeps all my life. And people will see me and say, "There goes Assieyatu in her new Jeep. What a fine life she has."'

'How did her child die?'

Assie shrugged. 'She was a child. She died.'

'Yes, but how?'

'Americans always want to know the answers.'

'I'm not American.'

'She is the best singer in the world, is it not so?'

'Yes. It is so.'

'She will be there tomorrow.'

'Where?'

'On the beach.'

'Who invited her?'

'The beach is free. No one invites.'

'She doesn't like me. I have no intention of spending the afternoon with Esther Cole if she's in the same mood she was tonight.'

'She will be there. It will be a fine, fine day. We are the lucky people. Yes indeed.'

I drove home enraged.

If Esther Cole thought she could speak to me like that again, she had another think coming. Voice or no voice, the woman was a bitch. I'd find an excuse for not being there tomorrow. I'd seen Esther for the first and last time. I set my face to the road and drove on into the dark.

2

Esther didn't like the ocean. She said it was too big. In fact, she complained all afternoon: it was too hot on the beach; white people were the only ones who lay out in the sun with the mad dogs; Lady was too young to be swimming in the ocean – a wave could come and take her out to sea and it would be all my fault. What kind of a mother was I to treat my baby in this manner?

Most of the time I pretended I was utterly bored. I yawned twenty or thirty times. She was goading me. Assie had probably told her that I didn't want her to join us at the beach. She arrived a few minutes after we did with an entourage – a young girl of about fourteen who was her cousin or sister, a young man who looked to be in his early twenties, and an elderly woman Esther introduced as her mother. Later I learned the woman was a distant relative who'd come to the city to buy fabric. They all attended to Esther Cole's every whim. They seemed to consider me lucky to have Esther's company for a whole afternoon. I tried to make it clear from my expression that their idol made me sick.

Esther held audience on the beach. She gave speeches and issued commands. She was solicitous toward her maternal relative, doting over Lady, and reasonably kind toward Assie. The rest of us she treated like dirt.

On the beach, Esther's darkness was more pronounced than
it had been when she'd worn the red and white gown the night
before. On this day, she was dressed in yellow – a shocking
yellow. The word 'fragrant' came to mind because it was a color
deep enough to possess a scent. She had a matching yellow
headtie wound round her head, and the gown was drawn tight
underneath her full breasts so that it hugged her waist. She
used her hands when she spoke and they were covered in gold.
Her skin was like black water – a dark mirror. I sat there hating
her and loving her at the same time. She could afford to make
proclamations about Africa because Esther Cole was Africa dis-
tilled – at least that's what she'd have you believe. And, looking
at her, I found myself drawn into her creed, all the while hating
her for convincing me of it. Esther came from the land and she
would return to it, and Africa would open its arms to her in
welcome.

'You do not care for your child, Jacinta Moses,' she told me,
waving a regal hand across her face to bat away an insect. 'You
let her swim in the ocean with the waves. Is she a child or is she
a fish, Ma?' She turned to her relative to ask the question. All I
could see was her back. Her 'mother' tittered. I'd had it. I poked
her shoulder with my index finger.

'Listen, you, I've had enough. Lady's *my* child, get it? I do
what I want with her. She has nothing to do with you, okay?'

'All children are my children,' Esther said, raising herself up
proudly.

'The hell they are! Not my child anyway.'

Assie ran back just then with Lady in her arms. They were
both wet and laughing. Assie handed Lady to me and fell down
at Esther's feet. Esther put her hand on Assie's head and began
stroking her braids.

'The water is hot! Hot like ice!' Assie cried.

'Ice is cold, Assieyatu,' the young man told her.

'Ice is hot. It burns you when you hold it. Just like fire. Ice is
hot. And the water it is hot too.'

'The waves are strong,' Esther cautioned. 'You could get
pulled out to sea. The child is too young to be in the ocean.'

'I thought I told you to mind your own business.'

Esther narrowed her eyes and tried to stare me down. I stared back.

'You see!' Assie shouted, pointing at us both. 'You are the same.'

'No we're not!' My voice sounded childish. I wished I'd kept quiet.

Assie grabbed Lady again. 'Come on, little fish,' she said. 'We must go back into the ocean. It is calling us.'

Esther looked out after them. 'Children,' she said softly. Then she shook her head.

'I had a child,' she began.

'So?'

'I had a child just like your Lady.'

As if on cue, Esther's entourage stood up and walked off to another part of the beach. The young man led the elderly relative, and the girl skipped along ahead of them until they were all the size of my fingernail. Assieyatu's squeals were carried to us on the breeze. We sat under the umbrella Esther's people had erected for her and felt the sun through its shadow. No one else was nearby. This was siesta time. Most people had the sense to remain inside. I turned to look at the yellow of Esther's gown and the black of her eyes but she was still gazing after Assie and Lady.

'I had a child,' she repeated like someone who had memorized a poem and was ready to recite it. I waited for the next move. I thought of a chess game – Esther Cole as the black queen, me as the white one. I couldn't be black because she was; I was metamorphosed into her opposite. My own fragile link to the continent was made more fragile still.

Esther reached out during the pause and grabbed my hand.

At first I wanted to jerk it away. Then I noticed the coolness of her fingers. I didn't pull away. She began to stroke my hand from the palm to the tips of the fingers. Then she massaged the whole hand. Her fingers pulled on mine and I thought about cows and how we can milk them dry with the right techniques.

'What do you want?' I asked.

'I want only to tell you a story. Do you want to hear it, little Jacinta Moses?'

Her fingers were working my own. Now she ran them across my wrist and I thought of hummingbirds.

'Once upon a time there was a young woman. She was a black, black one, and very proud. She had a magic voice. When she sang the animals would listen, and the people would cry because it made their hearts large to hear her. This young woman traveled all over the world. Men took her. Men she met. And women too, if they had money enough. She came back to Africa filled with ideas. She had a baby. A little girl called Florence.'

'Florence?'

'Yes. Florence. A fine name. Better than giving a child the name of a dog.'

I pulled my hand away. She roared with laughter, then cut the sound off as if her will were a knife that could slice anything in two.

'Florence was a beautiful child. She could run like the wind even though she was only two or three years old. Her mother was proud of her. One day, her mother went away with one of the men she knew. She went to Paris. Everyone loved her. She came back. Florence had been in a fever for three days. She lifted up her little baby and kissed her. Hot. Hot. She held the baby in her arms until Florence stopped. When she stopped it was very quiet. The white doctor came. He said, "You are lucky. You came back in time." "In time for what?" she said.

'It was two days before she could give the child up to the earth. For two days she carried Florence around with her and sang to her. She was not mad; she knew her baby was dead. But she did not want to let her go until she was ready. On the third day she let go. Since that time the woman has grown old. She does not travel away from the land anymore because Florence is there. Good mothers do not leave their children behind.'

'I'm sorry,' I said.

'You have a girl too. She is alive today. She may be alive tomorrow. I cannot say those two sentences. Some people are lucky; some are not.'

'Some people would look at Lady and say I was very unlucky. Some people would pity me.' The bitterness in my voice took me by surprise.

'Why unlucky? Because of an arm!' She spat on the sand in disgust. 'People are fools. What do they know? What is an arm or an eye or hair or a nose? Nothing. The child *is* the child. Her blood is the same as yours. She lived inside you. She *is* you, is it not so? Her rhythm is your rhythm. And people who tell you she is not beautiful are ugly people themselves. Their hearts are sad. When they hear the rain they think of daggers, and when they see the sun all they know is thirst.'

She was drawing me close again. She had become the singer whose voice could make you strong. Her next words slapped me in the face:

'You know nothing, Jacinta Moses. You are a fool. We are not the same.'

I stood up without saying a word and walked down toward the sea. Lady and Assieyatu were sitting on the edge of the ocean where the surf met the sand. Lady screamed with delight whenever the waves reached her toes. The sun was fierce on the water. Lady had thrown off her sun hat; I tried to get it back on.

'She needs a sun hat in weather like this, Assie. Why doesn't she have it on?'

'She does not like the sun hat, girlfriend. She will not wear it.'

'Then it's time to leave,' I said, picking Lady up and marching off with her in my arms.

It took them a few seconds to catch on to what was happening; then they both began to cry.

'It is early. Mr. Murphy is expecting us. He has cold Star beer waiting at the bar. He will be too happy to meet Miss Esther Cole. He will never forgive us if we leave now.'

'Me want water! Me want water!' Lady cried.

I told them both to shut up. It came out before I could stop it, and then I couldn't take it back because I could feel Esther's eyes boring into my back. I didn't want to give her the satisfaction of seeing I'd lost control. Assie was stunned. We swept past Esther and headed for the Jeep. When I'd strapped Lady into her car seat, I turned to Assie to apologize, but she took off running before I had a chance to find the right words. 'Damn Esther Cole!' I said. 'Damn her to hell!'

Lady was still crying. At least I knew what to do as far as she was concerned. 'Cookie,' I said.

'Cookie! Cookie!' she cooed and stopped crying instantly, as if she were a faucet. Out of the corner of my eye, I caught sight of Assie skipping back to where Esther was sitting. It was obvious where her loyalties lay. I'd been a fool giving her all the money I earned. In return, what did she give me? A prima donna who thought she owned all the children in the world. I would never be able to stand Esther Cole; her ego didn't allow you in. This would be the last time I would see the woman. She was nothing more than an opinionated fool. I turned the ignition in the car and drove off fast enough to make the road howl.

Manny was in his study when we arrived. It was more a closet than a study, but he talked about it with pomposity, and I often envied him the tiny space he had all to himself. The electric typewriter was clicking itself to a frenzy. I didn't bother to let him know we were home. We didn't speak much unless it was necessary.

He emerged from the room when Lady began wailing again. She wanted Assie. She wanted the water. She said a word that sounded like Esther.

'What in Christ's name is the problem here?' Manny said as he walked into the kitchen.

I gave Lady a cookie and she was quiet. Her chest was still heaving but there was a grin on her face. She had what she wanted.

'How come you're back so early? Thought you were planning on making a day of it,' Manny said irritably. It was clear that he was counting on having the house to himself.

'Lady wouldn't wear her sun hat on the beach. I brought her home.'

'Where's Assieyatu?'

'She wanted to stay on the beach.'

'Are we paying her for this little vacation?'

'*We* never pay her at all, dear. And no. *I* am certainly not paying her for this afternoon.'

Manny sat down at the table with the bread and meat he'd taken from the refrigerator. He began to eat. I could see his jaws from the back as he chewed and swallowed. I was married to this man. I could hardly believe it. I used to want his tongue in my mouth and his hands all over my body. Why? I knew the writing wasn't going well. He'd told me a few weeks before that he was at a tricky stage in the novel – trying to orchestrate a confrontation between the boy and his father. He was up to page one hundred and eighty, he'd said. It was slow going, but he was making progress.

Lady was getting heavy on my lap. I stood up and put her in the high chair. She began to howl. She hated being confined, so meals were always a battle. I tried to ignore it, but I could feel the tension growing inside my head. I bit my lip to stop myself from swearing at her.

'How's the novel?' I asked, putting a spoonful of cereal into Lady's squalling mouth, trying to find something to take my mind off her behavior.

'It's a bitch.'

Lady spat out the oatmeal.

'How much did you get done today?' I asked absentmindedly, forgetting that Manny hated to 'talk pages' as he called it.

'Jesus, Jazz, that kind of thing isn't quantifiable, you know. A lot of fiction writing is thinking things through, mulling them over. Does she have a shirt to wear?'

Lady was naked from the waist up. Manny hated seeing her that way. I didn't think he'd ever touched her stump.

'She's happy like that.'

'She's half naked.'

'If you don't like it, you know what you can do.' There. I'd said it. For a moment it tasted good, then the good feeling evaporated and all that was left was bitterness.

Manny shoved back his chair and stood up. He still had bread and meat in his mouth. He spoke through it.

'Look, obviously you're in a rotten mood. Just don't take it out on me, okay? I'm going to the office. I was taking the afternoon off, it's so damn hot in that building. But at least it's peaceful. Salamatu doesn't nag me to death. I'll see you tonight.'

I was sitting in the echo of slammed doors for several minutes before I realized that Lady was screaming for more cereal. I handed her a cookie and put her in the playpen. For once, she didn't protest.

Salamatu was Manny's assistant – or rather, she was the assistant to many of the low-level contract workers for the nonprofit organization. When I'd visited the office once she'd told me how handsome my man was. 'I like the blond people,' she'd said. Her dress was so tight you could trace each one of her ribs, her navel, and both nipples. I had no doubt that Manny was right: Salamatu never nagged him to death.

Heat lay on the house like a blanket. The air-conditioning was noisy, and the air it sent out through old filters was stale. A sluggish fan turned in the living room, and the lights dimmed whenever the refrigerator kicked in or the a/c revved up. The house had too few windows. We had a spectacular view of the beach and another over the city, but the small windows didn't take advantage of it. The old vinyl on the floors had lost most of its original pattern, and the furniture was standard contract issue for those ex-pats of the lower order – those whose skills were needed but not prized. Yet we lived like royalty in comparison to most of the people in the country. We were the lucky ones. I laughed bitterly. We were the lucky ones.

Lady began to scream again. It echoed through the house and leaped back at me off the walls. 'Shut up!' I said to myself. 'Just shut up, for God's sake!'

I ran over to the playpen and yanked her up and out. Once again, her crying stopped instantaneously. Where was Assie? She should be here. She knew how to keep Lady quiet. I hated to admit that motherhood wasn't especially appealing on many days of the week. I wanted time just like Manny did. I too had writing to get done – a university press was interested in seeing a collection. I was more than a year behind now that motherhood and teaching had taken over. Manny claimed it would all be worth it once 'Sophie' was finished. It would make us a small fortune, he once said. A six-figure advance, a movie option. Three agents were already interested now that they'd seen a few chapters. I couldn't claim that for poetry. No one made money from that. So I'd become a woman who gives a man time to realize his dreams while stifling her own. Jesus, it had better pan out the way he says it will, I thought.

I walked into Manny's study. It wasn't a deliberate act – it just happened. Usually he kept it locked. He said he didn't want Lady getting into his things, but I knew it was me he wanted to keep out. I didn't care. But today I wandered in there and then found that a raging curiosity took over.

It was dark in his writing closet. The whole room was taken up by the desk, a chair, and a small bookshelf. I flipped through the pages on his desk. The manuscript, as expected, was called 'Sophie.' It began with a description of a woman –

He saw her emerge from the water – hair on fire, limbs as wet as mirrors – and he thought she was the most beautiful creature he'd ever seen . . .

I flipped over the pages. The chapter was ten or twelve pages long. The next chapter began

He saw her emerge from the water – her hair on fire, limbs alive with the sea – and he thought he would like to marry something as beautiful as that if he had the chance.

I hurried to the next chapter. Another version of the opening paragraph, a few more pages of notes. I looked around. This couldn't be his novel! He had written nearly two hundred pages. He'd told me so. Where was the rest?

And then I stopped looking. Suddenly I knew I wouldn't find any more because he hadn't written any more. 'Sophie' would never be written. Manny couldn't do it. My hands were shaking. He'd tricked me! He'd mocked my own achievements in poetry while staring at blank sheets of paper for years! He'd lied to me. Emmanuel Fox would never be a writer. The last vestige of respect I had for him fell away.

I didn't notice Lady. I didn't notice that she had a cookie and a cup of grape juice in her one hand. She came running up to me and planted her hand on the desk. The grape juice splattered all over Manny's pages. It looked like blood.

'O my God! Lady! You little fool! You are so stupid!'

She looked at me with eyes wide open and took it all in. Then she looked down and took three deep breaths. Then she turned around and stumbled out into the living room. I looked at the pages – they were ruined. He'd know what I'd seen. All the masks were off. I put my head in my hands to steady them.

Several minutes afterward I went out to the kitchen to fetch a cloth. I'd wipe up what I could; the rest would just have to be Lady's fault. He left the door open; she got in. No one was to blame but Manny.

I'd forgotten all about Lady. When I entered the living room, I saw her pulling wildly at her tiny left arm. 'Bad, bad, bad!' she whispered. Then she'd slap it and start rocking back and forth, back and forth.

I rushed over to her and picked her up.

'Lady! Lady, don't be sad. It's Mummy's fault. *I'm* the bad one. You didn't do anything.'

'Bad, bad,' she said softly, pulling on her arm.

'No. Not bad. Not bad. O, Lady. I've messed everything up. It's me, not you. It's *me*. I was forgetting.'

I held her against me. She was small and warm. I kissed her left arm and she pulled it away. I kissed it again. I didn't know how to comfort her. When she'd been hurt before, I'd been able to do something; I'd always found a way. But her voice was unlike any I'd heard before. It was a cry of despair. It was as if she'd looked in the mirror for the first time and seen how she was. But the mirror had been me. And I had failed her.

We sat in the living room for a long time. The air-conditioning chugged through the vents like a train and the fan labored to turn the heavy air. The sounds of distant traffic came up the hill and Lady pulled on her arm until it was red.

I wished for Alfred and for Louise. I wanted to make sure that the toddler in my arms would never suffer the way I had, but already it was too late. I thought of the stares she would endure, and I thought about her looking at her father's expression as he covered her left arm with empty sleeves.

'We can't stay here, Lady,' I said. 'It's too dangerous with your father. He's not whole and he breaks us into pieces. We need to get out. We need to find a safe place to go.'

Just then the doorbell rang. I stood up with Lady in my arms. On the other side of the door were Assie and Esther.

'We have come to take you to Murunghi,' Esther said, as if I'd been expecting them. 'My mother lives there. She would like to meet you.'

I looked at them and smiled.

Assie propelled me into the bedroom while Esther played with Lady.

'She likes you very much,' she said. 'Only her most favorite girlfriends are being taken to see her mother in Murunghi.'

'Supposing I don't like her?'

'Her mother is indeed a wonderful old woman.'

'I don't mean her mother. I mean, supposing I don't like Esther? And I don't like her, by the way. I think she's a bitch.'

'Shhh! She will hear you and then where will we be?'

'Better off.'

'Shhh! She is *famous*. We are *very* lucky. Do you not want to see this country? I thought you wanted to travel and find things?'

'I do want to find things out. I do. But things haven't turned out the way I thought they would, Assie. It's all ruined. There's no book. Nothing. And the grape juice – all over everything. He'll kill us when he finds it. It wasn't supposed to be like this. O God, Assie, I'm so lonely I can hardly bear it. And now I'm just like my mother after all, so what will happen to Lady? Where did all the dreaming go? . . . Assie . . .'

She held me while I cried. She didn't ask me why I was crying. Esther must have heard me, but she didn't come in. Assie said we should go to Murunghi, that everything would be better once we'd done that. I was too tired to argue. 'I ha-hate him,' was all I could say. And she nodded and told me to hurry before he got back.

Esther was gentle with me when we climbed into her car. She drove fast down the hill, swiveling round to me and Lady to relate stories about the beauty of Murunghi. I didn't know whether I was leaving my husband or not. I felt tired and stupid.

You should know when you're separating from your husband. It was a final thing, dramatic. I knew nothing; Esther was right.

I looked back. I could see our house way up on the top of Hill Station where white women had lived in houses built on stilts for more than a century; where white men had come to get away from the blackness of the city. But I didn't know the city from up there. It was a distant thing – something I could escape from. I didn't ride in crowded poda-podas or eat potato leaf soup and foo-foo. I lived White. Esther had been right about that too.

Lady leaned back into my arms. Manny had the car seat with him in the Jeep so I held her tight as we dodged huge potholes. Esther suddenly stopped talking and began to sing:

When my baby carries water
On her head in her mother's pot
Don't let devils come to take her
She's my baby, she's all I've got.

I fell asleep to the rhythm of her song and the rhythm of the road and the rhythm of my baby's breathing. I wouldn't look back anymore. Lady was my baby; she was all I had. Simon was my father and I had to trust him to show me the way home. Manny was the devil coming to take her away from me. 'We can let her die,' he'd said. 'It's for the best. She's not beautiful. No man will ever want her.'

The path is narrow to the river
She is young and foolish too
If they get her, the angry secrets
I'll know all my fears were true.

Esther wound her voice around her song and the car wound around the roads through the hills and over to the coastal village of Murunghi. There were rivers everywhere, and some of them were invisible. Angry secrets lurked behind the bushes and turned shadows into vengeance. No one loved my baby the way I loved her, unconditionally. I would keep her safe. I would be the mother my mother couldn't be.

The only road to take was the one that led into the heart of my father's Africa. Esther Cole was a capricious guide, but I didn't care. I'd go with anyone who could take me away from the white house on the top of the hill and show me what darkness meant. There was something I had to find in the bush. I was still the child on the elephant – the girl in my father's story. If I tried hard enough, I could swing Lady up onto the elephant with me; together we could find comfort in the sweet, dark warmth of the bush where our names were etched into the fronds of the high palms and trodden down into the earth by old elephants making their long way home.

3

Murunghi was one of the most beautiful places I had ever seen.

Its beauty reminded me of my first days in Virginia when I'd been struck dumb by the glory of the place. Esther's home was a small fishing village hidden in the dense bush that skirted that part of the coast. Floating over the wattle-and-daub huts and the concrete slab bungalows came the sound of the ocean. There were stories Esther told me that she said came from the ocean's mouth. If you listened carefully, you could hear the lost children under the sea moaning for their home. All Africa's stolen people could hear the sound, she said. It was inside them when they were born, but some of them could never identify it. She called it the reminder of loss, and she had found it when she'd traveled to America and heard the blues singers down in New Orleans. Now the ocean was never quiet, she said, because once the ears were open to suffering they could never completely close themselves again.

The dust road through Murunghi was orange in the early morning and pink at dusk. It was made firm by the bare feet of women carrying water and wood on their heads.

After the sun had gone down, the village people gathered on their porches or by the open cooking fires and told each other how they were. Kerosene lamps gave out a kind of fluid light that softened the edges of things and made me warm. I lost track of time. I didn't know whether Lady and I had been there for a couple of days or a week, and I didn't care. No one wore a watch. I discarded mine soon after I arrived because it tied me to a way of thinking that was out of place in Esther's village. It harnessed my imagination to schedules. My concept of time in England and America hadn't allowed me enough room for poetry. But in Murunghi, without watches or clocks, deadlines or dates, I could listen instead to the irregular beat of the land and the sea; I could time my arrivals and departures by the arcing of the sun or the moon; I could measure distance by what was in between one place and another and not merely by the length of the road. I was free.

Esther's mother was a beautiful old woman. The strong lines in her face made me trust in her experience. Her face told me she had tackled life head on and not lived on its surface. She had eight teeth and a bridge she inserted before eating. Her extra teeth, which she treated with reverence the way some people would treat a work of art, were kept in a glass on a shelf in her living room. She seemed to wear them out of respect for her dentist whose photo she kept next to the denture glass. Esther said her mother had been fascinated by the time the man devoted to other people's teeth. Her mother thought of his vocation in terms of great sacrifice, for who in his right mind would want to spend most of his life inside other people's mouths? Esther's mother pointed out the photo soon after I arrived. In it she was standing next to a stout Indian man dressed in white who was smiling at the camera. The photo had curled up with age, and the humidity had affected the color so that both subjects looked as though they were standing on an ocean floor. But it was a happy portrait – one of the few I'd seen in which the subjects seemed totally satisfied with each other.

Esther's mother was called Di. I asked if it was short for Dianna. No, Esther said. I asked if it was spelled 'D-i-e.' I was used to the unusual now – perhaps people here would be more comfortable with a name like that than I would. Esther said I was a fool. I asked her what the hell the name was short for, if anything. She said the name was, of course, short for Diamond. Her mother's name was Diamond Cole. When I thought about it, I wondered why that hadn't occurred to me before. Her name was as delightful as any other name I'd heard of, on a par with Lady's and my own mother's name. I was glad Diamond Cole had been given a name that reminded us of how slow the process of her making had been and how brilliant the result.

Ma Di made us foo-foo and bitter-leaf soup one night. Was it the first night? No. We were too tired then. We fell on to the palette bed in one of the windowless rooms and were asleep in minutes. The foo-foo had the consistency of dough before it's been cooked. It had the flavor of yogurt, and Ma Di put wells in the high white mound of foo-foo on the communal plate and poured the bitter-leaf soup over the top. The choice pieces of fish and meat in the soup were picked out for me and Lady. We ate like pigs, using our hands as spoons. The palm oil in the soup was startlingly orange. Mango orange. I told Esther that the orange in mangoes, papayas, and palm oil would be the color I'd take back with me to America. For me, that color was the recurring theme sung by the land. I fancied it was an echo of the tropical sun caught in the fruits of West Africa. I saw it repeated on women's block-dyed clothes; and I imagined that, if one day I were to try and paint the faces I'd seen, I would layer burnt sienna over a blood orange to re-create the light in the dark faces of my father's people.

We all ate the foo-foo with our right hands, as was customary. Assie had to constantly remind me to accept things with my right hand. As I was shy about the scar on my right palm, the custom was a trying one for me. But Lady, of course, ate with her right hand because it was the only hand she had. She ate with astonishing grace for a two-year-old, and everyone, especially Esther's mother, praised her for her dexterity.

Later on that evening, Assie played with Lady while I went with Esther down to the beach. She took my hand and led me down to the water. No one was there. The moon was full. The light cast on Esther's face and arms was alabaster, which made her skin by contrast darker than ever. I too was dark in the moonlight. I looked at my arms – thin shadows.

Esther began to take off my clothes. I put my hand up to stop her. 'Shh,' she said. 'It is only fabric. What will happen when it is not there? Will Jacinta Moses disappear?'

Yes, I thought. Jacinta Moses may disappear. Then what would be left after that? A wisp of regret curling like smoke up to the stars, and a deep love for a child.

Esther took off my clothes and led me to the edge of the water. The ocean was flecked with light – white birds' wings glimmering under the moon. The ocean was still warm. She told me to sit down. I was conscious of the fact that my clothes were behind me, farther up the beach. I was conscious of the size of my full breasts and conscious of the water lapping up between my legs, lapping me up.

Nothing happened except everything.

Esther talked to me. She kept her clothes on. She didn't need to be naked because her clothes were not cumbersome like mine. One day I wanted to wear clothes the way she did, but I had to find something out first. When I discovered her secret, my clothes would be light on me – as light and intimate as skin. She told me that without saying it. I believed her.

If I could have fallen in love then, I would have. But love for me had always been a question of timing. And, in spite of the silenced watches at Murunghi, I had come from a time of marriage and a time of obligation. I couldn't love. And when Esther's hand came to me I pushed it away. She only laughed and mocked me for being a coward. We looked up at the moon; she wasn't angry. I lay back in the sand and let the moonwater kiss me and was glad.

Esther told me stories. We felt the pull of the sea. I asked her whether she could hear the lost children moaning under the water. She said children were never lost as long as they were remembered. I took that idea and held it to me. Lady's arm was remembered; Lady's arm was not lost. Florence was remembered; Florence was found. At the drive-in funeral home in Virginia, Quasar Hicks remembered little Leonora, his drowned relative; she was not lost. If loss was forgetting, our duty was to remember.

'I want my poetry to be like your singing, Esther.'

'How so?'

'I want it to make people remember the forgotten things. I want happiness to come through the sorrow like that mango orange that shines up through the land and the people.'

'Then you will have to write inside fire, little Jacinta Moses. And you will get burned.'

'I'm already burned.'

'You are not even half-baked yet, girl.'

'How do you know?'

'Because you are ready.'

'Ready for what?'

'Ready for love.'

'So are you.'

'No. I am not ready. I am past ready. That kind of love is not a part of my life anymore. I have myself alone. I do not waste time chasing after some romance from the West. I live instead.'

'I thought you were chasing after me.'

'That's because you're a fool, Jacinta Moses. I would merely like to try you, that is all. If you too could find that interesting, then we should do it. If you could not, then we should put you back into your clothes.'

I didn't know what to say. I was unused to her type of bluntness.

'I would like to be friends with you, Esther. That's all. I'm tired. Just friends. That's all.'

She shrugged. I couldn't make out her expression in the moonlight. Then she took my hand and kissed it.

'Okay,' she said. 'It is probably better this way. I do not think you could cope well with Esther Cole. You are too white.'

'I do not think I could cope well with Esther Cole because she is too arrogant.'

'Ha, ha! Is it so? And tell me, Jacinta Moses, what is poetry but arrogance? We have no visions worth telling without it.'

'You sound like William Blake.'

'Who?'

'A friend of mine.'

'Ah. Well, this friend of yours was very wise. Did he sing?'

'Sometimes.'

'Sing one of his songs.'
'I can't. But I can recite one.

"Tyger! tyger! burning bright
In the forests of the night,
What immortal hand or eye
Dare frame thy fearful symmetry?"'

'He was a good singer, this Blake. I would like one of his tapes. Yes. I like him. He is not afraid to be afraid, is it not so?'
'Yes. It is so.'
'People are afraid to look. They keep their eyes closed. You, Jacinta Moses, for example. You are one who keeps her eyes closed when making love.'
'How do you know what I do when I make love?'
'It is clear. I see it here.' She touched my forehead. Her hands were wet from the surf.
'Do you keep your eyes open?'
'Always. Even when I am sleeping.'
'Are you mortal, Esther Cole?'
'Yes. I am mortal. But I cannot die.'
'How can you be mortal, then?'
'It is a secret.'
'I think you are an arrogant, rude, selfish, magnificent woman, Esther Cole.'
'Good. You are beginning to know me.'
'I never want to leave. My husband is one of the frightened ones. He is pulling me down with him. It's like drowning. He's lied to me. He doesn't look at Lady. He's afraid.'
'Then do not go back.'
'Just like that?'
'How else is it that you leave someone? You leave or you go back. No middle way. There is never a middle way.'
'Yes there is. You're wrong.'
'I am never wrong, little girl.'
'Now you've just been wrong twice.'
'Ha, ha! I am liking you more and more, Jacinta Moses. Perhaps I will let you love me one day. Who knows?'

'Perhaps I will have forgotten you by then.'

Esther stood up suddenly.

'We go now,' she said. 'Get your clothes.'

I wanted to say I was joking, but her tone was imperious and I resented her for it. She had hurt me on many occasions, yet she couldn't carry her own hurt with dignity. I fetched my clothes and hurriedly put them on. She watched me in the moonlight. I felt embarrassed. I couldn't pull my bra up over my damp skin. I threw it down in disgust and just put on my shirt. Esther picked it up.

We walked back to the house in silence. Just before we entered through the door, Esther pushed me up against the wall of the house and whispered something in my ear.

'What? What?' I said. But she was gone through the door.

Later that night as I lay next to Lady I tried to capture what Esther had whispered to me. I thought I could reach the last words: '– the moon.' Something, something the moon. Don't something the moon. That was it. Don't what the moon? Don't . . . don't . . . don't forget! Yes! Don't forget the moon. Was that what she'd said? I couldn't be sure. Damn! I couldn't be sure. Was she asking me not to forget the night? Or was Esther Cole the moon, waxing and waning in the black sky, as full as the holes in the world, as empty as the open mouths of the dead?

4

Lady, Assie, and I left the next morning.

Esther didn't seem to care either way. She was indifferent when she wandered out from her bedroom as we were about to leave. I thanked her for putting us up. I thanked her mother. Esther's mother had tears in her eyes when she embraced Lady. Lady called her Ma Esther instead of Ma Di because she'd become oddly attached to Esther's name. Sometimes she'd repeat it over and over like a chant. Sometimes she sang the name as if it were, all on its own, a ballad.

Esther's hair was matted and her eyes were red. She said she needed a Bloody Mary. She kicked a nearby dog and Lady hid between my legs.

Assie whispered to me: 'Esther is in a hard place without the Bloody Mary.'

And I knew at that moment that Esther had a weakness that could topple her, and I felt sad and victorious all at once because she wasn't invincible after all.

I kissed her good-bye. She barely acknowledged me. 'Go, go,' she said.

'I'll call.'

She shrugged.

'I need to go back. I didn't leave a note. I need to go back.'

She didn't say anything.

We'd come in Esther's car. Assie had set out early in the morning to find a ride. The taxi she'd found was a small Toyota sedan stuffed with five passengers. The three of us would make eight. Assie had reserved me a seat up front. In between my legs was the gear stick.

'I can't ride that way, Assie,' I said.

'The back is too many. You will be squashed.'

'But the gear stick –'

'It is okay. It is always this way. The driver, he does not mind.'

'Great,' I said. 'That's just great. I'm so glad he doesn't mind, Assie.'

A crowd gathered. Women and children from the village began to point and titter. I heard the word 'Poro.' They were calling me white. I was making a fuss the way all white people did because I was having to endure the things Africans endured every day. I picked Lady up and scooted across the front bench seat. When the passengers in the back caught sight of Lady's arm, some of them clicked their tongues in their mouths as an expression of distaste or sympathy. I'd heard that sound often since I'd arrived in Africa. It made me sick. I glared them quiet. Assie squeezed in beside us. I stared at Esther, who was gazing at the car from her position on her mother's porch. Her own, air-conditioned vehicle was parked to our left.

'She never even offered to drive us home,' I said to Assie.

'Esther does not like to drive in the morning time,' Assie said. 'We should have waited until the afternoon or the night-time.'

I screwed up my mouth in disgust.

Ma Di was at the window, handing us oranges. She was crying and smiling. Her sullen daughter sat with her head on her hands. She looked nothing like the Queen of Africa she played so well. She looked like a washed-out, middle-aged singer with a bad hangover. She was no more powerful than I, after all. I looked away. The driver climbed in, reached down between my legs for the gear stick and shifted dramatically into first gear.

'We are on the go!' he cried, laughing. He was a short, powerful man with a build similar to my father's. His hand remained on the gear stick; the muscles in his forearm were defined by the sweat on his skin. He wore new Levi's – a status symbol of which he was proud. 'New jeans, eh, Missus,' he said. 'You like?'

I ignored him. He looked at Lady and said something in Krio about deformed children. Assie began to shout at him. Ma Di, still stooped over beside the car, began calling him names. He turned the key in the ignition and stopped the engine. He stared ahead.

'What is it?' I whispered to Assie.

'Ma Di called him a fool.'

Like mother, like daughter, I thought.

'We have to get out,' Assie said. She was scared.

'I'm not going anywhere. He said he'd take us. We've paid, haven't we? If he's not going to take us, I want my money back. I'm not leaving until I get it.'

Assie jumped out. 'Please, Jassie,' she begged. 'He is very angry. You must get out. He has been insulted. He is a Christian Muslim and –'

'A *what*?'

'He does not like to be insulted.'

'He insulted us, didn't he? What did he say about Lady? What did he say, Assie?'

Esther appeared at the other side of the car. She was leaning into the front seat, her mouth close to the ear of the driver. She spoke down into the car in a voice that hushed the onlookers and made the passengers in the back shift in their seats.

'Le' we go, woman. Eh, bo. Le' we go,' one passenger pleaded. Esther ignored him and spoke into the driver's ear.

'He said they leave babies like Lady in the bush to die. He said her arms do not match,' Assie told me.

I was so angry I wanted to hit him. Before I could react Esther had yanked open the car door. Her forearm was over the man's throat. Her mother had rushed round to rummage through the driver's pockets. Some of Esther's friends from the village were standing to attention around the car. Some of them were smiling.

'Big mistake,' one man said, shaking his finger at the driver.

'You no know Miss Esther. Big trouble. She na one bad woman. Big mistake.'

I don't know how much money Esther's mother took, but the driver didn't argue. As soon as Ma Di had found sufficient cash, Esther let go of the driver. I scooted out from the front and Assie hurried round to the back to get the bags. The driver threw the keys for the trunk on the ground at Assie's feet. She picked them up. Everyone except the driver and me laughed. My legs were shaking. Assie reached into the trunk and got the bags. Before she'd closed it, the taxi had taken off at full tilt through the village, the trunk of the car clapping in the wind. The onlookers congratulated Esther and patted her on the back. Esther took the money from her mother, walked over to where I was standing with Lady in my arms, and handed me more than twice what I'd paid for the fare.

I wanted to thank her, but there was a lump in my throat.

Esther said she would be ready in five minutes.

It took her two hours to get packed and dressed, but I didn't care. It took almost that long for me to stop shaking. Assie said the driver was from the north. 'They are bad up there,' she said. 'They have no manners.'

Lady played in the dirt and sang her Esther chant: 'ES-ther CO-le. ES-ther CO-le.' Assie, realizing I was sensitive about Lady's difference, tried to make me feel better.

'Lady is a fine-fine swimmer, yes? She can swim like fishes. She is too smart.'

Ma Di brought out more foo-foo and bitter leaf and tried to make us eat. She took me on one last tour of her small home, showed me the real glass windows again that Esther had bought her, the fine new tin roof – another gift from Esther; the generator (something she rarely used) locked up in a small shed, again the result of her daughter's generosity; and English lace curtains Esther had brought back during the period when she used to travel. I admired everything, even her partials and the photo of the dentist. I felt sad having to say good-bye all over again. I felt sad because a dumb idiot of a man had said my daughter's arms didn't match.

In a tiny back room overlooking the yard where Ma Diamond

cooked the meals was a chest of drawers. It looked like a piece of Victoriana I remembered seeing in Alfred's flat. It was an ugly piece, incongruous in this little fishing village in West Africa. Ma Diamond opened one of the drawers with great care and pulled out a scrapbook. She looked around furtively and drew a potato sack curtain across the doorway.

She opened the book to the first page. It was another photograph, this time of a beautiful young girl with a baby in her arms. The girl was Esther; the baby, of course, was Florence. Ma Di didn't say a word. She just pointed and nodded.

I looked hard at the photo. I wanted some clues to the woman who could fell me at every turn, who could make me feel like dancing on air or like crawling in the dirt. Esther's young face was Esther's older face. The only significant difference was in the eyes, which looked at you with question marks in them, the way eyes can when they don't yet know what kinds of solutions they will find. The eyes were expectant. Alcohol had not yet clouded them. I wished I could have met Esther back then. I would have been a child. She could have shown me who I was. I hadn't thought enough about my mother's race and my own. I was mixed race; Louise Buttercup was white, my father was African. Yet I wasn't simply a bringing together of opposites. I was me. Distinct. A race apart. I didn't just want to know Esther; I wanted to know other people like myself. It would be a luxury to talk with someone who understood what blackness meant from a white perspective and what whiteness meant inside the dark.

Assie and Lady slept all the way back to the city. Esther and I didn't talk much; she was still hung over. She took four aspirin at a time. She washed them down with Star beer.

She drove fast, almost recklessly. I couldn't remember whether she'd done that on the way there or not – I'd been too exhausted to care. She turned the radio up loud, and then played tapes of Sabanoh '75. The taut guitar strings and the frenzied beat of the music raised my spirits. I pictured the driver left to die in the bush. Ants were eating his generous forearms. He was crying out to me for mercy; I pretended not to hear.

'Revenge is often unwise,' Esther said without preface.

'I'm not . . . I mean, I was just . . .'

'He will know what it means to suffer, little Jacinta. You do not need to waste time thinking about a man like that. He is already dead.'

We careened around a corner. A huge pothole in the road forced us to swerve to the right. Assie hit her head on the window and moaned before she went back to sleep.

'Why do you drive so fast?'

'Why not?'

'You could kill all of us.'

She shrugged.

'Don't you care? Do you have some kind of death wish or something?'

'If I wished to die, I would die. I am alive. I like to drive fast. I like the world to rush past me. It is exhilarating. Sometimes I drive slow. Sometimes I drive medium. It depends.'

'Drive slow today. Please. These roads make me crazy. They're lethal. And people here drive like crazy people. They're all kamikaze pilots. It's nuts. Lady doesn't have a car seat, so she could fly right through the windscreen if I were to let go –'

'Okay, okay! Calm down. See. Now I drive as slowly as a hearse.'

She slowed down to a crawl.

'Not that slow.'

'Okay.' She sped up.

'Esther! That's too fast!'

'You see. How can I please you? There is no way, is it not so? You are a difficult woman.'

She did slow down after that. Assie only hit her head three more times. I was grateful but still uncomfortable driving with a woman who was high on Bayer and last night's vodka. I needed the Jeep back. Without it, I was at everyone's mercy. I felt pulled toward that vehicle as much as I was pulled toward the house. It was my means of escape.

I tried to take in the scenery. I stared at the women who seemed to fly by us with tree limbs on their heads. They would make fires in the afternoon and cook with other women. The ones with the babies on their backs carried as much wood as the others. The babies were extensions of their bodies; the women, in turn, extensions of the land they walked upon. If I were ever to paint them, they'd merge with the bush and people would have to ask me where the women were. When I'd point them out, people would say, 'Yes! Of course! There they are! How stupid we were not to see them before!' The palm fronds waved languidly in the slight breeze. Here and there a child darted out from the bush and ran along beside the car. Esther would slow down to greet them, then speed up, leaving them behind in the dust clouds we created. None of the children had shoes. We passed old men who walked bent over with their eyes on the ground. Some had sticks to help them. One blind man was led by a child who had him on a piece of rope. The boy stretched out his hand when he saw us. Esther threw something out of the car window. In the side mirror I saw the child fling himself on it and stand up smiling and waving.

'The taxi driver is very generous today,' Esther said, making me laugh.

Heat held us inside the vehicle. When we had to stop at the army roadblock, it leaped into the car with us and blanketed the cool air in seconds. The soldiers knew Esther Cole. They joked with her respectfully, then waved her on. One of them asked for my phone number. Esther said in Krio that I was a married woman, faithful to her husband. She said it mockingly. I tried not to think about it.

It seemed to me on that journey that the country was peopled with women walking through the bush with great loads upon their heads. It seemed as though the weight from the loads was what pitted the roads and made them seem endless. I imagined myself as a woman like them, carrying load after load from the bush to my village. Perhaps I would know another life because of rumors I'd heard or infrequent market trips to the city. And if I knew, perhaps each step I took would be to the beat of my yearnings. Or perhaps I'd know the secrets of the bush. If I'd found its center, perhaps I'd be blessed with calmness. Why didn't privilege bring peace? Measured in terms of these women's possessions, I was wealthy beyond belief. I'd wanted wealth growing up. I'd wanted privilege. I had it. It wasn't enough.

Lady stirred in my arms. She was sweaty. She had several mosquito bites on her arm. Supposing I had made her sick by taking her to Murunghi? I held her closer to me.

'Your baby is well,' Esther said, surprising me again. 'You do not need to be afraid.'

'Thanks.' I eased up on my hold of her. She was strapped into my lap. I knew I'd crush her in an accident. You weren't supposed to travel this way. I wished I'd brought the car seat.

During the journey, I tried not to picture Manny's face. There were too many empty spaces in it. It was my responsibility as his wife to fill them. I would fail again. I took an eraser and rubbed him out.

Because Manny had been erased completely by the time we arrived in the city and rounded the bend at the crest of the hill, I cried out when I saw him, as if he were a ghost.

Esther placed a hand on my knee and patted it. Lady woke up.

'Daddy!' she cried.

Assie woke up then too. 'My Jesus God!' she cried. 'It is Mr. Manny! Tell him that going away was not my own idea!'

Manny didn't come up to the car. He stood by the open gate and watched us pull into the driveway. He had on a pair of white shorts and a white T-shirt. His hair was bleached a lighter blond. His skin was the color of new leather.

He didn't say a word. He opened the gate for us and Esther drove up the driveway. He followed us with his hands in his pockets, his head bowed.

'Daddy! Daddy come home!' Lady cried, as if it had been Manny who had left us.

Guilt swept me up in a great wave. I didn't bother to ask Esther in. I told Assie she could have the day off. They drove away as soon as I'd gotten my bags. Manny still hadn't uttered a word.

Inside the house, the rooms were surprisingly cool. I walked to the bedroom and put my bag on the bed. Lady wrenched herself out of my arms and ran to her father. He picked her up and kissed her. I couldn't look at him.

'I had the air fixed,' he said.

'Yes. I could tell. It's much cooler.'

'Yeah. Not so loud either. Should have fixed it before.'

He kissed Lady again.

'I've made lunch,' he said.

'How did you know we'd be back?'

'Just hoping, I guess,' he said.

Guilt caught me again and made me weak.

'Put Lady in the playpen, Manny. We need to talk.'

He obeyed immediately. I heard Lady protest, then he handed her something – a cookie maybe. It was quiet again.

He came back to the bedroom and stood in his place at the door.

'Come and sit here,' I said, indicating a place on the bed.

He came in and sat down beside me.

'We need to talk, Manny. We're in trouble. We –'

'I know. I know all about it, and I don't blame you. You read the book – what there is of it. I could see you'd been through my things.'

'I'm sorry. Really I am. It was an accident. I –'

'Don't apologize. To tell you the truth, Jazz, it's a relief. It was driving me crazy lying to you about what I'd gotten done. The thing is, you've been lucky with writing and all, and I haven't. You sit down and it's written in a few minutes. For me it takes weeks – months. So I lied about the novel. Said it was done when it wasn't. You didn't give me a choice. I'd gotten so caught up in lying, I didn't know myself what was real. But now I do. I've thought about nothing else in these few days. You're real, Jazz. And I want you back.'

'What about Lady?'

'Lady's real too. Sure she is.'

'Manny, you don't even know her. You pick her up once in a while and you think that makes you a father. It doesn't. And I don't care about the writing. I never cared as long as we could be happy. But it's too late.'

'No it's not, Jazz! You're wrong! I'm going to prove it to you. You'll see. You've come back and we can make it work. I know it was wrong to lie about "Sophie," but I can make that work too. I'll write the damn novel; I'm just kinda stuck, that's all. All

I need is a bit more time. I'm out with these damn farmers day in, day out, and it's tough trying to focus on writing when you get back home at eight or nine. And Lady's a sweet kid. I'll play with her, you'll see. And we can have others. There's no reason why all the others couldn't be perfect.'

'You really don't understand, do you, Manny?'

'Understand what?'

'I met a man like you earlier today. He said Lady's arms didn't match. He said we should have left her out in the bush to die.'

'O, for Christ's sake, Jazz! Have I ever said –'

He stopped in mid-sentence and looked away.

'We can still make it work,' he said softly. 'We've got to.'

'Why, Manny? We don't bring you any joy. Why do you need to make it work?'

'When I was a boy, something terrible happened to me. I don't need to tell you what it was. It's over now. But it changed everything. I'd lie in bed – I was ten years old – and I'd wish I was dead. I'd try to will myself dead, if you must know, but it never worked. My mother had given me a radio for my tenth birthday. One of those big ugly things. I'd wanted a transistor to carry to school, but she'd found this thing at a yard sale and carted it home. It wasn't pretty, but it turned out better than I'd thought it would because it picked up all kinds of stations. And there was this one station that played black music – blues and jazz. And I'd listen and try to pretend I was inside the radio with the guitars and the pianos. It wasn't like other music; it was like my life.'

'Esther sings that way,' I said. 'She can make her music your life too.'

'Esther's the woman who drove you home?'

'She's a singer. Esther Cole. She sings like that.'

He shrugged. 'Never heard of her. Anyhow, I'd listen to the music and there'd be certain women singers who could . . . I don't know how to say it. . . . They could turn the air around me into a flight of stairs and make me go on up to the top and look down on everything terrible. And then I wouldn't be afraid because I'd risen above it. Do you see what I mean?'

'What happened to you, Manny? What was so terrible?'

'Doesn't matter. It's over. But I wanted you to understand why –'

'How can I understand if you don't tell me?'

'Look, I am telling you. I'm telling you that *you're* the voice on the radio. You're the jazz I heard. You are. Your name, your face, everything. When I make love to you, I'm not afraid. You can take me up the stairs. I need you, Jazz. I don't know how to live without you. You've got to help me with Lady. Okay, okay. I know I don't play with her much, but you don't let me in. You've built a wall around the two of you. Assie gets in. Looks as though this Esther woman gets in too. Why not me? I'm your husband. Doesn't that mean anything to you?'

I thought about it. Did his being my husband mean anything? He was working himself up into anger. I'd seen him do it before as a kind of release. It bored me. Sweat stood on his temples, and he moved his hands along his thighs like someone trying to rid himself of a stain.

'Look, Jazz, I'm not an unreasonable guy. I know it's been hard for you too, having Lady the way she is. I know it's a pain that will never go away.'

'Manny, you're a fool,' I said, looking him straight in the eye.

I thought he was going to cry. The lower half of his face caved in, and he blinked hard.

I didn't back down. Too much had been pent up for too long. I couldn't stop myself.

'This is how I see it, Manny. I see a man who's scared stiff of himself and of the world he's in. I see a man who doesn't even begin to know what it means to have a child like Lady, who still thinks we can measure her by the length of her arms. I see a man who has never focused on anyone else's pain. I see a man who's tired of life, hanging on for fear of drowning, willing to risk other people's happiness to ease his own, self-induced pain. I see a man who told me we should kill our daughter. I see a father who will make his child ashamed of who she is. Do you know what it's like for a child to be ashamed of who she is? I was a child like that. My mother was mad. For several years she didn't know which way was up. You have to love children unconditionally and then love them even beyond the unconditional.

You have to make them feel they can move mountains if they want to. If you look at them and see what's not there, they carry that space with them – they're empty for the rest of their lives. I was never my father, you see, and in my mother's eyes for years that was my failing –'

'And I was never tall.'

'What?'

'My father was ashamed of me. I was too damn short.'

'O yes. Lydia mentioned something –'

'That bitch should learn to keep her mouth shut!'

He looked at my expression and softened his own. 'It's my life, not hers. She had no right to tell you that.'

The room was filled with rage. It ran down the white walls like blood. We both had to pause for a while. Lady called out from the living room. I went in to her. She'd finished whatever it was she'd been eating. I turned on the television. There was a local, self-help broadcast – 'How to Build a Village Well.' As usual, Lady was mesmerized by the screen. I handed her a bottle of juice and went back to the bedroom.

Manny looked small on the bed – almost as small as his father must have made him feel. His features were delicate, like his hands. Clean nails – an air of fastidiousness about him. Out of the blue, I was overcome with the notion that something brutal would put an end to his studied refinement. He and Alison Bean merged into one. It was Manny twisted up in the middle of the road, fly undone, blood oozing out from under him. It was closer to a vision than a daydream. I was so certain of its reality that I had to go and touch him to check that he was still whole.

'What's wrong?' he asked, grabbing hold of my wrist as I touched his cheek. It wasn't ripped and bleeding. It was only my imagination.

'Nothing's wrong,' I lied, seeing Alison again, hearing the obscene screech of the bus's brakes. Maurice Beadycap was there, telling me it was my fault. My best friend had been killed before I had a chance to tell her I was sorry. Killed because of me.

'I'm sorry,' I said.

Manny looked up and smiled. In that moment I'd spoken to the dead, and two words had changed our lives. We'd been going in one direction, but now we swerved off along another road.

His face lit up. He buried his head in my chest. 'I love you, Jazz,' he said. 'Without you, I'm lost. I need you to get me through this hell.'

He took me in his arms and positioned me on his lap. He was passionate. He tore off my buttons and buried his face in my neck. He hadn't shaved since we left and his beard was rough on my skin. He rocked me and cried out to me. We were dying again – the two of us plunging farther and farther into loss as he took me down with him to the darkness and begged me to hold his hand. When he reached a climax, he was sobbing. I cradled his head in my arms and felt the weight of a man's fear.

After he calmed down, he wanted to make me promise to stay with him until he died. I couldn't answer at first.

'Please, Jazz. I need to know you'll be here through thick and thin. We can grow old together. I know we can be happy. Please. Give me another chance. I have a trip to take next week. To Lunama – Assie's hometown. Why not come with me – you, Lady, and Assie? We can make a vacation of it. You're always saying you don't get to see anything. I want to make you happy, Jazz. I know I can do it. Please. Give us another chance.'

'Okay,' I said, and it was as though someone else was speaking. 'Another chance. But I can't promise a lifetime. I just can't promise that. Things have happened. I'm not the same as I was when we got married.'

'That's okay. I don't care about that. As long as you're here. As long as you keep holding me.'

Lady cried out: 'Mama! Mama!'

Manny told me to rest. 'I'll get her,' he said. 'My wife needs her sleep.'

He walked out of the room and closed the door quietly behind him. I heard him talk to Lady. They were both laughing. The white walls of the bedroom seemed to step back several feet and I floated up toward the ceiling.

My husband was playing with my child. Maybe he could love her after all.

Sometimes when you've waited for something for a long time, it doesn't materialize in the manner you thought it would. Manny's pledge to me and Lady was like that. I'd wanted to hear him say he could love us for a long time. Now he'd said it, and I felt nothing but weariness. I'd sat with Esther on a beach and watched the moon light up our skin. I was beginning to know my father's country. I'd swung my child round and round in the ocean and watched her scoot forward through the waves in a movement fashioned from grace. I was writing poems full of words whose shapes Manny would never appreciate. I'd left him behind. But he wanted to come too. I reasoned I had a responsibility to him because of the vows we'd made. Wasn't that why I'd come back? Or was it fear? Was Esther right in thinking I was a coward? And if I was, what right did I have to dismiss the man I'd married because he too was afraid? And deep down, there was my own fear, snapping at my ankles, telling me I couldn't make it on my own. Louise's voice saying women needed a man. Society's voice telling me I was the one who was weak.

I listened to the man and the child in the other room. The air-conditioning made muffled protestations to the heat. I wanted to step aside from my life for a while and watch myself pass by, but I couldn't be anything but a participant. I was being rushed off in a direction I hadn't consciously chosen. I wanted time for me and time for Lady, time for my writing, time to know what gender and race added up to in this country. Wifehood was a scheme designed to ensure that there was never time to unravel yourself from the threads of obligation. I was married. Manny was playing with Lady in the other room. He was taking us to Lunama. He would try and love us. I had to be content for a while longer. All my wishes had come true. Over the rainbow was here and now. No going back. The trains were coming in my head. Just like poor Hubert Butcher, I'd have to wait for them to arrive. In the meantime, the important thing was to hold the skull together while it endured the vibrations of a machine careening on its way from past to future tense. No point in falling apart like my mother had done when she understood the sad inevitability of her present tense. Whatever happened, I planned to endure. If not for my sake, then for Lady's. I'd lost a mother once; I refused to become a mother who was lost.

Lunama. A place of moons and legacies. I could meet Assie's family. I could try to find out more about my own. Lunama was near my father's village. Nothing had changed. I was still on my way home. I got up quietly, found a pen and paper, and wrote:

Dear Alfred:

You were right about unconditional love. I am trying to live accordingly.

If you still pray once in a while, pray for me. I am not as strong as I should be.

I am going to begin looking for my father's house in earnest. We go to Lunama soon – a town whose name is full of promises. I will write from there about our adventures. I have a feeling that life has just picked up speed. I have visions. Do you believe in them? I am trying not to.

Give my love to Louise. Give her Lady's love too.

This is short. There isn't time to write – so much to do. I should never have been angry with Louise for being tired for all those years. Now I understand. Please tell her I'm sorry. I've met a woman who reminds me, strangely enough, of Louise, of you, of Alison Bean, and Simon. She is marvelous and dangerous all at once. Sometimes she hates me. Sometimes she makes me glad. I miss Alison Bean. I think about you and Louise and Vera Butcher and Hubert – even the Beadycaps – and wonder how it is I've arrived here at this place when I began over there on a different schedule on a different train altogether. I think about poor Hubert with the trains coming in his head, and I think I understand his torment. I think about Maurice Beadycap and wonder if evil is a style we inherit like a way of walking or speaking, or whether it's acquired when we lie in the seams of bitterness and regret. He did some terrible things. I think of his twin sister and I shudder.

I've learned to love Lady not 'in spite of' but 'in the light of' her difference. Her lack of an arm seems incidental to her many talents. She is simply beautiful. I don't love Manny anymore. Did I tell you that? I've forgotten what you know and what you don't know. We have been apart too long.

You taught me about the accident of gender and Simon taught me about the profundity of race. Louise taught me how to gather myself up and 'screw myself to the sticking point' and so avoid utter failure. I hope it will be enough.

I love this country.

Manny is a particular kind of white male. It's only just occurring to me that perhaps this is significant.

I wish my father were alive now in this country so that he could show me who he was in Africa. I see him in the faces and in the land, but it's too little, much too late.

This sounds sad. I'm not sad. I have Lady. Manny says he loves us after all. We are blessed, aren't we? And all the roads not taken cannot come to haunt you if you keep your eyes fixed on the path ahead.

Is it not so? That's the phrase they use in this country at the end of almost every sentence. Is it not so? Is it not so? And often, it is indeed so.

Lady is crying for me. I must go. I can hear the crickets in the bush and the ocean calls to us over the hum of the city. The night is shot through with fireflies – they look like small explosions – minutiae in their necessary mating dance.

Thank you for being the voice I can always write to.

My dear almost mother and father, my dear Alfred Russell-Smythe.

Cinta

5

Lunama was as ugly as Murunghi had been beautiful.
Assie began to complain about it when we still had ten
miles to go. It was clear she didn't want to be associated with
her hometown, now that she saw it in the light of the city. It was
also patently clear that Assie was a snob.

'The town it is a shame,' she said from her seat in the front
of the Jeep. 'It is certainly a very ugly place. The sewers run in
the road and there are rats. Some of the rats are as big as pigs.
There is a story of a family who hear a big noise in the night.
They are nervous. They get up and go to the kitchen. They are
from India. They look in the kitchen. They say, "We are aghast.
Look at the rats!" And indeed, a hundred rats have eaten a
hole in the screen itself, that same one, and here they are in the
kitchen eating the food for the month. The man and the woman
and the servant take brooms and hit the rats unconscious. It is
too sorrowful. No one survives.'

'The rats killed them!' I say, horrified.

'No. Of course the rats are the ones who are dead.'

'O.'

'Rats do not kill people. Only babies,' she said.

'Aren't babies people?' Manny asked.

Assie thought for a minute: 'No. I do not think they are
people as such. They are bits of people. One day, when they

grow, they will be real people. When they are babies, they do not speak. They suck titty. That is the end.'

'Seems to me they're people all right. Isn't your son a person?' Manny asked.

'No,' Assie insisted, 'they are not people as such. But they remember how to be people and that is why they will become them.'

Manny winked at me in the rearview mirror. This was one of the moments when we were supposed to laugh at Assie's ignorance. Yet I liked the idea of babies remembering how to be people. It seemed sensible. How else would they know where to go once they'd shed their infancy?

'But Lunama is the most dirtiest town in the northern province,' Assie continued, determined that we should know she forfeited all claim to the place. 'Many a time I have been telling people there to clean the roads, but it is not done. And now here is the St. Peter Boy, which is to ask us for money. For years he begs on the road. It is not good.'

Manny slowed down as a young man approached the vehicle. At first, I wasn't sure what I was looking at. The man's limbs were so altered as to be hard to recognize. Assie saw my surprise. 'He is a polio,' she said, much too loudly.

The young man was at the window. He thrust his hand inside the car. I jumped back and made Assie laugh.

'It is only St. Peter,' she cried. 'He is here at the intersection every day. Do not be afraid, Jassie. He is crazy.' She rolled her eyes in her head and laughed again.

'Shut up, Assie,' I said.

She looked scornfully at me, then closed her mouth tight and stared ahead.

St. Peter's hands were huge. He had three fingers on one hand, two on the other, and their size compensated for their number. His legs were twisted into boomerangs. His left leg curled under so far that he couldn't put his weight on it. He walked a step, then crawled another step – walk, crawl, walk, crawl, all the way from the roundabout in the center of the intersection to the car. 'Du ya, Missus,' he begged. 'Gi me ten cent.'

I reached into my pocket. I found a coin. As I handed it to

him, Manny jammed his foot on the accelerator and we sped off.
St. Peter's hand was caught in the gap between the window and
the top of the car. I screamed to Manny to stop, but before he
could respond, Saint Peter had pulled it back from harm.

'What the hell – he could have lost his arm, for God's sake!
What are you doing, Manny?'

'If you encourage them, they never leave you alone,' Manny
said. He was trembling. I remembered what he'd told me about
having to leave Africa because of the lepers. I was disgusted.

Assie tittered. 'Ah, that St. Peter he is always having to beg.
It is not good. The priests give him money, the nuns, the
tourists. He is too happy.'

'He didn't look too happy to me,' I said. 'He looked pathetic.'

Manny had recovered his composure. He lectured to me in
his calm, arrogant fashion about the importance of consistency.
If we gave it to one, we should give it to them all.

'We do give it to them all,' I said. 'We screw them right and
left.'

Assie tittered again. I was beginning to hate her. She and
Manny belonged together in the front of the car. Two snobs
mocking the unfortunate in unison. I wanted to spit.

Manny asked Assie why he was called St. Peter.

'It is a good reason,' she said. 'He was adopted by the priests.
They gave him a wheelchair. It says "Donated by the Church of
St. Peter the Rock, in the Name of Jesus the Lord Christ
Almighty." It is in white letters on the side. It is a very proud
thing. So we call him St. Peter from the time he get the wheelchair. But he doesn't like to use because then it is that the tourist
see he has friends in high places. He will be more richer if he
does not ride.'

Manny smiled. 'He is a wise man.'

'No. He is crazy,' Assie said.

One of Manny's rice projects involved a Peace Corps volunteer named Lionel Saucer. He was the person we were to stay
with while we were in town. There were no hotels now that the
iron ore mines had closed, but at least there was electricity in
some homes, and occasional running water – part of the legacy
of the German mining company.

We had to pass right through the main thoroughfare in order to get to Lionel's house. The main street was named after the current president. It was a politically correct thing to do, especially as he was Temne, and Lunama sat in the heart of Temne country. Besides, a town in the south that had refused to name a street after the previous Mende president had been attacked one night by soldiers. Five of the councilmen who had voted against the naming were dead by morning. People learned from others' mistakes. The presidential street sign in Lunama was three times as large as the other signs, and all the councilmen were famous for their peace of mind.

Assie told us the main street had once been asphalt. Now it was mostly dust and rocks. In the rainy season, the road was a mud hole. Assie told us that Lunama was sick in the rain because the sewers overflowed, and the electricity came on less frequently than usual. The marketplace stood off to the side of the road, mostly housed under a big shed roofed in sheet metal. Vendors with rickety wooden stalls, who hadn't been fortunate enough to have a place inside the market shed, set up shop along its outside walls, while their children slept under tables with dogs and flies and disease. Some of the stalls' total produce was worth little more than two or three dollars – four or five piles of old 'Irish' potatoes; a modest selection of mangoes; perhaps a dozen yams and a mound of rice. Other stalls were piled high with merchandise from China: cheap perfume, colorful fabric, beads, knick-knacks, hairpins, nylon twine for braiding. Poverty echoed around the market – in the cheap plastic sandals people wore and the holes in their clothing. It echoed in the obsessive care with which the consumers purchased goods, counting out their cents one at a time and knowing what it meant to give them up. Poverty was there in the acceptance of a debilitating heat and in the open gashes on the hindquarters of dogs. But poverty couldn't smother the spirit of many of the women, who sat on stools and told each other what they knew. Their laughter traveled over the heat and entered us. A few boys of five or six rushed up with oranges and begged us to buy them.

We bought three oranges. Manny told us to douse them in

bottled water before peeling them. We ignored him. Assie pointed to a woman at one of the nearby stalls. The woman was dressed in yellow gara cloth. The patterns on the cloth swirled in brown toward the center of her body, making me think her navel was a whirlpool. At her feet was a massive bowl of palm oil. Assie wanted some to take to her mother. She jumped out of the Jeep. The woman filled an old jam jar with the orange oil, which shone like gasoline and smelled like thatch. It would give the food a distinctive flavor. It would make you imagine that the meat and fish and chicken and rice had been cooked under the earth because palm oil when it's fresh has a deep-down taste of old nutrition.

In spite of Manny's protests, I got out of the Jeep to watch how the women poured the liquid from a dipping can to the jar. 'Liquid gold,' I murmured as it slid from one container to the other – shimmering, glorious, Africa orange. The woman selling the palm oil heard me, and I watched as laughter traveled down her throat. She handed the jar of oil to Assie, stood up, and came over to me. She was small – about my height. She placed her hands firmly over my breasts and squeezed. I was too surprised to push her away.

'Very nice titty,' she said. 'You give me the bra?'

Assie burst out laughing. Manny rushed up and shoved the woman to one side. I turned on him.

'What are you doing?'

'I don't want some market woman manhandling my wife.'

'She wanted my bra, that's all. She didn't hurt me. Do you want my bra?' I asked her.

'Jacinta, get in the car,' Manny said.

'Do you want it?' I asked her again.

She nodded.

I reached up under my Mickey Mouse T-shirt and unclasped the hooks.

'Jazz! What in Christ's name –?'

It was easy slipping it off. The T-shirt was extra large. My bra had black cotton cups trimmed in lace. In Paris, Manny had told me he could live inside it happily for the rest of his life. He'd said it would be dark and warm like I was.

'Here,' I said to the woman. 'It's yours.'

The woman was thrilled. She put it on over her blouse. She thanked me over and over and hugged Assie. Manny stormed off to the Jeep. I decided to walk around for a while. Assie came with me.

People recognized Assie and called out her name: 'Eh, Miss Assieyatu! Eh, Miss Assie!' One Lebanese shopkeeper called out from her store: 'Miss Assieyatu, hi! You bring your friends to us. We will give them cold Star beer! You bring the Americans to us.'

Assie said something in Krio, then she turned to me. 'The Lebanese want all the Americans to take money back to their children in the States. They need the dollar bill. They need them for the tuition schooling fees. That Mrs. has four girls in the colleges in the United States. There is never enough money. Lebanese are thieves.'

I told Assie she was racist.

'I cannot be racist. I am black,' she said simply.

'You're still racist,' I said.

'You do not know how the Lebanese treat the black in this country. You do not know what I mean.'

'Some Lebanese people must be okay.'

'I do not know one,' Assie said and set her mouth again in a deliberate move to shut me up.

We returned to the Jeep. We'd kept Manny and Lady waiting in the scorching car. Manny barely glanced at us. We were being punished. Assie climbed into the front again. 'I am riding again in the front!' she said. 'It is a wonderful thing.'

We were a few blocks from Lionel's house. We reached the end of the main road and saw ahead of us a building that must have been flown in from Italy.

Assie brightened. 'Look! There is the St. Peter Catholic Church, Jassie! You see it! It is the largest church in all of the northern province, built here in Lunama. Father Marco from Italy built that church. My own father, he was the one helping with the construction. He himself was the one who place the cross on the top of the spire. Look up! See how high this man was climbing! It is a miracle!'

St. Peter's was a huge building that dwarfed the rest of the town. It stood inside a large, well-kept compound. Assie pointed out the priests' house and the convent, which stood to the right of the church. They were painted a weak sky blue. The church was a white monolith against the heat of the day.

'When the Germans were here, this church was full every Sunday. The Germans and the Italians and the British, they all came. They wore nice hats and shoes. The town was very much having fun. At the mining compound there is tennis courts and a swimming pool.'

'*Swim!* Lady *swim*, Mama! *Now!*'

'No, Lady,' Assie said to her. 'The pool is closed. Weeds grow in the bottom now because the Germans have gone. They were the ones who made it work. Africans are no good to make things work. There is no water in the pool now. But in the old days, it was full. When I was a child, I swam in there because my very own mother was the main worker in the foreman's house. Those were the good old days.'

I shook my head.

Assie took offense. 'We had water and electricity with the Germans. Now we have nothing. Lunama is a dead town full of old Africans. Soon I will go to the United States. You can carry me back with you. Then I will live like Assie used to live. Then I will be happy.'

Manny couldn't resist the temptation to preach. He told Assie that happiness did not rest upon material wealth. He told her that she wouldn't like America – that it was one of the most racist countries on earth. I asked him if that meant he didn't plan to go back after all.

'Maybe I'll never go back,' he said. 'Maybe I'll die here. Africa's growing on me. I'm in tune with things here. As soon as we find your folks, I plan to look into buying some land. I like it here. It's unspoiled.'

Assie interrupted him. He hadn't made a dent in her desire to live in the United States.

'I do not care about this racist business. The foreman's wife used to make cream caramel. I want cream caramel in my own refrigerator. I want to eat it every day until I am sick of cream caramel. In America I will have all the ingredients. Everyone has a refrigerator in the United States. I am asking them each time if they have one and they say yes. It is true. Some of them have refrigerators you can walk inside. That is what I want. But I do not care if it takes me many years to get a big, big one. When I first go there, my refrigerator will be small because I will be saving to bring over my son. Michael will stay with my mother until I am ready. He stays with her now and he is happy. Often it is only me and you and Lady at the beach, is it not so? And we are happy. So I will leave him for a few years and get an education and a refrigerator. Then I will send for him. Then I will be happy, yes?'

Lionel Saucer wasn't home.

We knocked on the door for ten minutes because Manny was convinced that the young man from Minnesota was still asleep.

We sat on the porch and waited. Lionel lived on the outskirts of town in a concrete-block, single-story house with brown shutters and an outhouse. Assie explained that most of the houses had indoor plumbing because of the mines, but now that the water was mostly turned off, there was nothing to flush them with. 'It is too sorrowful,' she moaned.

I took Lady round to the outhouse. It was several yards away from the house at the end of a tiny bush path. Draped across the top of the makeshift wooden structure were two fat black snakes. I stood looking up at them, fascinated.

'Sake!' Lady cried. She was shocked at first, then we both began to laugh.

Manny had heard her cry and came rushing round the side of the house.

'Stand clear! Stand clear!' he cried.

We stood clear. Assie screamed. And then none of us knew what to do.

'Kill them, Mr. Manny,' Assie suggested.

'With what?' he said. It was a practical question.

'With a gun,' she said.

'I don't have a gun, Assie.'

'All whites have guns,' she said.

'Only in the movies,' he told her. 'Do you really need to go?' Manny asked me.

'Yes.'

'You went just before we left the last town.'

'That was hours ago. I need to go now.'

Manny put his hands on his hips. He'd been relatively patient for an impatient man since I'd come back from Murunghi, but now he was becoming his old self again.

'I'm not risking life and limb so that you can take a piss,' he said.

'Fine,' I said. 'Then I'll do it.'

'This I must see,' he said.

I walked off in the direction of the house. I hunted around for a big stick. When I found one I carried it back with me to the outhouse.

'And what do you plan to do with that?'

'Here, take her,' I said, handing him Lady. I wanted to do something grand. Manny was impotent; I wanted to make him feel his inferiority. He'd tricked me into staying with him and I wanted to make him pay. I knew I could kill the snakes. I wasn't afraid.

'Jazz, put that stick down. You'll hurt yourself. Is this some kind of statement or something? First the tossing of the bra, then the killing of the phallic symbol. Is this what this is about?'

'No, dear,' I said. 'These snakes are not your penis. I only wish . . .'

He looked away. I'd hurt him. Revenge felt warm inside me.

I walked up to the outhouse and whacked both of the snakes off the doorway at once. They fell writhing to the ground and I jumped back. One had almost brushed my toes.

Assie was screaming. I told her to shut up. Manny was calling me an idiot. Lady was laughing. Just then we heard a car pull up. We all forgot about the snakes and rushed round the side of the house in time to see Lionel Saucer get out of a crowded taxi. What he did next was odd, to say the least. He leaned down into the Toyota sedan and hugged each one of the passengers. He was crying. I assumed someone had died. My first thought was one of selfish annoyance. Several days with a grieving Peace Corps volunteer would not be pleasant.

The taxi pulled off slowly, and Lionel walked over to his front porch and sat down on the steps. He didn't seem to know we were there. Manny tried to introduce us, but it was a while before Lionel understood who we were.

'O, hi,' Lionel said. Then he was gone again.

'What's the matter with you?' Manny said, all of his impatience coming to a head.

Lionel looked up at us, bewildered. He wasn't seeing us; he was looking out beyond us to somewhere in the distance.

Manny repeated his question: 'What happened? What's the matter with you, man?'

'I'm – I'm sorry. It's just that . . . something amazing . . . We saw . . . amazing.'

'What did you see, Lionel?' I asked, strangely excited by his mood.

'We saw . . . and she was . . . I mean . . . *huge.*'

'Who was?' I asked.

'She was,' Lionel said. 'Huge. And we thought at first it had to be some kind of mirage and then we realized we'd all seen it! I mean . . . well . . . fuck!'

'The boy's drunk,' Manny said, heading off to the Jeep to unload the bags. Lionel jumped up.

'No! You're wrong, Mr. Fox. I'm not! I'm not drunk! Look!'

To Assie's delight, Lionel attempted to walk a straight line. 'See!' he said. 'See!'

'Okay, so you're not drunk. Will you help me unload the Jeep then and cut all the crap?'

Lionel flinched.

'I'll help. But I want you to know I saw it. We all saw it. And it's real.'

'What is?' I pleaded.

Lionel Saucer gazed down the road into the heart of the bush. 'The dinosaur. It's out there. We saw it.'

Lionel was agitated for the rest of the day and into the night. The only thing he wanted to talk about was the dinosaur. Manny dismissed his story out of hand. He muttered something about

Lionel and pot, and then refused to listen to him. I, on the other hand, was fascinated by it. Whatever he'd seen out there, it was obvious it had changed him. Every few minutes he'd stop in mid-sentence as if he'd been struck dumb by the shock of his vision.

After dinner, once I'd put Lady to sleep on the bed Lionel had given over to his guests, I suggested he try to draw the creature he'd seen. We couldn't call it a dinosaur in Manny's hearing; the word drove him crazy. 'Dinosaurs are extinct, for Christ's sake!' he'd exclaim, and then storm off. Why it made him so angry I didn't know. But I had a nasty suspicion that Manny was jealous of Lionel, especially when he saw how moved I was by his story.

Lionel drew the picture with great care.

His creature looked like a cross between a brontosaurus and a giant lizard. Lionel said he wasn't an artist. He said we should go to the library in the city and see if they had any books on dinosaurs. I asked him if the creature he'd seen could have been one of those giant lizards found in Indonesia or Papua New Guinea or some such place I'd read about. He shook his head.

'Mrs. Fox . . . I mean, Moses –'

'Jacinta.'

'Jacinta. This wasn't some lizard. I swear. This was unlike anything I've ever seen in my life. It must have been thirty feet long and fifteen feet – maybe eighteen feet high. And yet it moved softly. None of the ground-shaking crap you see in the movies. This was *real*. We all saw it. Some of the women and some of the men began to cry. I was crying. There was something about it. It came on to the road. We saw its head first and we all gasped, and then the rest of its body emerged from the bush, and the driver said "Monster" in this whisper and we all kinda froze and he jammed on the brakes. We nearly hit it. No kidding. We nearly hit the thing. And then it kept on going, right across the road. But before it disappeared into the bush on the other side, it turned its head and looked at us. And it seemed to be saying, "What the hell are you doing here?" And then she was gone.'

'She? Why do you call it a "she"?'

'I don't know. Didn't know I was.'

'Was there something female about it?'

'No. I mean, yes. I don't know. I guess . . . it's just that she seemed . . . I mean *it* seemed like a female. I half-expected to see a baby trailing behind it. She had an air about her. She looked like a goddess. I guess you think I'm crazy, don't you? Calling some animal a goddess?'

'No. I think that some creatures do live in a state of grace. We have a lot to learn from them.'

'Thanks,' he said. 'God, I'm glad you're here.'

'What are you going to do?' I asked him.

'Well, I know one thing for sure. I can't forget it. Something has happened to me, Jacinta. I'm not the same person I was when I set out this morning. I'm not. I've been changed. I'm from Minneapolis, for God's sake! I mean, this kind of thing doesn't happen to guys like me. Coming here was about the most adventurous thing I've ever done in my life. I plan things. I map them out. I try to anticipate. I'm going to be a field engi-neer. I like logic. I've always liked logic. My father, Lionel Saucer the First, liked logic. Things like this don't happen in my world. I feel like those wise men in T. S. Eliot's poem –'

'"The Journey of the Magi."'

'Yes, that's it. Do you like poetry?'

'Very much. I write it once in a while.'

'You do. Neat. That's why you're not laughing at me. My poems go from A to B. They're logical. I like fancy metaphors, but only the kind someone like John Donne would use. The ones that join mathematics, say, with romance. I think I'll go see John tomorrow.'

'John Donne! He's dead, Lionel.'

'No! Not John Donne! I'm not crazy. I know I must seem crazy, but I'm not. I'm talking about John Turay. He's African. A good friend of mine. Works up at the old mines.'

'I thought they were closed.'

'They are. He, like, keeps things oiled and stuff. Maintains the place in case they ever decide to come back.'

'The Germans?'

'Anyone. Doesn't matter. This town is dying.'

'Why did they leave?'

'Taxes. The government got greedy.'

'What do you think John will say about your creature?'

'Don't know. But I think he'll say something wise. He's about the wisest person I've met over here. He studied in England at the University of London.'

'So did I! When was he there?'

'Don't know for sure. But he's older than you. Now he reads and reads. Reads just about everything. Has a daughter – or is it a niece? – but no wife. Don't know where she is. Cooks the best venison around. Hey, would you like to come with me tomorrow?'

'I'd need to bring Lady. Assie wants to visit with her family.'

'That's okay. John loves kids. Want to come?'

'Yes. I do.'

'Great,' he said. Lionel looked at me shyly. I knew he liked me, and I didn't want to lead him on. He'd seen the way Manny treated us, and I could tell he wasn't impressed with him. But I had to make Lionel realize I wasn't looking for anyone else – at least until I'd determined what to do about Manny. Something in Lionel's eyes told me I needed to let him know that fast. I'd tell him tomorrow at the mines.

I wished him good night and went to join Manny and Lady in Lionel's bedroom.

The flimsy bed creaked when I climbed in. Lady was in the middle of the bed. Her small left stump was nestled up against Manny's mouth. I could see them by the light of the moon that shone through the window. It looked as if Manny were kissing her. He woke up briefly when I lay down.

'How's the visionary?' he whispered sleepily.

'Lionel's okay. He really saw something, you know.'

'Maybe. But it wasn't some damn dinosaur, that's for sure.'

'How do you know?'

'Jazz, grow up. Dinosaurs have been extinct for eons. What the hell would one be wandering around West Africa for?'

'Some people say the Loch Ness monster is some kind of dinosaur.'

'And some people say there are UFOs, but most of us aren't dumb enough to believe it.'

'Do you only believe in what you see with your own eyes?'

'I believe in rationality. Dinosaurs in this day and age are not rational.'

'But you're a writer. Don't writers transcend the rational world?'

'No. We leave that kind of thing to lunatics and poets.'

He turned over. The conversation was finished. Lionel's dinosaur didn't make sense. Lionel's dinosaur was a fabrication.

'I'm going with Lionel to the mines tomorrow. There's a man there he needs to see.'

'Suit yourself,' he said. 'See if you can keep your bra on this time.'

With my one gesture of giving the bra away, I'd triggered in Manny a retreat into meanness. There would never be a time when I would be able to please him. I knew that now. He'd pretend for a while and then his love for us would dissipate. He couldn't help himself. Weak people are always the most dangerous.

I lay awake for hours listening to them breathe. Manny moaned once or twice in his sleep. I thought about Murunghi and pretended I was still there. Esther was holding my hand and the ocean was spilling into me like absolution. Everything about the air and the stars and the beach and me was clean. I went to sleep listening to Esther singing. Her voice merged with Murunghi's ocean until there was no distinction to be made between the waves and her melody.

In the morning I woke up early, got Lady up and dressed, and headed up to the mines with Lionel before Manny had finished breakfast.

'You'll love John,' Lionel said. 'There's no other man like him.'

I didn't listen much. I was thinking about Simon. I'd hardly begun looking for his family. Time was running out. Again I had the sense of things speeding up. Perhaps this John Turay person could help me. He knew the land. And he sounded like a nice person. I'd tell him about my father. Yes. He'd be the one to help me.

I kissed Lady and sighed.

'We're going to meet the man!' Lionel cried.

'Yippee!' Lady cried in her sweet baby voice.

'Yippee yi yay!' I shouted back as I put my foot on the gas pedal of the Jeep and sent us flying along the road that led to the mines.

6

John Turay wasn't home.

We knocked on the door several times. Eventually an old man came around from the back of the house and greeted us.

'Where's Mr. John?' Lionel called out.

'He is at the club. It is breakfast. I am Mr. Charm, the gardener. You remember me, Mr. Lionel?'

'Sure. Charm. I remember.'

'Mr. John will be home quick quick. You want to wait in the inside?'

'No. We'll go find him. Thanks, Charm.'

We got back into the Jeep and Lionel gave me directions to the club. He became garrulous. It was obvious he'd wanted to find John Turay at home. He fidgeted with his glasses, pushing them on to the bridge of his nose, taking them off and cleaning them. He tried to be a good host, pointing things out along the way, but his heart wasn't in it. He'd begin sentences and then his voice would trail off into memory.

'When the iron ore mines were open, this place was booming, so they say. . . . Everyone talks about the good old days with the Germans. There's one of the old conveyer belts. Looks pretty rough, doesn't it?'

'Yes, it does.'

'Things rust out here overnight. John does the best he can, but he's one man against the bush. God, can you believe it? I mean, like, it doesn't make sense. It's not logical. But we all saw it . . . amazing. Where was I?'

'You were talking about John. One man against the bush.'

'O yeah. Well, that's what it's like. One man. And then the bush creeping up on you. That's what it's like. Old John, he's an oddball in a way. I think he kinda likes the idea of the bush taking over again. Never did think much of the industrial age. Never wants to go back to Europe. Says he's had enough.'

We passed the old tennis courts. Lionel said they were still used by some of the wealthier people in Lunama – the Lebanese shop owners, the bank manager from the city. The cement had risen up on one of the courts as if there'd been an earthquake. On either side of the net, you'd be playing uphill.

Yet there was something beautiful about the mining compound. The rusty edifices to the west brought me back to where Lionel was – with his dinosaur. They were peaceful. The hills around the abandoned buildings were dotted with gorgeous trees covered in crimson-pink blossoms. Each blossom was larger than my fist, and five or six were grouped together on each stem. Limbs of trees were hidden by hundreds of flowers.

'What are those blossoms called?' I asked Lionel.

'Don't know. John calls them "In the Name of the Fathers," but I think he's just kidding. He's always kidding around. Says they put him in mind of the father, son, and holy spirit. Says they look like the glory of Christ's blood.'

'Is he a religious man?'

'John? No! Hates religion – Christianity anyway. Says it screws everything up.'

We approached the swimming pool. I was glad Assie was spending time with her family. Seeing the state of disrepair the pool was in would have caused her real pain. Weeds grew up through the cracks in the cement, and a dark green fungus lined the sides of the walls. The fence around the pool was rusted, like everything else. I stopped the car to take a closer look. Lionel tried not to burst.

'We don't want to miss John,' he said. 'He'll be off on his rounds in a minute, checking on this and that, oiling things. We don't want to miss him.'

I assured him we'd only stop for a moment. There was something hypnotic about the place. It was returning to nature. The white men had lost.

With my face up against the fence, I could block out everything except recent history. I heard the European expatriates telling the 'native boys' to get their beer or their cocktails. I saw Assie with a white girlfriend laughing in the shallow end of the pool. A few wealthy Africans sat at tables under striped umbrellas. They laughed with the rest and forgot what was down in the town below them. St. Peter wasn't at the pool, of course; neither was his wheelchair. And the lepers I'd seen at the market in the city were absent too. There were guards by the gates chatting up the girls who were looking after the white women's children. Boredom, hedonism, race, class, gender, and heat combined to color everything.

'Assie says it was beautiful,' I told him.

'John says it was shit,' Lionel replied.

I shifted Lady from one arm to the other.

'Can I take her for a moment?' Lionel asked.

I hesitated. I never gave Lady over to anyone easily. She'd been attached to me for too long. Only Assie had free rein with her.

'I'm fine,' I said. 'Let's go on to the club.'

Lionel seemed hurt. He must have sensed that I didn't really trust him.

As we climbed into the Jeep, he asked me what had happened to Lady. I detected spite in his voice; he was trying to get back at me for refusing to allow him to hold her and for delaying him here at the pool.

'Nothing happened,' I said.

'Was she born that way?'

'What way?'

He let the matter drop.

'Which way to the club?'

'Straight ahead, then turn left at the intersection. You'll see it there on the right. It's a two-story building with large glass windows.'

We drove on in silence.

The club looked like the post office in the city, except it was on stilts – large concrete columns that held it up like a trophy for the bush to see. It had probably been grand a few years ago, but now it was eroding like the rest of the mining compound. The odd roach scuttled across the verandah, and the green paint on the wooden shutters was peeling. Ants had constructed small mounds in corners, and when we walked inside, we were greeted by the sweet-stale smell of mildew.

John Turay was sitting at a table in a lounge that a few years ago would have been crowded with Europeans. He was watching TV – news about the upcoming OAU conference to be held in the country in a few months' time. I saw him from the side. His hair was tight against his head so that the shape of his skull was clear. His dark skin shone. He was sitting under a fan eating rice and soup with a spoon, and he had a newspaper in his hand. He was dark in the poorly lit room. A fan whirred over his head.

'Hey, John! How are you doing, man? I've brought visitors.'

John Turay stood up and walked over to us. He was of average height and build. His shirt was open almost to the waist. He began to button it up on his way over to us. His rich brown skin made the white of his shirt brighter.

'John Turay, Jacinta Moses and Lady. They're staying with me for a few days while Jacinta's husband works on the new rice project.'

John Turay shook my hand. Lady wanted hers shaken too. She leaned over in my arms and reached out with her left stump. He took hold of it gently and shook it.

'Delighted, I'm sure,' he said to her. She giggled.

Immediately, I liked him.

He invited us to join him. Lionel began his story before we'd sat down.

'I swear, John, it was the most amazing thing I've ever seen! Huge! Massive! At least thirty, forty feet from head to tail. And calm – as if we were like ants or something. It's changed me. Everyone saw her. Everyone.'

'Hey, Lionel. Slow down. We've got all day. What was forty feet?'

'The dinosaur, John! I saw a fu – I mean, I saw a dinosaur.'

I interrupted: 'Lionel keeps referring to it as a woman.'

'It was female, I tell you. I'm damn sure of it now. The more I think about it, the more it makes sense. She was distracting us from her young. Her eyes . . . they were . . . feminine.'

John Turay didn't laugh. He called over to the only other person in the room – a man cleaning glasses behind the bar who stepped out from the shadows and smiled. John asked for three more bowls, spoons, and more rice and soup.

'I know white people eat Kellogg's cornflakes for breakfast,' he said. 'But now we're in Africa, we do as the Africans do, is it not so?'

'I am African. My father came from here.'

'Is that so?' he said. 'Well, then, Miss Jacinta, welcome home.'

I had been made to feel welcome before in Africa – many times, in fact. But John Turay's welcome, simple though it was, outshone the others I'd received. It warmed me up like oatmeal, opened me up like the blossoms we'd seen on his trinity trees.

We ate cassava leaf stew. It was dark green – almost black – peppery and good. Even Lady liked it. John said she was a real African if she liked cassava leaf. That was the main test of heritage, he claimed. And she had passed.

Lionel showed John his drawings. The more he talked about the creature, the more animated he became. I wished I hadn't been rude to him about Lady's arm. I was too sensitive. He'd brought me to meet the man, and the man was worth meeting. I was grateful. As breakfast continued, we began to talk without barriers between us. Lady talked too. She chattered on and on. Then, out of the blue, she climbed down from my lap and toddled over to John.

'Me sit,' she said, looking up at him.

'My God, she wants to sit on your lap!' I said. 'She never does that with strangers – especially men.'

'I'm glad she doesn't,' John said, scooping her up and placing her firmly on his knee. 'She will be too pretty to make that request in a few years. She will get into trouble. I hope her mother will teach her to look out for men of wicked intent.'

'She will,' I said.

Lady fell asleep on John's lap, we ate two or three helpings of cassava leaf, and still we talked.

Lionel was the one who spoke the most. He wanted answers.

'So what do you think, John? Is it possible? We all saw her – every one of us in the taxi. They could all verify my story. What do you think?'

'I think you need to talk to Isatu.'

'The girl I met last time I was here?' Lionel asked.

'You and she need to talk.'

'Who's Isatu?' I asked.

'She is a girl with a story,' John said. 'Come on, let's go and find her.'

Isatu lived on the mining compound with her mothers and father. Her natural mother was Mr. Charm's senior wife. We found Isatu in a small house behind John's place. She was thrilled to see us. She was about twelve years old, with finely braided hair and a beautiful, inquisitive face.

John explained who we were. Isatu said she remembered Lionel from last time. 'But he has grown taller,' she said. We all laughed.

'I think I stopped growing a few years back,' he said.

'Yes,' said Isatu, unperturbed. 'You have indeed grown, Mr. Lionel.'

'Isatu,' John said, 'tell Mr. Lionel and Miss Jacinta the story you told me the other day.'

Isatu drew herself up. Clearly, she liked the attention.

'My story is this. I was walking through the bush and it was hot. I was so hot I was sweated very much. I was over there by the river and so I said, "Isatu, go for a swim in the water." This is what I did because I was too hot. I took off my clothes and jumped in. I am, in fact, a good swimmer. Mr. John has been my teacher. Now I swim like the fishes.'

'Swim! Swim!' Lady begged.

'And I was in the swim for many long minutes until I was

tired. Then I went for a rest on the little island in the river. It is a small island, and I am happy there because I can think about my life and make dreams. So I am lied there in the sun, mind you, when all of a sudden I hear something. It is not much. It is like this.'

Isatu bent down and scuffed up the red dust with her hand. 'It is like this, but it is more loud. And then I sit up and I see something amazing.'

I looked at Lionel. He seemed to be holding his breath. His eyes were wide open and his glasses sat on the end of his nose.

'What was it?' he asked in a whisper.

Isatu shrugged. 'Who knows?' she said.

Lionel was exasperated. 'Well, what did it look like, for Christ's sake?'

Isatu shrugged again. Then she said, 'It looked like this.'

Slowly, very, very slowly, she raised herself up on tiptoe, stretched out her neck, and stared through us to a place beyond all horizons. Slowly, very, very slowly, she began to turn her head. When she saw who we were there was a brief moment of recognition, then she dismissed us, all without a word, and slowly, very, very slowly, she turned back to face where she had been before.

'Christ,' Lionel said. 'You saw her too, didn't you?'

John looked from Lionel to Isatu and back again. 'Well, it looks as though we have a genuine mystery on our hands. Why don't we go inside and talk about it some more?'

John Turay's house was a modest one: a vinyl sofa in the living room; a wooden table with four chairs; an old TV and a rug. Isatu and Lady made themselves at home. John said I could relax and let her run around. 'It is safe in my house,' he said. 'I like children. My niece brings her little friends and Charm's family is always here.'

He brought us iced tea with mint leaves. The drink was delicious. He said the wives of the mining crews loved the drink. He'd learned how long to steep the tea from them. He'd learned well. I wondered how many wives he'd known. I thought about the buttons on his shirt and how he'd done them up when he approached us this morning. I wondered how many women had seen him undo them. I wondered at the depth of the dark in his skin.

We talked for hours about monsters. Isatu elaborated on her story, though it began to be difficult to tell how much was made up, now that she was in the limelight. She'd certainly seen something. And her impersonation had been uncanny. It had sent chills down all of us. I thought I understood for the first time what Lionel meant when he'd said his dinosaur was female.

Lionel asked if they should report what they'd seen to the authorities.

John laughed. 'You are talking like a white man, Lionel. Which authorities do you mean? The police? They are living in hovels. Many of them have not been paid for four months. They are thirsty for revenge. They do not want to hear about monsters. Or do you mean your authorities? The people at the American Embassy? The people at the British Consul? What is the term you use – psycho-vacked. Yes. You would be psycho-vacked back home in the blink of an eye.'

'It's hopeless, then,' Lionel said.

'No. That I did not say. We have one thing in our favor.'

'What's that?' Lionel asked miserably.

'We have some people here who know the bush inside and out. If your dinosaur is in this area, Lionel, I think we stand a chance of finding her.'

'You mean, you're willing to go on a hunt! With me! For something you've never even seen?'

John shook his head. 'Lionel, you must always remember a phrase that the white people have put into their Christianity: "Blessed are they who have not seen and yet still believe."'

'Are you blessed, Mr. Turay?' I asked him.

'Yes. I had a mother who loved me and a sister who did not die before she had a beautiful daughter for me to remember her by. And now I have met you and Lady. I am blessed,' he said.

Lionel looked at us both. His mouth was hard. When he spoke, his voice was clipped: 'Your husband will be back soon from the rice fields. I promised I'd take care of you. We should be getting back.'

When we climbed back into the Jeep, the sun was halfway down the side of the sky. It was mid-afternoon. We'd been talking for almost a whole day. We agreed to return early the next day and begin the hunt. I'd leave Lady with Assie, who had been wanting to take her young charge to see her family – this would be a good opportunity. Lionel, Isatu, myself, and John Turay would set out toward the river. I was to bring a bathing suit. John would pack us a lunch. We could head east, toward what I thought was the area my father's family had come from. John hadn't heard of any Moses from there, but he knew many of the villagers out beyond the third set of hills, and he could ask for me.

Once again I was on the road. Moving fast toward a destination whose coordinates escaped me. I was chasing a dream-monster with Lionel Saucer, Isatu Charm, and John Turay. If we found her, what the hell would we do? Our only weapon was a camera. But I already knew that, if we saw her, and if indeed she had the kind of grace that Isatu had displayed in her divine mimicry of the monster, I would never shoot her with film. I would let her go. Having seen her once, I would be blessed.

When we returned to Lionel's house, Manny was sitting on the front porch.

'You're late,' he said.

'We hadn't agreed upon a time,' I told him.

'You're late,' he repeated. 'I've been waiting for hours.'

'What about the farmers?' I asked him.

'Sleeping. Say they won't do a damn thing on an afternoon like this. Say it's too hot. We're way behind schedule. I need to go down south and pick up some extra tools.' He stood up and headed inside. 'We'll leave early in the morning,' he called back over his shoulder. Lionel and I looked at each other in horror. Then I followed Manny inside with Lady in my arms.

'I'm staying,' I said quietly. 'We have plans for tomorrow.'

'*We?* Who the hell are *we*?'

'Me, Lionel, a man named John Turay, and a young girl named Isatu. We have plans.'

'It's always someone new, isn't it, Jazz? First this Esther Cole

woman, now John what's-his-name. Pathetic. Look, I'll say it
once more: We're leaving tomorrow morning. Early.'

I went up to him and stopped a foot or so away from him.
Heat sat on the tin roof of the house like a curse.

'Tomorrow, Lionel, John, Isatu, and I are going out into the
bush to look for Simon's village. Lady will stay with Assie.
She'll be fine.'

Manny looked at me. Hatred lined his eyes.

'Do what you like. I guess you'll be taking the Jeep?'

'I guess I will.'

Manny laughed. 'Who gives a shit?' he said, and walked
through the back door to the outhouse, grabbing a roll of toilet
paper from the table on his way out.

'Maybe you should go with him,' Lionel suggested. 'He is
your husband, after all.'

I'd had enough of sulky men. Enough of people telling me
what I should do.

'Go to hell, Lionel,' I said. 'You know nothing.'

Lionel walked out on me too, only he went through the front
door into the heat-white light of a tropical mid-afternoon. Lady
stayed behind, happily playing at my feet, bringing me some of
Lionel's treasures to look at: an old pair of socks, a dog-eared
photograph, a pen or two, and a feather. Each one fascinated her.
She cooed and clucked and ran the feather over her tiny left
limb, which seemed to be more sensitive than her other, long
arm.

I picked her up and held her. Behind us I heard the crunch of
Manny's footsteps as he came back from the outhouse. The
snakes hadn't gotten him. Damn, I thought, before I could stop
myself.

He was silhouetted in the doorway, looking taller than he
was.

Even though his face was in shadow, I could just make out
his expression. He looked pained. I felt a pang of guilt. My
words had hurt him. I was about to apologize when he spoke:

'This is all I need' – his voice a long, thin whine – 'one day in
Lunama and what do I come down with? Diarrhea, that's what.
It never rains but it pours. How am I supposed to get down to

the southern province like this? I guess I'll just have to stay here and stew for a coupla days. This is peachy. This is just great.'

That night Manny made fourteen trips to the outhouse. By morning, he was exhausted. I offered to stay with him; but, to my relief, he told me to go on. The illness had softened him. He told us to have a good time. He instructed Lionel to look after me. 'Don't let her get into any trouble,' he called after us. I didn't know Emmanuel Fox. He was one man and then he was another. I wanted to stay for a while and ask him what triggered his episodes of kindness and fury, but it was time to go on a journey again. The road wouldn't wait.

I left Lady with Assie and her mother. Assie's little boy, Michael, had been taken to Lunama by a cousin several weeks before, and Lady was delighted to be reunited with him.

On the way to the mines, Lionel repeated his story about the sighting of the dinosaur. As usual, his voice shook as he remembered the way she'd turned her head to look at him. I was struck again by how much this had meant to the young man from Minnesota who had been touched by a miracle and whose life-long quest, it seemed to me, would be a desire to be touched again.

John and Isatu were waiting for us when we pulled up in front of the house.

'You two are late,' John said, but there was no resentment in his voice, only joy at our arrival.

We didn't waste time talking – there was too much to discover. We had a rough map drawn by John, and Lionel's depiction of our dinosaur. We set out in the Jeep singing and laughing. John Turay drove and I sat with him in the front. Soon we had entered the bush and were driving along paths barely wide enough for the Jeep to get through.

After a while, Isatu got tired of using the binoculars she'd been so thrilled by early in the day. Lionel took them back and used them himself, urging John to stop whenever he caught sight of a shadow. John was patient, coming to an abrupt halt each time. But nothing was there. Only Lionel's need for confirmation.

As the journey progressed, Lionel became increasingly impatient.

'I saw it, I tell you,' he said, as if we were disputing the fact. 'She was real. Where the hell is she?'

I began to hope we wouldn't find anything. I realized that Lionel was a wild card – that he could just as soon try to harm her, cut off a piece of her to take home with him to Minneapolis. He began to talk as if she belonged to him, as if his sighting of her was more significant than the fact of her being there at all. He began to talk the way white men have talked on that continent for hundreds of years.

The river was an olive ribbon of light and dark. It cut through a section of the land that rolled up on either side of it in gentle banks and ridges. John said crocodiles came there at certain times of the year, but that we were safe now. I had my bathing suit on underneath my clothes, and I didn't think twice about slipping off my sundress and stepping into the warm water. Lionel didn't want to swim, however. He wanted to continue looking for his dinosaur. 'She's round here somewhere,' he said. He sniffed the air like a dog. 'I smell her.'

John told him to go off on his own and come back for us in a couple of hours. Lionel wouldn't take any food. He was too wound up to eat. He walked off into the bush by himself, muttering something about women. Isatu spent her time swimming back and forth from the island to the bank. In the end, she perched herself on an outcropping of rock and waved to us from time to time. She was not much more than a small black dot the size of my little finger by the time John and I climbed up onto the island in the middle of the river.

We were breathless. We'd raced. I'd won because he'd been carrying food above his head so that it wouldn't get wet. We both fell down on to the sandy bank and laughed.

He told me about his family. Most of his immediate relatives were dead. He'd been to the University of London years before I was there. I estimated him to be about forty-five. He wanted a copy of my father's stories. He wanted my poems too. He told me I was beautiful, and I returned the compliment. I told him about Lady before he asked. I don't know why. I told him about

Manny too and, for some reason, I told him about Maurice
Beadycap. Not all of it, just the part about Alison Bean and his
accusation. I needed to tell someone, I suppose; after all these
years his words had burned a hole in me. For some reason, I
knew that John Turay would understand. When I finished, we
lay in silence for a while. Then he said:

'Don't be sad, Jacinta. There is much to be happy about in
this world if we look for it. You have done well. It is time to stop
trying so hard.'

'How do you mean?'

'I mean that you can give yourself permission to be happy. It
will be all right. You will see. You will not fall.'

He put his warm hand on my thigh and began to move it up
and down. I thought briefly about stopping him. I was married.
I saw Manny's face in my head telling me he didn't give a shit,
telling me I was late, telling me I'd failed, telling me fiction
was harder than poetry, telling me Lady's arm was still missing
and what was I going to do about it? Telling me his novel was
nearly completed, telling me he would never be there when I
needed him because his body was full of holes. I could plug
them for the rest of my life and still the anger would spill out of
him. And now here was a man saying I didn't have to try so
hard, giving me a kind of dispensation. Not since the days when
I used to kneel in the confessional and be cleansed of my sins
had I felt so light. If my body had levitated off the ground then
and there, I would not have been taken aback. I let John Turay
touch me because in his fingers was forgiveness.

Soon he had eased my swimsuit up between my legs, and I
let his fingers know me. If I had died then, I would not have
been regretful. There, by the warmth of the olive river, near the
land where my father grew up, I lay with a man who touched
me, that was all. And that was all I wanted. He didn't ask for
anything more than that. His fingers were never urgent; they
were persistent and gentle. He didn't kiss me or make me look
at him. I closed my eyes and focused on his African fingers.
They were dark licks of light. I shifted position so that my face
was to the sun. Isatu was too far away to notice us; Lionel was
in the bush searching for redemption; Manny was in Lunama

with diarrhea; and Lady was with Assie and Michael, making friends all over again. I lay back into his fingers and shivered.

Afterward we ate lunch together. He didn't ask me how I felt or if I minded what he'd done; it would have been a silly question. Every so often, when a pang of guilt grazed my cheek like a light wind, John seemed to sense it, and he would nod and smile at me, and tell me it would be all right. Something made me believe him.

A boy in a hollowed-out log paddled past us on the river. 'Kusheh-ya!' he called. We returned his greeting. Not more than ten years old, he maneuvered himself through the water with tremendous skill. John told me he was the ferry boy. People from the next village used his little boat almost every day. He was happy we were there, even happier when he caught sight of Isatu. He spent his time circling around her as she sat on the rocks. He hurled compliments at her in Temne, some of which John could catch if the breeze was blowing in the right direction. 'The poor boy is in love,' he said.

'Has he met Isatu before?'

'I don't know. Does it matter?'

'I suppose not.'

'Love is never a question of time, is it not so? Love has a home outside that circle of fire.'

'Have you loved, John?'

'Yes.'

'Many times?'

'No.'

'Why not?'

'No one can love many times. You love once, twice, three times, if you are lucky. The rest is just playing. This is the first and last time we will be together, is it so?'

'I don't know.'

'Me, I know.'

The ferry boy circled around Isatu and called out his love to her over the water. The sun warmed us and time beat upon us like a climax. We fed each other bread and fruit and dried fish. The fish was roasted with hot peppers and lime juice. It burned my lips and tongue.

Lionel came back just before we'd finished eating. He was angry. He hadn't seen anything. He called to us from the bank, telling us to hurry. It was already afternoon and we had a long way to go, he said.

I didn't tell him I'd found what I'd been looking for.

We called out to Isatu, who had finally gotten tired of her place on the rocks, swum back to land, and fallen asleep under the shade of a tree. She woke up with a start, claiming she had had a terrible dream.

'Our monster was a monster,' she said. 'She chased us and then she killed us all, every one. Except for Miss Jacinta. Miss Jacinta was left alone and crying. And the monster went away with us in her mouth. As for me, I would rather be the one she is eating than the one she is leaving behind. Because then it was the night and Miss Jacinta was all alone in the bush with death.'

John could see that Isatu's dream disturbed me. Gently, he urged her to be quiet. Nothing like that was going to happen, he said. The monster wouldn't eat any of us. Lionel's picture quite clearly showed a dinosaur with vegetarian preferences.

We drove on toward Simon's place of birth. It would be impossible to reach the exact place, even if I were sure of where it was. But we could come close if we drove pretty fast. Lionel kept asking us to slow down. Again and again he grabbed the binoculars from Assie and jerked them up to his eyes. Each time, nothing.

At last we pulled into a clearing. Around the circle of cleared land was a group of huts. A man came up to greet us. John and he embraced. We were introduced. When John told the man my father's name, he whistled through his teeth, then he called over his shoulder to his wife.

'Fatmata, come on out here. Quick! Quick! We have a guest. The daughter of Simon Moses!'

His wife came up to us. She was a woman of about fifty with strong features and an ironic expression.

'The daughter of Simon Moses,' she repeated. Then she said something in Temne. I asked John to translate. He didn't want to at first.

'She says he . . . that he . . .'

'Go on.'

'She says your father was ashamed of his people. She says your hair . . . proves it.'

I looked at the woman. She looked back at me. Then her husband stepped forward. 'Come, Miss Moses. Come and eat with us. We have potato leaf and plantain. We have pawpaw and palm wine. This was not your father's village, but it is close. Only a half day away. But now his fambul is dead. All dead. There was a terrible illness in that village twenty years ago. Very terrible. Half of the village is gone. I do not think there are any Moses left now. Except for you.'

'I have a daughter,' I said. 'Her name is Moses.'

'That is a good thing,' he said. 'Now there will be a way to keep on to tell your story. Come. We have palm wine and chicken grun'nut. Plantain too. . . .'

We ate with the people from the village. The woman who had taken a dislike to my mother's whiteness mellowed. She began to talk about Simon as a boy. She came from his village too. After a while, I understood they had been sweethearts. But then she'd been betrothed to Mohammed, and Simon had won a scholarship at the missionary school and gone off to study in the city. No one else could remember much about him apart from the name that his family had taken. Moses because of the missionaries, they said. The old name was lost now; they couldn't remember it. Simon's father had been Christopher Moses for as long as they could remember. They'd heard that Simon was a writer when they had learned of his death. They said a countryman studying in England had gotten word to the village about it when he'd read my mother's memorial to him in *The Guardian* newspaper. They said Simon's old mother had been sad beyond sad to hear of it. They said she died soon afterward. I'd understood that my paternal grandmother had passed away when Simon was a child, but I didn't mention it. I suspected that part of what I was hearing was stories made up to comfort me, but I didn't care. I was finding it more and more difficult to distinguish between what actually happened and what we dreamed had happened. I wasn't faithful to Truth in the old way anymore.

I'd brought a copy of my father's stories with me. I gave it over to John's friend, Mohammed. He didn't put it down for the rest of the evening. Once in a while he'd gasp at something he'd read. Once he shouted out, 'Na me, oh!' meaning 'That's me in there!' He read with incredible speed, turning over the pages as though all the secrets of the bush were caught inside them. Often he was silent for fifteen or twenty minutes at a time; then he'd burst out laughing or sigh like an old man. He liked the story about the elephant best of all. He said he'd show it to the principal of the local secondary school and get him to add the book to the syllabus. Perhaps the whole country would soon be reading Simon Moses for their O levels, he said. 'We are very very tired of Charlotte Brontë and even our own writers sound too much like Englishmen. We need someone who is remembering us too well. I will tell Mr. Bangura, our principal. He will take it from there. Yes, I am about to remember the elephant story again. Ha, ha! That girl on the elephant back. What a warrior! Your father has a photogenic memory. Indeed it is a miracle, is it not so?'

When darkness came, we climbed back into the Jeep and headed for home. Mohammed and Fatmata told us to come back soon. They would find out more about my family, they said.

John asked me whether I was satisfied with what I'd found out about my father.

'Yes,' I told him. 'I found everything I've been looking for today.'

My response irritated Lionel: 'Well, I sure am thrilled you found what you were looking for, Jacinta. Because none of the rest of us did. And now we've wasted so much time we'll never find her in the dark.'

As we drove through the pitch dark of the bush, John asked me again whether I was disappointed. I couldn't help but think he was doing it on purpose to tease Lionel. I repeated the fact that I wasn't disappointed. If I were to die now, I said, I would be happy.

'Not me!' said Isatu from the back. 'I want to live a long, long time. I want to be a great typist or a singer. I will not die in this place. It is too far away.'

'Too far away from what?' I asked her.

'Too far away from where you are,' she replied.

Just then, Lionel called out again. We were all so used to it by now that we barely reacted, even though his cry was frantic.

'Stop the car! Stop! Look! Jesus Christ, look over there!'

John slammed on the brakes and we all jerked forward in our seats. We looked out over the dense blackness of the bush to see where he was pointing.

To our left, not more than fifty feet away and higher than the tops of small trees was a form, huge and ponderous, making her way toward us, shaking the earth as she came.

7

Isatu screamed. 'The monster! She is coming to eat us! Help! Help!'

I was frozen. The thing moved toward us through the dark. Forty, thirty, twenty feet from the hood of the Jeep. 'Simon!' I whispered.

'Jesus Christ!' Lionel cried. 'Get the camera!'

I felt a hand pull me out of the car. John had rushed round to my door, opened it, and was dragging me out. He was yelling at us:

'Get out, all of you!'

I reached over the seat and grabbed Isatu's hand. She was whimpering. 'Do not let her eat me, Miss Jacinta! I am only a child!'

We were out in seconds. Running, running as fast as our legs could carry us. All I could hear was my own heart and my breathing and Isatu crying to me not to let the monster eat her. I stopped suddenly and Isatu ran into me.

'Where's John?' I cried.

'I . . . I . . . I . . .'

I shook her until her teeth clicked together. 'Where is he? He dragged us out. What happened? Shh! What's that?'

'I . . . I . . .'

'Shh, Isatu! For God's sake, shut up! I'm sorry. It's okay. It's okay. What the hell was that?'

Behind us was the sound of voices – dozens of them. Men's voices. Screaming and shouting. And another sound. A bellow sadder than any sound I'd ever heard. A bellow that rocked the land we stood on and made my eyes sting.

'We must go back!' I cried, pulling Isatu after me.

'No! No! Please no, Miss Jacinta! She will be eating Isatu Charm! Do not do this to me! I am your friend!'

I dragged her back down the bush path we'd taken, calling John's name. I could hardly see in the dark, but I didn't care. I couldn't run away. He had saved us. I had to know what had happened to him. There were lights up ahead. A circle of fire. And men. Twenty or thirty men encircling the monster.

And the monster was dead.

John rushed up to us. He hugged us. He wanted to know whether we'd been hurt. I caught sight of Lionel sitting on the ground, his head between his knees, sobbing.

'These men are from Lunama,' John told us. 'They've been chasing it for days.'

I walked up to the form on the ground. Even on its side, it was huge. I reached out and touched the skin. 'An elephant? Is that what we've been chasing?'

Lionel heard me and called out to us in a voice seamed with despair: 'That's not what we saw! You think I don't know an elephant when I see one? You think I'm too stupid to tell the difference between an elephant and a dinosaur! She's the wrong one, I tell you. I never saw her before in my life.'

Isatu came up behind us. Her fear had changed to fascination.

'A real elephant,' she said. 'This is a miracle like the Eucharist. I have been in a miracle. For years, ever since I was a little girl, I have been chasing for elephant. My father, he tell me there are no elephant left in Lunama. No elephant in the whole country. I tell him he is wrong. He laughs at me. And now who is laughing? Isatu. Isatu Charm! I have been in a miracle! I have seen the elephant alive!'

'And now she's dead,' I said.

'*He.* It is a male,' one of the men told me.

It didn't seem to matter much.

I asked John why they killed it. He told me they probably wanted food and ivory. Elephants are dangerous in places like this, he said. There was no room for them anymore. It was a great pity that the elephant had strayed so far from home.

'It didn't,' I said. 'We did.'

They cut the elephant up. We watched for a while because Isatu wouldn't leave and Lionel was too distraught to stand up. We saw them slice through the trunk and score the flank with knives. The blood shimmered like mercury in the light from the torches, a mercury river that poured from the creature's body and soaked the ground. Soon our shoes were squelching in the mud created by the slaughter. I thought of butchers. I thought of racks of meat hanging from hooks. I thought of tiger skins and lions' heads, antlers, and goatskin rugs. I witnessed butchery on a huge scale, and I knew I was in no position to speak. I had killed and eaten for years. My own wealth was predicated on the poverty of my father's people. Who was innocent? I looked over at Isatu. She was. Lady was. We had been in a miracle. I wished I could say that without irony the way she could.

Lionel staggered over to us. His voice was staccato with rage.

'I'm not crazy! I'm not! We all saw it. Ask any of them. And it wasn't some . . . some . . . rogue elephant.'

John placed his hand on Lionel's shoulder to quiet him.

'We believe you, Lionel,' he said. 'We'll look for the dinosaur on another day.'

We had to drag Isatu from the scene. She begged to stay until morning. She said she wanted to see the size of the carcass at sunrise. She said the bones would be as big as a house. She wanted to play inside them.

John lost his patience. He told her to get into the Jeep and be quiet. I suddenly realized how scared he'd been – how scared we'd all been. The elephant could have killed us.

The Jeep was intact. There was a dent in the door on the passenger side, which meant that it couldn't be opened from the inside. Apart from that, it looked okay. Some of the men ran ahead of us for at least a couple of miles. They wanted to guide us home. In the headlights their dark legs were beautiful. They ran like gazelles, and I thought of the kind of life my father must have known growing up in a land close to itself. By the time the men left us, Isatu and Lionel were fast asleep in the backseat. They were leaning on each other for support. Lionel's glasses had slipped to the end of his nose. They winked at me in the dark.

'I heard the elephant's death cry. It was a terrible sound. I don't think I'll ever forget it,' I said.

'Yes. It was terrible.'

'Why didn't you come with us?'

'Lionel and his stupid camera. He wanted photographs.'

'Why didn't you just leave him behind? You could have been killed.'

'He is my friend.'

'He's a fool.'

'That does not make him less of a friend.'

'In my book it does. Supposing you'd been killed?'

'I was not killed. The elephant was killed.' He sighed. 'It is funny,' he said. 'Saying those sentences should make me feel good. But they do not make me feel good. The elephant is dead. I am not dead. Those words are sad ones. I saw them with their rifles. Army rifles. I saw them coming. I saw the wound in the eye. The eyeball burst and then the elephant made the sound you heard. It fell at our feet. At first, I thought we were lucky. Now I don't know. It's sad to think what is happening to the world. Once upon a time, elephants roamed this land. They lived here in West Africa with us. And then we hunted them. And the white men hunted them even more than we, without regard to who they were. Now it is only your grandfather or your uncle's uncle who has seen an elephant. They do not come here anymore. If Lionel's dinosaur is real, I hope it runs away into the darkest part of the bush. I hope it stays there like the Loch Ness monster, and never comes out again. If it comes out, we will surely kill it. White and black, that is our way.'

I placed my hand on his knee and patted it. He put his hand on mine. We rode together that way until we reached the out-skirts of Lunama. Then we took our hands away because I was returning to my husband, and John Turay had no legal claim to me like Manny did.

Manny was in bed when we walked through the door. He hadn't waited up for us. He came out sleepily and asked what time we thought it was to be coming back. Then he gasped.

'You're covered in blood!' he cried.

And it was true. All of us had been spattered by the elephant. We told him the story. He listened for a while, then got up quickly and headed for the back door.

'Damn diarrhea!' he said. 'Where's the toilet paper?'

John stood up to go. He said it was very late. I said I'd drive him home. He said it wasn't necessary. I insisted. When Manny came back, I told him I was driving John and Isatu home. Manny began to offer to drive them home himself, then he had to make another hurried exit. I didn't wait for him to come back.

Lionel was already asleep on the sofa.

'We could have walked,' John said. 'It is only a few miles.'

'You're not walking after a night like this. Besides, Isatu certainly doesn't want to walk, I'm sure. Don't worry about it. It's no big deal. Just a ride home, that's all.'

But I was lying. I knew I had no intention of dropping them off and coming straight back to Manny. I hated Manny. He turned me into a monster when I was with him.

The moon came out during the journey home. It cast a watery light on the road. It made me think of Murunghi and what Esther had whispered about the moon: 'Don't forget the moon.' I looked up, found it, and made a wish.

I drove slowly. I didn't want the night to end. John fell asleep. When we pulled up to his house, Mr. Charm and his wife were waiting by the door.

'We are being afraid,' Mr. Charm said. 'You are indeed late.'

'Yes. I'm sorry. We had an adventure,' I told him.

Isatu snapped herself awake and John soon followed. Her words tumbled out of her. She ran to her parents, chattering about miracles. Her mother smiled and reeled her in like a fish. John quickly explained what had happened and told Charm he was sorry for keeping Isatu out so late. 'Forgive me, old friend,' he said. 'It was unwise to take a child on such a journey.'

'Isatu has not been a child for years,' the old man replied. 'She is here, is it not so? Then all is well.'

'Yes,' said John, smiling. 'All is well.'

Inside John's house it was dark. He moved to flick on the lights, but I wouldn't let him. I took his hand and led him across the living room. I had caught a glimpse of his bedroom when we'd been here yesterday. Even in the dark, I knew where it was. I don't know what made me so bold with the man from Africa I barely knew. It would be easy to dismiss it as a symptom of frustration or a play at vengeance. But in truth, Manny was the farthest thing from my mind at that moment when I dared to reach for happiness. I didn't care what I was risking because it would be worth it to have lived without restraint with this man for an hour or two. Alfred taught me to live in the present and use the memories to bless the future. If I had one night with John Turay, it would compare to the day I had had with Louise at the museum. Most of us don't have many such days or nights to live by. Most of us cannot become the day like Hubert Butcher could. Tonight I would become the night with John. No line between us and the dark.

John steered me away from the bedroom. At first I thought he wanted me to go home, then I realized he was leading me to the bathroom. It was a tiny place – room only for a toilet, a shower stall, and a sink. He took off his clothes, throwing the blood-stained shirt on the floor in disgust. Then he helped me take off mine. I still had my swimsuit on. He eased the shoulder straps down my arms. When he saw my breasts in the moonlight, he put his forehead on mine and thanked me.

We showered together. There was no hot water. He apologized. I hushed him. After the first shock of it, the water felt good. The soap was Palmolive – a soap I'd used in England. It took me back to Lavender Sweep and the first time I'd taken a bath in our new bathtub. In the light of the moon, our bodies looked like paintings. When we toweled off we were both shivering.

In his bed the sheets were cool. He held me tighter than hunger. I didn't let myself think of Manny. He was a dream I'd had once. I'd woken up now. I felt the urgency of John's tongue and thought about his blackness and my own. He knew what to do without my saying anything. He listened to the way I responded and took his cues from me. I had never felt so lucky in my life as I did that night in John Turay's bedroom. My life had turned around at last. He'd opened me up, given me courage. If love could be like this, then there was no settling for anything less than triumph.

Afterward, John asked me why I'd said my father's name when we'd seen the elephant.

'I don't know. I didn't know I had. I suppose it just came to me. He'd written about the same thing, if you see what I mean. It was as if we were entering his story, as if we had become the characters he wrote about. And the girl, Jacinta, the one who rides the elephant, she was me and she was Isatu as well. I don't know. It doesn't make sense. The elephant was Simon – just for a second. I'm not mad.'

'I know.'

'Maybe I am mad. I feel like someone who's in a story, and the story is going to turn out badly. I've read the end, you know, but I can't change it. Someone else has already written the words. Sometimes I think all people of color feel like that – as if the words have already been written and the story always runs backward, to pain. Then, at other times, I convince myself I can write the end and that it will be a good one. The elephant was one of the most beautiful things I've ever seen. I wish they hadn't killed it. I wish we hadn't. I wish he hadn't died. Why did we do it? There's no goodness in the world anymore. Everything turns to dust.'

'Shh, Jacinta. That is no way to talk. Look at you. You have talent and beauty and a lovely child. You were born in the West – you are more privileged than three quarters of the world. And you have a heritage to come back to. Africa is not going anywhere.'

'Africa's a mess.'

'Yes. But it is also Africa.'

'Yes. I've committed adultery.'

'Yes. Does it make you sad?'

'No.'

'Good. Because from what you have told me, you are married to a fool.'

'I was raised Catholic. I should feel guilty.'

'Okay. Let us feel guilty for the next two minutes. Then we must make love again.'

'Why?'

'So that we remember why you sinned in the first place.'

'You sinned too.'

'Perhaps. But I will take my punishment like a man and never say it was not worth it. Will you regret this, Jacinta?'

'No. You don't believe me.'

'You were raised as a Roman Catholic. It is hard to over-come.'

'Did you hear the way the elephant cried out? It sounded like old pain, you know what I mean? Forest pain, centuries old. It was all I could do not to fall on the ground and try to bury myself just to get away from it. There shouldn't be that kind of pain in the world. It's too much to bear. My mother . . . there shouldn't be that kind of pain.'

'The other side of that pain is bliss, Jacinta. Without one, there cannot be the other.'

'I think that's ridiculous. I don't need pain to be happy. All I need is a few kind people and a lot of luck.'

'You can have all that and more,' he said. 'I will be kind to you, Jacinta. Let me be kind to you.'

I didn't stay all night. I left at around two or three. Saying good-bye was torture. I went back three times. Each time he wanted to begin all over again. He said I could live with him. He said he would protect me. I told him I could protect myself. He asked if I'd protect him, then, in that case. When I drove away, I saw him in the rearview mirror. He was standing in the door-way waving. I had the strange sensation that he was on a boat, or I was – one of us was leaving on an ocean voyage. Parting was so painful that I thought of slave ships and departures the land had seen long before we had been born.

On the journey home I wondered what happened to residual pain. The elephant's death cry was joined to the cries of my father's people, their bones shifting on the ocean bed after a hundred thousand Middle Passages. Lionel's dinosaur, her face held between grace and suffering, walked off into the distances where miracles lived. Lady's left arm swirled under the tides with Manny's pet goldfish, its fin the arm of a baby. And Louise's cry echoed the elephant's roar, for my mother too had loved a man like John Turay, and she had loved him for nearly a decade, become accustomed to his smell and his touch, before he was torn from her like a limb and sealed into the quiet earth. No wonder she went mad. Poor Louise Buttercup. No wonder my mother went mad.

And then there was the other side. Always, that was the light to cling to. The other side of the Middle Passage, which had resulted in a hundred new cultures sprung from the old. Jazz and blues and Martin and Baldwin and Zora and basketball and a kind of vast reservoir of glory that traced its roots to here. Here, where I was tonight. Driving back from love. On a road in a town called the moon.

Manny was snoring in bed, his arm cradling Lady. I climbed in softly. He moaned. I couldn't hear what he said. Tomorrow, I'd tell him about John Turay. I couldn't pretend to keep trying. I hadn't loved Manny for a long time. It was time to tell him that as gently as I could. I wasn't afraid. It was time. It would be obvious to both of us that there was nothing left to work with.

When I woke up, vultures were crash landing on the roof. The click-click of their claws sounded like a woman's high heels.

Manny was sitting up in bed. He said he was too sick to continue with the project. He told me he had to get back to the city – see an American doctor before this country killed him. I got up and packed our bags. As soon as we got home, I'd tell him. I stared at him for a while trying to see whether this was some ruse he'd made up, knowing that the end was near. But his face was almost green; and, if he was acting, it was the best act I'd ever seen. We said good-bye to Lionel and drove away from Lunama in a cloud of dust.

Lady was sick on the way home, sicker even than Manny. I cursed myself for not giving strict instructions to Manny to collect her from Assie's house before evening. The mosquitoes

had probably gotten to her there – Assie's family had no screens
on the windows. I drove fast. Manny moaned about his stomach. Assie moaned because her vacation had been cut short.
Lady moaned in pain.

By the time we reached home, I'd been driving for six hours
straight. The roads had slowed me down. The early rains had
increased the potholes left from last year's rainy season. We'd
had three near accidents and my head was pounding with the
stress. As soon as we got in, Manny went to bed. I saw to Lady,
with Assie's help. Soon she was asleep. We'd take Manny and
Lady to the Peace Corps doctor in the morning. Assie lay down
with Lady. I went to the kitchen to make some tea.

I sat down and watched the steam rise from the cup. I would
tell Manny when he woke up, if I could find a time when he
wasn't sitting on the toilet. God, life was absurd! I could still feel
John's fingers running across my body. I didn't know how I
would contain my own happiness. If it was wrong to love him,
I didn't care. It had never been right to give myself to Manny,
who could only be part of a man. One sin begets the other. And
what was sin anyway but a code created by a flawed group of
men determined to have power?

The doorbell rang. For some reason, I knew who it was as
soon as I heard it. There was only one person I knew who would
ring the bell like that: Esther. I was happy. Esther would understand what had happened. While the house slept, we could
talk. She'd never be pious. She'd talk about sex without obligation and tell me again how good it could be.

I rushed to the door and opened it.

The man standing on the doorstep was white and clean-
shaven. His clothes were immaculate. It wasn't until he said my
name that I remembered him.

'Hello, Cinta. Remember me?'

I took several steps backward and nearly tripped over one of
Lady's toys. He rushed up and grabbed me.

'Careful now,' he said. 'It's only me. You look pretty shaky. Sit
down.'

I opened my mouth to speak.

Only one word would come.

'Maurice!'

Then the room went dark.

When I woke up, Maurice was holding my hand. He was patting it gently, as an old friend would pat it. I tried to pull it away, but I was too weak.

'Who's this John fella?' he said.

I opened my mouth, but no words would come.

'Hubby's sick too. So's the kid. What's happened to her anyway? Some kind of accident?'

I tried to sit up.

'I wouldn't try that, if I were you. You're too sick. Malaria. Doc says you'll be weak for several days. But don't worry. Nurse Maurice is here to take care of you. Good job I showed up when I did. God knows what would have happened to the little Foxes if I hadn't appeared on the scene at just the right mo. That Assieyatu is a sweetie. Washed my undies for me. Think she rather fancies old Maurice Beadycap. Good with the kid too. Shame her name sounds like a sneeze. Still, can't have everything, can you?

'S'pect you're surprised to see me here like this. Well, Jacinta, I've been planning this visit for a long, long time. Thought I'd be visiting you in Virginia, then you moved on me. Got all the news from Mum. Did you ever get my postcard? Sent it from Madagascar. Yeah. Been on my mind a lot over the past years. I've done well for myself. Very well. Did you hear about Mary? A complete loon. Had to put her away. Always thought the poor sod was doomed. Alfred's still as queer as ever, so I hear. Prancing around in those purple negligees. Never did understand what you saw in him, myself. At least your mum isn't as nutty as she used to be. Let's see . . . who else? Hubert is as happy as a sand clam. Still a retard, but harmless. I was back there last month. They couldn't believe it when they saw what had become of me. Remember what I used to look like? Vera Butcher says I've turned into a movie star. My mum can't get enough of me. Dad thinks I'm Superman. I earn more in a year than they've made in a lifetime. Gave them a few thousand

pounds. Ten actually. Should've seen their faces. Mum cried for
three hours solid. Yeah. I've done okay for myself. Funny, isn't
it? You were always the superior one, the one at the convent
school. We were the comprehensive school kids – the dumbos.
Remember when Mary spat in your school hat? Took her two
and a half hours and she still couldn't fill it up. And now I talk
like you and act like you, and no one would know there was
ever any difference. Funny – what goes around comes around.
What? Are you trying to say something?'

'Go to . . . hell, Maurice.'

'Now, Cinta, that's not nice. Here I've come all the way from
Nigeria – Lagos, actually. I'm in computers now. Did I tell you?
Traveled thousands of miles to see you, and you insult me. I'm
quite miffed. If you don't behave, you won't be getting the
pressie I brought you. Funny, isn't it? You, Jacinta Louise
Buttercup Moses, having a handicapped child. Bit of a come-
down, isn't it? Must have just about blown you away when it
happened. Was she born that way, by the by, or was it some kind
of accident?'

I tried to reach up and scratch his eyes out, but I couldn't
raise my arm more than a few inches. I felt tears on my cheeks
and tried to wipe them away before he saw them, but again my
arms let me down. I still couldn't believe that Maurice Beadycap
was sitting on my bed, stroking my hand, filling me with
poison. I wanted to call for help. But how would I explain to
Assie that this good-looking, cultured Englishman was evil?
She would never believe me. The only thing to do was turn
him off until I was strong enough to maim him.

'Don't cry, Cinta,' he said. 'I'm not going anywhere. I'll stay
with you all and nurse you back to health.' He ran his index
finger along my neck and down the middle of my chest. 'Always
did like thirty-four B,' he said. 'It's my favorite number.'

Then he stood up abruptly and walked out. I heard him
whistling in the kitchen. He was singing the song Lily Beadycap
used to sing at Lavender Sweep, 'Pack Up Your Troubles.'

But it wasn't Lavender Sweep; this was West Africa. And I
wasn't the Jacinta I used to be. I'd moved on, hadn't I? Where
had Maurice come from? He was history. He couldn't invade my

present tense. He had no power over me. I would not be afraid
of him. I would not. And if he harmed a hair on my angel's
head, if he even *touched* Lady, I'd kill him.

It took three days for me to recover sufficiently from malaria to
be able to sit up. I had the usual symptoms – uncontrollable
shakes, high fever. I vomited into a bowl held for me by Maurice
Beadycap. He tried to give me a bed bath, but I summoned up
all of my strength and bit him. He nearly hit me, then changed
his mind because Assie came in. Assie gave me the bath. She
asked Maurice to leave, but I saw him peeking in through a
crack in the door.

Manny got stronger before I did. He must have lost ten
pounds during his bout with what was either malaria or intestinal flu, the doctor never could say for certain. He looked like a
skeleton when he came into the room. He'd been sleeping in
Lady's room on the spare bed, while Maurice had moved into
the guest room. I was grateful for the fact that he'd been there
with Lady. At least Maurice couldn't get to her at night. As soon
as I could string some sentences together, I asked Manny to turn
Maurice out of our house.

'I thought he was a pal of yours.'

'I hate him.'

'He's been pretty good to you since you've been sick. Besides,
I like the guy. We have a lot in common.'

'Maurice Beadycap is a pervert. He is dangerous, Manny,
and . . . he's in love with me.'

'Ha, ha! Seems to me that he's gotten over you pretty well.
Seems to me he's focusing on younger blood these days. Got
quite a thing for little Assieyatu. Took her out on the town last
night. Sorry to burst your bubble, but I don't think Maurice
Beadycap has the hots for you anymore. To be honest, Jazz, you
don't look too pretty throwing up in a bowl in bed. You really
don't. By the way, that John Turay has been calling here. I told
him to get lost. Lionel tells me you didn't get back until the
early hours that night you dropped them off at the mines.
Maurice tells me you've got quite a reputation along Lavender

Sweep. Not in so many words, of course. But now a lot of things make sense. I'm willing to let bygones be bygones, Jazz. You're not all you were cracked up to be, but then neither am I. We've both had to settle for less than we'd hoped for. But we have a child, and maybe it's about time we both grew up. I'm your husband. We belong together. John Turay is an African has-been. Lionel tells me he'll never amount to much. In the government's pocket, so they say. And even the locals don't treat him with much respect. Got some kid he passes off as his niece and three women in the town he visits on different nights to satisfy his urges. Anyhow, it's your choice. Maybe I'm not such a bad catch, after all. I've always been faithful to you, Jazz. Always. Even when you spat in my eye. Even when you turned your back on me and wouldn't give me any . . . even then. You owe me. You owe me big time. Think about it.'

I threw up all over him. It came out in a flood of venom. It gushed out of my mouth and splattered his face, arms, and chest. He stood up in fury, shouting something to Assie about clearing the shit up. I fell back to sleep, glad I'd been able to respond appropriately.

The next day I got up and took a shower. I washed my hair and changed my own sheets. No one seemed to be home. I looked in on Lady, but her little bed was empty. By the time they came home from a trip to the beach, I had made the phone call I'd been desperate to make ever since Maurice's arrival.

Maurice walked in with Manny, Assie, and Lady. He was telling some filthy joke. Manny was laughing. Manny looked at me and grinned. It was clear he wanted to use Maurice as a weapon. It was clear Maurice liked being used.

Assie put Lady down for a nap. Manny told me I was looking more human. But I was too thin. Need a little flesh on those bones, he said, pinching me in the side. I slapped his hand away. The two men laughed.

'Was she like that when she was a kid?' Manny asked.

'Worse,' Maurice said. 'A real spitfire. Uppity too. Glad she found a man who could keep her under control.'

Manny grinned again, then tried to pat me on the head. I jerked my head away and then had to steady myself by holding on to the table. I looked at the clock. Surely the phone call would pay off soon.

Manny and Maurice helped themselves to what was in the refrigerator. Manny was talking about making another trip to Lunama – asking Maurice if he wanted to come too.

'Not much there, Maurice. But it's got a few things to recommend it. The Germans used to have iron ore mines up there. Closed down some years ago. There's this crazy Peace Corps volunteer we could stay with. Thinks he's seen a dinosaur.'

'You're joking.'

'God's truth. Ask Jazz. She accompanied a merry band of explorers on a trip to find the thing. Got pretty beat up along the way. Turns out it was some damn rogue elephant. Guess Lionel had been eating too many brownies.'

'Lunama, eh? I'll think about it.'

'Don't take too long. I want to leave the day after tomorrow. Got a million things to do. Had to come back early with this damn intestinal flu. I'm way behind schedule.'

Maurice began to eat some cold meat and bread. Manny joined him. I watched their mouths while they chewed. I thought of Maurice's tongue and Manny's lips. I thought about how easily I had given myself over to some of the men in my life, not understanding how dangerous it was to open yourself up to those who were not ready to receive you. I thought about violation and about Maurice's twin sister, Mary Beadycap. I thought about what madness meant and how vital it was for some people to enter into a pact with insanity if they were to remain on this earth. I thought about evil. I didn't know how to fight it. It made me weak. Evil was the void they never prepared you for in school. The nuns had taught me to be good and obedient. They had betrayed me. Good and obedient made you a slave. You had to fight. Alfred had been wrong too. He'd seen good in everything. Sometimes, when good wasn't there, he'd had to invent it. But I'd learned my lesson at last; I wouldn't be inventing it anymore.

I looked at the two white men consuming the food Assie had prepared without regard to the flesh they were eating or the trouble a black woman had gone to in making them something to appease their fat appetites. I thought about Lady growing up to please a man. *I would not let her do it.* The only person she would please would be herself. At four or five she'd be enrolled in karate. I must have begun to smile because Manny asked me what was so funny. He was always afraid I was laughing at him. I smiled more broadly.

'I want Maurice to leave my house and never set foot in it again,' I said in as matter-of-fact a way as I could muster. 'I don't want him ever to contact Assie or come near Lady. I want him to leave now without finishing the food he has stuffed into his foul mouth. Go and pack your bags, Maurice. It's time to go.'

Manny had a wad of food in his mouth. He opened his mouth to howl with laughter. Bits of meat and bread sprayed out over the table. Maurice simply stared at me, one eyebrow slightly raised.

Manny recovered at last.

'Jazz, Jazz, Jazz, you're delirious. First, this isn't *your* house, it's *our* house. In fact, I pay the rent, so I guess, if I were being picky, I could claim it as mine. Second, I kinda like old Maurice. He's opened my eyes to a few things since he's been here. He's been good to me. Besides, you should be grateful. He took care of you for days. And you were not a pretty sight.'

'I'm asking you one more time to leave, Maurice,' I said, trying to stand.

'And what will you do, Jazz, if he doesn't?'

A voice boomed out behind Manny's head, almost making him choke.

'She will ask her good friend, Esther Cole, to kill him.'

Esther stood in the kitchen doorway. Visible behind her were two large members of her entourage.

'Where the hell did you come from?' Manny asked.

'As Jacinta Moses can tell you, I came from hell, Mr. Manny. And now I plan to take a few people back with me, if I find it is a necessary thing to do.'

'Who is this bitch?' Maurice asked.

The two men who had been standing behind Esther moved forward into a position on either side of Maurice Beadycap. He turned whiter and appealed to Manny.

'What's going on here, man? Who are these people?'

'Time to leave, Mr. Shittyscrap,' Esther said. 'Jacinta is tired of you. Jacinta thinks you are a mess in her house. We have come to escort you to the hotel. If you come back to visit at this house, we will find you and boil each one of your testicles. After this, we will detach them from your body. Now it is time to go.'

The two men yanked Maurice up and led him out. Manny just sat there like a stone. Out of the corner of my eye I saw Assie with her mouth open. Manny stayed in the same position until he heard the door close, then he got up and went to the phone.

'I'm calling the police,' he said.

I told him it would be unwise to call them as Esther was a close friend of the police chief. He cursed me and slammed the phone down. He ranted and raved for several minutes, but I could never recall what he said because I was too bored to listen. At last he left me alone and went to his study. Esther called an hour later to say Maurice was safely installed in one of the city's more expensive hotels. One of her people would pick up his bags tomorrow and drop them off there. When I tried to thank her, she wouldn't let me. She said we were friends. She said it was nothing.

That night, for the first time in ages, I slept peacefully for several hours, until there was a knock at the bedroom door at three A.M.

It was Manny. I told him to bugger off. He began to cry. He knelt down at the side of my bed and told me he knew how bad he had been. He told me he was sorry – that my illness had driven him out of his head. He told me he still loved me but that he'd panicked when he'd thought he was going to lose me. He said he was nothing without me – that over the past few months he'd grown to love Lady. If he lost her now, it would kill him.

'She's beautiful,' he said, finding my main weakness and exploiting it. 'In the ocean today, she was gorgeous. I've never seen a tiny kid swim like that. To be honest, I've always hated it when people saw what she looked like. . . . I was embarrassed . . . ashamed . . . as though it was my fault. You never seemed to care. But I've always felt that beauty is important. I mean, we're beautiful people, Jazz. You can turn anyone's head. And we should have had a beautiful child. At least that's what I thought. But today, when we took off her shirt and she ran into the water, she looked like a little mermaid. And I couldn't remember why I'd wanted more than that. I know you've been trying to tell me how lucky we were. You think I didn't want to hear you, but I did. The thing was, I was afraid. Handicapped people have always made me afraid. Once I went swimming and this kid came along, not much older than me, and he had this artificial leg. He took it off and dove in the water, and I swear I nearly threw up. Had to get out. Ran all the way home. I was terrified. And then when she was born, she took you away. Day in, day out, all you could think about was Lady – when should she get a prosthesis, what kind of physical therapy did she need, how could we teach her to swim? But I think I'm starting to feel the same way you do about her. You think I can't. I know you've given up on us. But you must believe me, Jazz. I didn't know. I mean, I just didn't know her. She's my daughter too. She's the only thing I've ever loved without wanting anything back. I'm proud of her. I didn't know I could love like this. Please. Don't take her away. Why don't we begin again? I have to go back to Lunama. Come with me.'

'That nice vacation with Maurice. I remember.'

'No. He can go to hell for all I care. I've been sitting thinking about a lot of things. Maybe Maurice isn't the monster you make him out to be, but he's not to be trusted either. There's something about him that makes you say things you don't mean – makes you – makes *me* into someone I don't know. I can't explain it. I wanted him here to get back at you. I'm . . . I'm sorry. Will you come to Lunama again? Could we try one more time to get it right?'

'I don't love you.'

'Why not? Esther Cole, is that who you love? They say she does it with anyone. Or is it the mine man? I'm sorry. I'm sorry. See what you've made me say? Shit, this isn't coming out the way I'd planned. Look, let's go to Lunama. Hell, I'll even sit down with you and John and talk things over. I'm not unreasonable,

Jazz. And I love you. I love you and Lady more than I love the air
I breathe. I'd die if anything happened to you. But I'm not a good
man. I never claimed to be a good man. I'm just a man. I have
faults. I can't always tell you how I feel or what I need. You're
strong, Jazz. You're like Esther. You see something and you go for
it. You've got to be patient with people who aren't like you. I'm
Lady's daddy. I love her. I love every inch of her. Don't take her
away from me. Please.'

I told him we could go to Lunama. He buried his head on my
neck and thanked me over and over.

He thought we were going to try to patch things up. But what
he'd said about Lady had sent ice through my bones. I'd imagined it would be easy getting custody of my child. But now he
was trying to sabotage that. He knew that Lady was his hold on
me. I didn't trust in his sudden conversion to fatherhood. So I
was cautious in my response. I needed to talk this over with
John. He'd know what to do. I could consult with Esther too.
Among the three of us we'd find a way to rid me of the man who
was weeping in my lap.

I didn't tell Manny we were going to Lunama because the
only man in the world who could open me like the blossoms on
trinity trees lived there; I didn't tell him I would use anyone,
including my husband, to get to see him again.

8

We arrived in Lunama in the early afternoon, about a week after the incident with Maurice. It took me longer to get better than I'd thought it would. I was still weak by the time we pulled up in front of Lionel's house.

Lionel was there to greet us. He looked at me sheepishly. He knew I knew he'd told Manny what time I'd come in that night. I didn't even bother to say hello.

'You've been ill,' he said. 'You look thin.'

'I'm better now,' I said icily.

'Let's not open up old wounds,' Manny said. 'What's past is past. No harm done. Nothing happened, Lionel. They just talked, that's all. In future, you need to learn to keep out of my wife's affairs.'

The pun didn't seem to have been intended. Manny and Lionel both blushed, then looked away. Manny sniffed. 'Damn congestion,' he said.

After that auspicious start, we all trooped into the house. Lionel tried to be ingratiating. He'd spent most of his meager Peace Corps salary on treats like mayonnaise, mustard, canned clams, and honey. He told jokes to lighten the mood, but the only one who laughed was Lady, and then only because she seemed to be amused by the sound of his voice. Lionel offered to walk Assie to her family's house. He played with Lady. None of it made any difference in my mind. He'd betrayed me once, he could do so again. When he began to talk about his dinosaur, I cut him off.

'Enough's enough, Lionel. No one believes that story anymore. What you saw was an elephant and now we've killed it. Do you have a Heineken?'

I had to see John Turay. To my amazement, Manny suggested we all go up to the mines to visit with him. Assie wanted to go. She'd missed out on the trip to the mines last time, and she had no intention of missing out again. I didn't know whether I liked the idea of us all going together, but at least it meant I could see John. After resting for a couple of hours, we got in the Jeep and drove up to the compound. I knew Manny had an agenda. His sudden turnaround was unconvincing. Once in a while he'd forget the new role he'd adopted and revert to his old, irritable self. But whatever plans he had, I knew I was safe. Nothing he could say could harm me anymore. As far as I was concerned, we were already divorced.

John was at home when we knocked on the door. He opened it and saw Manny first, then the rest of us. I couldn't tell whether he'd been warned that we were coming. He seemed relaxed. He welcomed everyone and hurried to get us sodas and beers.

Manny was nervous and the nervousness slipped into condescension. He wanted to demonstrate his superiority because he was in competition with the man before him. He spoke in the tone he'd used in creative writing workshops in Virginia. He asked John questions about the mine, then made fun of the answers. He commented on the size and location of John's house – neither of which was satisfactory. He asked after John's niece, and wondered how often John got down to Lunama to socialize. It was a deliberately pointed question designed to embarrass John, but it failed. When Manny saw how angry I was getting, he changed his tune, complimenting John on his way with children.

Lady was ecstatic to see him. She wouldn't let him put her down until Assie distracted her with a new coloring book I'd bought her.

John said he'd found out some more about my family. Would I like to go with him to meet an old woman who claimed to be my aunt? I looked over at Manny. Manny smiled. His whole face ached with the effort. I told John I'd love to go. We'd set out the next day with Lady, while Lionel and Manny worked at the rice project. Manny suggested Assie go with us. 'The girl needs a change of air.' It was such a stupid thing to say that Manny blushed when he'd finished the sentence. We could hear Assie's voice coming from the bedroom; she was playing with Lady, trying to teach her to count to ten. When John agreed it would be nice to go with Assieyatu, Manny was visibly relieved.

On the way back to Lionel's house, we passed by St. Peter's Church. I asked Manny to pull over. The red disk of the sun hit the side of the church, turning it salmon. The road looked like a river that shone in the dark, and the air was washed with a phosphorescent haze. This was the time of magic – when light seemed to resurrect itself from the bowels of the earth to stage a brief, glorious drama for those who cared to watch.

The nuns were scurrying back and forth in the church compound. We walked up to join the crowd of faces lined up along the high metal fence. Something was drawing people to the church. I pushed my way to the gate with Lady in my arms. On the grassy area in front of St. Peter's, the nuns were setting up a life-sized depiction of the crucifixion. The statues were white plastic with lightbulbs inside – giant Tupperware glowworms of Christ on the cross, the Virgin and the disciples. The sign above the cross flashed on and off: KING OF THE JEWS, KING OF THE JEWS, KING OF THE JEWS. It is beautiful, Assie said, placing her hand over her heart.

The nuns saw us. They came over and invited us to step beyond the gates. I refused. It felt uncomfortable to be singled out because we were not 'natives.' The Africans were told to stand back; we were invited to come through the gates. The nuns wanted to know us. Did we teach English? They were looking for good English teachers. Were we Catholic? They looked at Lady and were glad. 'All children are God's children,' said one of the sisters as she reached a hand through the bars and placed it on Lady's head. Manny told them I was Roman

Catholic. 'Come in, come in,' they said. I told them we had to be getting back. Lady was tired. We had an early start to make the next morning. We lingered for a few minutes, watching the nuns try to light the Virgin. She kept blowing a fuse. The nuns laughed at the trickery of electricity and one hurried off to find Father Marco. 'He is the one who built the church. He is a great fixer of problems,' Sister Renata told us. The nuns were from Spain, Mexico, Italy, Ireland, and Japan. The one from Ireland was nearly in tears when I refused to visit with them. She asked me if I'd ever been to Dublin. When I told her no she said I had missed seeing the most beautiful city on God's earth. She asked us if we planned to come to midnight mass the day after tomorrow. 'We'd be traveling back home then,' Manny said. She looked down at her feet and swallowed hard. 'It is difficult here,' she said softly. 'Very few visitors from the British Isles. There was one young man a couple of weeks ago. From Nottingham. Nice young man. Liked the shortbread Sister Eunice baked. Ate twelve pieces, can you believe that, dear? AVSO. Taught over in the eastern province. Just passing through, that was all. A nice boy. Protestant, but a really nice boy.'

I had forgotten it was Easter. I had forgotten that Jesus Christ would be risen in a few days. The organ music resonated in the minor key across the dusk – an anomaly passed from one world to another. We watched the light on the Virgin flicker on and off. When we got back to where we'd parked, the St. Peter Boy was waiting for us. He had climbed up on to the hood of the Jeep and had his crooked hand outstretched for pennies. Assie shooed him away.

'The polio is always begging for money. It is not good. He is everywhere in Lunama. He is putting off the tourists.'

I was afraid to go after him. I had Lady in my arms. Disease pitted his face.

Behind me the cross burned on the lawn, and I gave nothing to the St. Peter Boy because I was afraid.

When we returned to Lionel's house, Manny found a way to get me alone. He took my face in his hands and covered it with kisses. He wanted to push me on to the bed and make love to me, but I told him I wanted to be left alone. 'I love you,' he said, over and over. 'You know that, don't you? You're my life.'

I pretended to be asleep when he climbed into bed that night. He was drunk. He and Lionel had been playing cards and he'd lost every hand. I'd listened to him railing against his own misfortune as Lionel beat him over and over again. He stubbed his toe and swore at furniture in the dark. 'Damn wimp. Who's he think he is, anyhow? A cheat, that's who. Coulda slaughtered him if I'd wanted to. My daddy taught me how to play. Taught me how to *win*. I'm a *winner*. Emmanuel Fox knows how to play cards.' His muttering woke Lady. She sat up in bed. I held my breath. If he knew I was awake, he'd want sex. Tonight I was lucky – his mood swung from resentment to sentimentality when he saw Lady sit up in the dark.

'Hush, sweetheart, it's only your very own daddykins,' he said.

'Daddy,' she replied, nestling into his chest. 'I love Daddy.'

Soon they were both snoring. I wondered how Lady stood the stink of him. When I turned over, her cheek was up close to his mouth. He was breathing cheap rum all over her sweet black curls. I pulled her toward me. He called out something in his sleep, farted, and rolled over.

I was up before five and ready to leave at six. Lady rose early too. She ran around the house singing John's name. Manny tried to keep calm. Assie had refused to go with us. She said she wouldn't travel to that village 'up in the far beyond.' She said there were secret societies up in the hills that stole young girls like her and used them for sacrifices. She'd told me some time ago about the Bundu society – the secret women's organization that had performed female circumcision on her. She wouldn't say much about it apart from that. When I'd tried to find out more, she'd clammed up. Later it had occurred to me that it was her business, not mine. I stopped passing quick judgments and learned to value her privacy. Now Assie restated her fear of the 'bush people,' as she called them. 'They are not civilized like us. I am a city girl now. I do not go back to primitive ways. I am advancing with the rest of you.'

Manny tried to convince her that she was being foolish. She

set her mouth and sucked through her teeth. She defeated him. The only chaperone John and I would have would be Lady.

'Be good,' Manny told me when we were about to leave. The sentiment seemed ridiculous. I just looked at him.

He hugged Lady again. 'Daddy loves you, Lady. You're Daddy's girl, aren't you?'

Lady put her arm around his neck and kissed him. He tickled her under her arm stub. I strapped her into the car seat and got behind the wheel. I was going to spend the whole day with John Turay! I wanted to dance. It took every ounce of restraint I had not to laugh out loud.

We drove off in a flurry of dust. I didn't tell Manny what time we'd be back because I didn't know myself. He wanted to ask but restrained himself. A part of me begrudgingly acknowledged that he was handling things with unexpected dignity. Soon, however, I'd forgotten about Manny. I was going to meet the man again! Each time I said that to myself, it felt like flying.

At the mining compound, John was waiting for us. He was leaning up against one of the trinity trees outside his house. He was in deep shadow. When he stepped out as we approached, I imagined the tree had given birth to him. On his head and shoulders were a few wide petals. He brushed them off, and they fluttered to the ground like fuchsia wings.

'Hello, Miss Jacinta! Hello, Miss Lady!' he called out to us. His face was alight with happiness.

'Hello, Mr. John!' I called back.

We had arrived. A whole day together.

We climbed down from the Jeep and stood looking into each other's faces. John bent down, picked a handful of petals up from the ground, and handed them to Lady. She threw them up in the air and watched them fall. 'Rain, rain!' she cried. 'Lady make rain!' The petals fell on the three of us. John Turay took my hand and squeezed it.

'I heard you were sick. I wanted to come to you.'

'Who told you?'

'Assie wrote to me. She sent the note with her cousin.'

'Assie? My God. She knows, then.'

'Yes. Of course,' he said. I felt like a fool.

'Does she know everything?'

'She knows how we feel. It is not the same here as it would be where you are. It is not a scandal. I cannot believe you are here. I was sure I would never see you again. Now I am beginning to believe we will last for a long time.'

John wanted us to ride in his van instead of the Jeep. He said he was more comfortable driving his own vehicle, especially after the dents he'd put in the Jeep the last time around. We sped away from the compound like thieves.

It took several hours to get to Simon's village, though the distance was relatively short, because the roads were becoming treacherous. The week before, an absurdly early rainstorm had washed away a bridge in the eastern province. Five people had died. We drove slowly, trying to avoid potholes, plunging into some that stretched the width of the road. The villages we passed through were filled with children. They ran up to the side of the van and banged on the doors. 'Eh, Mister. Gi' we somting! Eh, Missus, gi' we koppoh, du-ya!'

Women waved to us as we drove past. They turned slowly to greet us, not wanting to disturb the baskets, the wood, or the bowls on their heads. They turned with the kind of grace Isatu had employed when she impersonated the dinosaur.

The leaves on the bushes and trees were a hundred different greens: yellow-green, purple-green, grass-green, black-green, water-green, mud-green, shimmer-green, turquoise, and viridian. When gradually the land raised itself up and away from flatness, I heard monkeys chattering from tree tops and felt a cool breeze on my face. The humidity of Lunama was left behind and things passed by us in sharp focus. Little had changed in this area for centuries. This part of the country belonged to the bush, which would reclaim things again once we had moved on. For a moment I tried to pretend that it made me happy to be a fleeting thing, but I was lying. I was like all the rest; I wanted to win. I wanted to find a way to make Lady and me a permanent fixture on the face of the earth; I wanted to change its expression. I didn't want us to be shadows no one would remember. I needed to be connected to the land so that there would be a way to pass things on.

Lady was playing happily in her car seat. She had her coloring book open on her lap. It was a counting book. She was looking at the picture 'Two.' There was a little girl in the picture. She was black. The writing above her head said 'Two ears, two eyes, two legs, two hands, two arms, two feet.' Lady was smiling. Her one hand was tracing the contours of the word 'two.'

'You know what "two" means, Lady?' I asked her. She looked up at me – her big eyes were black and curious. 'Two means the two of us – you and me.' I made up a song about our being together and sang it to her.

Lady joined in. She stomped her feet on the seat and slapped my hand with hers to the beat of the made-up song.

What is the sound of one hand clapping? Just the same as two.

'No one can spoil it, Lady. That's what the book means. Two, you see it there? You and me.'

We drove on singing our song, adding John's name once in a while if the rhythm allowed it.

Stupidly I had thought that John and I would be fastened on to each other's bodies by now. I had forgotten that, in a relationship based on friendship, desire is secondary to intimacy. As we drove along the dust roads, I looked over at him; his profile was framed by the bush. I fancied he was making the bush happen – that when he turned and spoke to me he created more of it with his words. As long as he kept on speaking, the bush would keep happening. On and on we could drive, on to the edge of the world, and still the bush would occur because his words had made it so.

'I am in love with Africa,' I said.

'And she is in love with you,' he replied.

'I will never leave.'

'Or perhaps you will leave. Soon,' he said.

'No! You're wrong! I've found something here. I've found peace. I've never had it before. Most people in England and America don't know what peace means. We take seminars on it and workshops and find cult leaders or TV gurus who will give it to us for a price, but really we don't know what it means. The bush is the quiet place in the center where everything stops. I'll never leave. Or if I do, I'll come straight back. I need to see my mother. There's so much to tell her. She'll want to know about my father's family – at least I think she will. And I want her to know I found him here. Because I feel him when I'm with you. I feel his stories and the power of his eyes. Last night I heard his voice telling me the story about the elephant. I was riding on its back through the bush. Me. Jacinta Moses. The African.'

John laughed. 'You have a vivid imagination,' he said. 'It is very obvious your father was a storyteller.'

'I don't lie, John. I mean it when I tell you I can't leave this land now that I've found it. It's mine now. I have no intention of losing it again.'

The village was a pause in the density of the bush. We came upon it unawares. We were talking and there was the bush surrounding us: we were talking and there was the village. My heart seemed to stop and I looked around almost expecting to see my father come toward me to let me know that the earrings he had bought me on my fifth birthday had made a difference. I was African like him after all, and he was proud of me.

John told me that Mohammed had contacted the villagers, so they were expecting us. I wondered how he had done it. The road had turned to little more than a bush path some fifty miles back. How did people learn about the outside world in this tiny place? What news came to them that could begin to touch the way they lived?

When we pulled up, children ran off to fetch their elders. I took my father's book from the front flap of my rucksack. On the back cover was his photograph. I gave it to John. He pointed at it and then spoke in Krio and then in Mende to the group of people that had gathered around us. Some of the older ones nodded their heads. 'Simon Moses. Simon Moses,' they said. My father's name sounded holy coming from their lips. They propelled us toward a small house made of mud at one end of the village. Before we had reached the doorway, an old woman stepped out to meet us.

John greeted her. She replied in formal, somewhat stilted English.

'Yes. I am the one. This is my daughter, no?'

'Yes,' said John.

'And this is her daughter, no?'

'Yes.'

The woman raised her hands to her face and laughed like a girl. 'This is a great day, my friends. Look!' she said, holding up the book with Simon's photo on the back. 'Simon Moses has come home.'

Everyone laughed and cheered. They led us into the house. The circle had come home. It would never be broken again.

The old woman was not my aunt in the Western sense of the word, but she was distantly related to Simon. Eventually John was able to discover that she was the daughter of my grandfather's third wife. But she did remember my father, and she welcomed her newfound family with a joy that touched me.

Miss Regina had only a few scraps of furniture in her house, so we sat outside where she cooked and talked about what life had been like before disease had wiped out most of the village. It sounded as if the culprit was cholera, but no one knew for sure. She remembered my aunt Jacinta – the one who had run away from the nuns. She said she'd left some time after Simon did. She said she was a typical daughter of Christopher Moses: full of fire. Once she crossed the paramount chief and had to pay a steep fine. She didn't remember what happened to Jacinta. Like her brother, she had left them, never to return until now. When Miss Regina said this, I was struck by the ease with which she relegated death to the margins of existence, and by how easily she adopted me as the messenger of the late Simon Moses. Curiosity and then death may have snatched Simon away, but his family could bring him back from the dead. This Easter, he was resurrected. I wished Louise could have witnessed the miracle.

While we were talking I realized my aunt would be an old woman by now; that, if my father had lived, he'd be over seventy. On average, you were in your forties when death claimed you in this country. The elderly were the middle-aged, and youth was old before it had a chance to grow up. But because Simon's death was premature, I could see my father as he had been. Frozen in time, my parent became my peer, and then, at last perhaps, my young relative who never allowed age to rust his brilliance.

We were taken to the palm wine bar at a place a mile or two inside the bush. Miss Regina led the way, and a dozen or more of my new 'family' came with us. We met Mr. Kargbo at the palm wine bar, which was a lean-to in the middle of a clearing. A rough-hewn bench was all the furniture Kargbo had at his bar, but he had mugs and a metal tea strainer with which to remove the maggots from the palm wine. I'd tasted the drink before and hated it. This time, however, it was kinder to me. It sat on my tongue in layers – bitter like lemon juice, then sweet like honey. Mr. Kargbo was the principal of the boys' school situated ten miles up the road. He was a loud man, full of his own dictums. He claimed he was a good friend of my father, but he spoke about him as if my father had left the village last week, so I knew he was lying. I wasn't angry. It felt right to be sitting in the heart of the bush drinking palm wine out of a mug that said 'Jesus Saves.' Miss Regina would not let go of my hand. Her own was large and warm. A grandmother's hand. She asked me to carry her daughter's child back with me to America. She said there was nothing here for young people. She didn't seem to be pinning her hopes on my agreeing to take her grandchild, however, and she was pleased when I said I'd write instead. 'And send books?' Yes. I'd send as many books as I could afford.

On the way back along the bush path, John Turay asked me how I was going to send books from America if I wasn't going back there. I told him I would go for a visit and buy them then. 'You will go back soon,' he said, his voice low in his throat.

'How many times do I have to tell you, John? I'm here to stay. I've come home. Even if I go back for a while, I'll return. This is where I belong.'

We ate with Miss Regina, her daughter, and her daughter's daughter in the clearing outside her small house. We had groundnut stew made from fresh-ground peanuts, goat meat, and onions. Lady ate three helpings. Everyone admired her appetite.

I looked around while we ate because I was afraid I would forget some detail, which would spoil everything. I wanted to be able to write about Miss Regina's talent for giggling like a teenager and welcoming us all with the grace of a matriarch; I had to capture the hands reaching for food in a rhythmic, soothing gesture of community; I mustn't forget the old mission schoolhouse in the background, long since abandoned by the priests who had come to teach the boys how to read and write in English and how to pray in English too; and I must remember the shadows and the light that played on the ground and in the air like a symphony of lighter and deeper darks. I put Alfred and Louise into the picture with me. They ate and were glad. Simon joined us then, dressed in local clothes, humming the song his mother had hummed before him, watching us eat like a family, white and black together.

Just then, Miss Regina stood up. She had remembered something, she said. She went into her house and brought out an old black book with tattered edges. Carefully, so as not to displace any of the treasures glued inside, she turned the pages until she found what she was looking for. She pulled it out and held it up for me to see. Simon, in a white shirt, was standing in the bush, his face a wide, bright smile, the palm trees black behind him. She told me Simon had the same, the very same photo himself, but he'd given her a copy. She was his auntie, she said. They were friends together.

She told of the time when Simon had gone on his first hunt. Not more than a small boy, he had traveled with his father into the bush to hunt. 'He could not do it,' she said.

'Do what?' I asked.

'Kill. He could not kill. When they came upon the elephant – and there were elephants here in those days – many elephants –' (the old people at the feast nodded in agreement) 'Simon Moses tried to save the animal. Can you imagine it? He ran in front of them and told them no. A priest was hunting with them. A Christian man who later was the man who helped Simon go to school in the capital. It was he who nearly shot your father by accident. Everyone laughed at Simon. He was too tenderhearted. He would never be strong enough to be a hunter like his father.

But Simon did not care what people said. He was a strange, strange one. He did not want to be like all the rest. It is no surprise that he left us. And it is no surprise that he has come home.'

After the meal, we pulled ourselves away, leaving just enough time to get back to Lunama before dark. I'd brought gifts with me. I left photographs behind, and magazines, two Timex watches, four bras, five T-shirts, and eight packs of chewing gum. It was little. I was ashamed when we were thanked again and again for such small gifts.

The journey home seemed quick. To my dismay, I fell asleep on the way home. When we reached his house, John woke me. 'We're here,' he said.

'O no! It's too early.'

'It is late. See. The sun has gone down. It is dark, but I think there will be a moon tonight.'

It was true. It was dark. Lady was fast asleep. Around us the air was shot with fireflies that played upon your sight like motes of brilliance. The night air hummed with crickets and the bush seemed to be a place where secrets were safe.

Reluctantly, I put the car seat in the Jeep and said good-bye.

'We'll be back soon.'

'When?'

'Next week. I plan to tell Manny tonight. We're leaving tomorrow. Then I'll come back next week, okay?'

'Let me be there when you tell him. It is not safe for you to tell him alone.'

'Manny's not dangerous, John, believe me. I know him. He wouldn't hurt me. I know it will be hard for him, but I've sorted it all out. I'll let him see Lady. I'm not going to make things difficult. He just has to let me go, that's all.'

'It is never as simple as that.'

'It will be this time,' I said.

'You are young.'

'And you are patronizing. I know Manny. Take my word for it, Lady and I will be back within a week, and Manny and I will be separated by then. I have a part-time job, and I still have some savings. We'll be okay.'

'You can reach me at the post office if there is an emergency. Call Mr. Kline. He is a friend of mine. He knows the situation.'

'He does! Why didn't you just broadcast it over the BBC? Okay, okay. I suppose it doesn't really matter. Besides, the whole world will know soon. God, I hate to leave. We haven't even . . . we haven't . . .'

He touched my hand. 'Do you want to come inside?' he said.

I had been waiting for him to ask, but now, when he did, I wasn't ready. 'I don't have anything. Do you?'

'Condoms? Yes. I have some.'

He'd had some last time. They'd been there in his bathroom. Was it true then about the women in the town? Had he been with anyone else since then? What did I know about John Turay apart from having witnessed his courage, and felt the profound dark beauty of his body and his mind? I knew nothing. Suddenly I felt anxious. What if this man were like Manny? What if he went mad like Louise and turned on me, enraged by something I'd said or done? These thoughts flashed by in a moment, then they were gone. In their wake, a residual insecurity, enough to turn the tide of our lives.

'Let's wait, okay? I want to tell Manny. Once I've done that, I'll feel better. It's driving me crazy, lying like this. I can't do it.'

He put his finger on my lips and hushed me. He told me he understood. He told me if I decided to come back, he'd be waiting. But I knew from his tone that he never expected to see us again. I felt superior as I drove away. It would be fun proving him wrong. How surprised he would be when the taxi dropped me and Lady off next week. Everything was possible now that I had come home.

Manny wasn't back when we arrived at Lionel's house. Assie was there instead, swinging in Lionel's hammock on the verandah. She rushed up to the Jeep when she saw us approaching.

'He is here!' she cried. 'At the Lebanese shop!'

'Who? Who is here?'

'Your enemy. Mr. Maurice Bodykip. He is here!' She sounded excited. I remembered what Maurice had said about Assie and his underwear. I wondered whether she had been his informant.

My hands began to shake. I asked Assie where Manny was.

'He is with Mr. Lionel at the palm wine bar. They are merry-making.'

I told her to go home. I told her we'd leave tonight – go back to the city and tell Esther what had happened.

'No, I am not leaving this place at this time,' she said, a new confidence rising in her. 'I am not afraid of Mr. Maurice. He has been kind to me. He and I are the same one. He was a poor boy who made it good. He is my friend who will take me to see Lagos, isn't it so?'

I took hold of her shoulders and shook them.

'Listen, Assie! For Christ's sake, listen to me! Maurice is evil. He is a bad, bad man. He will eat you up, Assie. He is not kind. He will use you. He doesn't even respect you. He told me as much. He is using you to get at me.'

'Ha!' she said, loosening herself from my grip and raising her eyes skyward. 'So he is like all men, then? He is in love with Miss Jacinta from the United States of America and not Miss Assie from Lunama. Well, I do not think it is so. I think you are very much in the error of your ways, Jassie. And I do not care what you think. I am on the up and the up. He is one man who will be helping me to get there.'

I took some money from my purse and shoved it into her hand.

'Okay, then, fine. Take this and keep it somewhere safe. It may come in useful if you need to get away.'

She was ecstatic. She threw her arms around me and kissed me full on the mouth.

'Esther taught me that one!' she cried. 'Esther is a fine, fine woman, is it not so?'

I urged her again to be careful, but it was useless. She said she'd be back in the city in a few days.

I grabbed Lady's car seat, being careful not to wake her, hurried into the house, and threw our things into a bag. I asked myself again, why was I afraid of Maurice Beadycap? John was here. Manny was here too. And yet who would Manny side with were I to ask him for a divorce? I'd wait. Ask him once we got to the city. Better still, I'd ask him when Esther was there. Nothing bad could happen with Esther Cole around.

I knew I was behaving like a coward. I could hear Esther's words on the journey back from Murunghi:

'Why go back to an idiot husband who has only a dick to recommend him? You are strong. You are free. Do what you want. Why stay with an old rag when you can have a new mop?'

My explanation had been weak then; it was weaker now. When it came right down to it, the reason I stayed was because Manny was the devil I knew. ('Better the devil you know,' my mother used to say, 'than the devil you don't know.') Manny was my familiar demon. I had lived with him for several years and I knew what he was and wasn't capable of. I knew also that he would never be able to stop me when I made up my mind to leave. That was my comfort. That gave me the strength to take my time. Feminist friends of mine, like Barbara Simpson in the writing program or Esther Cole herself, would certainly mock my faulty logic. I didn't care. In a way, I was like Assie and like Simon – bullheaded. Besides, and here was the rub, supposing underneath our play of domesticity lay a kind of violent subtext – a violence that could suck strength from me and make me as weak as I had been when the bastard who was flirting with Assie had shoved me against the flowered wallpaper on Lavender Sweep? Ever since Maurice's tongue had salivated over my innocence, and ever since my mother's hands had clutched my neck, a part of me waited for violence to make its grand entrance again. I could pretend to dismiss Lydia's story about Sophie, but way in the back of my head, in a place I was only now admitting to, was a deep-seated fear. It was only a fish, I told myself, but I had dreams about Manny's pet writhing on the floor, a mermaid this time rather than a fish, gasping unto death as he drew the contours of her pretty glitter tail. Evil could come at you from anywhere. Why hadn't Alfred warned me about its power? His stories of goodness and light, crafted morality tales, didn't help one damn bit when this fear hit me. We like to think that we are the brave ones, but most of us are not. I was not like Esther, and that's why I valued her as a guide, in spite of her vicious tongue. She didn't seem to be afraid of much at all. Esther, I thought, I wish you were here with me tonight.

'Mr. Manny is making you very sick,' Assie said. 'I know this is true. It is he who has made you to cry. I remember this. You are Esther's girl now, and Mr. John's. They will not let him do a harm to you.'

'I'm not Esther's girl, Assie. I'm no one's girl. I'm Jacinta Louise Buttercup Moses. I'm me. That's all. Do you understand?'

'Exactly. Esther will not let a man touch you.'

It was my turn to raise my eyes skyward.

'Good-bye, Assie,' I said. 'I'll see you next week. Don't go anywhere with Maurice, you hear me? The man is evil. He is dangerous. He hurt me. He will hurt you too. You understand?'

'Yes,' she said. 'He is a naughty man. I know this.' She winked at me. 'And he has a face like one of the movie stars who is in the movies, is it not so?'

I gave up. She would never be aware of the danger she was in. I couldn't help her anymore. I said good-bye again and took the sleeping Lady to find her father.

I found him where Assie said he would be – at the palm wine bar on the far end of town. He was dancing with a young woman from the town. He had his arms around her and he was kissing her on the cheek. I couldn't tell whether or not he was drunk. When he saw me drive up, he pushed the girl away and giggled like a child who has been caught with his hands in the cookie jar. I wanted to tell him I didn't care who he went with as long as it wasn't me, but we were in a hurry; and, as well as that, he had an annoyed expression on his face when he turned and saw me. I'd seen him give his mother the same look.

I called to him to get in the Jeep. Lionel joined him from his place at the bar. 'Go away, Lionel,' I said. 'We're going back to the city.'

'We're going *where*?' Manny asked.

'We're going to the city. Get in.'

'What's the rush? I'm not driving on those roads at night, Jazz. Don't be ridiculous. What happened?'

'Nothing happened. We just need to go back, that's all.'

'Well, I'm sorry, but there's no way in hell I'm driving a hundred miles along shitty roads –'

'Maurice is here.'

'What?'

'Who's Maurice?' Lionel asked.

Manny shuffled his feet on the ground, pulled at his hair, tried to look brave, then changed his mind. 'Okay, okay. Do we need to get our things?'

'They're in the back.'

'Who's Maurice?' Lionel called as I shifted into first gear.

'Someone you don't want to meet,' I called out to him. 'If he comes looking for us, tell him we went to Timbuktu.'

I was surprised that Manny had agreed to leave so readily. When he got in the car, however, he told me he'd seen Maurice hanging around our house after "that madwoman" had thrown him out. At first he assumed he was after Assie. Then he found Maurice peeking in through the bedroom window one night, watching.

'He saw you naked,' he said, between his teeth. 'You should learn to close the goddamn curtains. Sorry,' he said, as if surprised by the spitefulness of his own voice.

He went on to explain how he'd chased Maurice off, and threatened him with prosecution the next day when he caught him trying to peer into our windows again. He said the man gave him the creeps. I asked him why he hadn't mentioned all this before now. He hadn't wanted to scare me, he said, but now he thought we needed to do something. The whole thing was getting out of hand. 'You're *my wife*, for God's sake!' he said, pushing a strand of blond hair from his face.

Not for long, I thought.

Manny changed his mind about leaving when we were on the edge of town.

'Why run from the bastard?' he said. 'It's only Maurice Beadycap, not Jack the Ripper. Whose wife are you, anyway? We could tell the police.'

Realizing how they would laugh were we to go to them with a story like this, he sighed. 'What's he going to do to us anyway?' he said weakly, and I realized Manny was even more frightened of Maurice than I was.

I pointed out that the man he thought was harmless had followed me all the way over here. 'He is insane,' I lied, wanting nothing more than to get back to Esther and her bodyguards so that they could boil Maurice's testicles as they'd promised. 'I saw him with a gun in the house.'

That was enough to convince Manny we should continue our journey. He sat back in the seat and his leg shook like a leaf for several minutes. He kept glancing toward the side mirror to see whether Maurice was high-tailing it after us. When he was sure we were safe, he began to puff himself up again like some silly bird. And I had been afraid of this man! I almost laughed out loud.

I hadn't planned to tell Manny about me and John until we got home. But, after I gave up the driver's seat because Manny was a better driver than I in the dark, I had a chance to think about things. I climbed into the back with Lady. Manny was a nervous passenger, and he'd made me nervous too. Sitting in the back I listened to his monologue. There was nothing in Lunama, he said. Nothing but a few has-been Africans. He asked me about my trip to Simon's village but didn't wait to hear my reply before he was ranting again about Maurice Beadycap.

'The man's crazy. Who the hell does he think he is? Hanging around our house with a gun, for Christ's sake! Saw him at the supermarket too, coupla days after I threw him out. Hanging around the checkout. Didn't think much of it at the time, but it all adds up now. Man's insane.'

At that moment I looked up and saw the moon. Round and majestic, she appeared briefly, then was enveloped by clouds. Held up against her glory, Manny's words seemed even triter than they had seemed before. I checked to see that Lady was asleep, then leaned forward and began speaking before I'd fully formed the words in my head. They tumbled out into the humid night air. I told him I wanted a divorce because I couldn't love him anymore.

'I was afraid to tell you, but I shouldn't have been. It wasn't fair to either of us. I'm sorry. You need someone else. I'm not good for you; neither is Lady. You can see her as much as you want. This isn't about revenge or anything. It's just the . . . the sensible thing to do when people don't love each other any-more. Do you understand?'

He didn't seem to hear me at first. He tapped some tune out on the steering wheel, and I thought I'd have to repeat myself. Then he bit his bottom lip until blood came, balled his hand up into a fist, and flung it back behind him. It caught me on the mouth and sent me flying back on to the seat. I looked down into my hand. There was blood trickling from my bottom lip. Manny was accelerating round curves, calling me a bitch and a whore. I kept staring ahead because I didn't know what to do next. He'd hit me! Manny had hit me! I shook my head to try to clear it. I looked over to see that Lady was okay. I didn't want her to see what had happened. Her mother being hit by her father. I never wanted her to see that. I shook my head again. I had to remain calm. He was at the wheel. He was driving. He was banging his fist on the dashboard. He was swearing. He was cursing me to hell. I looked down at my feet. There was a crow-bar. Manny carried it in case we got stuck out on the road somewhere. I thought about hitting him with it. No! No! What was wrong with me? He would calm down soon. I should have listened to John. I should have waited. I tried to picture Esther's face. She wouldn't be afraid. I looked up to find courage in the moon but the clouds had covered her again so her light was eclipsed. Soon we'd be there with her in the city. Lady and I would stay with her. We'd be fine. The two of us. Fine.

Manny was pulling over. He was getting out and coming round to the backseat. He was opening the door. He had me by the hair. Now I was up – up against the hood of the car and my skirt was in my mouth! Dear God! He had his hands between my thighs and he was telling me to love him. 'You . . . owe . . . me!' Each time he pushed me deeper into the metal. My child was sleeping in the backseat of the car. If I made a noise, I'd wake her. Lady was sleeping. If she woke up and saw what he was doing, how would she forget it? I was quiet. I studied the moon, which had emerged above his head like a fingernail halo as he banged himself into me. I could see the moon rise and fall behind him as if it were a yo-yo on a long string. I focused on the moon. I watched. I turned my body numb below the waist and watched the rise and fall of a star. A car zoomed by. He threw me down when he caught sight of the headlights. We were on the ground, scrambling in the dirt. He was trembling, asking me if that's the way I liked it. I didn't say no, because how do you say no to horror? Asking me who was better, Turay or him? I found the moon. There she was. I brought her closer to me, close enough to swallow. White, warm moonlight down my throat. It was okay. Esther was there with me in the moon-light. I hadn't forgotten the moon.

Manny was kind to me after that. He helped me up and asked me if I was hurt. He found my panties and made me step back into them while he knelt down at my feet. He found a cloth and wiped my nose where it was bleeding and my mouth where it was covered with the wet light of the moon. When I couldn't stop shaking, he rummaged in the back of the car and found some rum that he made me drink. He said I was getting sick. He said it was probably malaria all over again. He said he'd take care of me.

'My father never took care of me, Jazz. That was the problem. That's why I've been . . . I mean, I'm so damn depressed and that's the reason. He used to like . . . he was a bad man. Evil. Evil. When I was ten, he came to my room. Are you listening, Jazz? He came in. He'd left us, but he was visiting. He was always leaving us. It was the last time I let him touch me. The last time. He tore up my paintings. The ones I was working on. I was drawing a girl I knew at school. They were good drawings. My best ever. He tore them up. He said all I'd ever have for a girlfriend would be my pet goldfish. I had a goldfish named Sophie. He went round to the other side of the bed and bent down so that he could look at me through the fishbowl. I kept the bowl. I always kept the bowl as a memento. His eye was as big as a fist. 'Sophie's your gal,' he said. 'You and Sophie. Two of a kind.' Then he laughed into the fishbowl and his mouth was fucking huge because of the glass, and you could see each one of his fillings, and the brown stains left by the chewing tobacco. Ugly teeth. Ugly as shit, my dad. I never let him see me again after that. And now I'm okay about it. I've read the books. I know how to deal with it. I'm okay now. But men's hands . . . I never like looking at men's hands, you know what I mean, Jazz? Jazz? Are you okay, honey? C'mon, let's get you home.

You'll catch your death of cold out here. There's a storm coming.' He helped me into the car and covered me with a blanket.

Lady was still asleep in the back of the Jeep. I thought about taking her out of the car seat and holding her to me, but I still had the moon for comfort. I unwound the window partway down and peered up at her. She was a clean eye against the dark. I let her wash me.

'We're in for rain,' Manny said. 'Hear the thunder? Better step on it if we're going to beat the storm home.'

His voice was far away. It was mixed up with a woman called Sophie and someone's fist. It was all mixed up with music on the radio and a baby's flipper arm. The moon was a hole punched into the dark tent of the sky. I hummed 'Moon River' and dreamed the road into rapids. We were in a boat. There was a harbor just around the corner. We couldn't see it yet, but the moon would guide us home.

He drove faster, dodging potholes that were sometimes small craters.

'This road is gonna be shot by the middle of the rainy season if they don't start filling in some of these things.' He swerved from one side of the road to the other in an effort to avoid the worst of them.

'I saw a work crew back there before night came on. Let's hope they're repaving the damn road. It's a bitch.'

I watched the scene as it flew by us watched by the moon. The road was barely wide enough for two cars. I wasn't nervous about the rain or the condition of the road. Manny was an excellent driver. I wasn't nervous about anything. The shaking had stopped. I was calm. Thunder rolled across the sky and shook the land like a brief stampede.

Manny's words tumbled over each other like penitents. I had to understand what made him tick, he said. There were things that made people act in a certain way. It wasn't their fault. 'He was always drunk, my father. One time, I heard him come in. I crept to the bedroom door and cracked it open. He had my mother by the hair and he was banging her head against the wall. Bang. Bang. Bang. Her head didn't sound human, you know. It sounded like a basketball. Then he did some other things. I watched. They didn't see me. I saw them. Disgusting. He was drunk.'

Manny reached back and placed a hand on my knee. He told me to scoot forward; I obeyed him. He let his fingers crawl up my thigh, leaning back in the seat so that he could reach far up into me. I didn't move or say a word. I was looking at the moon. She was more beautiful than ever.

'You've got to understand, Jazz, what it was like living with a madman. It changes you. But we don't have to be that way. I mean, your mother was kinda crazy too, but you turned out all right, didn't you? We're the same, you and me. That's why we belong together. We've been through hell and come out on the other side, and we're okay. We have Lady. We have each other. We can begin again. Put all that behind us. Okay?'

I kept staring at the moon.

'What are you looking at?'

'The moon.'

'Did you hear what I said?'

I focused harder on the moon. I let myself dissolve into the eye of the bright disk. I had become the moon. It was easy.

We rounded a bend at the crest of a hill. Hurtling toward us on the wrong side of the road was a pair of blinding headlights.

Manny jerked his hand back to the wheel. He swerved the Jeep over to the left, rode partway up a bank, and came down again on all four wheels.

'Are you guys okay?' he cried, slamming on the brakes. In his voice was the same concern I'd heard when he'd pulled up my panties.

'Yes,' I said, pulling myself away from the moon. 'We're fine.'

Lady was still fast asleep – totally unaware of how close we'd skirted disaster. She was sucking her thumb. Her juice cup was nestled in her lap.

Manny cursed the driver, though he had disappeared into the night without evincing any sign that he'd seen us.

'They drive like jerks in this country. Probably some taxi driver. Those are the worst.' His voice was tripping over itself. Things were happening too fast, he said. No time to think. 'Let's get home, Jazz, and sort all this out. We can get on the right track again. We're safe, that's the main thing. We've got a second chance. I love you, you know that. You and Lady. We're gonna make it. Things are always darkest before dawn. My mom used to say that.'

I looked up at the moon. She was still perfect. I turned Manny off. Click. He was gone.

After a few more miles, my body was yielding to the way the car moved along the pitted road. I sank into the curves of sleep and dreamed about the moon.

When I was jerked awake, the first thing I thought about was Lady.

We were careening through the air and Manny was yelling something that sounded strange. A word, said in slow motion. 'Jeeessuus!' No. It wasn't that. It was my name stretched out like elastic: 'Jaaaazzz!' The word wound out from his mouth like fishing line before his body was hurled up against the steering wheel. Earth inside my mouth or the powder of shattered teeth. Which?

Lady!

Lady!

Crying.

When I opened my eyes, it was pitch dark. The Jeep was leaning over slightly, as if we were riding along the side of a steep river-bank. No. It wasn't pitch dark. There was a faint light coming from somewhere and there was a trinity tree in the car. Its branches scratched my neck.

'Lady!'

No reply but the moon.

I opened my eyes again and saw the tree in the car. Not a trinity tree. No blossoms. Just a simple tree. Or part of a tree – yes, part of a tree. This time, someone was crying. The noise came to me convulsively, as if I were coming up for air every so often and could only hear sound in gulps before my ears were filled with water. I reached out toward the sound and caught hold of what felt like a spatula. It was warm. I recognized it. I'd never been so happy to feel the warmth of Lady's flesh before. I'd found my child's signature in the dark.

And it was beautiful.

Lady was alive and crying. I held on to her tiny arm for as long as I could before passing out again.

I came to for good when the rain was just beginning to come down. My head hurt so much that I must have sobbed myself awake. I was still sobbing. I thought it was someone else making all that noise, but it was me. I knew in the first few seconds that we'd had a terrible accident and that Lady had been crying the last time I opened my eyes. I was able to move my right hand. I reached over to where I thought Lady would be. Nothing.

'Lady!' I screamed.

'Mama?'

Lady's small voice a few inches from my hand. I groped toward it. There was my child's hair, her eyes, her mouth and nose and neck. Thank God! Thank God!

I tried to move from beneath whatever was pinning me down. There was part of a tree in the car. I hadn't been dreaming. It was a tree. Branches had smashed through the glass.

I called Manny's name. Nothing.

Limbs from the tree were wedged between the driver's and the passenger's seats in the front. It was impossible to see through them to the driver's seat. I concentrated again on Lady. I began to talk to her – silly, nonsense things that would soothe her. At the same time, I worked on freeing myself from underneath the debris. I was crazy with fear – something could tumble down on top of Lady. I didn't know what the hell was among the branches. I didn't let myself think about it.

After a long struggle, I had most of my body freed up. One of my feet was wedged against something and there was still a kind of wall between me and Manny, but I was able to reach over at last and unstrap Lady from the car seat. I pulled her out.

I could see a little better in the dark now that my eyes were used to it. My hands were bloodied and trembling as I felt all over my little girl for signs of injury.

Right leg – fine.

Left leg – fine.

Torso – no cuts, no gashes.

Right arm – fine.

Left stump – fine.

Thank you, thank you, thank you! I never want any more than this! Just this, and I will be grateful!

Lady wanted to cuddle me, but I had to help Manny.

The rain was steady overhead. Wherever we were, we were shielded from it a little. Maybe we'd crashed into some huge tree, which was giving us some shelter from the rain? Water dripped through the smashed windshield, but it didn't pour down upon us even when the wind picked up. I was grateful a second time.

My head was throbbing as I picked at the mess piled up along the center of the car. Every so often I called out his name. After forty or fifty calls I did it out of habit, with no hope that he would be able to respond. If he was badly injured, I'd have to risk taking him to a hospital. But white people said it was better to die than to go to one of the hospitals up-country. For a moment, I was paralyzed with fear. Then reason took over again: he may not be badly injured. I should find out first, then worry about getting help. I didn't even know if he was still in the front seat. He could have been thrown into the bush. I saw his neat body thrown into a high arc, then smashed into obscene disintegration. My vision. It had come true. I started to giggle. Then it became laughter. Someone was laughing like Rochester's wife, like Louise – and it was me. Then it stopped. I wouldn't be afraid. I had Lady with me. She was alive. That would be enough.

I worked from the top, slowly, slowly, leveling the wall between us.

Stones, rocks, great clumps of earth, twigs, branches, limbs of trees – only limbs of trees, please God – all the things that had been launched into the car upon impact. I found Manny's briefcase and one of Lady's little sneakers. Then I found a square box. Tupperware. Some of Lionel's food I'd packed in case of emergencies. I put it to one side for Lady, shocked by my ability to remain relatively calm.

Until I found the top of Manny's head. I could feel it when I reached over the wall. Lady crying. 'Shh! Shh! Mama's here. Don't cry.'

A cut on something sharp – a piece of metal. Part of the bloody car door! O, Jesus! 'Manny! Manny!'

My foot freed itself quite suddenly – I didn't know how. I leaned back and swiveled my legs up as high as I could. I had a tight hold on Lady. A hammer still pounded my forehead. I scooted up between the seats, glad that I was small enough to fit into the narrow space on her side of the wall. I pushed on the wreckage with my feet, calling his name into the dark. If I pushed it hard enough, I could create a space to slip through. I'd tried climbing over the top; it was impossible. The roof had been opened up like a tin can and jagged pieces of metal would have cut me to pieces. If only the elephant hadn't damaged the Jeep. I could have gotten out on the passenger side and tried from the outside. No, you fool! The Jeep was crushed on that side too. It wasn't the elephant. Don't blame the elephant. I cursed myself instead – all the errors I'd made, over and over, learning nothing from the time before. I cursed Manny, while I was trying to save him, for coming to me in pieces and telling me to pick them up and make a man out of them.

And then I'd done it! The wreckage collapsed under the weight of my feet, falling around us in a clatter. Manny was visible, slumped over the wheel.

Part of his face had been sheared off and the part that remained was staring hard into his lap.

'Manny? I just want you to know a few things.'

The rain had stopped but we were still in the center of the night. I thought it would be safer to stay there and hope someone would spot us than to try to pry the rest of the door open and go for help. I probably couldn't get out anyway. The door was a mess before the accident – impossible now. Lady was sleeping against me. I didn't turn to look at Manny's silhouette when I spoke because it no longer made sense to me now that so much of it was missing. Every so often I could've sworn it moved. I fixed my eyes on the bent hood of the car and the lessening rain, and imagined beyond the darkness the brilliant light that shattered into stars. It was the night sky that was over-laid on to a long bang of light – a fabric overlay so that we could bear the whiteness of things.

'Manny, Lady is fine. She is fine. I wished you dead and then you died. Walt Disney knew: Dreams can come true if you wish for them hard enough. He was right. They do. My head is killing me! You called out my name! Bastard! You called out my name! Why? I know. Maurice again. Accusing me. You did it, Cinta! You are the killer again . . .'

Wild animals! They can smell blood from miles away. Listen! Something out there in the dark! Eyes staring from the bush! Look! There they are! 'Lady! I've got you! Don't cry! Please don't cry!'

A howl rushed out of the dark from somewhere nearby. I jumped, and Lady began to cry.

She was hungry and thirsty. I pushed the fear and the pain in my head into the background and found the Tupperware container. I fed her bits of Lionel's stew with bloody fingers. There was beer in a cooler somewhere. I couldn't find it. Lady was thirstier than ever after the stew. There were puddles of water from the rain. One puddle on the seat by the door. I scooped some rain up in my hand and managed to get a little into her mouth. Then I thought about breast feeding. I had no milk, but it would quiet her. 'Titty,' I said. 'Do you want some titty?'

Lady sucked. I listened to the bush and the silence beside me.

Two people breathed: that detail changed everything.

I was in the Jeep again, racing along the road with Manny. Suddenly he cried out:

'Look! Over there! Dear God, Lionel was right!'

I followed his arm. Twenty, thirty feet away, no more, the

monster. A silhouette. Neck as long as a bridge. Towering over the bush.

'Jesus! We saw her, Jazz! She's real! She's –'

Brakes! Brakes! Like the screech of an animal in its death throes.

Eyes in the headlight. Baby eyes. Mirrors. As round as saucers. Jeep swerving to the right! And suddenly we were flying! Yes, flying to the right! Up over the bank, then down, down into trees.

What was that in the road? What was it? Bigger than a small elephant, frozen by headlights in the middle of the road? Rump. Leather. Wrinkled. And the smell . . . ancient. Ancient past Egypt, past the Benin Empire. As ancient as the moon. Lionel's voice: *I told you she was a mother.*

Then my father came to me. His face was elongated into pain – three feet from his hair to his chin. Raffia around his neck. Eyes – slits in the dark. Behind him drummers, pounding on skins, heating up the air. A wild dance in the mask of death. Drums playing midnight. Hands on drum skins – the wings of hummingbirds. The sound of crickets whirring in the bush like clocks. We were in the dance! Lady and me. In the dance with my father, Africa! I looked up at the sky: a constellation in the shape of a monster. Glory be! We'd seen it! We'd seen the Thing Itself rise from the ashes of time to fill the land with grace! No need to launch wishes like boomerangs anymore. Simon was with me, dancing with death in the night.

Simon opened the door from the outside – the only way doors can be opened – and pulled Lady and me from the Jeep. He carried us gently up the embankment and laid us on the side of the road. I asked him why he had risen from the dead.

'I was never there,' he said. 'You were only dreaming.'

He told me to rest. 'Help will come soon,' he assured me. 'All will be well.'

I fell asleep smiling.

9

They said they found us in the morning as the sun was coming up. A crew was working on the road. The foreman was British. We must have been thrown from the car, they said, when they found us lying by the side of the road – though how we had traveled so far from the Jeep and sustained only minimal injuries, they couldn't say. It was a miracle. They never would have found us if we had remained trapped in the vehicle. The Jeep was covered by the bush. No one could have found us if we hadn't been lucky. They said we must have swerved off the road. Did I remember anything? they said. Yes, I told them. I remembered my father. He was wearing a mask as long as exile. No one heard me.

They put us in the back of one of the trucks and drove us to a place whose name I cannot remember – the nearest town with a mission hospital. I was fully conscious all the way there. I wouldn't let anyone else touch Lady. At first they thought she'd lost her arm in the accident; they tried to hide it from me. I told them she was born with it. Once they understood, they were happy for me.

Soon after we arrived at the mission hospital, John came to us. He was with Assie and Lionel. He held me like a lover. The nuns at the hospital were shocked. 'It was your husband who was killed in the accident?' they asked.

'Yes,' I said. 'This man is my brother.'

They let him stay.

They kept us in the hospital for two days. They said they needed to observe me. John stayed with us. Assie stayed too. I slept with Lady. I wouldn't let anyone touch her. When the nightmares came, John held me. When he asked me about the accident, I said I couldn't remember anything. He said it was a blessing.

'Yes,' I said. 'I'm lucky.'

They took us back with the body. We rode in the front of Father Marco's truck. Assie and John rode in the van with Lionel. I had wanted to ride in the van, but the nuns insisted I ride with Father Marco. Father Marco was a good driver. He would take care of Lady and me.

Some of the nuns followed in a car. They were kind to us. The journey was like a dream. Manny's body bounced around in the back. I heard his coffin bang the side of the truck. Father Marco tried to talk over the sound so that I wouldn't hear it, but I heard it. I asked him to hear my confession as I drove. He listened while I told him I had killed Manny. I left out the part about John Turay. I left out everything except Manny's anger and my wanting a divorce.

Father Marco said I was typical. He forgave me. All wives blame themselves, he said. It was not your fault; it was the Lord's will. It was an accident. I didn't know how to reconcile the three statements.

We dropped Manny off at the old church down by the docks. The funeral would be held tomorrow. There was a strange smell coming from the back of the truck. People wore masks as they lifted the coffin. Lady asked me where Daddy was. 'In heaven,' I lied. 'Daddy's gone to heaven.'

Esther was waiting at the house. The nuns didn't argue when she took over. She and John and Assie and Lionel took care of us. Esther treated me like a baby. John's face appeared in the doorway of the bedroom, then disappeared again.

'Lady is safe,' Esther said. 'That is the main thing.'

The funeral was blurred. Someone had it out of focus. I tried to adjust the lens, but it was too late. Manny was already buried in a little plot in the Creole cemetery. The priest got muddled up, said it was Manny's father who was African. Told the story of a man who went on a journey to find his father. In his sermon, the man found peace.

After the funeral, I got a call from Alfred, who had just learned through the British Consul what had happened. He wanted to fly out. I told him no. Louise was on the phone then. 'My poor baby,' she said. 'Let us come and be with you.' 'No,' I said. 'We're fine. Our friends are taking care of us.'

Alfred spoke with Esther. I don't know what she said. When I took the phone again, he was calm. 'She is a good woman,' Alfred said. 'Yes,' I answered. 'She is looking after us.'

We stayed in the city for two more weeks. Esther stayed with us, so did Assie. Lionel left one day. I can't remember when. Before he went away, I asked him about his dinosaur.

'There never was a dinosaur, Jacinta. I was a fool to believe it. It was an old elephant, that's all. I know that now. It's funny. It was Manny who helped me see that. We talked about it – at the palm wine bar the night you left. . . . He helped me see the light. Was driving me crazy. I think your husband's common sense may have saved me. I'm peaceful now. Easy.'

'I envy you,' I said. But I didn't know whether I was being sincere.

We never spoke after that.

Soon after Lionel had gone, things came back into focus. I looked around me: Lady was playing at the foot of my bed; Esther was with Assie in the living room singing a song with her in a language they shared; and John was in a chair in my room waiting for me to recognize him.

'You have been in and out of things. The sedatives,' he said, 'and the painkillers.'

'Am I better now?'

'Yes. I think you will soon be better. Will you tell me what happened?'

I opened my mouth to speak, but nothing came out except a sentence or two of mumbling.

'Who is Sophie?' he asked me.

'A fish,' I was able to reply.

'I don't understand.'

'Neither do I,' I said.

'Do you want to sleep?'

'No. I want to watch everyone.'

'Okay,' he said.

He cradled me in his arms and I watched Lady play with her toys. When I fell asleep it was in his embrace, and when I woke he was there by my bedside, where he promised he would always be.

Gradually I got stronger, and John said he had to return to Lunama and the mines.

'Will I see you again?' he asked.

I told him I believed we would see each other again, but that first I needed to be alone for a while. When I tried to apologize, he placed a hand gently over my mouth.

'You are you, Jacinta. You decide which road you take. If you want me to ride with you, I will come. If you want to ride alone, I will wave good-bye and await your return. It is not complicated. It is what should be done.'

Then he broke down and cried because once there had been trinity trees and storytellers and elephants, and now there would only be a conjuring up of these in the memory of the ones who were there.

When he left, it was as if he had taken a limb of mine with him.

Esther remained with me and Assie. Assie had come back from Lunama as soon as she'd heard about the accident. She and Esther would help Lady and me get ready for the trip back to Virginia. We would spend time with Lydia, then perhaps I would find work. I didn't know. Tom Brandon in the writing program was going to help. Lydia had contacted him, apparently. There would be space in Virginia to absorb the enormity of what had happened here.

The day before I left, Assie handed me two notes. One was from Maurice. She told me she'd been afraid to give it to me after what I'd said about him. She told me he was sorry. 'You must forgive him,' she said. 'He is a poor man like Assie.'

The other note was from John.

I read Maurice's note first.

Dear Cinta,

We just heard about the accident. Let me know if I can do anything. Probably you hate me. But I want you to know I came to Lunama to apologize to you and to Manny. You bring out the worst in me, Cinta. You always have. I don't mean half the things I say. I just want you to know Mary and I were not monsters. If you and the kid want to visit me in Lagos, that would be great. Bring Assie too. I'm not a monster, Cinta. Just someone who didn't 'love wisely but too well.'

Come and see me in Lagos.

I'll be waiting.

> *Yours ever,*
> *Maurice*

The second note was very different.

Jacinta:

I know that things happened on the road from Lunama that you will hold forever in your heart. I am sure that the horrors of what happened will, in some way, accompany the other journeys you will make. But I urge you to remember that Lunama was not just a tragedy. It was also a love story, Jacinta, one that you and I dared to tell.

When you go home (Assie tells me you leave on Monday. Without good-bye?) know that nothing is lost if it is remembered. I will carry you and your pretty Lady in my heart. I will remember the scent you wear and your hair covered in In the Name of the Father's blossoms. How can pain last in a world where such bliss has been shared? It is too early to talk about you and me. But one day it may be too late. When you too can say, 'I am ready,' let me know. I am ready now. I will be ready then.

> *Always yours,*
> *John Turay*

I burned the first note. I watched the flames curl up from the burner on the stove and lick the note to death.

The second note I put carefully in a plastic sheet. Then I placed it in my diary with the other treasures of my life.

During the last few days of my time in Africa, Esther would hold me and shush me to sleep when the nightmares came. When I woke up the night before I was due to leave, I cried out:

'I did it, Esther! It was me! He was right. I did it.'

'No,' she said, not needing to understand what I was referring to. 'Whoever told you that was a fool. We cause little in this world, Jacinta. The world makes itself happen, for the most part. Then there are people like Maurice Shittycrap who can throw bad luck around like dice. They can make a few things happen once in a while. So you are on your guard, and you protect your little girl from idiots like that. Lady, she is what you have got. Keep her, Jacinta Moses. You had a husband. He was killed in an accident. You will have another. That is your story.'

'Esther?'

'Yes, child.'

'I saw you that night. You were in the moon.'

She smiled and stroked my head with her hand.

'Will I see you again?' I asked her.

'Maybe,' she said. 'If you come home again.'

'Manny is dead, but I feel nothing. I am evil. I feel nothing.'

She hushed me, but I needed to speak.

'I saw Simon in the bush. He had a long face with raffia at the end. I dreamed he saved us.'

'Perhaps it was the Poro or one of the other secret societies. They wear masks like that. Or perhaps your father made them come to you.'

'Could he do that?'

'The dead can do anything, silly child. They teach you nothing at the white schools.'

'You're angry with me. Don't be angry. Don't you love me, Esther? I don't think you love me anymore.'

She held me in her arms. 'Little Jacinta Moses,' she said. 'You know nothing.'

Lady and I left the next day.

The day after, we were back in Virginia.

When Lydia saw us at the airport, she ran toward us like a woman who understands the need to comfort another. I was grateful.

'You poor children,' she said. Then, 'Did he suffer?'

'No. It was instantaneous.'

'Good. That's a blessing. He was . . . I don't know. I don't really know who he was.'

'He was the father of little Lydia Fox, my Lady Moses,' I said, remembering how words can comfort us if we let them.

'Yes,' she replied, her face lighting up as she looked at her pretty grandchild. 'That's worth something. Isn't it?'

10

A few days before she dies, I am holding her hand when she begins to speak.

'My name is Louise Buttercup Moses,' she says. 'I have not been a good woman, but I have tried hard. I fell in love with a man called Simon Moses. People thought it was strange because he was a black man from Africa and I am a white woman from England. But it was not strange. We were like the moon and the night. We made each other brighter. Really, there was no difference between us. People are fools if they don't know what I mean. I never spent time looking for difference. I just made love to it. What else can you do? When he died I loved his little girl, Jacinta. She was like the sunshine. Is that you, Jacinta, all grown up? Now I'm going to go and be with him. I will be buried in the grave where he lies. They dug it deep enough for two. I am happy. Never be sad about this. The cancer is a blessing. It takes me back to where I want to be.'

This is what I must carry with me. Not the accusations or the outbursts, not the guilt or the sense of loss. Only this:

Just around the corner, my mother waits for me, the way parents wait for their children who are still making the journey they have already completed. In the bend of the night, she and Simon are there, arms entwined, waiting for their wayward child to come home.

As Alfred has entreated, I pick up a pen again and write. This time it is an answer to the question that had troubled me:

> *If life is only a brief journey toward great loss in a*
> *small room, what will I tell my child when she asks me*
> *again, just as she did at five years of age, 'What is the*
> *meaning of life, Mama?'*

At the funeral, I read my response to the small group of people gathered to remember what mothers mean.

'I will tell my daughter the same thing my mother told me: that it is worth the coming back in order to be with those we have made. The joy we find with them, however brief, is the thing "of great constancy" Shakespeare wrote about. Louise Buttercup built something amazing with Simon Moses on Lavender Sweep. Unwittingly, she handed the passion to me when she railed against his loss and refused to accept that the small room of mortality equaled separation.

'In memory of Louise Buttercup Moses, I refuse to accept it too. Likewise, I refuse to accept that the light cannot house the dark, and that night is not blessed when the moon's whiteness kisses it. We will not fly away from one another anymore. When I am here so is she, because I remember her.

'Love cannot happen in a small room, that's the secret. And the journey is only brief if you segregate the tenses. Her past is my present is my daughter's future. The beloved together are the meaning of life. There is no more than this.'

After the funeral, Alfred, Lady, and I sit in the living room again and plan the future. I have a long-overdue trip back to Africa to make. Alfred wants to come. He insists his arthritis will not bother him. 'I am still a young man in here,' he says, pointing to his large cranium.

Lady is thrilled to hear we three may go back in the summer. She wants to ride an elephant. When I tell her elephants are gone from that part of Africa, she tells me I'm wrong and rushes to the bookshelf. She returns with her grandfather's story collection.

'Read it!' she commands. 'You'll see, Mom. They *are* there. You have forgotten.'

I begin to read. She is right.

They are there after all.